Blindside Beauty © 2024 Lex Martin

All rights reserved. No part of this book may be reproduced or transmitted in any form or by any electronic or mechanical means, including information storage and retrieval systems, without express written permission from the author, except for the use of brief quotations in a book review.

Without in any way limiting the author's exclusive rights under copyright, any use of this publication to "train" generative artificial intelligence (AI) technologies to generate text is expressly prohibited. The author reserves all rights to license uses of this work for generative AI training and development of machine learning language models.

This is a work of fiction. Names, characters, businesses, places, events and incidents are either the products of the author's imagination or used in a fictitious manner. Any resemblance to actual persons, living or dead, or actual events is purely coincidental.

This adult contemporary romance is recommended for readers 18+ due to mature content.

Copy editing by RJ Locksley

Proofreading by Julia Griffis, The Romance Bibliophile

Cover by Najla Qamber Designs

Model Photograph by Lindee Robinson

First Edition

ISBN: 978-1-950554-19-5

ABOUT THE BOOK

The single dad next door is my biggest temptation.
After I accidentally plow my car into Nick Silva's bumper, I can't blame him for not hiring me to be his daughter's nanny, but I'm still salty about it. I need the money to go on a trip of a lifetime, one my ex didn't want me to take.

The worst part is Nick just moved in next door.

I'm sure he associates me with my dirtbag ex—his former teammate—so I try to avoid my neighbor whenever possible.

But when his new babysitter gets locked out of the house, leaving Nick's four-year-old alone inside, I attempt to rescue her by breaking in through a window.

Unfortunately, I have a wardrobe malfunction and end up flashing my goodies to the whole neighborhood, Nick included.

Because of my embarrassing heroics, Nick's now convinced I'd be a great nanny.

The trouble with football players is they're very persuasive, so I agree to take the job but immediately regret it.

Who needs to see a gorgeous, shirtless man jumping rope and doing push-ups in gray sweatpants? Who wants to watch a sexy, single dad snuggle his little girl and read her bedtime stories? Who enjoys working closely with a walking, talking thirst trap every single day?

Fine. I do. I want all of that, but I already swore I'd never date another jock after the last one stomped all over my heart, so this bookworm needs to play it safe.

But rumor has it Nick has a new girlfriend, which helps me maintain appropriate boundaries.

Because I won't be blindsided by another quarterback again.

Blindside Beauty **is an angsty nanny romance featuring an adorable, accident-prone bookworm and a struggling, grumpy single dad. If you enjoy close proximity, enemies-to-lovers vibes, opposites attract, small towns, and college football, you'll love this steamy final addition to the** *USA Today* **bestselling series Varsity Dads.**

EPIGRAPH

"I was in the middle before I knew that I had begun."
— Jane Austen, *Pride and Prejudice*

PROLOGUE
APRIL

ABIGAIL

I'M in such a rush to get to the interview on time, I trip as I get out of my old Corolla, land on my knee, and tear a hole in my khakis.

Dang it.

Maybe he won't notice the blood. At least it matches my red cardigan, which I button.

Limping across the parking lot, I tug my messenger bag up my shoulder and hope my résumé didn't get squished. I really need this job, or I'll be stuck waiting tables all summer. That would be fine if I hadn't waitressed all through high school *and* college.

I just need to do something different for the next few months to save money for my trip. If I'm really lucky, he'll want me to keep working this fall, but I don't want to get my hopes up.

I graduate this winter and need to get a teaching position, so this is my only chance to work as a nanny before I get a more permanent job.

The rich smell of dark roast hits me as soon as I swing open the door to the Rise 'N Grind Cafe, which is my favorite place in Charming to get coffee.

I scan the restaurant, which is also a bookshop. I spot him along the back at a two-top, parked in front of the rack of magazines.

Nick Silva.

At the sight of him, my heart beats wildly.

Not because I like him or anything, though he is ridiculously handsome. It's just... I've had really bad luck when it comes to quarterbacks, and Nick is the six-foot-three-inch starting QB for the Lone Star State Broncos. He's a single dad with a young daughter who needs a nanny.

Please don't ask me about Ezra.

Roxy is always telling me to be optimistic. As I replay the pep talk she gave me last week about turning my life around, I push my clear-framed glasses up my nose and pat down my messy bun. I can do this.

He seems to be wrapping up an interview, so rather than stare like a weirdo, I get an iced coffee, but I start to second-guess this decision when my hands shake as I'm reaching for my beverage.

Calm down, Abigail. He's not going to throw you into a pit of snakes.

I take several sips as I wait for the pretty brunette at Nick's table to get up. They're smiling at each other, and he's nodding.

Shoot. I hope the position isn't filled yet.

As I walk to his table, I make a concerted effort not to run into anyone or trip. When I get to his table, he's shuffling through a stack of résumés.

"Hi, Nick. I'm Abigail, your one o'clock appointment."

He looks up and nods, but before I can sit, his eyes go right to the hole in my pants.

Ugh.

I start to sweat.

When he doesn't say anything, I feel the need to fill in the silence. As I slide onto the chair, a string of word vomit bursts forth. "I tripped, but I'm fine. Just ignore the blood. I didn't have time to get a Band-Aid." Dang it. Maybe he thinks I'm not prepared to take care of children. "I usually carry one in my bag, but it must've fallen out. Did you know that some cultures use wet clay as a poultice? Once, when I was little, I tried using mud, but I... just got... an infection."

Shut up, Abby!

I expect him to kick this off with some random chitchat. In fact, I practiced this morning in the mirror. *I'm from San Antonio. I love knitting and working with kids. I drive a manual stick shift. That's cool for a girl, right? My friends and I love playing Scrabble. Did you know that the highest two-letter word score is "za?" As in pizza? It was officially approved as a word in 2006. And I adore cats! I had one named Mr. Darcy, but he died. Do you have any cats?*

"Tell me why you want this job."

What? Where's the chitchat or softball questions?

Swallowing, I sift through all of the responses I worked on, but for some reason, I draw a blank, which means I have to wing it.

Winging it is not my strong suit.

His jaw tightens. "Because if you're just interested in football—"

"Oh, God, no." I snort-laugh. "Football is the *very* last thing I want to talk about."

Now he's looking at me weird. Great.

But then he flexes his hand, and it draws my attention to his taut, muscular forearm that's attached to thick biceps, which stretches his black polo.

I'm staring. My focus snaps back to his eyes, which are narrowed on me.

He has a rugged jaw and gorgeous green eyes, the color of light sea glass, but they're not the friendliest.

I clear my throat. "Can we start over? I'm super nervous because I'm not great at interviews, but I love kids. I babysat through high school and college, and all of my references will vouch for me. I'm not a great cook, but I can make a mean peanut butter and jelly. And I've been watching *The Nanny Whisperer* since I was little. That show is why I want this job." I also need to save more money than waiting tables will allow me to do.

Before he can say anything, I pull out my résumé and list of former employers. "I'm an elementary ed major, and I already did my student teaching last spring. Here's a list of the families I've worked for." I suck in a deep breath before I pass out. "I have other references too."

As he looks over my materials, I stare at him again.

I've heard girls on campus talk about how hot he is, but I've never met him in person until now.

And I can one hundred percent agree with their assessment.

Nick Silva is a looker.

His thick, dark brown hair hangs in his face until he blows out a breath. It's short on the sides and longer on top. But those bottle-glass-green eyes are his best feature. Like, pow, they hit you with force.

Also noteworthy are his great ears and nice nose.

Ears and noses are important because the older you get, the bigger they get. Fun fact.

But his above-average looks are not why I'm here.

Handsome men are all fine and good until they cheat on you. Ask me how I know.

"I need someone reliable." I'm so focused on his obnoxiously attractive jaw, that his voice startles me. "Sometimes I'm unavailable because I'm at practice or playing in a game, and I have to trust in my nanny's ability to make good decisions and keep my daughter safe."

He's talking about the job. This is a great sign.

"Of course. Child safety should always be the priority in any situation."

Picking up a pen, he scribbles some notes on a legal pad of paper. "Your CPR accreditation expired."

"Really?" I pull out another copy of my résumé and, sure enough, it lapsed last month. "Huh. You're right, but does that much change in CPR techniques from year to year? You do thirty chest compressions for every two breaths to the beat of 'Staying Alive.' That's an old song by the Bee Gees. My mother loves them."

I sing a few lines because maybe he doubts me, but all he does is glance at me and scribble some more.

Ugh. Maybe that was the wrong answer. "I mean, I'm planning to renew it. If you were that concerned, I could do it next week."

A group of girls walk by and pause at our table. A gorgeous redhead puts her hand on his shoulder. "I'm looking forward to our date tonight."

He winks at her before she walks away, and I roll my eyes. What is it with football players? They're such fuckboys.

Not that I would ever say that to Nick's face. Or to anyone really. I'm trying to curb my language because future elementary school teachers shouldn't swear.

He reaches for his glass of ice water, takes a drink, puts it down. His lips go flat. "Look, I'm not sure—"

"Please don't hold it against me."

His head tilts. "Hold what against you?"

"The fact that I dated Ezra Thomas." His brows lift, but he doesn't say anything, so again, I fill in the silence. "That's your reservation, right? That he and I dated. Well, technically, we were engaged, but I had no idea he was a total P.O.S. He was a completely different person in high school and when he came home to visit. I'm just saying that if you're worried about him because y'all had bad blood between you, please know that I haven't seen him in months."

Nick opens his mouth and then closes it.

I've rendered the man speechless.

"You're his ex-fiancée?" He chuckles, but it lacks humor.

"I swear I'm great with kids. If you want, I could come by to play with your daughter, no charge. Just to see if you think we vibe."

His intensity as he stares at me makes goosebumps break out on my arms. "You'd be willing to do that without pay?"

"Absolutely. I'm not just doing this for the money. I mean, yes, the money would be great, but I'd rather work with kids than sling chicken-fried steak all summer."

His eyes turn up to the ceiling, and I get the feeling he's talking to himself. "What the hell? Okay, fine. Let's give that a shot."

Inner high five to me!

∾

SQUINTING IN PAIN, I wave my hands around as though that will stop the sting in my left eye.

Son of a biscuit with gravy.

Tonight isn't going the way I thought it would.

When my phone rings on the bathroom counter, I accidentally knock it on the floor and bang my elbow on the cabinet.

"Abby? Are you okay?" a voice shouts from my cell.

"Roxy!" I yell as I rub my arm. "Hang on. I'm having a crisis." Once I'm able to function again, I grab my poor beat-up iPhone. "I don't think I'll be able to make that blind date. I can't get my second contact in, these fake eyelashes look like caterpillars glued to my lids, and I'm running late."

"I bet it's not that bad. Just wear your glasses. You don't have to get all dolled up. It's just drinks."

The high I was riding this afternoon from getting the thumbs-up from Nick to play with his daughter crashed and burned once I got home and remembered I have a blind date tonight.

It's on the tip of my tongue to tell Roxy about my interview, but I don't want to jinx myself. I'll tell her after I get the job.

I pout in the mirror. "I suck at this. You know I can't dress myself." With a groan, I press down on the front of my khakis. "I don't think pleats are my friend."

She chuckles. "Abs, it'll be fine. You're a beautiful woman. Now get your ass in gear before I head down there and drag you to the Cactus Cantina myself." Her voice softens. "You can't mope about Ezra forever. It's time you get yourself out there."

She's kind enough to not say what we're both thinking. That my ex is banging everything with two legs and has been for a while.

Even when we were together.

Once upon a time, that included Roxy. Only she didn't know he was in a relationship until she crashed our engagement party. Ezra did us both dirty. He knocked up Roxy and wanted nothing to do with her baby. When I really think about it, she probably had it worse than I did. I was just the heartbroken fiancée.

It's been more than a year, and I'm still not over it. I made everything exponentially worse by transferring to his college, Lone Star State, right after he proposed. I was so excited to spend more time with him and help him prepare for the draft. It didn't matter that some of my credits didn't transfer. I just wanted us to be together.

Which was dumb as fu—*fudge.*

A few weeks later, we broke up when I learned that he'd been cheating the *entire* time we'd been together.

And because I'd been an idiot—A.K.A. head over heels in love—and didn't care that I'd lose college credits when I transferred, now I have to do an extra semester to graduate.

I don't have enough curse words for that... that turd.

My friendship with Roxy is the one good thing that came from being cheated on by my high school sweetheart.

A thick knot forms in my throat, and my vision blurs. "I hate him," I whisper.

"I know, babe. It'll be okay."

"He wasted so much of my time." Not to mention he was a bad boyfriend. He never held my hand or kissed me in public. Never invited me to his college football games. Never did anything sweet or romantic. I had a long-running fantasy that he'd finally get me tickets to see him play, and after the win, he'd jump into the stands and kiss me. Total foolishness. Someone should've knocked some sense into me a long time ago.

"Don't let him waste any more. By you going on this date, you're proving that you're over him."

I nod and reach for my lip gloss. "You're right."

"I know it. Now get your cute little ass to the bar. And hey, look on the bright side. That asshole probably won't get drafted."

Roxy doesn't mean to hurt my feelings, but those words cut me deep. Because somewhere during the four years Ezra and I dated, his dream of playing professional football became my dream too. I would've done anything to help him.

Ugh, I really need to get a life.

"Get going, Abby. Call me later and let me know what happens."

"Okay, and hey, thanks for hooking me up with Paige. She seems really sweet." Since I can't afford living by myself anymore, Roxy helped me find a roommate. I'm moving in with her friend from cheerleading this summer.

"You're going to love her. She's fun and outgoing and will push you out of your comfort zone."

"I need all the pushing. Especially since you're leaving soon." Roxy is literally my only friend at Lone Star State. Her fiancé Billy is about to get drafted, and they'll be off living their dream lives.

"Don't jinx us!"

I rap my knuckles against the cabinet. "I knocked on wood. There'll be no jinxing."

After we hang up, I take out my one contact, strip off my lopsided lashes, and throw on my glasses. Roxy's right. I have to start living again.

But two hours and four cups of coffee later, my heart sinks when I realize I've been stood up.

"Would you like another refill?" the bartender asks. At least he didn't give me the stink eye when I didn't want booze.

"I'm pretty jittery. I'd better pass, but thank you. I appreciate you letting me sit here all night."

"Sure thing, honey."

Glancing around, I close my book and tuck it into my bag. Self-conscious, I push up my glasses and pat my messy bun. Did my date take one look at me and bolt? Did he see me reading and think I'm a nerd?

For the record, I am a giant bookworm.

Also, I'm not the most fashion-conscious person I know. I tend to wear jeans or khakis and button-up sweaters. I suppose you'd call my look a librarian vibe. So maybe it's not super sexy, but does one really need to look sexy on a first date with someone you've never met before except via a dating app? Really, my simple cardigan and tan pants seem like the smart thing to wear. Stranger danger and all that.

But no amount of self-pep-talking makes me feel any better. My legs feel weighted down like concrete pillars as I trudge out of the cantina. The night air is chilly, and I wrap my sweater tighter around me. At least I tried, right? That has to count for something. Plus, I enjoyed reading that new romance novel. Enemies-to-lovers gets me every time. There's just something so hot about a guy who hates you seeing the real you and falling in love when it's the last thing he wants.

Someone shouts my name, and I freeze. That voice sounds familiar. Too familiar. Icy cold dread slithers down my spine when I realize why, and I close my eyes.

"Abigail, hey, do you have a sec?"

Maybe this is a bad dream, but when I open my eyes again, Ezra is still standing there, looking as handsome as ever. Except I know that underneath his pretty facade is a pitch-black soul.

Funny how I used to think he was my prince. The truth is, he's just a frog with a million warts, and I'm a hopeless romantic who's read too many fairy tales.

"I don't have anything to say to you." Until I found out he cheated on me, I never really stood up to him when he was being an asshole. I always brushed off the little things. I won't be that girl again.

With my jaw clenched, I march toward my white Corolla, which is parked on the far side of the lot behind the bar.

It was packed when I got here hours ago because there are several restaurants in this quaint shopping area, but now that it's late and dark, I'm creeped out. Worse, the live oaks around the perimeter form a canopy that blocks out the streetlamps, making it hard to see.

"Ace, come on. I need your help."

"Don't call me that." I never understood that nickname. It had something to do with me getting good grades and helping him with his essays, I suppose.

He juts out his lower lip. "Please."

Ugh, I hate his effect on me. All he has to do is give me that puppy dog expression, and I cave. Against my better judgment, I pause next to my car. "Make it quick."

He rubs his hands together and nods. He's never nervous, but he is right now for some reason. "I probably won't be drafted next weekend, but my agent says he can get me into some open tryouts. You know how good I can be. You've always had my back. Always believed in my talent."

If he knew that, why did he sleep around? I swallow down my emotions and blink quickly to try to clear my eyes. At least it's dark, so he can't tell I'm two seconds away from bawling. "What's your point?"

"I was hoping I could talk you into coming with me."

"Go with you... where?"

"To the tryouts. You know, so you could cheer me on."

He has some nerve. After the way he led me on for *years*? After how he treated me when I moved here? After the way he stomped all over my heart? "Why don't you take one of the five thousand girls you banged while we were dating?" I jam my keys into the lock, but I'm too flustered to get it open.

"Ace, don't be like that. You were so far away, and I was stressed out. I needed a release. It was just sex. It didn't mean anything."

So many lies.

Even though we both got accepted to Lone Star State, Ezra didn't want me to attend with him. He said it would distract him, so I went to a local college in San Antonio. But really, he wanted to sow his wild oats and be a fuckboy. Roxy shared all the promises he made to her and showed me their texts. "Ezra, I can't with your bullshit anymore."

The lock finally turns, and I jump in and slam the door shut, but he grabs the handle and flings it open again before I can hit the lock. "Wait. Please." I glare at him and am surprised by the desperation in his eyes. "Okay, you're right. I was a dog, but I really need your help. You were always my good luck charm, my lucky ace. If you come, maybe I'll make a team."

His good luck charm?

Blood rushes to my ears.

Ezra is the most superstitious person I know. Especially on game days. He wears the same socks for every game, eats the same foods, and does the same warmup.

Then it dawns on me. Why he dated me.

Because that always perplexed me. I'm a straight-up nerd. I love Jane Austen, school, highlighters, color-coded homework, and triple-word Scrabble scores. The library and bookstores are my happy places. I love thrift shopping and bargain hunting. I'm literally the opposite of this man in every way to the point that Ezra dating me in high school was a huge shock to our classmates. Heck, it was a huge shock to me. The gorgeous quarterback who fell for the quiet bookworm? I felt like I was living in one of my romance novels. Or maybe that movie my mother loves, *Pretty in Pink*. I'm like Andie the geek, someone no one appreciates except other geeks. And really nice people like Roxy.

Ezra and his lies.

The words feel like gravel as I spit them out. "I'm part of your game day routine." In other words, I'm the reason he thought he won.

He was a third-string quarterback when I started tutoring him. Then, one afternoon, we made out in the library—my first time kissing a boy—and the next day, when the two other QBs got injured in a game, he took the field and won against all odds.

We dated ever since.

Until I broke up with him.

And the day after our breakup, he injured his shoulder—because he got a blow job at some party, stood in front of an open window, leaned back too far and fell. Which meant he couldn't go for the draft his junior year like he'd planned. Ezra had just won a national championship. He should've been a shoo-in. Instead, he struggled during his last year of eligibility until Coach Santos replaced him with Nick Silva, a new transfer at the time.

My vision blurs. "Say it. Tell me I'm right. Admit the only reason we dated is because you thought I had something to do with your winning streak."

Ezra blinks.

I growl. "Say it!" On game days, he always had me call him exactly two hours before he played, just like that day in high school.

He shrugs. Then, finally, nods. "Yeah." He holds out his hands. "I know that sounds terrible, but I want to make it up to you. Come with me to my tryouts, and I'll pay you. I know you need money for that European trip you want to take. Your mom told my parents."

Is nothing sacred? I love my mom, but she blabs way too much. "Ezra, let me make this really crystal clear for you. I fucking *hate* you. You ruined my life! I never want to see you again."

His eyes go dark. "Don't be so goddamn dramatic. You're being such a bitch. You were nothing when we started dating, just a little nerd with too much time on her hands. The only social life you've ever had is because of me."

My chest constricts. *What did I see in this man? And why the hell am I sitting here listening to this crap?*

As I slam my door, I hear someone yell at Ezra, but I can't make out what he says, and I'm not sticking around to figure it out. I throw my car into reverse and back out fast—*way* too fast. I don't realize there's a dark SUV parked behind me at a weird angle until I clip it and take off their front bumper.

Holy crap.

You'd think my night couldn't get any worse.

I roll down my window and lean over to get a better look. Damn, there's a couple in the other vehicle. Not that I was going to just drive off, but I would've preferred writing an apology note with my phone number rather than have two other people witness me freaking out at my ex.

Awkwardly, my driver's window is right next to the other driver, and based on the fact that a disheveled girl is sitting in the lap of some jock, I put two and two together and realize I've just interrupted their hookup.

"Sorry!" I wave helplessly. "I didn't mean to interrupt your... your... sexy time."

Sexy time? Really, Abigail?

The woman sticks her head out of the window and screams down at me, "What the fuck is wrong with you?"

I flinch, and it takes everything in me not to sink to the floorboards when I realize she seems familiar. "I'm so sor—"

"Have you ever tried using a rearview mirror? I'm calling the cops."

"Larissa, calm down," a deep voice says.

"Calm down? She ran into you!" A minute later, she hops out of the other side of the vehicle and yells, "Your bumper is on the ground!"

My tongue feels thick in my mouth, and I'm suddenly sweating. I want to explain I didn't see their car because it's really dark and they were parked at a bad angle, but I can't seem to spit out any words. I wring my hands, hating how I get tongue-tied when people yell at me.

Ezra starts laughing and calls me a cockblocker and asks "Douche McLoser" if he always gets laid in dark parking lots. Leave it to my ex to make everything worse. I swear I never saw this side of him before I moved to Charming.

That's when I finally get a good look at this woman's date. Dark hair, chiseled cheekbones, and a beautiful rugged jaw.

I close my eyes.

The universe hates me.

Because Nick Silva's glaring at me from the front seat.

I rest my forehead on my steering wheel and try to hold back my tears.

But it doesn't take a genius to figure out he won't be calling to follow up on my interview.

I just lost my chance to be a nanny.

1
NICK

JUNE

Sometimes I can't get over how different Charming is from Dallas. It's still Texas, but somehow worlds apart.

Although Charming has all the trappings of a big college town, with dozens of bars and coffee shops downtown lined up along cobblestone streets, it's quaint as hell. Locals tell you 'howdy' and call you 'sir' or 'ma'am.' There's a farmers' market on every corner in the spring and summer. And the baristas always remember your name and order.

But what I really like about it is how it feels safe. As I drive to our new house, I notice kids playing in cul-de-sacs and riding their bikes and families out for picnics in the park.

Just as I'm about to turn onto Cottage Street, a car blows through a stop sign, and I slam on my brakes to avoid hitting him while I quickly reach back to make sure none of the moving boxes tumble over and crush my daughter. Fortunately, nothing budges back there, but the point is they could have.

Motherfucker. This is a residential neighborhood. That guy could've killed someone driving like that.

So much for being safe.

"Hazel, are you okay?" I glance back at my four-year-old daughter. I'm grateful I splurged on the top-rated car seat. It set me back, but nothing is more important than Hazel's safety.

"I'm hungwy, Daddy."

I blow out a relieved breath. She's always hungry. "The guys said they're bringing burgers."

"No onions."

"No onions, kiddo."

"They huwt my tummy. And then I have to poop."

I chuckle. "I know, munchkin. I'll check your burger to make sure there are no onions, and if there are, I'll peel them out."

"You pwomise?" She can't say her Rs yet. It ticks her off when people mention it even though everyone thinks she's adorable.

"Cross my heart."

After double-checking to make sure there's no traffic, I turn, but it's a little too sharp, and the driver's side tire rubs against the panel, making a horrible sound. It's bad enough I had to tie my bumper back on after Abigail Dawson hit me this past spring, but that sound is a reminder I can simply be sitting in my SUV and bad shit happens. It makes my blood pressure shoot up every time I hear it. Like I need another reason to be paranoid about driving.

My jaw tightens when I think about that night.

I hadn't been with another woman since my girlfriend Gemma died our sophomore year. I hadn't hooked up or messed around with anyone. I wasn't ready. Plus, I had my hands full raising my daughter. But last spring my teammate said his friend wanted to go out with me, and it made me realize that maybe it's time to stop being a monk.

Larissa and I talked on the phone for a few weeks and finally set a date.

After she and I grabbed a bite to eat, we sat in my SUV and

talked. Talking turned into kissing, which, to my surprise, turned into her crawling over the center console and straddling my lap. And that was turning into something interesting when Ezra Thomas once again fucked up my life by pissing off his ex-girlfriend so much, she threw her car into reverse and plowed into me.

The memory of him harassing her still pisses me off. At the time, I didn't know it was Ezra and Abigail. I thought it was just some douchebag yelling at a woman. I'd rolled down my window to ask if she needed help, and that was when she hit the gas.

I work my jaw back and forth.

Larissa and I have been in an awkward place ever since. Maybe it's for the best. I'm probably not ready for anything serious. I might never be ready for something serious, if I'm being honest.

What I need is peace and quiet. A safe place for my kid to play and somewhere I can study my playbook and film uninterrupted.

I only have one more shot to make the NFL, and if I can't get my shit together, I'm royally fucked. I can eke out the grades to play, but no one would call me an Einstein. I have no fallback if football doesn't work out for me. I'm a business major with no real aptitude for it. When my friends were figuring out what they wanted to do with their lives, I was changing diapers and mourning the loss of my girlfriend.

A few minutes later, I pull into the driveway of our new rental. It's a small two-bedroom house on a sleepy suburban street, which is perfect.

I'm getting Hazel out of her car seat when a little red sports car pulls in behind us and Larissa gets out.

"Why is she he-a?" Hazel asks, her eyes going squinty.

"You don't like Daddy's friend?" Because at this point, that's all we are. We've both been busy, and after our makeout session got interrupted, we haven't had many chances to hang out.

Hazel shrugs and goes into koala bear mode, wrapping her arms tightly around my neck.

"Hey, cuties." Larissa gives me a wide smile and tickles Hazel, who pointedly ignores her by burrowing her face into my neck.

I gently jostle my daughter. "Hey, kiddo. Say hi."

"Hi," she says, her voice muffled.

I roll my eyes. "Hey, Larissa. How's it going?"

She's a tall redhead with legs for miles, a pretty face, and a good sense of humor. She's starting law school at UT this fall and has been interning for some high-caliber lawyers for the last year. I like that she's motivated. She seems like the kind of woman I should go for.

That's what Gemma was like. My girl was going to take life by storm.

My throat gets tight, and I shove that thought down deep. Memories of my high school sweetheart still hit me hard sometimes. Gemma and I had our ups and downs, but at the end of the day, I adored her.

Suddenly, I wish Larissa hadn't shown up.

A U-Haul truck parks in front of the house next door. I guess our neighbors are moving in too.

Two girls hop out. One is a cheerleader I recognize from our games, and the other is...

Oh, hell no.

Abigail freezes when she sees me.

Please tell me she's not moving in next door. I don't want any more drama from her and Ezra. That asshole was supposed to go for the draft as a junior, leaving the QB1 slot wide open for me last year. Instead, he got injured in the offseason, couldn't participate in the combine, and decided to stay our senior year. I had to ride the bench for the first three games until he sucked so bad, Coach Santos finally gave me a shot.

And while I had a decent season and the Broncos made it to the national championship game, my stats weren't anything noteworthy. If I'm being honest with myself, I can admit we had a spectacular defense that got us to that game, which I then promptly lost.

So now I have to use my last season of eligibility to play football and try to get drafted instead of graduating like I should've last May.

Trust me when I say that playing another year of college football while I juggle being a single father is the very last thing I want to do this fall.

Something tells me having Abigail Dawson next door won't give me the peace and quiet I'm looking for. Especially if Ezra flips out on her again, and I get thrown in jail for kicking his ass because I have zero tolerance for men harassing women.

I pinch the bridge of my nose. It probably doesn't help I didn't hire her for that nanny position. She's likely still pissed about it. But I'm not gonna hire someone who drives like a bat out of hell when the job might require picking up Hazel from daycare or preschool this fall. Even if Coach's daughter Roxy vouched for her last spring, I can't bring myself to hire her. I need a responsible driver.

Shit. I really hope Larissa doesn't recognize my neighbor.

I didn't like how she flew off the handle when Abigail took off my bumper. It's one of the reasons I have reservations about her. While I was pissed Abigail hit my SUV, there was no need to curse at her.

"Hey, Nick. I'm Paige," the pint-sized cheerleader says. I'm not surprised she knows my name. All the cheerleaders know the team. She nudges Ezra's ex. "This is Abby."

"We've met," Abigail says quietly as she tucks a strand of her dirty blonde hair behind her ear. Her whole body is rigid, and animosity wafts off her.

Yup, she's still angry about that nanny job. Too fucking bad. Oksana has thirty years of experience, is certified in CPR, and is some kind of Russian martial arts expert. If anyone can protect my child, it's her. So she lacks a little warmth. Her cold personality is the price I pay for my kid's safety.

When Larissa doesn't say anything, I realize she probably doesn't recognize my new neighbor. It was pretty dark that night. After Larissa flipped out and called the cops, I put her in an Uber so I could think straight and deal with the situation.

Paige leans over to say hi to Hazel. "Hey, peanut. Aren't you adorable?"

Hazel smiles shyly and giggles. I don't miss the frown on Larissa's face. I want to tell her I can't help who my daughter likes or dislikes. Hopefully, Hazel will warm up to her soon. Aside from family members, Hazel's not used to women being in my life. She probably just needs some time to adjust.

It's not like I'm going to bring over a different girl every weekend. I've been talking to Larissa since the spring, and I'm open to seeing where things go with her. As long as we keep shit casual and she doesn't plan our wedding behind my back or poke holes in my condoms, we should be cool.

Because I'm absolutely positive I don't want more kids. I have a hard enough time keeping this one safe.

My attention drifts back to Abigail. Her oversized t-shirt and shorts are smudged with dirt. She looks at me, glances at my Frankenstein bumper that's still wrapped to my old Outback with duct tape and bungee cords, and looks away.

Yes, you did that.

While her insurance paid out, I needed that money to move. Our old apartment complex was loud, and Hazel was constantly being woken by late-night parties. I could've tapped into our savings, but I was worried about cashflow when I might need to put down a big deposit on a rental. I make a mental note to make that repair a priority.

Really, I shouldn't be upset with Abigail anymore, but car accidents, even fender benders, always fuck me up a little.

Now that I can get a good look at Abigail during the day, I see why Ezra dated her. She has big blue eyes, a heart-shaped face, and long, dirty blonde hair that cascades down in a tangled ponytail. Those glasses don't do her any favors, but she's still a beautiful woman behind that shy demeanor and baggy clothes.

Larissa hooks her arm into mine and introduces herself. "Hi. I'm Nick's girlfriend."

I lift an eyebrow. *Girlfriend* is probably a stretch, but I don't want to embarrass her, so I don't object. Although maybe we need to have a conversation about where we really stand.

My daughter tries to push her away. "Daddy doesn't have gulfwends."

I kiss the top of her head. "Be nice, munchkin."

Larissa leans closer. "Isn't it time to break the seal, *Daddy*?"

Holding back a cringe, I give her a tight smile. I suspect she's trying to be sexy, but being called Daddy is not a turn-on, especially when I'm carrying my daughter.

Abigail snorts and looks away while Paige tries to hold back a laugh.

Thankfully, the guys pull up in another U-Haul before things get any more uncomfortable.

Jinxy jumps out of the truck with a bag of burgers. "Food's on, bitches."

"Dude, language." I point to my daughter. "Hazel doesn't need to learn your colorful vocabulary."

"Oh, sorry, Hazy Daisy." He trots up to her and hands me the burgers. Pausing, he looks around. "Is Miss Trunchbull here?"

"Who?"

"Your scary-ass nanny who looks like the schoolmistress from *Matilda*."

"She's not that bad."

"So you say." He turns to Hazel, holds out his hands, and she jumps into his arms. "Did you miss Uncle Jinxy?"

She nods with a giggle.

"Not too high," I warn because I already know what he's gonna do.

"Oh, ye of little faith. I got this," Jinxy says just before he tosses my daughter into the air. She squeals and laughs. Larissa frowns the whole time, probably upset Hazel hasn't warmed up to her.

But Abigail watches my little ladybug with a sweet smile.

It catches me off guard because that smile changes her whole face. She instantly goes from pretty to downright gorgeous.

Except her grin promptly disappears the moment our eyes connect.

Yeah, she's not over losing the nanny job.

ONCE ALL OF our crap is moved in, I video-chat my father because if I don't call him, we'll never talk. I should also call Gemma's parents, but her mom always gets so emotional, and it drains me and upsets Hazel.

It takes three tries, but he finally answers. "You okay?" he immediately asks, half-asleep.

"Sorry we woke you."

Hazel sticks her head in. "Hi, *abuelo!*"

"Hi, *mija. ¿Cómo estás?*" How are you?

"*Tengo hambre.*"

It's funny that she can roll her Rs in Spanish but can't quite pronounce them in English. I grab my kid in a gentle headlock and scruff her hair. "She just ate, but she's already hungry." Hazel rolls off the couch, and I reach over so she doesn't bang into the coffee table. Jesus, this child is gonna shave a decade off my life.

My dad gives us a tired smile. "Reminds me of someone I know."

"Nothing's changed," I joke. When he doesn't say anything, I prod a little. "How's work?"

"*Lo mismo.*" The same.

"Did they give you a raise for all that overtime?"

He shakes his head. "Those tightwads turned me down again."

My dad's a bricklayer. José Silva slaves in hundred-degree Texas heat, six days a week. He crafts gorgeous fireplaces on million-dollar mansions while he lives in a hovel. His hands are cracked and weathered, his skin the color of sunbaked leather, and he looks twenty years older than other men his age.

"Why don't you try getting a job with a different company?" It's a question I've asked a million times.

"Don't wanna screw up my retirement."

The problem with my father is he's too loyal, and his boss takes advantage of his back-breaking work ethic. "Dad, you're so good at what you do. Have you tried to get customers directly?"

He runs his dirty hand over his face. "You know I'm not good with people like you are."

It kills me that he thinks so little of himself. In the right conditions, my father is charming, but he clams up when he has to sell his skills.

What's scary is that, in my own way, I'm a bricklayer just like him. I'm only good at football, and if I don't get drafted, what else will I do?

"Please make sure you take water breaks. Don't land yourself in the hospital again."

He holds up a weathered Gatorade squirt bottle. "I have to piss every ten minutes when I drink that much, but you're right."

My father almost worked himself to death last year. He got so dehydrated on the job, he passed out and ended up in the ER. Now he's having a hard time handling those medical bills. *"Cuídate, papá."* Take care of yourself.

I used to resent how much he worked because that meant he never came to my games when all the other parents were in the stands, but when I had Hazel, it finally sank in. He needed the money to pay the bills and feed and clothe me. No one else was gonna do it.

Worried, I rub the back of my neck. "I still have some insurance money if you need—"

"No. I told you, I'm not taking Gemma's money. That belongs to you and Hazel. You're gonna need it for the extra year at school."

"I'm graduating this winter."

"But the draft isn't until April. Be smart."

"I can get a job second semester 'cause I won't have classes."

He shakes his head. "What if the baby gets sick? What if you have an emergency? No."

Those are good points, but I hate that I can't help him yet. "Fine, but when I get drafted, I'm paying off your mortgage and making you retire, old man." His hoarse chuckle makes me smile.

Now I just need to have the best season of football of my college career.

No pressure.

2

ABIGAIL

AFTER PAIGE and I drag in the last box, we collapse on her couch the football guys were nice enough to move for us.

Nick was noticeably absent in that effort. Whatever. He can go suck a lemon.

At least his girlfriend didn't remember me.

Paige laughs. "Did you notice Nick's expression when Larissa called him Daddy? I almost died."

I crack a smile. "Yeah, he looked pretty uncomfortable, but who says that in front of a man's daughter?" Some people have no boundaries.

I can fully admit I'm jealous of Larissa and her silky red tresses and designer clothes. Reaching up, I tuck a loose strand of hair into my lopsided ponytail. Some of us go with the natural look, and that's okay too.

Paige takes a long drink of her bottled water. "Nick's not my type, but seeing him cuddle his little girl did things to my ovaries."

"We can't help but find that appealing. My science teacher used to say that women are hardwired to be attracted to males who can provide security for their children. That it's biological.

So don't give Nick too much credit." When she doesn't say anything, I turn to look at her. She has a strange expression on her face. "What?"

"Did something happen between you and Nick?"

"Like what?"

She nibbles her bottom lip. "I don't know. That's why I'm asking. I feel like you guys had a vibe."

"If you mean he hates me, then yes, we had a vibe."

Her mouth drops open. "Oh my God. Something *definitely* happened. You'd better dish, roomie."

"Ugh, it's too embarrassing." I sink deeper on the couch and drag my arm over my eyes.

She squeals and wiggles in her seat. "I have an idea. Let's have a girls' night. We'll do facials and manicures and you can tell me all about the reasons why you're vibing with our sexy neighbor."

Did she miss the part where I said he hates me? Or the part where he has a girlfriend?

But seeing as how I don't have any friends at Lone Star State, I don't want to pass up the chance to hang out with Paige.

I've never done a girls' night before. My friends back home play Scrabble or Pictionary or annotate their favorite novels in their free time. "Can we do facials without discussing Nick Silva?"

She smirks. "Nope. I want all the details."

Great.

An hour later, after we've cleaned up and ordered Mexican food, we're both slouched on the couch again, but this time in our robes.

I wiggle my nose. "This mud mask itches."

"That's the price of beauty." She holds up her glass of wine. "To a fun summer."

"Cheers." I clink her glass with mine and take a sip. "Can I ask you a question?" After she nods, I debate how to ask this. "Don't take this the wrong way because I think you're really fun and super cool, but I was wondering why you'd want to live with me instead of some of your cheerleader friends."

Her mouth twists as she runs her finger over the lip of her glass. "I've had a hard time clicking with the team. It's super competitive, and when Roxy quit last year because she got pregnant, some of the girls didn't like that I took her place as a flyer."

"What's that?"

"I basically leap off of giant human pyramids."

"Holy crap. That sounds terrifying."

"It was the first time I did it, but I wanted to be the best at something. I have two brothers who are super smart, and then there's me. I struggle to get Cs. It's embarrassing."

"How about we help each other? I'm a big nerd and love school, and you're hands down the coolest person I know in Charming." Well, her and Roxy, but Rox just moved to Chicago because they drafted her fiancé Billy. "Maybe you can help me be more social and less awkward, and I can help you with any class stuff you might struggle with. Tutoring is my jam."

She gives me a wide smile. "I'd love that." Holding out her glass, we clink again. "Okay, so dish. What's the deal with Nick?"

I groan. "I hit him with my car."

Her eyes bulge. "When did this happen?"

"He was on a date with Larissa last spring, and Ezra was hounding me to go with him to some NFL open tryouts. I was upset and gunned it in reverse." I cringe when I think back to that night. "Nick and Larissa were obviously trying to find some alone time in a dark parking lot, and I clipped his car with mine."

Paige busts out laughing. "Oh my God. I mean, I can laugh since no one was hurt."

"I want to crawl under a rock whenever I think about it. And me being me, I shouted something like, 'Sorry I messed up your sexy times!'"

The look on my roommate's face is so funny, I start laughing with her. She grabs her stomach and bends over hooting. "Abigail, that's the best story I've heard all year." She pauses. "Is that why his bumper is all jacked up?"

I nod, and we both break out into hysterics again. Once I catch my breath, I tell her the rest of the story and move my hands to show her how I nearly t-boned Nick. "At the end of the day, I guess I'm lucky all I did was clip his bumper and dent the side of his SUV a little." I make a face. "But Larissa was sitting in his lap, and they were obviously hooking up." I cover my mouth as I admit the rest. "I think I interrupted some dry-humping."

Paige folds in her lips, but her face is red from laughing.

"The worst part is I had just interviewed to be his daughter's nanny. Obviously, I didn't get the job, and now I'm waiting tables instead of taking care of Hazel, which I was really hoping to do because I love kids."

If Nick hired someone like Miss Trunchbull, like his buddy mentioned, then I never had a chance anyway. I'm definitely more like Miss Honey.

"Bummer. That sucks."

"But it gets worse because when I crashed into him, Ezra kept shouting stuff at Nick, calling him names. I kind of hate myself for dating him for so long. But in my defense, he never behaved that way in front of me. It wasn't until I transferred here last year that I got to see Ezra for the asshole he is. And if I have to look on the bright side, that moment in the parking lot flipped a switch in me. Whatever residual affection I had for that man instantly shriveled up and died."

"I can't get over you being engaged to Ezra Thomas."

Sighing, I shrug. "I know. I'm not really his type."

She touches my arm. "That's not what I mean. It's just that he's an arrogant ass, and you're such a sweetheart."

"Thanks. It sucked to find out he slept around behind my back."

"He didn't get drafted, did he?"

"No, but he got a walk-on position with some team in Florida." I guzzle down my wine. "I'm just glad I won't have to run into him anymore."

"Nope. Now you just have to live next door to Nick."

She gives me a look, and we both crack up. "Talk about an icebreaker. Now you know one of my most embarrassing stories, and I have some doozies."

Paige shakes her head. "I can beat that."

"No way."

"When I was fourteen, I tried to warn my brother's best friend Rhett that his fiancée was cheating on him. Danny and Rhett are older than me, but I've always had a huge crush on Rhett, literally since I laid eyes on him when I was like five."

"Oh, gosh, that long?"

"Yup. But I was a kid, and that's how he'd always seen me, as Danny's little sister. Not that it made any difference to how I felt about him. So he got engaged to his long-time girlfriend, a woman I never liked. Then a few weeks before their wedding, I saw her talking to some guy, and based on the way they jumped apart when they saw me, I knew something was going on. So I finally worked up the nerve to tell Rhett…"

I clutch my stomach. "Did he believe you?"

"He said he was sure it was just a misunderstanding." Brows furrowed, she shakes her head again. "It was the one and only time my brother didn't take my side. Danny said I was just a kid and didn't understand what I saw. That I was letting my feelings for his best friend cloud my perception. And of course, he said it *right* in front of Rhett. I wanted to crawl under the couch and die."

My eyes get wider and wider as she tells me her story. "So what happened? Did he marry her?"

"Yes, and I was so distraught on the day of the wedding, I faked a stomach bug and stayed home to cry."

I reach over to hug her. "I'm sorry. Heartbreak is heartbreak. It doesn't matter if you're young or old, it hurts regardless. Are things weird whenever you see Rhett?"

"To this day, I try to avoid him at all costs."

"Jeez. I don't blame you. Were you able to repair things with your brother?"

Her eyes turn down. "Yeah. He apologized after Rhett caught his wife cheating. Unfortunately, Danny had leukemia and was sick for a long time. He passed last year, but we'd worked through our issues long before that." She waves a hand in front of her face. "Sorry, losing my brother still feels fresh."

"Paige, I'm so sorry." I hug her again, and she wipes her eyes. "Well, you're right. You win the most embarrassing story."

She laughs through her tears. "No more crying tonight. Tell me what you want to work on socially. You said you need help."

That's easy. "For one, I can't dress myself. I never know what to wear. My closet is full of baggy clothes, mostly because Ezra didn't want me to change my style."

Her eyebrows pull together. "Why?"

"He's superstitious."

"I don't get it. What does that have to do with your clothes?"

"Because when we started dating in high school, that corresponded with him winning his football games. And because he secretly viewed me as his lucky charm, he didn't want me to change anything about myself. Like, *anything*. That's why I still have these geeky glasses instead of something cuter. Keep in mind I only recently figured this out, but that's the reason he strung me along for years. So he could win football games."

Her mouth drops open. "What a dick."

"My goal before I graduate is to do everything he said I shouldn't. Wear contacts, buy more form-fitting clothes, maybe highlight my hair. Just... all the stuff girls do to feel pretty and less like big book nerds."

"You're already beautiful, and there's no shame in loving books, but I'm happy to help with a makeover. It'll be fun."

"We just have to do it on a budget. I didn't plan to do an extra semester here at Lone Star and I can't afford a semester abroad, but I'm also hoping to gift myself a graduation trip to Europe. I've always wanted to go to England to see where Jane Austen lived. I'd love to check out the holiday markets and take one of those double-decker bus tours. I gave up on that dream when I started dating Ezra. He didn't want me to do a semester abroad because the only time it would've worked for my academic schedule was in the fall, which is football season."

What I don't tell her is that taking this trip will help me reclaim some of my pride after all those years I dated someone who didn't appreciate me. That's why I'm desperate to work as much as possible between now and when I graduate this winter. I need to put myself first and achieve one of my dreams instead of investing in someone else's.

"Well, fuck Ezra Thomas. You can do so much better than that asshole." She tilts her head. "I just discovered *Pride and Prejudice* last year. Want to watch it with me? I love the Keira Knightley version."

"That's my favorite." I hop in my seat. "Let's do it!"

3
NICK

AUGUST

THE AUGUST SUN IS RELENTLESS. I swear it's cooking my brain. After I wipe the sweat from my forehead, I slide on my helmet.

Training camp started a few days ago, and while the long days have been tough, things will only get more challenging once classes start. Even though I have enough credits to graduate, NCAA rules require that I'm a full-time student in order to play, so I can't slack.

When the guys reach the huddle, I call the play, we clap, and everyone jogs to their positions.

Bowser huts three times and snaps the ball. The second I get it in my hands, I drop back into the pocket and check my options. Maverick makes the tight cut, but two defenders block my path. Jinxy is gunning it down the field, but he has someone hot on his heels too. Dax stumbles, so that leaves me with Finn, who's cutting in twenty yards away.

It's a sure bet, and I like certainty.

When he catches the ball and runs it in for another ten yards, I shout my approval. That's a thirty-yard gain.

But when we break for water, Coach Santos doesn't look happy. He takes me aside and puts his hand on my shoulder. "Nick, that was fine, but I want you to aim for traffic next time."

I frown. That makes no sense. "You want me to throw to someone who has a defender on him?" I have to clarify because, in my opinion, it's always better to make the safe pass rather than risk losing the ball.

He nods once.

I'm confused, but I do what he says. On the next play, Dax runs his route as he tries to shake off his defender. My throw to him is a little hard, and it bounces off his hands.

After two more tries with similar results, we finally nail it, and Coach blows his whistle. "That's enough for today. Good practice. See you tomorrow, gentlemen. Just a reminder, I want lights out by ten p.m. An assistant coach will be by to make sure everyone's accounted for."

During training camp, the guys stay on campus, but I have permission to sleep at home because I can't take Hazel to the dorms.

As I'm about to head for the tunnel, Coach calls my name. "After your shower, meet me in my office. I want to talk about a few things."

This can't be good. I thought I'd done okay out there today, but if Coach wants a one-on-one, I must've screwed up something.

Twenty minutes later, after I've cleaned up and changed, I sit across from Coach in his office, which is immaculate. Folders are color-coded and lined up straight in a silver organizer on his credenza. Our thick playbook is the only thing that sits on his desk. Behind him are awards he won in college and MVP plaques he got playing in the NFL. Santos is a legend, and I'm honored to play for the man.

He leans back in his chair. "How's Hazel doing?"

Debating how much I should say, I nod slowly. "She's acclimating."

"Is your babysitting situation good?"

It pains me to admit that Hazel hasn't warmed up to Oksana yet. "I'm working on it." I scrub my face and decide to level with Coach. Maybe he'll have some good advice. "Trouble is, she isn't crazy about her nanny. Thinks she's too strict, but strict keeps her out of trouble, you know?"

"I can relate. Roxy was a hellraiser when she was little." He chuckles, his eyes going soft as he thinks about his daughter. "I was lucky my wife wanted to stay home with the kids and that we could afford to go off one paycheck." He frowns. "Not sure I've said this enough, but I'm sorry for the loss of your girlfriend. That had to be tough."

Today, it is. I'd do anything to have Gemma to talk to right now. "Thank you, sir."

"Do you have family nearby who could lend a hand?"

I shake my head. "My dad's up in Dallas, and he works a lot." I don't mention that my mom passed when I was young because he already knows that, and I don't want any more pity.

"What about your girlfriend's family? Can they help out?"

"Her parents gave me the insurance money from the accident, and that's helped a ton, but they live in Fort Worth. Sometimes Gemma's sister checks on us, but she doesn't live nearby either."

"If you're ever in a tight spot, you can call me and the missus. As you know, we've had some recent experience with kids." He reaches behind his desk and hands me a framed photo of him and his granddaughter Marley.

"She's a beauty."

"That she is. Probably will be a wild child like her mother. Lord help Roxy and Billy." We both laugh as I return the photo to him. "Okay, I know you didn't come in here to look at baby pictures. Let's get down to business, Nick. Why do you think I picked Billy to throw that Hail Mary against UT last year?" The question catches me off guard. "Granted, I wasn't a hundred percent sure it would come down to that, but if it did, I wanted the ball in his hands."

And not yours.

Ouch. He doesn't say the words, but I feel them nonetheless. *It's not like he benched you. Chill out.*

I try to remove my emotion from the scenario and consider his question. "Because substituting a defensive player would throw off the defense."

"Partially. But that's not the main reason."

Billy Babcock was one of the best defensemen on the team, but he was also a stellar quarterback in high school and has an arm like a missile. He might've been one of the last guys drafted in the spring, but I had no doubt he'd go pro. "Because he has a longer range than I do?"

An admission that pains me to make.

"No." Coach taps on his desk. "You're every bit as good as Billy at quarterback. I've seen your range, and it's nothing to sniff at. I chose him because that boy is fearless."

Flashes of our loss in January have been playing like a broken loop in my mind for months. Knowing you're the reason for the biggest defeat of the season is a bitter pill to swallow. "You're saying I lost the championship game because I played it safe."

Coach stares down at his desk for a brief moment, but it's enough to tell me I'm right.

He sighs. "We made a lot of mistakes that day. It's not all on your shoulders. Would I have preferred you take a few more chances? Yes, but not if that meant turnovers. Ultimately, I don't want you looking backwards. That never serves anyone. But moving forward, we need to learn from our mistakes. I'm working with the team on what we can do better this season, and that includes helping you step outside your comfort zone."

"Yes, sir. I'll try."

"Do or do not. There is no try." His expression is so damn serious, but finally he cracks a smile. "Don't you recognize that quote from *Star Wars*?"

"You've been joking around more lately." I give him a look. "It's weird."

He laughs. "I'm trying to relax more. That health scare a while back put things in perspective. I love football, but it can't be my entire life."

I nod. I get it. Kinda. I do what I do for Hazel, but I have to be obsessed with football if I want to make it to the pros.

Coach Santos steeples his fingers. "Son, you have a lot on your plate. Keep your eyes on the prize. Hang out with the guys when you can outside of practice. Build that camaraderie. Spend quality time with your daughter, and forget the draft for now. To be clear, you absolutely have the potential to get drafted, but thinking about it now, at the beginning of the season, is just added pressure. What's that saying? 'How do you eat an elephant? One bite at a time.' So keep your focus on the game ahead of you. The good news is you're my main QB this fall. You don't have to share it with Ezra Thomas."

"That's a relief."

"It is."

Coach has been tight-lipped about his feelings toward Ezra, which is weird because if Coach is upset with someone, he lets that person know it. Conversely, he never withholds praise.

When he doesn't say anything else, it makes me wonder if the rumors are true. That Ezra Thomas is Roxy's baby daddy, and that's why Coach iced him out of his circle of trust last fall. Because Roxy is Coach's daughter and his obvious pride and joy.

If some douchebag knocked up Hazel and then left her high and dry, like I suspect Ezra did to Roxy, I'd be out for blood.

I'm told Billy and Roxy were friends long before they announced they were dating and having a baby, so no one really questioned her pregnancy at the time. But now I'm wondering if Billy throwing that pass was about more than just winning a game. Maybe it was Coach rubbing a little dirt in Ezra's face for being such an asshole.

Whatever the case, Coach is right. If I wanna get drafted next spring and have the life I want for my daughter, give her the security I never had growing up, and help my father retire, I have to change how I play.

I hope I won't let them down.

∼

AFTER I PICK up some dinner for me and Hazel, I book it home. She should go to bed soon, but if I don't see her in the evenings, I won't see her all day, and that's not okay with me. It's bad enough she's down to one parent. The least I can do is love up on her and make sure we hang out a little.

When I pull into my driveway, I notice that my neighbors aren't home. The girls are rarely there. I think Paige teaches gymnastics and has cheerleading practice. I'm not sure what Abigail does. I'm surprised I haven't seen her much this summer.

When I walk in the house, it's spotless. The floors are clean, the house smells like lemon Pine-Sol, and everything looks neat and orderly.

Oksana is sitting on the couch, knitting.

"Hey. How'd it go today?" I glance around again, looking for my little gingersnap, as I drop my gym bag by the door. "Where's Hazel?"

Oksana doesn't bother looking up from her knitting needles that click, click, click. "That child is obstinate. She would not put her toys away when I asked, and she did not like what I made for lunch."

My heart sinks. Sometimes, those two get along, and other days they butt heads. "What did you make?"

"Borscht. A staple in my country." She sniffs. "But she wanted chicken nuggets."

Hazel can be picky. That's why I have a wall of nuggets in the freezer. "What did she end up having?"

"Nothing. She would not eat the soup I made, so I sent her to bed early."

I wait for her to say that's a joke, but she doesn't. "So she went all afternoon without anything to eat?" I can understand not wanting to waste food, but my daughter is young and pretty slender. I'm not sure she should go that long without any sustenance.

"Do not fret. I gave her bread and water."

My brows lift. "Like she's in prison?"

The click-clack of her needles stops as she finally looks up at me. "You are too lenient. She needs rules." Oksana pulls her hair back into a tight bun, so her eyebrows are always raised.

"Rules, yes, but she's only four."

After another ten minutes debating the topic, I scrub my face, and we agree to disagree. Once my babysitter leaves, I head for Hazel's room and poke my head in. I find her curled up in the corner of the room on the floor, wrapped in a white fuzzy blanket, listening to music with my giant headphones. On the nightstand is a plate of uneaten bread and a full glass of water.

What the fuck? Oksana never checked to see if Hazel ate even a bite, which means my daughter hasn't had anything since eight this morning.

Squatting, I tap her shoulder so I don't scare her.

She lifts her little head. "Daddy."

"Hi, pumpkin," I whisper and remove the headphones. Her little arms go around my neck, and I sit in the rocking chair. "Heard you had a rough day."

She nods but doesn't say anything.

"Wanna tell me about it?"

"No."

I pat her back and rock and try to think of what to say. There's no handbook that tells you how to deal with your child when she doesn't want to eat what the nanny prepared.

I suppose we should start with the basics. "You hungry? I could make us some sandwiches."

Her head pops up. "Peanut butta and jelly?"

"Sure." Not really what I want to shovel into my child, but I suppose it's better than nothing.

"Okay."

I hug her tight because I think we both need it. "Dad had a rough day too. Wanna hear about it?"

"Did you thwow the ball good?"

"Eh. So-so."

"Gotta thwow it hawd, Daddy."

"Not too hard. That's a problem sometimes. I need to work on it." I kiss her forehead and carry her into the kitchen, where I set her up in the booster seat and nestle her in at the table. After I make our sandwiches and pour two glasses of milk, I sit kitty corner to her. "Tell me what happened with Oksana's borscht. She says you wouldn't eat it." Because we've talked about trying everything before we say we don't like something.

My daughter's shoulders slump. "I twied to, but it tasted funny."

"Funny how?"

Her nose wrinkles. "Like onions. I didn't wanna poop."

That makes sense. The last time onions snuck into her food,

she had diarrhea all night. Not that it was the onion's fault. Some other ingredient in that meal might've done it, but Hazel thinks all her problems stem from onions.

"Sorry, kiddo. I'll talk to Oksana again about not putting onions in your food."

Hazel stares at her half-eaten sandwich. "She doesn't like me."

My heart cracks. No one tells you how much it pains you as a parent when your child is hurt. "Of course she does, honey. But she's old-school and thinks kids should eat what's put in front of them. Grandpa is like that too."

She shakes her head. "Do we have to have Oksa?" Hazel can't pronounce the nanny's full name.

I let out a sigh. I don't blame her for wanting a different babysitter. I'm pretty pissed at Oksana right now too, but I don't have anyone who can step in. "I'll talk to her again, but let's see how things go. I need someone who can keep you safe, and while Oksana isn't the friendliest person, she does make sure nothing bad happens."

"Like what, Daddy?"

Too many things to count. Shit that keeps me up at night, frankly. "In the meanwhile, why don't I put a few snacks in a drawer for you? That way, if you have trouble with her cooking, there's something you can eat. I don't want you going all day without eating." Hazel hasn't gained much weight lately, and I don't want this trend to continue. "Just as long as you try Oksana's food first, okay? We don't want to be rude."

"Okay." My daughter smiles, and it's everything.

4

ABIGAIL

"I wish we had the money to go shopping every week. That was so fun. Well, everything except twisting my ankle," Paige says as she fiddles with the radio. It's Friday evening, and we have the windows rolled down and the radio blaring.

"We'll ice it when we get home. Is it swollen?" I ask as I turn down our street.

"A little, but hopefully it'll be okay by morning."

"Like you always say, there's a price for beauty."

She chuckles. "Our first game isn't for a few more days, so I should be good to go if I rest it. Don't tell my coach, but finding that dress was worth it. Plus, it was a steal."

"I adore this pattern." I run my hand over the thin fabric covering my thighs. "I never would've had the courage to try this on, but I love it." We went thrifting this afternoon, and Paige found this beautiful floral tube-top dress. It's much more daring than anything else I own, but I feel so pretty that I had to wear it home.

"You look fab."

I pull the top higher. "I'm just afraid I'm going to flash someone."

She smirks. "That's half the fun."

"You're sure this is okay without a bra? I feel so nipply."

After a quick glance at my chest, she shrugs. "The dress is mostly black. I'd say go with a strapless bra if it really bothers you, but I think you have the boobs to hold it up, so why not? Besides, nips are in these days."

We giggle, and I shrug. Nips are in.

Ezra would hate this dress, which means I'm absolutely going to wear it braless.

When we pull up to our house, I have to be careful getting out because the dress is a little short, but with these new wedge sandals, I feel pretty stylish. Before this moment, no one would ever describe me as stylish. The best part is I only spent thirty dollars on the whole ensemble.

A loud banging makes us turn toward Nick's house where his nanny is hammering on the door with her fists. "Open the door right this minute, little girl!"

Paige and I look at each other, and I motion toward the nanny. "Sounds like she needs help."

We walk over, and the nanny turns toward us with a huff. "I got locked out."

"Do you want me to call Nick?" I offer. Paige lifts her eyebrow at me, and I laugh. She thinks he and I are secretly pining for each other. I hate to rain on her parade, but I'd rather date a cactus than Nick Silva. Plus, he's seeing that beautiful redhead. Why in the world would he be interested in me? "For your information, I have his info because of that fender bender."

Nanny Meany Pants scowls. "We do not have time. I have something on the stove, and I am worried how much longer it can boil."

I frown. "Why can't she hear you?"

Meany Pants' eyes turn into little slits. "She listens to music too loud with those things on her head." She motions over her ears.

"Headphones?"

"Headphones. It is bad for her hearing."

"Okay, that's probably an issue for another day. Have you tried the back door?"

She rolls her eyes at me. "Of course. Do you think I'm stupid?"

All right then.

That's when I sniff the smoke, and my eyes widen. I turn to Paige. "Call the fire department. Better to be safe than sorry." I pull up Nick's number and get his voicemail. "Hey, neighbor, it's Abigail. We have a little situation at your house. Your nanny got locked out. We're calling the fire department, but I wanted to let you know what's going on." That's when I notice the awning window above the giant picture window in the living room is cracked open. "I'm going to try to crawl in through your window. Call us back."

I toss my phone on the ground and point to the window. "Paige, could we lift you up there?"

"Yeah, but I'm worried about coming down on my ankle."

Ugh. "That's right." Nanny Meany Pants would never fit up there. It would be a tight squeeze for me, but maybe I can try. I turn to her. "Think you could hoist me up?" I point to the open window.

"I will try." She leans over and laces her fingers together. "Put your foot here."

I do as she asks, and then she hoists me up. As quickly as possible, I lift the window. Fortunately, it opens outward, and I shimmy over the ledge.

Oh, God. Hanging halfway over a super narrow window ledge hurts like a mofo, but that's not the worst part. It's really breezy, and I'm pretty sure I'm flashing the girls behind me.

Whatever. We're all women. They can deal.

"Hazel!" I call out. "Can you hear me?"

From this angle, I can't see the kitchen, but something is definitely burning on the stove. Hopefully, I can get to it before it gets worse. The fire alarm starts blaring, and I'm hoping she hears it and runs out, but when she doesn't, I realize I'm wasting precious time.

I wiggle and try to get my hips over the edge, but I can't seem to scoot over. After another attempt, I manage to get them over.

That's when I realize my dress isn't making its way over with me.

"Ah!" I'm about to flash my boobs along with my ass. I try to cover my chest, but that's just slowing me down.

Cue the fire truck blaring down the street. Son of a biscuit. This is worse than hitting Nick with my car.

Don't think about yourself, Abigail. That child needs you.

I do my best to fling myself over, but I get stuck with my boobs out and smashed against the window. And the more I try to kick myself over, the more my skirt rides up over my ass. Paige is trying not to laugh, and Meany Pants is frowning at me.

"Y'all, I'm stuck!" My glasses fall off my face and crash behind the couch.

I'm upside down when I see several firemen stalk up to the house as I make one more attempt. I'm not totally sure since everything is blurry without my glasses, but maybe it's better I can't see well.

There's yelling outside, which I assume is Meany Pants explaining what's going on to the fire department.

I push off one more time, and suddenly, I'm airborne. I go flying with a scream and land in a heap on the loveseat, but I come down at a funny angle on my neck.

Groaning, I crack open my eyes to find three super-hot

firemen staring at me from the other side of the window. I mean, I assume they're hot, but without my glasses, I'm not really sure.

This is mortifying because my beautiful floral tube-top dress is bunched up at my waist. Awesome.

This is probably why I should've worn a bra.

My one consolation is at least I'm not wearing granny panties.

"Ma'am, are you okay?" one yells as he bangs on the window.

I roll off the couch with a pained moan, land on the floor with a thump, and wiggle around until my nips are tucked away. I wobble to a stand and stumble toward the door while I try to cover my ass.

After I unlock the door, the men come rushing in. One scoops me up and carries me out.

"Put me down. I'm okay. But can someone get my glasses? They fell behind the couch."

After I slide down the mammoth's body, Paige reaches over to hug me.

"This is bullshit," Nick yells next to me as another firefighter holds him back. "Let me in to find my daughter."

"Sir, no one can go in until the premises are deemed safe. We'll get your daughter."

I'm not sure when Nick arrived, but I'm glad he's here for Hazel. Hopefully, he didn't see my boobs streak across his window.

A long, anxious minute later, someone carries out Hazel, who's crying. Her dad rushes to her and pulls her into his arms. In between sobs, she wails, "Da—Da—Daddy, the loud noise scawed me!"

Hot tears fill my eyes. It's a touching moment.

The mammoth hands me my glasses. "Here you are, ma'am."

I sniff quickly and slide them on my face. "Thank you."

"What the hell happened?" Nick yells to Meany Pants.

"I got locked out. Obviously. And your daughter would not open the door."

Hmm. That's technically true, but if Hazel couldn't hear us banging, it wasn't deliberate. "Um, Nick. Sorry to interrupt, but I was told Hazel was wearing headphones and listening to music, so I don't think she knew her nanny got locked out."

Meany Pants scowls at me, but I'm not going to let Nick's daughter get in trouble for something that was clearly an accident.

Another firefighter, who looks like Clark Kent, comes out with a black pot that's still smoking. "We got here in time. It helped that Wonder Woman here got the door unlocked for us quickly." He gives me a wide smile, and I blink. Yeah, this guy definitely saw my boobs.

Awkwardly, I flap my hand. "Don't give me too much credit. Nick got here in time with his keys." If I had just waited another few minutes, he could've unlocked the door himself.

Paige hooks her arm in mine and peers up at the man. "Are you single? Because my roommate Abby is single."

Um, no. This is not the way I want to meet a man.

But then Clark Kent reaches out to brush a strand of hair away from my face, and I freeze. This guy is flirting with me, right? That would be cool, except I don't like strangers up in my space. I try to smile, but I'm sure it comes out more like a grimace.

In my peripheral vision, I catch Nick watching the interaction. Those bottle-glass-green eyes sweep over me, and it sends goosebumps down my arms, but when I turn to him, his jaw tightens, and he looks away.

∼

"How are classes going?" my mom asks.

"Fine, but we haven't even had a full week of school yet." I set the books I'm going to need for tomorrow on my desk.

"Are you still waiting tables? You know how much I hate when you get out of work late from the diner."

"I'm still working at Moe's and keeping an eye out for other jobs." And sometimes, when I'm feeling extra adventurous, I climb through stranger's windows and flash the neighborhood. I shake my head at myself. I'm definitely not mentioning that to my mother.

"It's a shame you can't be a nanny." She sighs. "I know how much you were looking forward to building a family with Ezra, but if you take care of children, that might really help fill the void."

My throat gets tight. "That's not why I want a nanny job. You know I love that show *The Nanny Whisperer*. It looks like so much fun, and I already love babysitting. It's just more of that." I've seen every episode except last season, but I've been too busy to watch it.

"Hmm."

"Mom, there really isn't a deeper reason other than I like working with kids." My mother is a high school guidance counselor, and she loves to ferret out the root causes of problems. She's like a damn hound dog sometimes.

"If you say so. Before I forget, your father said he wants you to help him format a Mathletes study packet. He says you always make his handouts look better." My dad is an award-winning math teacher, which means he's a bigger nerd than I am.

"Sure. Tell him to email it to me."

"What about your trip? Are you still planning to go this winter?"

"That's when the holiday markets are, so yes. If I can afford it."

My mother hums again. "Your father and I don't want you to

go by yourself. Have you looked more into that exchange program?"

"It's too late to apply for this fall, and you know I can't swing a spring semester."

She groans. "I hate that it didn't work out for you. I feel like I failed you. A semester in Spain would've been *hermosa*!"

"I'm going to England, Mom. I don't speak Spanish well enough to go to Spain." My mother only knows, like, ten Spanish words, so I don't understand why she wants me to go there. "Besides, it's not your fault. I'm the dummy who transferred schools." She warned me it was a bad idea. She said I'd regret losing credits. Did I listen? No.

"You know, I just spoke to Beth—"

"We're not talking about Ezra." My mom's best friends with his mother Beth, and they're both heartbroken he and I didn't work out. "He *cheated* on me, Mom." I never gave her the full story, because it was too painful to talk about, not to mention embarrassing.

"I'm not trying to rationalize his behavior, but I'm guessing he's matured a lot since that happened, and he definitely regrets how he treated you."

"That's doubtful. Look, I need to go."

"Darling, wait. I'm sorry. I won't bring him up again. You're doing what's right for you, and I support that. I'm just sad."

I nod. "I'm sad too." Not because I lost a fiancé, but because I lost what that meant—having my own family. Having someone who supported me the way I supported him. Really, what my parents have. "But I'll survive."

"I know, sweetheart. You're strong."

No, I'm not, but I'm getting there.

5

NICK

"Daddy, these awe so pwetty," Hazel says as she leans in to sniff the roses I bought for our neighbors.

"Don't squish them, honey. You can carry them if you promise not to drop them."

Her eyes light up. "I can do that."

After I grab the pizza box, I open the front door and follow my daughter outside. As we reach Abigail and Paige's house, I realize my hands are clammy. I wipe them on my jeans before I knock on the door.

How do you thank the women who possibly saved your daughter's life? Surely pizza and flowers aren't enough, but maybe it's a start.

Paige opens the door with a smile, and I hold up the pizza. "Hey, Paige. Hazel and I wanted to thank you guys for everything you did the other day. We're really grateful."

My daughter hops up and down and knocks a few petals to the ground. "We bwought you flowas and pizza."

I clear my throat. "Yes, flowers and pizza." I read somewhere it's better not to outright correct my child so I don't embarrass her, but rather to model the proper pronunciation. "Hope you guys like pepperoni."

"Why don't y'all come in?" Paige opens the door wider. "Abby!" she calls out behind her. "Our neighbors brought us food!" Paige grins at me. "Abby was just telling me she was craving pizza."

"Perfect."

Their house is basically the mirror image of ours. Same living room setup. Same dining room. Same picture window. I glance up. Same awning window above it.

I chuckle to myself when I remember how Abby squeezed through mine. Damn, that was a sight. If I hadn't been shitting my pants, scared to death something bad was happening to my daughter, I would've appreciated the moment more. Because her legs? They were a thing of beauty. Her ass? Round as a summer peach. Her tits? Fucking gorgeous.

I shake my head and try to clear my mind of the memory because it would be really awkward to walk in here with an erection.

You're here to thank Abby, asshole, not perv on her.

She trots out wearing duck pajama pants, a t-shirt, and giant bunny slippers. She looks adorable. I can't quite keep track of her style. One second, she's got a bloody knee and a hole in her khakis, the next, she's a vixen in a tiny little dress, and now she's ready for a pajama party.

She slides to a halt when she sees us. "Oh, hey." She pushes her glasses up her nose and tucks a loose strand of hair that's fallen out from her messy bun behind her ear. "Is everything okay?"

"Sorry to intrude, but Hazel and I wanted to thank you and Paige for coming to the rescue the other day. So we brought you some dinner." I hold up the box of pizza. It was a fluke that I was close to home when I got her message. I honestly don't know how to thank her for what she did.

She takes a tentative step closer. "Um. Thanks. You didn't have to do that."

"Of course we did. Hazel." I nudge her forward. "Give the girls their flowers." My daughter runs up to Paige and hands her the white roses, then heads for Abby to give her the red.

Abby gets down on her knees. "Thank you, Hazel. This is so thoughtful. I'm just glad you're okay."

To my surprise, my daughter throws her arms around Abby's neck. This must surprise Abby because her eyes widen as she looks up at me and returns the hug.

"I was scawed, but Daddy said you got the doo-a open. Thank you."

Abby blinks quickly and nods. "I'm just happy we got there when we did."

Paige motions to their small dining room table. "Do you want to join us for dinner?"

I hold up my hand. "That's okay. You guys enjoy it."

Hazel races up to me and tugs my arm. When I lean over, she whispers in my ear, "Can we stay, Daddy? I want pizza."

I distinctly remember her saying she did *not* want pizza an hour ago when I ordered it. Before I can respond, Paige pulls out a chair. "Sure thing, Hazel. Grab a seat. The more the merrier. Right, Abby?"

Abby's eyes meet mine and then dart away. "Of course."

I try not to be disappointed that Abigail isn't enthusiastic to see me. I can't blame her. I haven't been the friendliest.

My daughter clambers into a chair, but she's too short to reach the table, so I scoop her up and put her in my lap. "That better?"

She nods. "Thanks, Daddy."

Paige hands us paper plates and sits across from us, and

Abby takes the chair next to her. Then Paige growls. "Where are my manners? What would you like to drink?"

"We'll take water, thanks." I lean over and grab a napkin and tuck it in my daughter's t-shirt. Otherwise, I'll be scrubbing marinara out of it later.

Abigail serves my daughter and then moves the box to me so I can grab my own. When she leans over to get her own slice, I notice tape on the corner of her glasses and bruises. Lots of them.

I motion to her arms. "Are those bruises from hopping through the window?"

She shrugs. "Yeah."

"Jesus, Abby, I'm so sorry. Are you okay?"

Paige returns with four waters. "That's nothing. You should see her stomach and hips. The poor girl is black and blue."

Abigail glares at her roommate. "I'm fine. Really."

If I hadn't come over here tonight, I never would've known she got hurt. Everything in me wants to march to the other side of the table and see where else she's injured, but I'm pretty sure she wouldn't welcome the attention. "Abby, how can I make this up to you? Do you need to see a doctor? I can pay for that."

"The bruises will heal. Nothing internal hurts." She takes a bite of her pizza and mumbles, "Except my pride."

I glance down at my daughter, who's happily munching away, and debate what to say. "It's just... the way you slid down the glass... looked painful." I'd just handed the firefighter my keys when she went flying over the ledge.

Abby freezes and her cheeks turn bright red. "You saw that?"

Shit. I had to open my big mouth. "I thought you noticed me in the window."

"Without my glasses I couldn't see much. They fell behind the couch. I thought you were a firefighter. You know, someone

I'd never have to see again, so I wouldn't have to crawl under a rock."

I chuckle. "You were really brave. I never would've thought to try that window. How the hell did you get up there?"

Hazel tugs on my arm. "Daddy, you said hell."

"Sorry, kiddo. How the *heck* did you get up there?"

Abby takes a sip of water. "Your nanny gave me a boost, so I wiggled through, got stuck, then slid tits first."

Paige chokes on her drink. "Okay, I have to say it. You've just beaten my most embarrassing story. And hey, look on the bright side, babe. At least those firefighters have been blowing up your phone all week."

Abigail snorts. "I already dated an elite athlete. No way will I go out with a firefighter."

I have to admit I'm not crazy about that scenario either. Abigail seems way too innocent to date one of those guys who strolled up on my lawn, but I'm curious what her rationale is. "Why's that?"

Her blue eyes sear into mine. "Because I read a statistic about how many of them cheat."

Knowing she dated Ezra, I can't blame her for feeling that way, but it's unfair for her to lump all elite athletes together. "I never cheated on my long-term girlfriend." I never bring up Gemma, and honestly, I don't know why I do now, but it's too late to take it back.

Her expression softens. "Then she was lucky."

Conversation is a little stilted after that, but fortunately, Paige brings up the game this weekend, and I can talk about football on autopilot. After dinner, I throw away the paper plates and toss the plastic water bottles in the recycling bin as Paige chats with my daughter.

Abigail is at the sink washing her hands when I tap her on

the shoulder. "Can I at least pay for your glasses to be repaired? That happened when they fell behind the couch, right?"

"It's fine. I was planning to get new frames anyway." She shrugs. "Sometimes things break for a reason, you know? It's like the universe's way of making the decision for me."

"I like your attitude." I smile down at her. Damn, she's so pretty. Abigail's not wearing any makeup, but her big blue eyes are stunning nonetheless. She has beautiful full lips and creamy skin. And Christ, she smells good. Like ripe summer peaches. "Just so you know, I feel like I owe you a favor now."

"Let's call it even. I ruined your bumper, after all."

I chuckle, which is a first for me. Until this moment, I hadn't found that bumper very amusing. Maybe it helps I finally got it fixed.

Her blush deepens. "I'm just glad I could help Hazel."

My attention drifts to my little munchkin, who's still chatting with Paige. "I didn't want to say this in front of Hazel, but I'm interviewing for a new nanny. Oksana and Hazel don't gel, and the incident this week underscored this issue. Hazel tends to listen to music when she's upset, but once she heard the fire alarm, she got scared and hid in the closet." I'm just so fucking grateful there wasn't a full-blown fire. "If she had a good relationship with Oksana, maybe she wouldn't have been trying to block out the world with those headphones. In any event, Hazel and I have talked about not listening to music so loudly because she needs to be able to hear me or her babysitter if there's an emergency."

Abigail gives me a sympathetic smile. "I know that was scary, but I'm sure she learned a valuable lesson. It sounds like you're teaching her all the right things."

"I can only hope." I feel like I fuck up a lot, and I really don't wanna mess up my child. I jam my hands in my pockets. "By the way, if you'd like the job, if you're still interested in the nanny position, I'd be okay with that."

Her eyes widen, and she shakes her head. "I don't think it would be a good idea."

My heart sinks. It's obvious my daughter likes her. Hell, the woman crawled through a window to help my kid. What more do I need to prove she'd be able to keep Hazel safe? But Abigail and I got off on a bad foot, starting with the car accident. And yeah, I wasn't terribly friendly during that interview. She was just so nervous, I thought she was a football fangirl, and I'm not interested in hiring someone who's here for the wrong reasons. "You think I'm an asshole."

She laughs, and the smile she gives me makes my heart beat hard for some reason. "You're a good dad, and I'm sure you're a great employer, but I don't think I want to work for anyone who's"—her voice drops to a whisper—"seen me ass up, tits out, hanging over their window."

I don't let my eyes drop beneath her gorgeous face, though, Jesus, I wanna look. Unfortunately for both of us, I remember that moment down to the light berry color of her very hard nipples as they streaked across the glass.

I've thought about that more than I'm comfortable admitting.

But she makes a good point. I have seen *a lot* of Abigail, and I don't want things to be weird between us.

Her cell rings on the counter, and I frown when I see the name. "Clark Kent Fireman is calling." Is that the guy who was flirting with her after they evacuated my daughter? While I'm grateful the emergency crew was there that day to help, I'm not excited about him calling my sweet neighbor. I don't know why I feel so protective of her all of a sudden.

She rolls her eyes. "Paige entered his info. I changed it from Hot Firefighter."

"Are you going to answer it?"

"What's the point? If you're not going to swing at the ball, why take an at-bat?"

Damn, she knows her sports references too. My smile widens. "Why, Abigail Dawson, are you a baseball fan? I thought for sure you'd only be a diehard football fan."

She shakes her head. "I've given up on football."

I hold my hand over my heart. "That pains me to hear." Her cheeks turn that lovely rosy color. "If you ever change your mind and want to come to a Bronco game, let me know. I'd be happy to score you some tickets."

"Truthfully, I'm weaning myself off the sport. Too many good memories have been tarnished."

What the fuck is wrong with Ezra? He had the whole world in the palm of his hand. Not only did he have a bright football career ahead of him, but he was dating this beautiful, smart woman. And he blew it. For what? A seedy blow job at a dumb party? What an idiot.

I want to tell Abby that not all men are like that, but it's not my place. I don't want to make things more awkward between us.

She clears her throat. "Anyway, good luck at your game this weekend. It's against Mississippi State, right?" When I nod, she tugs at a strand of her hair. "Watch your blindside. Those guys blitz like crazy."

I shouldn't be surprised she knows this. She dated Ezra for years, and she obviously cared enough to pay attention to the teams he faced. "Are you going to the game? Or will you watch it on TV?"

"I, um... probably not."

Damn. That shouldn't bother me, but it does.

As Hazel and I walk back home a few minutes later, she skips next to me. "I love Abby and Paige."

"I know, honey."

I just wish there was something I could do or say to convince Abigail to be my daughter's nanny. Because it would make Hazel's day.

And maybe mine too.

6

ABIGAIL

"Order ten, up!" Moe calls from behind the counter.

I hustle to the other side of the diner to grab the stack of pancakes. Moe's Diner is a greasy spoon that serves breakfast until midnight. Since we're close to campus, this place is always busy, especially on Friday nights. It's a cute restaurant with vintage cherry-red booths, mini-jukeboxes at all the tables, and the classic black and white checkered floor.

The only problem is the meals aren't expensive, which is great for customers but lousy for tips. And I'm not a fan of the waitress uniform. At first, I thought this diner dress was cute, but since I tend to spill things, I wish it wasn't pink.

"Here you go, Mr. Pearson," I say as I slide his meal in front of him. "Do you need me to warm up your coffee?"

He runs his thumb through the top strap of his worn overalls as he smiles at his food. "Nah, I'll never get to sleep tonight if I have more than one cup. But I need a to-go container. You know how much Essie loves her pancakes."

Essie is his pet goat.

"Sure thing." After I drop off the container, I double-check his order on my notepad, tear off his copy, and tuck it under the condiments. "No rush."

As it gets later, I notice all of the cute couples walking hand in hand, and it makes me sad I'm single. Now that I know what the real Ezra Thomas is like, I'm grateful I found out the truth about him when I did, but it makes me wonder if I'll ever find someone special.

The bell over the door rings as I'm taking another order, and internally I groan. We're understaffed tonight. I don't know what it is about this place, but people constantly call in sick. I'm flying solo—again—which means I'll have to haul ass to cover all the tables. That stinks because no one gets good service, and customers take it out on me by not tipping.

Moe says he's hired some new people who start next week. I only hope they're reliable.

Loud male laughter makes me turn my head, and I groan again when several jocks in their black and white letterman jackets make their way to the back booth, which is a large circular table. Reluctantly, I head down there to take their order.

I scribble the table number on my notepad as I greet everyone. "Hey, guys, I'm Abby. Welcome to Moe's. What can I get you to drink?"

"Abby. Hey."

I look up to find Nick smiling at me. Oh, good gravy. Why the heck couldn't Whitney show up tonight? This is her dang table, not mine. I don't want to wait on Nick and his football friends.

It's been two weeks since he and Hazel dropped off pizza and flowers, and I'm embarrassed about how many times I've thought about this man. I was good when he hated me for screwing up his bumper. Why did he have to go and be concerned about my bruises and wonky glasses?

At least I had the good sense to turn down that nanny job,

though I'd much rather take care of his adorable daughter than wait tables all semester.

But the man has seen my ass and nipples, for Pete's sake. With that thought, heat rises up my neck. Great. Now I'm blushing. For some reason, I always go as red as a fire hydrant around him.

"Hi, Nick. What would you guys like to order?"

The guy next to him leans forward and looks me up and down. "That depends. Are you on the menu?"

"Cut that shit out," Nick says as he elbows his teammate. "Abby's my neighbor."

The third guy, I think his name is Maverick, gives him a look. "Is she the one whose dress—"

"You told them?" My mouth drops open. Why in the world would he tell people about my outfit fail?

Nick holds up his hands. "I swear it wasn't me."

I give him the stink eye until his friend Jinxy pipes up across the table. "Everyone's been talking about how you rescued our little Hazy Daisy. And the subject of your great... dress... might've come up."

Nick sighs. "One of our neighbors saw everything go down from across the street."

Awesome.

I stare at my notepad and will myself not to cry because I freaking hate this place sometimes. I've never felt like I belonged in Charming. Transferring to Lone Star State for Ezra is the biggest mistake I've ever made. Maybe things would've been different if I'd started here freshman year, but nothing ever works out for me at this school. I can't seem to make friends, I never know how to act, and I'm constantly embarrassing myself.

"Abby," Nick says softly as he slides out of the booth and walks me a few feet away with his hand on my back. When we stop, I look up into his concerned eyes, and some of my anxiety melts away. Good Lord, he smells good. Would it be wrong to lean closer and sniff him? "Sorry my friends are making this weird. Do you want us to leave?"

Weird is me wanting to brush my nose against his neck.

Wait. What did he ask me?

"It's fine." Do I wish he and his friends would leave? Yes, but I also know that despite how busy this place is, Moe needs every one of his customers to stay afloat.

"Are you sure?"

I nod.

"You probably didn't get this from my teammates' comments, but you're the hero in that story. I'll always be grateful for you stepping up to help Hazel. She's my whole world."

My throat gets tight, and I try to smile. "Th-thanks."

"I'll keep everyone in line, okay?"

I fidget, not knowing what to say, so I blurt out the first thing that comes to mind. "You've been playing great this season."

He lifts a brow. "Have you been watching my games?"

I roll my eyes. "There have only been two."

"And?"

"Fine. I've watched your games."

The smile he gives me stops my heart.

This is bad. Really bad. Having a crush on my next-door neighbor is a terrible idea. Because that's what this is, right? This is how things started with Ezra. He smiled and flirted, and I basically fell at his feet in a big puddle.

I scramble to think of how to justify watching him play. "I promised Paige I'd watch her cheer." Which is not a lie. It's just not the entire truth.

"Sure." He winks.

I hate this charming bastard so much. But, ugh, does he have to smell so freaking good? Like sandalwood and leather and a hint of citrus. I want to roll around in his letterman jacket until that scent rubs off on my skin.

Jesus, Abby. Could you be any weirder?

Taking a deep breath, I remind myself that he's just being nice. He's not actually flirting with me. This wouldn't be the first time I misinterpreted the intentions of someone being friendly.

The man has a girlfriend. I repeat that to myself three more times. That girl Larissa announced it on the day we moved in next door to him.

I follow Nick back to the table, where the guy who'd eyeballed me holds out his hands. "Hey, I'm sorry, Abby. Didn't mean to be an asshole. I'm Dax, by the way."

They go around introducing themselves to me, and I start to relax. Maybe this won't be so bad. I take everyone's order and drop it off in the kitchen before I deliver their drinks.

I'm just putting down the last glass when three cheerleaders come skipping up to the guys' table. I'm hoping Paige is here too, until I remember she has a date.

"Hey, lovers. Ya got room for us?" the pretty brunette says.

Dax pats his lap. "Right here, gorgeous. Climb on up."

She crawls over Nick, pausing to whisper something in his ear, and I take that as my cue to leave.

I hate this clawing feeling in my chest. I remember it well from all the times Ezra would flirt with other girls in front of me. He always said he was just keeping up appearances, but now I know it was more.

I've come to accept that I've got a streak of jealousy in me, which is why I can't ever date another professional athlete. They have women four rows deep begging for their attention wherever they go.

I don't care how handsome Nick is or that he makes my heart flutter. I never plan to stand in the back of that line again.

When their order is up, I line up all five plates on a giant tray and carry it over. One of the girls is squished between Nick and Dax, but she doesn't look upset by the lack of space. The other two girls squeezed in at the other end of the circular booth next to Jinxy.

I'm just glad these women aren't my problem anymore. *Go for it, ladies. Flirt all you want. I'm not going to lose sleep over it.*

I pass out the dishes and am about to ask the cheerleaders if they'd like something to drink when the queen bee sitting between Nick and Dax snaps her fingers at me. "I'd like a chef's salad, please. No tomatoes. With that diet vinaigrette on the side."

Did she really just snap her fingers at me? I bite my tongue until I taste the tang of metal. "No problem."

Nick gives her a look. "Be nice." She rolls her eyes.

One of the other girls orders fries, and Queenie tuts. "Sheryl, those fries are going to land on your ass, and no one will be able to heft you up the pyramid."

Poor Sheryl pales. "You're right. I'll have a plain salad."

The third girl kills my soul by following suit and ordering another plain salad.

I have to bus a few tables and serve up other orders before I get a chance to deliver their meals, and Queenie is pissed. "That took for-fucking-ever."

Nick murmurs something to her, but I can't catch it.

"Sorry about that. I'm the only one who showed up to work tonight. I'm doing my best." As Queenie eyeballs her salad, I slip a small plate of fries to Sheryl and make a "shh" motion with my finger. Jinxy smiles at me and steals one. I turn back to Queenie. "Moe makes a killer chocolate icebox pie. Would you like a slice? My treat for the long wait."

She flicks something off her salad. "God, no. All that processed sugar makes me want to yak."

Okay, then.

I might need to eat a whole one when my shift is over.

Dax nods. "Hell, yes. Bring on the pie. We'll pay for ours, obviously."

Nick motions to me. "Can you put my piece in a to-go box? I think I'll share mine with Hazel tomorrow."

Why does he have to be so sweet? I can see that moment now—Nick sitting in front of his large picture window with Hazel on his lap as they share the pie.

And why does he have to be so dang handsome? Tonight, he has scruff on his chin, and he looks so collegiate in his letterman.

Queenie interrupts my fantasy by wrapping her arms around his neck. "You're really hot when you talk about your daughter."

That's my cue. Turning on my heel, I head off to get the pie. When I drop off their slices, I place their check under the ketchup and beeline it to the cash register before I throw up from watching Queenie flirt with Nick.

You'd think I'd learn.

Well, I wanted to kill my attraction to Nick, and watching that cheerleader crawl all over him definitely did the trick.

Now we can go back to neighbors who occasionally say hi when we get our mail instead of whatever strange thing this is that makes my heart flutter.

Moe hits the ringer on the counter. "Order up!"

I still have another hour before we close, my feet are killing me, and a slow throb has taken up residence behind my temples. Another group of students comes in, and I want to cry. When will this night end?

I stare longingly at my new romance novel under the cash register. When things are dead around here, Moe lets me read sometimes. Obviously, that's not happening tonight.

My mom says I shouldn't read romance because it'll give me

unrealistic expectations about relationships. She doesn't understand that it's the one thing that gives me hope of finding my person, whoever he is.

Jinxy and Nick come up to pay the check, and I apologize as I ring them up. "Sorry for the wait tonight."

Jinxy smiles. "No problem, cutie. Dinner was great. Jinxy loves a good omelet."

Did he just refer to himself in third person? I try to hide my laugh. "Glad you enjoyed it. I'll tell Moe."

I don't make eye contact with Nick. I shouldn't be hurt that he's flirting with cheerleaders. He's not my boyfriend.

Before he can say anything, I take off to deliver another order. In the last ten minutes, five tables paid and left, and now I have to bus their tables since people keep coming.

Out of the corner of my eye, I see the football table leaving, and I let out a relieved breath.

I really need to stop getting emotionally invested in men. A good start will be not watching those dang football games. If only they weren't so good. Nick really is an incredible player, and I hope he goes all the way. Fortunately, he doesn't need my one-girl fan club to do that.

I decide right then and there that I need to build up an emotional wall so high no one can scale it, not even my ridiculously handsome neighbor.

With a groan, I heft the large gray bin to bus the tables when Nick walks up to me. I do a double-take as he shrugs off his letterman, revealing his ripped arms and muscled chest, and drapes the jacket over a chair at the counter. I finally find my tongue. "I—I thought you left." My eyes widen. "Why are you wrapping an apron around your waist?"

Ignoring my question, he takes the bin out of my hands and starts bussing tables.

Confused, I stand there for a solid ten seconds as I watch

him scrape leftover food onto one plate and then stack the others in the bin. "What are you doing?"

He glances at me over his shoulder. "Helping you clean your tables so you're not here all night."

"I can see that, but why?"

"Because you've been busting your ass since I got here, and I can't in good conscience go home when you have so much work ahead of you."

My eyes sting, and I look away and blink several times.

He lowers his voice. "Plus, I didn't like how Tiffany talked to you. I told her to be nice. That she needed to watch her snark. I should've said more, but she's like a rash. If you itch, you make things worse."

So Queenie's name is Tiffany. Good to know so I can avoid her.

Nick's t-shirt stretches over his arms as he reaches across the table to grab an empty glass. It's a mesmerizing sight.

"You have a game tomorrow. Shouldn't you turn in early?"

After he wipes down the table, he turns to me. "I'll survive, and if I don't, I'm a suck-ass athlete." He winks at me again, and my face gets hot. "Go do what you need to do. I got this."

"Don't you need to get home to Hazel?"

"The new babysitter is watching her. We're good."

I'm equal parts disappointed he's already hired someone and relieved the position is filled.

Standing here watching him just makes things more awkward, so I shuffle backward. "Thank you. I appreciate your help." My eyes get watery again, and I stalk off before he sees.

Doggone it. I need to build a bigger wall.

7

NICK

Red, blinking lights flash in my face when I crack open my eyes.

Why is it blinking one-thirty? My alarm clock never does this, which is the first indication that shit's not gonna go my way today.

We must've lost power this morning because bright morning sun blares through my curtains.

The realization that it's Saturday hits me like a hard sack.

Crap. What time is it?

I leap out of bed, nearly killing myself on one of Hazel's Lego sets, and scramble for my phone.

It's ten in the morning on a game day. I've usually showered, dressed, and gotten down to the stadium by now. Fuck.

I race out to the living room, where I find my daughter watching TV and eating a bagel. "Hazel, why didn't you wake me?"

Her eyes never leave the cartoon. "I twied, Daddy, but you we-a sno-ing." She giggles.

"I don't snore," I grumble.

Figures. The one time my kid lets me sleep past seven in the morning is the day I could've used my little human alarm clock. I don't have time to ponder how Hazel managed to make her own breakfast at the moment, but I'll pat the kid on the back for that later.

As I haul ass into the bathroom to wash my face and brush my teeth, a million questions race through my mind, but one rises to the top with blaring intensity: Why hasn't my nanny gotten here yet? She should've been my failsafe to wake up on time.

I hired two women recently: Denise, who watches Hazel in the mornings and drives her to and from preschool, and Felicia, who stays in the evenings. But since Felicia wanted to pick up a few more shifts, she said she could cover today.

I'm about to call her when I realize she's already left me a message. Thank God. Maybe she's just running late.

I put the message on speaker as I tug on some gray dress pants and a black Bronco polo. Fortunately, I set out my game day clothes yesterday.

"Hey, Nick..." Cough, cough. "Sorry I can't come in today, but I'm not feeling well." Cough. "Maybe Denise can watch your daughter?"

My eyes narrow. She seemed fine yesterday, and those coughs aren't terribly convincing, but I'll deal with Felicia later. I pull up Denise's number, but it goes to voicemail.

I don't have time for this. I need to get my ass down to the stadium before Coach has an aneurysm. He's very strict about us getting there early on game days because traffic sucks.

I've never had a babysitter bail like this.

Maybe Abby can watch her. I run out to the living room and glance out the window, and that little bit of hope withers when neither Abby's nor Paige's car is in the driveway.

Paige can't watch her, idiot. She has to cheer at the game.

Fuck. What am I going to do?

My phone rings in my hand, and I'm hoping it's Denise, but it's Jinxy.

"Where the hell are you, man?"

"My power died last night, the alarm didn't go off, and my babysitter bailed."

"Shit. What about your neighbor?"

"She's not home." I run my hands through my hair. "What do I do?" I've never asked any of my teammates for advice when it comes to my daughter, but I haven't been in this position before.

"What about Miss Trunchbull?"

"I fired Oksana. I can't call her up now. Even if she did come, what if she took out her annoyance with me on Hazel?"

"Good point. What about that girl you were seeing? Larissa."

"Things didn't work out. Besides, she lives kinda far, and even if she could teleport here, Hazel doesn't like her."

He hums for a minute. "Bring Hazy Daisy to the game."

"What?"

"Bring her. We have nine assistant coaches. I'm sure someone has a girlfriend at the stadium who can help out. Or maybe one of the locker room volunteers can watch her."

I'm not crazy about this idea, but it's better than nothing. "Tell Coach I'm on my way and that I have to bring Hazel." I cringe. "Or if you don't want to face his wrath, just tell him the first part, and I'll tell him about Hazel."

After I race around the house and shove as many toys, coloring books, and snacks in Hazel's bag as I can fit, I brush the crumbs off her pajamas and kiss her forehead. "Honey, I hate to do this, but I need to bring you to the game today because we don't have a babysitter."

Her little eyes light up. "Can I watch you play football?"

She means in the stadium. She's been asking to come, but I don't trust a babysitter to watch her in a crowd of seventy thousand people. Hazel's a squirmy little thing. It would be too easy for her to walk off and not be noticed until something terrible happened.

"I'm not sure where you'll be, but maybe we can put it on the TV in one of the meeting rooms." I try to ignore her pout, but it pains me to disappoint her. As I slide on her shoes, I go over everything I can think of. "There's money in your backpack for food if you get hungry. I also included a bottle of water. Be sure to hydrate. And remember that Daddy's phone number is in the front pocket, with all of the emergency numbers. So after the game, you can always have someone dial that number for you."

Saying those words strikes a panic in me I have difficulty shaking by the time we reach the stadium. I fucking hate that I don't have anyone in my life I trust to watch my daughter. This shit's not fair to Hazel, who I have to drag around town all day. She's going to miss her nap and be out of sorts at bedtime. Who knows what she'll get fed today? Stadium nachos and soda? French fries and ice cream? Crap and more crap.

I'm sorry, Gemma. I feel like I'm failing our daughter.

I never had a chance to see a therapist after my girlfriend died, but I got a few books on grief that helped as I waded through the five stages of grief.

This morning instantly slams me back to the anger stage.

I'm pissed that my daughter is still in her pajamas. That her hair's a snarled mess. That I didn't spend time with her last night because I wanted to take Coach's advice and hang out with the guys for once.

And even though Gemma's been gone almost three years, I feel guilty as fuck for flirting with Abby.

Which I don't understand. I didn't feel weird about going out with Larissa.

That bagel I gulped down before I left the house feels like it might surge back up.

What would Gemma tell me? She was always good at talking me off a ledge, but for the first time, I can't remember what her voice sounds like.

After I park, I get Hazel out of the car seat and jog with her into the stadium. The volunteer who opens the door looks relieved to see me and clicks his walkie talkie to say, "QB1 is here."

Coach is probably pissed if he wanted an update like that. I'm two hours late. Even though there's plenty of time before the game starts, we all have our pre-game routine, and Coach always emphasizes how important it is to mentally prepare, which is why he likes us to arrive at the stadium early.

When I reach the locker room, I pause. Can I take Hazel in there? Shit. I'm not prepared to do a biology lesson with my four-year-old today.

But when the door swings open, Coach Santos walks out. "There you are."

"I'm sorry I'm late, Coach."

He nods and smiles at my daughter. "Hey, darlin'."

She shoves her face in my neck, and I pat her back. "She's shy." Sometimes.

His eyes go serious again. "I have a stadium volunteer who can watch her. She's been with us for years, and I'd trust her with Marley if I needed to."

"Really? Thank you so much. I'm so fucking sorry—"

Hazel lifts her head. "Daddy, you said the f-wowd."

"Sorry, kid." I'm a giant fuckup today.

Coach motions down the hall. "Here's Norma now. We'll set her up with Hazel in one of the conference rooms, and then I want you to go get your head on straight. Iowa doesn't give a crap that your game day routine was shot to hell."

"Yes, sir."

"And Nick? I need your focus to be a hundred percent."

I nod even though that feels like an insurmountable task.

We win. Barely.

But I get my ass kicked.

8

NICK

SHARP PAIN RADIATES down my thigh as I wobble down the hallway. It's only six in the morning, but I can't sleep. Like a bad highlight reel, I keep replaying all the mistakes I made yesterday. The post-game press conference was brutal.

I grab an ice pack and some juice and collapse on the couch.

Because I'm a masochist, I flip on ESPN. It only takes a few minutes before they recap our game. Jinxy already gave me a heads-up that they ripped me a new asshole last night, but I needed a breather before I watched the coverage.

I brace myself for the beatdown from the commentators, Joel Clark and Bo Tyson.

JOEL: *The Broncos had a great defensive game. If only their offense could keep up.*

Bo: *Nick Silva couldn't buy a vowel, Joel. He completed only eight of fourteen passes, threw an interception, and got sacked twice.*

Joel: *It's a wonder Lone Star State pulled out a win against Iowa.*

Bo: *That speaks to Coach Santos's fantastic defense. It's hands down one of the best in the country. They shut down Iowa and converted on two crucial interceptions. But the Broncos need more than a killer defense to get to the playoffs. Can't help but wonder if we're going to watch Silva melt down this fall the way Ezra Thomas did last year.*

Joel: Or, heck, the way Silva melted down in the championship game last winter.

Bo: Having said that, Silva is one of those players I always cut a little slack.

SHIT. I know what's coming before he opens his mouth.

JOEL: That's right. Silva lost his long-term girlfriend in that terrible car accident right after his big win against USC. He was on fire that night. Thought for sure he'd be up for the Heisman soon.

I FEEL SICK. This right here is why I deleted all my social media after Gemma died.

With a curse, I click off the TV. I don't need their fucking pity. I have two strong wins under my belt this season and one rough game. You'd think I'd been shitting the bed the entire time. They're already comparing me to Ezra? Really?

"Daddy?"

Fuck. I hope Hazel didn't hear that dickwad. "Morning, honey." I toss the bag of ice into a bowl on the coffee table and hold out my arms. She crawls into my lap, and I pull a blanket over her little legs. "You're up early."

She nods against my chest.

Yesterday was a shit show for more than just my game. Hazel got antsy hanging out in that conference room all day, didn't nap, and got hopped up on sugar.

But the worst part was seeing her run around on the sidelines during the third quarter. I caught her out of the corner of my eye, did a double-take, and got sacked so hard, my ears rang.

Who the hell takes a small child down to the sidelines during a game?

When I limped back to the bench, I asked one of the assistant coaches to get my daughter off the field because I can't concentrate if I'm worried she'll be flattened by an out-of-bounds play.

Afterward, I found out Norma the volunteer had to go to the bathroom and had someone else watch Hazel, and this other person got called to the sidelines and took my kid.

By the time I got to Hazel after the game, she was having a meltdown in that conference room. I tried to calm her down for a few minutes. The look of betrayal in her eyes when I had to leave her again to talk to reporters cut deep, but I didn't think Coach would let me skip it after my mediocre performance.

"Wanna go to the park today? I could push you on the swings."

She shakes her head and starts sucking her thumb. Damn it. She'd stopped doing that last year, but I think the stress of having new babysitters this week and the chaos of the game has taken its toll.

I kiss the top of her head. "I'm sorry about yesterday, kiddo. Daddy screwed up the babysitting situation. Was Norma so bad? She seemed like a nice lady."

Her shoulders shake and big fat tears well in her eyes. "She yelled at me a lot."

Fuck. "I'm so sorry." She turns in my lap and wraps her arms around my neck. I rub her back as she cries. It's possible Norma just used a stern voice, and with a four-year-old, sometimes you have to, but my daughter has a hard time when that comes from strangers. "Hazel? Can you cry for my football game too?" I ask, wanting to shift her focus. "'Cause I stank."

Red-nosed, she sniffles and looks up. "No, Daddy. You played gweat."

My throat gets tight, and I hug her. "Thanks, gingersnap. You always know what to say to make me feel better."

It's times like this I wonder if I'm doing the right thing by putting Hazel through another brutal season. At least if I'm in the NFL, I can afford to hire a nanny through an agency and trust they'll be more reliable than Felicia, who posted her impromptu trip to South Padre with her boyfriend all over her social media.

Of course, she begged me not to fire her last night when I texted her not to bother coming on Monday. I was so angry, I didn't trust myself to talk to her when she called. She's the one who wanted the extra hours. I could've found someone else if I had known she wasn't coming.

A couple of my teammates say their girlfriends can help me out this week until I find another babysitter. I'm worried how Hazel will take that news, but I can't exactly haul her around to all of my classes and practices.

Hazel and I putz around the house, and I watch an ungodly amount of kids' shows with my daughter. As I'm sitting in the living room, the sun blares through that awning window, and I squint up at it.

Since the day of the fire alarm, I've left it unlatched just in case we have another emergency. I'd like to change the lock on the front door so it can't be flipped on the inside and lock you out, but my landlord won't let me.

Something about that window reminds me of when I was a little boy and my grandmother would take me to church. I remember the pastor would say that when God closes a door, he always opens a window.

I really fucking need an open window right now.

Around lunchtime, I'm done moping. "Hazel, would you like some chicken tenders and chocolate icebox pie?"

I think a visit to Moe's Diner is in order.

And since Abby's car isn't in the driveway, I'm hoping she's at work.

Because I have to ask her a huge favor.

9

NICK

As Hazel and I make our way across the street to Moe's, I do my best not to limp. The ice and ibuprofen have helped, but it'll probably take a few days before I can walk normally. There's no need to tip off people that I'm not feeling my best, though.

The doorbell rings above our heads as we enter the restaurant. It's busy, but not as bad as Friday night. I immediately spot Abby across the diner chatting with old Mr. Pearson. She laughs at whatever he says, and I smile. Most people write him off as a whack job because his best friend is a goat. I love that Abby treats him with respect.

She finally spots us, and when she does, she almost trips. Her cheeks turn that alluring rosy shade as she walks up to us. "Are you stalking me?"

I laugh. "How did you know?"

That color turns bright red, and she avoids making eye contact with me, opting to kneel down and talk to my daughter. "Hi, Hazel. How's it going, little neighbor?"

"We want chicken stwips."

Abby nods, takes my daughter's hand, and walks her a few

booths down. Her uniform fits her like a glove. Snug on her great rack, her trim waist, and her perfectly round ass.

Her hair is braided down her back in a long, thick ponytail. It makes me wonder what it would be like if I wrapped it around my hand and pulled her mouth down to my di—

I'm snapped out of the fantasy when she lifts my daughter into a booster seat and asks her, "Do you like to color? Because I just got a new pack of crayons. Would you like to use them?"

"Yes!" My daughter grins from ear to ear, and something about that sweet expression cracks my heart wide open.

Running my hand over my face, I turn away. *What the hell is wrong with me? I shouldn't be fantasizing about this woman.*

Abby drags a paper placemat with some kind of puzzle in front of Hazel and hands her a cup with half a dozen crayons.

I'm about to sit next to Hazel when Abby leans toward me and whispers, "Why are you limping? Do you need some ice?"

Her concerned blue eyes meet mine, and I freeze. "I'm okay."

She clucks her tongue. "Okay, tough guy, but if you change your mind, I have some ibuprofen in my purse." Turning to Hazel, she takes out her notepad. "Would you like some dipping sauce for your chicken strips?"

"Yes, please."

"Nice manners, Hazel." She winks at my daughter and then turns to me. "And what will you be having today, Daddy?"

Our eyes meet, and I lift an eyebrow. "Daddy?" That blush returns, and I chuckle. When Larissa called me that, I was embarrassed, but when Abby says it, I'm intrigued.

She flails her arms. "You know what I mean."

"Just messing with ya." For some reason, I really like messing with this woman. She's fun to fluster, but I don't want to come across as a creep, so I shift my attention to a menu. "I'll have a cheeseburger and a chef's salad, please."

"Let me guess. No tomatoes and that diet vinaigrette on the side."

It takes me a second to realize what she's talking about. "Abby, I'm so sorry for how those girls treated you. I should've stopped that crap earlier."

She shakes her head as she scribbles on her notepad. "It's fine. Just giving you a hard time."

The smile she gives me makes something hard all right. And that's fucking weird.

Before Abigail, a woman's smile has never given me a hard-on.

Jesus, maybe Jinxy is right and I need to blow off some steam and get laid.

I clear my throat. "I'll take ranch for that salad, and Hazel and I will also share a slice of that icebox pie."

Abigail tucks a strand of hair behind her ear. "Did she like that piece you took her the other night?"

Wincing, I shrug. "I might've eaten it when I got home."

Abby snickers. "It's good to know you're human. Let me get your orders. And did y'all want water or something else to drink?"

"Water would be great."

I watch her walk away. My eyes are glued to her ass as I remember her rocking that tube-top dress. Even her wonky glasses that are patched up with tape are adorable.

Damn it. There I go again. She's hopefully going to be my new nanny. As much as I like Abby, I can't go down that path.

A pounding starts right between my eyes, and I pinch the bridge of my nose as I promise myself I won't flirt with my sweet neighbor.

When Abby returns with our dishes, she has a whole plate of little sauces. "Hazel, I wasn't sure which dip you might like, so I brought you one of everything. We have the all-time champion ketchup, a very tasty barbecue, a lovely honey mustard, and my favorite, the chicken-fried steak gravy, which is delish. Try whatever suits your fancy, and feel free to ignore anything you don't like."

With a dead serious expression on her face, my daughter licks her lips and nods. "Thank you so much."

When Abby heads off to help another table, I turn away before I can check her out again and tuck a napkin into the neckline of Hazel's t-shirt. "You're doing so well saying please and thank you. Nice job, kiddo."

She's busy inspecting her sauces. "Can I stick my finga in these?"

I shrug. "You mean to taste them? Why not? Wait. Let's clean your hands first."

Dutifully, she holds them out while I whip out some wipes from her bag. Then she goes to town, determining that she also loves the gravy.

By the time Abby circles back to us, my daughter has gobbled down most of her food. "The sauces were a hit. Thanks for giving her so many options."

She slides that piece of pie in front of me. "It was nothing."

Shit. We're almost done here, and I still haven't brought up my proposition. "Can I ask you something? It's kind of a big favor."

Abby nibbles the corner of her enticing lip. "Sure. What's up?"

I slide out of my booth because I don't wanna disappoint Hazel if Abby says no. I motion a few feet away, and Abby follows me. "I had a situation yesterday. My nanny didn't show up, and I had to bring Hazel to the stadium with me."

She tilts her head. "That's why you were off yesterday."

I nod. "I was a fucking mess."

Her eyes go soft. "It wasn't so bad. You had a great recovery when Bowser messed up that snap. And you can't really take all the blame because your O-line wasn't having a great day either. You still got the W. That's all that matters. Next game will be better."

Instantly, my shoulders feel lighter, and I can take a deep breath. "Thanks. That means a lot. So... I guess that means you watched another game?"

She looks down with a smile. "Maybe."

"Truly, I appreciate the support. But do you want to know what I really need?"

"What's that?" Her big blue eyes tilt up.

"A great nanny. Preferably someone who cares about my daughter's fifteen hundred dipping sauces and comes prepared with crayons."

She nibbles the corner of her mouth again. "Are you sure that's a good idea?"

"Why wouldn't it be? You're obviously great with kids. You're super responsible. I can tell from how you hold this place together. And you're getting a degree in early childhood education. Frankly, you're overqualified, and I'm a total asshole for not hiring you over the summer."

That color returns to her cheeks. "I did take off your bumper while you were in the middle of your"—her hands flail again—"date."

I cover my mouth to cough, mildly embarrassed she remembers that Larissa was in my lap that night. "Yes, well. I did park at a weird angle, as I recall from the police report."

"Order up!" a guy behind the counter yells.

She points behind her. "I have to get that."

I gently grab her arm. "Are you still on the fence about babysitting?"

"I just..." She closes her eyes. "I had a really bad experience with Ezra, which turned me off of football and everything associated with it. I know you're a nice guy, Nick. You seem like a decent human being, but I can't shake the feeling that I'm setting myself up somehow. Plus, I'd have to work out my schedule here. I can't just leave Moe. He's been good to me even though the tips suck."

I frown. I'm not a fan of being compared to Ezra. "What can I do to make you feel safe? What can I do to prove I just want someone responsible and kind to watch Hazel? I have no ulterior motives. I swear things between us will stay strictly professional at all times. And we can absolutely work with your schedule."

She stares at me a long moment. Long enough for me to notice that the outer rims of her eyes are a light gray. "You promise not to screw me over somehow?"

I hold my hand over my heart. "I swear on football."

She's on the fence. This is probably playing dirty, but I can't take the chance she'll turn me down. I need someone who's reliable. Someone I can trust. Someone who won't flake out on me. So I take her hand and walk her back to Hazel, who's happily coloring again. "Hazel, how would you feel if Abby babysat you sometime?"

I'm deliberately vague. Sometime might mean "every blue moon" or "several days a week." Hopefully the latter. Although I don't want Abby to feel cornered into this, I'm not an idiot. I need to use my best weapon—my cute-as-hell daughter.

Hazel's eyes widen and she folds her hands in front of her chest like she's saying a prayer. "You would be the bestest!" She wiggles out of her booster seat and throws herself against Abby's legs.

While I knew my daughter would be excited by this possibility, even I'm caught off guard by her enthusiasm.

I hold out my hand. "You heard it yourself, Abby. You would be the *bestest*."

Her eyes go squinty as she stares at me. "You don't play fair, do you?"

Grinning, I shrug. "Does that mean you'll help a guy out? Pretty please with sprinkles on top?"

Reluctantly, she shakes her head with a laugh as she kneels down to hug my daughter. "Just as long as we're clear that I'm doing this for Hazel and not you."

Am I disappointed she's not doing this for me? Yes. But since I just swore to keep things professional, I need to lock away the memory of Abigail Dawson in that tube-top dress.

So I nod. "I'll take what I can get."

10

ABIGAIL

A GIGGLE COMES from behind a couch cushion, and I tiptoe closer. "Hmm. Let's see. Hazel isn't in the closet, and she isn't under the kitchen table. Is she behind the curtains?"

I whip it back and smile when she giggles again. "Could she be hiding in the bathtub?" Stomping down the hall, I make a big production of not finding her there before I march back to the living room.

Nick's house looks like a masculine version of ours, which basically means there aren't any decorations or throw pillows. Everything is utilitarian. He has a small flatscreen sitting on a beat-up buffet table that holds three baskets underneath with toys, Legos, and stuffed animals.

There's an old brown leather couch and a reading lamp opposite the TV and a loveseat in front of the picture window, the same loveseat that broke my fall from the awning window above it. That's where Hazel's hiding, squished underneath the baby-blue cushions like a tiny assassin, waiting to pounce.

It's been a couple of weeks since Nick and Hazel came to Moe's. After Paige gave me the behind-the-scenes version of what happened that Saturday when his babysitter bailed on him and I heard how distraught Hazel had been, I wished I could start working for Nick immediately. But I had to help train the new waitstaff at Moe's and make sure they could handle everything. I'm still picking up a few shifts, but nothing like before.

Now that I'm watching Hazel in the afternoon and evenings, I feel foolish for turning this job down initially. Nick doesn't have a thing for me. He's so tired, he barely looks at me when he gets home.

If a part of me misses those flirty smiles, well, I'll learn to deal with it.

I sigh and then stop mid-breath.

If I inhale too deeply, I catch a whiff of his sexy cologne, and I'd be lying if I said it didn't affect me, so I try not to do that often.

I nod to myself. Not sniffing my boss's belongings sounds prudent.

"Hazelnut, where in the world are you?" I wander over by the couch, where her little arms jut out and grab my leg.

I do a big fake Hollywood scream, and she leaps from the cushions with a huge grin on her face. "You caught me!" Picking her up, I twirl her around and nearly have a heart attack when the front door crashes open.

Nick's standing there with his chest heaving. "What's wrong? Who's screaming? Are you hurt?"

I fold in my lips to keep myself from laughing. "Hazel and I were playing hide and go seek, silly. And when she caught me, I got 'scared.'" I hope he gets I'm playing up the fear for Hazel.

Holding out his arms for his daughter, he stalks closer. She jumps at him with a laugh.

"You silly, Daddy." She plants a kiss on his cheek. "We-a just playing."

We're just playing. Hazel's so stinking adorable. I love this child. She's a pleasure to hang out with all day.

My nose crinkles when I realize it's only three in the afternoon. "What are you doing home so early, Nick?"

He kisses his daughter's sweaty forehead. "Today's practice schedule got shifted around, and I had a little time before I need to get to the field house. Thought I'd grab us some subs. Are you hungry, kiddo?"

Hazel nods even though she ate a sandwich two hours ago, but we've been running around the house all day, so maybe she's worked up an appetite.

Do I stay and watch them eat? That feels weird.

Awkwardly, I point toward the door. "Do you want me to head home and give you guys time to enjoy your lunch? I can come back when you're done."

He shakes his head, and a thick strand of hair falls rakishly over his eye. "I brought you a sub too. Unless you're not hungry."

My stomach chooses that moment to grumble loudly. I slap my hand over it as Nick laughs.

Holding his arm out toward the kitchen, he smiles. "Join us, Abby. I feel like I've barely seen you since you started taking care of Hazel."

"Stay, Abby!" Hazel yells. "We still have to make Play-Doh. You pwomised."

"That's right, I did promise, didn't I?"

As Nick tucks her into the booster chair, he glances over his shoulder at me. "Doesn't she already have, like, fifty-two tubs of that stuff?"

I chuckle. "Maybe, but I told her making your own is fun because you can mix whatever shade you want. I already bought the supplies, so it's no problem."

After he unbags the food, he motions for me to sit down across from him. "Save the receipts. I can reimburse you for whatever you spend."

"It's okay. Someday I'll be a teacher, and I'll never get reimbursed for school supplies." It's a never-ending complaint from my father. "Besides, it wasn't expensive."

"What grade do you want to teach?" he asks as he gets us three glasses of water.

"I'm not sure. Probably kindergarten or first grade. I want kids to enjoy their first few years. So many children dread going to school, but maybe if they have a fun teacher when they're young, they'll remember it's a good place where they can make fond memories."

Pausing, he smiles. It hits me like a sunbeam breaking through a cloud, and I'm momentarily dazed. "That's really sweet, Abby. I'm sure you'll be a great teacher."

I clear my throat as I unwrap my sub. "Thanks. I love children."

"You want a big family someday?" When I don't answer right away, he apologizes. "Don't mean to get too personal. You don't need to answer that if you're not comfortable."

"It's okay. But yes, I've always wanted a big family with lots of kids..." Until my fiancé turned into a giant cheating turd. Having kids was a dream I thought was in reach, and now I'll probably die single.

His eyes go soft, and I shake my head. "Don't you dare level me with pity, Nick Silva. And if you bring up that jerk's name during an otherwise lovely day, I'm going to clean your toilet bowl with your toothbrush."

He chokes on a laugh. "I wouldn't dare bring him up."

Ezra Thomas can go suck a lemon.

But now I'm thinking about how that man ruined me. Yes, it sounds dramatic, like I'm some eighteenth-century debutante who got debauched at a ball and now no one wants her, but that's how I feel.

I should keep my mouth shut, but since the whiff of Ezra is in the air, I can't help myself. "He hogged all of my attention during college, and now that I'm almost done with school, all I do is work, and I feel like I'm destined to be a schoolmarm with twenty cats."

Wow, that was some word vomit. Embarrassed, I get up to grab some silverware so I can cut up Hazel's sandwich. Otherwise, the filling will slide out the back.

Nick's brows furrow. "Do you need to reduce your hours so you can have more of a social life?"

"That's just it. I'm not really a frat party kind of girl. That's all anyone here seems to do." Hazel pulls out a slice of onion from her sandwich, and I hold out my hand and tuck it into a napkin.

Nick sighs. "I told the sub shop no onions."

"It's okay. I got this. Anyway, don't worry about the hours. I need the money."

"This is an extra semester for you, right? I had every expectation of graduating last May too. If I didn't have a football scholarship, I could never afford it."

After I swallow a bite of my roast beef hoagie, I nod. "It is expensive, but I'm mostly saving up for a trip. I'm hoping to go to Europe for a few weeks after finals. I have to make up for lost time since my ex didn't want me to do a semester abroad. I have a huge list of historical and literary sights I'd like to visit."

"Where would you go?"

"England, maybe do a solo trip to Germany or Austria to see the Christmas markets. Who knows? The possibilities are endless."

Nick frowns again. "By yourself?"

"Unless I find some classmates who want to go too."

The grooves between his eyebrows deepen. "That sounds dangerous, Abby."

"I wasn't planning to walk the streets of Whitechapel at midnight. Anyway, the only time I could do a semester abroad was in the fall, which Ezra hated because God forbid his little lucky charm wasn't available for him twenty-four seven."

He puts his sandwich down. "Lucky charm?"

Part of me feels like I'm betraying Ezra by sharing this, but then I remember all of the women he sank his dick into when we were dating, and my remorse instantly evaporates. "You know he was superstitious, right?"

After Nick takes a drink of water, he nods slowly. "He has a pretty serious pre-game routine."

"Sure. Let's call it that. Guess who was part of his ritual?" I wave my hand. "That's why he and I were arguing that night I knocked off your bumper. He wanted me to go with him to open tryouts if he wasn't drafted because he thought it would increase his odds of making a team."

It's on the tip of my tongue to admit that's why Ezra dated me in the first place, but it's too embarrassing to say out loud.

"Abby, your ex was an idiot."

Hazel's head jerks up. "Daddy, we don't call people idiots." She must be parroting something he says.

"Sorry, kid. You're right." When his daughter looks down, he mouths, "Idiot."

I laugh. "Anyway, I plan to do all the things he didn't want me to do. Go to Europe. Highlight my hair. Get contacts. Wear sexy—" I cut myself off when I realize what I was about to say in front of Hazel. "Wear fun clothes."

My God, Abigail. Shut up.

This is my problem. I overshare.

I shove my sub in my big, fat mouth before I say anything else embarrassing. Because Nick isn't interested in my Cinderella dreams.

When I brave a glance at him, he's smirking at me. "*Fun* clothes, huh? Like that tube-top dress?"

Heat blazes up my face. "We're not discussing my wardrobe malfunction, Mr. Silva. *Ever*."

He chuckles as he gets up. "Gonna go hide my toothbrush. Be right back."

I can't help how my eyes gobble him up as he walks away. His t-shirt stretches over his broad shoulders, and his jeans mold to his perfect ass.

While my ex had a great body, he was on the leaner side. Nick is taller and more muscular. Kudos to whatever weightlifting regime he's doing because Daddy Silva has it going on.

I wave a hand over my face to cool off and chug some water before I incinerate. Maybe I should've left Nick and Hazel to their lunch because lusting over my boss can't be healthy.

I do *not* need to be obsessed with another football player.

Hazel hands me a black olive, and I dutifully hide it in a napkin. I only have three more months until the end of the semester. I just need to keep myself occupied, then Nick and I will graduate and go our separate ways, and I'll have dodged a bullet.

That sounds like a good plan.

I smile at Hazel. I can do this.

11

NICK

Big, blue eyes turn sultry as Abby leans over to place my food in front of me. But instead of her pink uniform, she's rocking that tube-top dress that gives me a clear view of her killer cleavage. "Is there anything else I can get you?" she asks softly.

"There is one thing you can do." I pat my lap.

She gives me a flirty smile and straddles me. "Like this?"

I fill my hands with her gorgeous ass and grind her against me. "Come here. Let me kiss you." She comes closer, but like a whisper, her lips only graze mine.

"Are you sure we should do this?" Her blonde hair tumbles over her shoulders, and I take it between my fingers. It's like silk. I wanna feel it against my chest as I fuck her.

"God, yes."

Her fingers rake through my hair. "You're off limits."

I groan. "You are too, but you feel so damn good."

"But you don't even like me." Strangely, she doesn't voice the question, but I hear it nonetheless.

Gently, I grab her beautiful face and drag her mouth to mine. "I like you more than I should."

Between hungry kisses, she pants, "What if I slid my dress down a little? Like this..."

Yes. She should absolutely slide that dress down.

I swallow as she tugs the material that slowly reveals creamy white skin. Her tits are plump, and the first hint of her pink nipples comes into view—

Good morning, Charming! Rise and shine, mothercluckers! It's a beautiful day out there. Let's get to the traffic report.

What the fuck?

God, it's my morning alarm.

I groan and slap the damn thing until it shuts up.

Reaching down, I fist my morning wood. Christ, what a dream.

As I lie in bed, I replay every moment. Her sultry eyes, her beautiful full lips, her incredible rack. Eager to reach the finish line, I grip my cock tighter.

The dream slowly bleeds into reality, and I have to admit I enjoy spending time with Abby. That sweet, embarrassed smile she's always giving me gets me every time.

My kid's nanny shouldn't be so damn hot.

My kid's nanny.

Guilt instantly sets in. Fuck, I shouldn't be jerking off to thoughts of my neighbor. I swore I'd keep things completely professional. She already got screwed over by Ezra. She doesn't need me being a creep.

I jump out of bed and take the coldest shower I can endure. With angry swipes of my hand, I lather my body and rinse off.

I shouldn't have returned home for lunch yesterday. Things were going well until that point. I'd been coming in pretty late because I needed to get some research done at the library, and she'd give me a quick rundown of Hazel's day, then book it next door.

Part of me feels guilty for hiring Abby. She didn't want this job, not after I turned her down initially. My daughter adores her, though, and Hazel's safety and happiness have to be my priority.

But that doesn't lessen the guilt.

My cell buzzes with a text.

Coach: Do you still need a nanny? The provost's niece was runner-up on some nanny show. He says she's great. I'm sending you her number.

I'm about to tell him I'm all set, but then I reconsider.

Having three babysitters instead of two would give me backup options in case of an emergency. Then Abby could have more free time to socialize instead of being at my beck and call Monday through Saturday, which is more than she worked at the diner.

And if I'm being honest with myself, I really don't need to see her six days out of the week. That's probably a little more temptation than I'm prepared to handle. I don't know what it is about her that draws me in, but I need to put a stop to it.

She's clearly looking for a serious relationship, and she deserves to have someone in her life whose world revolves around her.

I'm not that man.

Abby and I have chemistry. An absurd amount of chemistry. In a different lifetime, I'd jump all over that, but I'm not the same guy I used to be. I won't put my heart on the line again. Not like I did with Gemma. It's too fucking messy.

For the foreseeable future, I plan to keep my nose to the grindstone, win some damn football games, and take care of my daughter.

Hopefully the provost's niece is the answer to that equation.

I dial the number Coach sent, and a bubbly, feminine voice answers. After we talk for a minute, Cadence laughs. "Nick, please tell me my uncle didn't bully you into calling me about this job. I'm looking for a position, but I don't want you to feel like you have to do this."

I chuckle. "I swear, no one is pressuring me."

We agree to meet in person. I have a good feeling about her.

As I get off the phone, Denise pulls into the driveway. She's a sweet older lady whose children are in high school, so her mornings are free. She can drop off Hazel at preschool and pick her up or hang out with her if she doesn't have school.

My daughter bounds into the kitchen just before I take off. I kneel down for hugs.

"Have a good day, gingersnap. Be sure to brush your teeth after you have breakfast."

"Okay, Daddy."

"And remember, don't listen to music too loudly. It's bad for your ears."

"Thumbs-up." She holds up her hand, and I help her hold down her four fingers.

By the time I reach the gym, I'm feeling optimistic. Maybe I can keep this ship upright for a few more months.

I'm two miles into my warmup run on the treadmill when Jinxy jumps onto the machine next to me.

"Damn, Daddy. Slow your ass down. You're making the rest of us look bad." He waves a hand behind him to Dax and Bowser, who are also jogging.

Sweat drips down Bowser's thick brows. "Fuck off. I'm on this team because of my quick hands and my size, which means I ain't gonna be sprinting on this thing."

Dax rolls his eyes. "I heard all about your *size* last night. 'Oh, Big B! You monster! Yes! Harder!'" he mock-screams in a high-pitched voice. "Bowser almost banged a hole through my wall with his headboard."

The guys laugh.

Sex. It must be nice.

When I'm done, I slam the shutdown button with my palm.

Jinxy points a finger in my face. "Speaking of letting off steam, you need to get laid already, bro, before you break something. You got that angry energy wafting around you like a bad fart." This asshole's always busting my balls.

"You'd know all about bad farts." Dax snorts.

With the back of my arm, I wipe sweat from my forehead. "I'm relaxed right now. I just ran three miles."

"You *think* you're relaxed, but your eyes are all squinty and you look like you wanna smash something."

I glance at Dax, and he nods. "It's true. You do look wound up."

Hmm. Maybe I should've just jerked off this morning after all.

"Get laid already." That's his answer for everything. Jinxy waves a hand. "How long has it been since you did a deep dick dive?"

Not this again. I rub a hand over my face.

"Damn, man. That long? Please tell me it hasn't been since your girlfriend passed away. What, like two years ago?" Actually, it'll be three this fall. He crosses himself. "RIP dead girlfriend, but, Bromeo, your life ain't over yet."

My jaw tightens. "Have some fucking respect. Gemma was the mother of my child."

"And would she want you hermetically sealed for the rest of your life? If she loved you the way you obviously loved her, she'd want you to move on."

I stare at him, not knowing what to say.

Move on from Gemma? I wouldn't know where to begin. Every morning, I wake up with our daughter, who looks just like her mom.

"It's not that easy, man," I grunt. "Gemma was amazing." Not that I'm still hung up on her the way I used to be, but her death broke something in me I'm not sure will ever recover.

He slaps my back. "I'm not saying you have to get into another relationship, bro. Hookups are not complicated. Insert the USB into the port, and voila." He frowns at me. "Please tell me you've hooked up with someone since you got here. Like, at least a blow job or a handy or something."

I lift an eyebrow. "Do you really want to know if I've gotten a hand job? Jinxy, are you obsessed with me?" I chuckle as the other guys crack up. It's tough to stay mad at this idiot.

"I'm just saying if you had some good dick energy, shit might work better for you on the field."

"We're undefeated, asshole."

"Barely."

"The only time I really struggled was against Iowa. My kid was on the goddamn sidelines. It was hard to concentrate. Cut me some slack."

Jinxy pokes my chest. "Do you want to just *barely* win? The last game was super fucking close until the end." My nostrils flare, and he holds up his hands. "Just saying if you got your wheel bearings greased, maybe your engine would work better."

"Wheel bearings have nothing to do with engines," Bowser points out.

"Whatever. You know what I'm saying." Jinxy rubs his hands together. "Now tell Uncle Jinxy about your dating problems, and I'll fix what ails you. I just..." He glances around. "I need a favor."

Here we go. Everyone always wants something. "What kind of favor? I'm not helping you do anything illegal."

As Jinxy and I stand off to one side of the treadmills, suddenly it's the most interesting place in the weight room because Bowser and Dax huddle up too.

"Tell us about this favor," Bowser says. "Did you knock up someone? Or catch some cooties? Is your dick gonna fall off?"

Wincing, Jinxy cups himself. "No, you shithead. My dick works fine. It's my taint I'm having trouble with."

Bowser shudders. "If it's swollen, that's out of my field of expertise."

"Nothing's swollen. It's just... stinky."

"Sticky?" I choke on a laugh.

"No, fucker. *Stinky*."

When Coach encouraged me to bond with the guys, this isn't what I had in mind. "Jinxy, take a damn shower and use some soap."

He rolls his eyes. "Do you think I'm a moron? I've tried that. I've scrubbed so hard, you could probably see your reflection in my balls. But Velva says it still smells even fresh from a shower."

"You're dating someone named Vulva?" I snicker.

"Velva. With an E. This is serious, man. She won't blow me until my taint smells better. At least I think it's my taint. Who knows? It's not like I can stick my head down there to sniff. Anyway, she's hot as fuck, and I wanna make her happy so she'll suck my dick."

Bowser whips out his phone and scrolls while the guys give Jinxy shit. Then he holds up a finger. "*Reddit* says to wash everything—your dick, balls, ass, and taint—with soap, then apple cider vinegar, then soap again to get rid of the vinegar smell."

Jinxy runs over to the trainer's table, grabs a pen, and scribbles something on the back of his hand, then humps the air. "Jinxy's getting the goods this weekend, my friends!"

I shake my head when I see "ACV" on his hand in giant letters. I'm headed to the locker room when he yanks on my shirt. "You're not outta the woods. I'm getting you off this weekend."

"Thanks for the offer. You're nice and all, Jinxy, but I usually go for girls with less leg hair."

He holds up the hem of his shorts and models his leg. "What are you talking about? I got nice stems." Dropping his shorts, he wraps his arm around my shoulder. "But I see what you're doing. Using humor to hide your pain. Leave everything to me. We'll go on a double date. I'll bring Velva and her friend Cricket. She'll be down to fuck or blow you without any strings, you'll feel better about breaking the seal, and we can win our damn championship this year."

He's told me I need to get laid for months, but I figured he was just talking shit. This time hits a little different. "Do you really think we didn't win last year because I'm wound too tight?"

He shrugs. "I don't know, but can sex hurt? What if you do it, and it relaxes you so much your concentration ramps up? What if you step out on the field this weekend and blast away the competition 'cause you dicked some girl through her bedroom wall?"

"You're crazy."

Snapping his fingers, he nods. "Think of it like a hard reset of your phone. You know, going back to factory settings. Like, the Nick Silva who won almost every game as a damn freshman minus all that shit that fucks up your head."

Jinxy is an asshole, and half the stuff he says is insane.

Except...

Motherfucker. What if he's right?

12

NICK

"Higha, Daddy!" Hazel squeals as I push her a little harder on the swings. Other kids go twice as high, but she's tiny, and if she goes any higher, I'm afraid she'll do something dumb like let go and try to go airborne like the other daredevils at the park.

"Hold on tight, Hazel. Don't let go."

Who knew the fucking swings could give you a heart attack?

We have a bye this weekend, and I hope to make the most of it with my daughter. I'm sure I'll regret not doing any homework tomorrow night, but it's too nice outside to be cooped up at home. I did a quick workout this morning, made breakfast, and then gave Hazel a few options for today. She wanted to run around at the park, so here we are.

After the swings, I help her climb the jungle gym. "Are you hungry yet? 'Cause I'm starving."

Eager eyes greet me as she nods, then runs off to play in the sand. I'm gonna have to hose her off when we get home, but I'll do anything to keep her smiling.

"How 'bout I grill us some burgers this afternoon? Did you like that salad Cadence made us? The ones with apples and strawberries and that homemade dressing?"

She nods again, her brow furrowed as she leans over to make a sandcastle.

Thank God she likes the food Cadence makes. She warmed up to the new nanny pretty quickly, which was a relief.

"Did you enjoy the crafts you did with Abby this week?"

"Yes! I liked making flowas."

Abby and Hazel made fake flowers with crepe paper and wire. I love that Abby always goes out of her way to do fun things with my daughter.

I haven't seen much of Abby since that day we had lunch. I miss hanging out with her, but it's probably better if we don't spend too much time around each other. There's no need to complicate our lives, and it's easier to keep things professional if we don't hang out.

I'm about to suggest to Hazel that we head home when my phone rings with a call from Jinxy.

"Hey, man. Why don't you text like a normal person?"

He laughs. "I can tell you're getting more comfortable with the team 'cause you give us shit now."

I smile as I watch Hazel make a moat around a mound, which I think is supposed to be a castle. "What's up?"

"You down for that double date tonight? I was thinking we could head to the Buck 'Em Brewhouse, have a few drinks, grab some appetizers, see where things go."

He makes it sound so simple. "Are you pimping me out?"

"The biggest stud on campus? Hell, yes. I'm charging Cricket a hundred bucks for a shot with you."

This asshole. I chuckle as I scan the park. "Just because I go out doesn't mean anything's going down tonight. I'm not into hook—" I stop myself when I realize what I was about to say in front of children.

"I got you. Like I said, let's see where things go. Look, you had fun when you went out last spring with Larissa, right?"

"Yes," I say hesitantly. Things were fun with her until she wanted to get serious even though I was honest from the beginning that I wasn't sure I was ready for a commitment.

"How is this any different? The more you put yourself out there, the easier it'll be to take the next step."

I can't believe I'm taking sex advice from Jinxy. "I have to get a babysitter."

He howls into the phone. "That's what I'm talking about."

"Let me see if I can get someone to watch Hazel. It's last-minute."

I'm almost hoping no one can cover tonight, but Denise immediately tells me she's free because her husband is having friends over tonight to play poker, and she'd love to get out of the house.

I guess that means I have a date.

13

ABIGAIL

I'M ABOUT to tell my new friends about the ticket to London I just booked when they stop to stare at me. Paige motions at my head and mumbles something to her friend Baylee, who nods.

"Y'all are scaring me." I'm seated on a barstool in our kitchen while Baylee highlights my hair.

Paige waves at my face. "I was just saying she should give you curtain bangs."

Baylee nods. "They're totally in right now."

"Do I need bangs?" I've never had them before.

"Yes," they say in unison.

"I don't remember the last time a professional cut my hair. I usually just have my mom trim my hair straight across the bottom when it gets too long."

Baylee gasps. "Oh, girl, no. I'm about to be your new BFF."

Baylee is Paige's best friend from her hometown. She just graduated from cosmetology school and offered to cut and highlight my hair at a discount if she could use before and after photos on her social media. For the price, I couldn't turn her down, even if I'm a little nervous to make such a big change.

Brow pinched, Baylee separates my hair, folds it into a foil strip, and spreads on the bleach. "I know you're worried about how this will turn out, but you have great hair. We're just accentuating it. Your boyfriend will be drooling when he sees you."

"I don't have a boyfriend." Admitting that still makes me sad. I'm all for girl power, but there's nothing like cuddling with your significant other.

Paige tuts. "An incredibly hot firefighter offered to take you on a date."

"After he saw my boobs and butt," I remind her.

Baylee stops with a brush full of bleach halfway to my head. "You flashed a hot firefighter?"

"It's not like it sounds."

"Let me tell the story," Paige says. "And she flashed *three* hot firefighters. They were basically arguing over who got to ask her out."

Paige is misremembering because they most certainly did not fight over me.

By the time she gets to the part where my tits are streaking across the glass, Baylee can't breathe because she's laughing so hard. "You poor thing. Are you traumatized?"

"Yes. I'm never climbing through an awning window again."

Paige elbows her friend. "And now she works for the hot dad next door whose daughter she saved."

"Trust me when I say that Nick Silva isn't interested." Because ever since we had lunch together, he's back to being stoic and grumpy. And he hired another nanny so I could 'have more free time to date and socialize.'

Which is fine. Totally, totally fine.

He said he wants to have more people Hazel is comfortable with in case one of us gets sick. I completely understand that. I just wish it didn't feel like I wasn't enough.

"Shut up." Baylee's mouth drops open. "You're the nanny for that hot-as-fuck Bronco quarterback? I saw a football commercial last week where he was running in slow motion and his thick hair was kinda sweaty. I think I drooled a little."

"He's not that good-looking," I quip, but then she smirks at me, and I laugh. "Okay, fine. He's hot."

"Are you making a play for him? Because if I were in your shoes, I'd totally be like, 'Oh, my, Nick, you're so big and strong. Look at your enormous muscles. Can I touch them?'"

We all crack up because she's being ridiculous. "He has a girlfriend," I remind everyone.

Paige tilts her head. "Really?"

"Doesn't he? I thought he was dating that girl Larissa, the beautiful redhead who was all, 'Daddy Silva, you scrumptious man, you.'"

That's why I took the job. Because he's taken, and I refuse to fall for a guy who's in a relationship. It's a solid cornerstone in my emotional wall, which I need. Because I'm starting to realize I have a type, and Nick Silva is one hundred percent the kind of guy I go for. I need safeguards in place so I don't do something stupid like fall in love with him.

My roommate snorts. "I forgot about Larissa." She takes a sip of the margarita we made earlier. "Are you sure they're still together? Because I never see him with anyone except the babysitters."

Baylee chuckles. "It's always the nanny. Anytime a celebrity cheats, it's the nanny. That's why if I ever marry a professional athlete, we're getting an old hag to watch the kids."

"Solid plan." I hold up my drink in agreement.

"Abby, are you the only babysitter?" Baylee asks as she foils another strand of my hair. "How do you balance that with classes?"

"Denise watches Hazel in the mornings, takes her to preschool, picks her up. I cover a few afternoons a week and every other Saturday, and since I only have class in the mornings, it works well. Cadence will be covering the other afternoons and Saturdays."

"Who's Cadence? Is she new?" Paige asks.

"He just hired her. She's super pretty and cooks gourmet." I met her briefly when she came over to interview with Nick as I was leaving. "I'm totally not jealous that all I can make is sandwiches."

Cooking just isn't in my wheelhouse. I can bake okay—with a box recipe, which probably doesn't count—but I always manage to mess up anytime I try to do more.

But the thing that really tweaks my jealousy is that Cadence was the runner-up on the last season of *The Nanny Whisperer*, which means she must be amazing.

That reminds me... "Paige, do you know a cheerleader named Tiffany? She's really pretty, but..." How do I say she's the meanest girl I've ever met?

"She's a straight-up bitch? Yes, unfortunately, I do know her. She's co-captain of the squad. Her family donated an insane amount of money to the school, so even though she's always stirring up shit, we have to put up with it."

"She came in to the diner a few weeks ago and sat with the football guys. She was so rude and snarky." If I'm being honest with myself, I'm still bothered that she had her paws all over Nick.

Maybe it's good that he's back to being distant and grumpy.

By the time Baylee finishes my cut and color, she blow-dries it until every strand is straight and sleek.

"I never blow-dry my hair," I confess. "You're spending so much time on me, and I'm just going to put it in a bun later." I can see it now. A big bun, a giant mug of coffee, my Scrabble tiles that I sometimes like to touch and rearrange, and a good romance novel. My idea of heaven. Maybe I'll splurge on some new annotation tabs or highlighters. There's nothing I love more than tabbing my favorite parts in a book.

"Messy buns are super cute, but I want you to know how good it can look if you spend a little time on it."

She shows me how to use the different brushes to get the same results on my own. My hair feels so soft, but I still have no idea how it looks because the girls haven't done the big reveal yet.

We're about to order some Chinese when Paige gets a text from her new boyfriend. "Marcus and his two friends want to know if we'd like to join them for drinks in half an hour. I told them we're starving, and they can get us dinner." She points at me. "You have to come and show off your new look."

"But I never know what to say when I first meet someone, and I come off as a bumbling nerd." Or, as my friends back home would say, adorkable.

"You're a beautiful nerd. Just own that. Besides, it'll be a good chance to mingle."

"Mingle?"

"Yes, it's what you do when you're playing the field."

"Do I want to play the field?" I ask, hesitantly.

"Definitely." Paige texts her boyfriend, then sets down her phone. "This is going to be so fun!"

Baylee nods. "I'm in."

When Baylee's done with my hair, Paige hands me another thrift-store outfit I haven't worn yet. This one is a halter-top dress. "Put this on, and don't you dare look in the mirror yet. I want to do a whole aesthetic so you can see that you're a beautiful little butterfly."

I choke on a laugh. "Okay, fairy godmother. Your wish is my command."

After I change in my bedroom, Paige gets out her needle and thread and makes a few quick adjustments to my dress.

Once she finishes, I run my hand over the smooth material that now sits snug to my body instead of bulging out. "You have secret powers, Paige. This is amazing."

"I love sewing, which was handy when I was growing up because we were poor, and I had to adjust my clothes from the donation box at church." She pats the barstool. "Let me do your makeup. I was thinking we should go with a smoky eye."

I slide onto the chair. "I tried that once and ended up looking like a raccoon." If raccoon eyes were in like curtain bangs and highlights, I'd be golden.

Fortunately, I got my contacts in before our girls' night started, so I don't have to fuss with them, but it's still unnerving to try something new.

Paige places her hand on my shoulder. "Trust me. Close your eyes."

Here goes nothing.

14

ABIGAIL

I shiver and tighten the thin shawl around my shoulders. "If we don't get inside before it rains, my hair is going to frizz up."

Baylee gasps. "Over my dead body. Get your ass in there."

Laughing, I jog alongside her and Paige.

Despite the sudden dark clouds that blot out the moon tonight, the Buck 'Em Brewhouse is packed. It's a popular spot near campus. Part bar, part restaurant, part dance hall, it's one of those places where peanut shells litter the floor, and it smells like comfort food and beer.

I've been at Lone Star State going on my fourth semester, and this is really the first night I've gone out with friends. I don't count anything I did with Ezra because he tainted those memories.

Even though I'm nervous, I feel like I'm finally taking control of my life.

Paige hooks her arm through mine. "Troy seems really nice. I think you're going to like him."

She waves at three guys at the bar, and my stomach twists into a knot. They're handsome. Dressed in dark jeans and polos, they look like models in a cologne commercial. I still don't know what I'm going to talk about. I doubt they'd be interested in the travel Scrabble game I got on Etsy the other day.

I'm just glad I have Paige and Baylee to lean on. We've had so much fun today with my makeover, so I'm not going to let self-consciousness get the best of me.

The dark-haired guy wraps his arms around Paige and kisses the daylights out of her. I'm guessing that's Marcus. He's come over to our house several times, but I'm usually working, or they're already crashed out in her room.

She lets go of her boyfriend with a laugh. "Y'all, this is my boy toy Marcus." Motioning to the two guys next to him, she says, "This is Troy and Dylan."

Troy is a handsome blond with dimples, and Dylan has dark hair and blue eyes. They're all striking.

I wait to feel a thrill like I do when I talk to Nick, but nothing happens.

Hmm.

Maybe I need to get to know Troy before I get the flutters, but he immediately turns to Baylee and kisses the back of her hand.

Dylan and I give each other an awkward smile. I hope he's good at conversation, or this is going to be a long night.

The waitress seats us at a long table in the middle of the restaurant. I sit at one end of the table. From here I have a good view of the bar and the dance hall behind it. Dylan sits on my right, Troy sits next to him, and Baylee takes the chair on the far end. Paige sits on the other side of me and Marcus grabs the seat next to her.

The guys order a pitcher of beer, and I cringe. I'm not really a beer drinker.

Paige taps on the menu. "Girls, how do you feel about sharing a pitcher of margaritas with me?"

"Sounds good," Baylee shouts from across the table to be heard.

"I'm in." I'm not sure who's paying tonight or if we're all going Dutch, but I have enough to pay for myself.

The guys order several appetizers for the table, and then it's like the girls don't exist. Funny that I was so worried about talking to new people tonight because since we got here, they haven't shut up about next week's Bronco game against Northwestern.

"Sure hope Silva has his shit together," Marcus says after he takes a long drink of his beer.

Troy pounds his fist on the table. "I got a hundred on that game. He'd better win."

"Have some faith," I say because I can't help myself. "He's a great quarterback. Remember that he took over halfway through last season. That couldn't have been easy. It takes time to gel with a new team."

People are so hard on the guy. They have no idea how hard he works. DI football is brutal.

Marcus chugs his beer, then shrugs. "Guess you have a point."

Leaning over to Paige, I whisper, "Marcus doesn't know I work for Nick?"

She shakes her head. "Figured that was your personal business."

I seriously love my roommate. "Thanks. I appreciate it." Since it's getting warm, I remove my shawl and drape it over the back of my chair. "Excuse me a minute. I'm going to find the bathroom."

When I stand, Dylan whistles. "Why the hell are you hiding yourself behind that scarf? Damn, girl."

All of a sudden, Troy stops talking to Baylee to check me out. Gross. He picked Baylee, so he should be focused on her.

"I'll be right back." Self-conscious, I pull my long hair over my shoulder as I walk between the tables.

In the bathroom, I make sure my eyelashes are still glued on and reapply some lip gloss. I don't recognize the blonde in the mirror. My hair is sleek and smooth and my eyes are intense, but my lips are pale pink. The girls wanted me to wear a blood-red lipstick, but that's not my style.

Paige let me borrow her gold hoop earrings, and I'm happy to say that the black halter dress fits great. I definitely look chesty because it has an empire waist, but the long skirt is more flattering than I thought it would be.

I smile at myself. For the first time maybe ever, I feel really pretty. I might be a big nerd, but I look like a normal woman out with her friends. Maybe if I pretend to be confident, people will think I am.

Tossing my hair back, I step out of the bathroom. That's when I hear a familiar laugh at the bar. Jinxy sees me and does a double-take.

"Abby? You're Nick's babysitter, right?"

I smile. "Yeah, that's me." He leans down to hug me, and I reciprocate. "Meeting up with friends?"

He's obviously been drinking because he wobbles a little when I let go of him. "Yeah, Nick and I are going on a double date. Figured it was time to get my boy laid, you know?"

His words make me freeze.

Nick's on a date? Here?

Across the bar, I spot him talking to a gorgeous brunette. She's laughing and touching his arm, and he's smiling down at her.

Ugh, I feel sick.

I press a hand to my stomach, hating that I care. Out of all the bars and restaurants in town, why did he and Jinxy have to come here tonight? If they'd just gone somewhere else, I never would've known about his date.

"I thought... I thought he had a girlfriend? Larissa?"

"That ended a while back." Holding out his hand, he gives me a crooked smile. "You wanna go say hi?"

I shake my head. "That's okay. I don't want to interrupt."

"Who ya here with?"

I point to our table. "My roommate Paige, her friend Baylee, and some friends of Paige's boyfriend."

"I forgot that you're Paige's roommate. She's a great cheerleader."

"She's awesome." I fidget, not knowing what else to say. "Well, have a nice time tonight."

He waggles his bushy brows. "Oh, I plan to."

Athletes are players, Abigail. When will you get that through your thick skull?

I rejoin my table and make an effort to talk to Dylan. He just graduated from UT and works at a bank. We have nothing in common, but he's a nice guy, so I just smile and nod when he talks about investments.

Finally, I think we're about to leave, but Paige wants to dance, so we head to the back hall where a band is playing. My eyes immediately find Nick and his date. He's twirling her around to some country song, and her head falls back as she laughs.

This is good. Great, even. Nick swore he'd keep things professional with me, and he has. It's not like anything ever happened between us, so I have no reason to feel butthurt.

Knowing he's out there playing the field, "mingling" with girls, will help me move on.

I don't know when I got so hung up on my boss that I now need to move on, but it is what it is.

So when a slow song starts and Dylan asks me to dance, I decide I'm not wallowing.

"I'd love to dance."

He immediately steps on me. "Shit. Sorry."

I laugh. "It's okay. I have two left feet too, so don't put too much pressure on yourself."

Dylan grins. "I like that you're laid-back."

"That's me. Miss No Expectations." Okay, that's a fib because I was hoping we'd two-step, but he just pulls me close, and we sway. At least his spicy cologne is nice.

I like watching the couples around me. Some stare into each other's eyes like they're in love, and it's swoony.

I want to be in love like that. I can now admit I didn't have that with Ezra. There was always something elusive about him, but I just thought that's how he was. Now I know it's because he wasn't ever fully committed.

As painful as that experience was, maybe I'm a little wiser now and won't make the same mistakes again.

Afterward, the guys start talking again, completely ignoring the girls. I'm about to call an Uber when I spot a familiar face.

"Hey, Abby. Remember me?"

It's Clark Kent. The firefighter I never called back. "Hi. How's it going?" I feel like a jerk for not remembering his real name.

"It's Shane, in case you forgot."

"How are you?" I wave awkwardly as Paige nudges me.

"I'm great. Would you like to dance?"

Paige nudges me harder this time, and I practically fly into him. He laughs. "I'll take that as a yes?"

Take life by the horns, Abby. Say yes. I nod with an embarrassed smile. Because why not?

When he takes me in his arms, I wait for that feeling, that zip of electricity I always experience when Nick's around, but again, I'm disappointed.

But he's a good dancer, and it's fun to be spun around the room.

When the song ends, I thank him for the dance before I turn and nearly run into a brick wall.

"Abby." Nick's hands land on my shoulders to steady me.

Dang it. I was hoping to avoid him.

His date, who's even more beautiful up close, immediately wraps her arm around his waist.

Chill, girl. He's all yours.

I back away and force a smile on my face. "Hey, boss. Funny running into you here."

His brows furrow as he looks between me and Shane, who sidles up next to me. Fortunately, it's dark, and Shane's yelling to one of his friends across the room.

I'm not sure what I'm supposed to say to Nick. Nervously, I tuck my hair behind my ear. When he doesn't bother introducing the woman he's with, I shrug. "'K, see you later." Then I grab Shane's hand and drag him back to my group. No way was I going to initiate introductions. Because really I don't want to know the name of the woman Nick's sleeping with tonight.

Shane hangs out with us for a bit, but I'm fighting a headache and just want to go home. By the time my friends and I leave, I don't care that it's pouring rain and that I'm immediately soaked through.

At least I'm not thinking about Nick and his date.

Who am I kidding?

That's all I can think about.

15

NICK

Jinxy takes me aside as the girls put on their sweaters. It's raining so hard, you can't see the cars in the parking lot.

Bleary-eyed, he leans toward me. "Are you sure, bro? Because Cricket is down for whatever you want to do, and it's not even midnight yet."

I pull out my phone for the tenth time to double-check that I don't have any calls from Denise. Then I click on the weather app. Everything's flashing red on the radar map, which means the rain won't be letting up tonight. "I don't want to keep my babysitter out in this weather. I should get going. There's a high wind and flood advisory."

Plus, thunder sometimes scares Hazel. I don't want her waking up and being afraid.

He leans closer. "Why don't you take Cricket with you? She can Uber home later."

Jinxy has had too much to drink and isn't thinking straight. "I'm not bringing a hookup to my house when my daughter is sleeping ten feet away. Someday, you'll have kids and you'll appreciate how wildly inappropriate that is."

Rolling his eyes, he tosses back his beer. "You've been pissy since you saw your saucy little nanny. Just admit it. Why didn't you tell me she's hot as fuck?"

Irritated, I tuck my phone in the back pocket of my jeans. "Abigail is beautiful. You know this already. You've met her before."

He motions to his face. "Nah, she did something. Makeup maybe? Her hair? That dress? I don't know, but she went from a seven to a solid ten."

"She doesn't need makeup. She's always been a ten."

Did she look extra hot tonight? Yes. Will I be the douchebag who slobbers all over her because she had a makeover? No.

"Ah-ha!" Snapping his fingers in my face, he bounces on his toes. "I knew you had a thing for her."

I can admit I was irritated to see her in the arms of another man, but she wants the happily ever after, and I'll never be that for anyone. "Have you considered that it's possible to find someone attractive without acting on it?"

"Why would I do that?"

"Never mind."

He smirks. "Just admit that you want to do her, and I'll shut up."

"Jinxy, she's my *employee*. She makes peanut butter and jelly sandwiches for my daughter and teaches her the alphabet. I will not 'do' her. Look, I'll see you on Monday. You're not driving, right?"

"Nope. I'll take an Uber."

"And the girls will be okay?"

"I'll bring them home with me." He pauses, his brows lifting. "You okay if Cricket comes to my house? Maybe sleeps in my bed with me and Velva?"

I bark out a laugh and smack him on the back. "As long as that's where she wants to be."

I say goodbye to our dates, book it through the rain across

the parking lot, and jump into my car. I reach down into my gym bag and pull out a towel to wipe my face.

As I drive home, I replay tonight. I tried to have fun with Cricket. I smiled and talked to her. Asked her to dance. But everything was forced because I didn't wanna be there.

After Jinxy told me Abby was there too, I couldn't stop thinking about her. She looked like she was enjoying her night, so I didn't want to interrupt.

And yes, she looked stunning. Like an amplified version of herself. So poised and beautiful. Like someone had flipped on a switch inside of her and made her beam.

It must've been her date. Lucky bastard.

I couldn't take my eyes off them while they were dancing. Although, now that I think about it, she danced with a different guy than the one at the table. He looked like one of the firefighters who hit on her in front of my house.

My heart sinks.

Damn. I bet it was that guy who called her.

I shake my head at myself. This is what I wanted, right? To keep distance between me and Abby?

Then why am I so pissed about it?

By the time I reach my neighborhood, my hands ache from gripping the steering wheel. The rain hasn't let up, and water rushes down the side of the street to collect at the drainage grates. Since I moved here, it's never rained this hard.

I pull into my driveway, relieved to see the lights on next door. I'm hoping the girls got back okay, but just in case, I send Abby a text.

Me: You make it back okay? The weather is terrible.

I don't let myself consider the possibility that maybe she went home with the firefighter. That's none of my business. Frankly, if she's seeing someone, that would be better for our situation.

Then I wouldn't feel so fucking tempted.

After I lock my car, I race up to the house. The wind is blowing so hard it nearly slams the door against the wall when I open it, but I catch the handle at the last minute.

Closing the door behind me, I wipe my face with my arm.

Denise is reading a magazine on my couch. "Did you have fun tonight?"

That's when we hear a loud roar, almost like a train. "What the hell is that?"

Her eyes widen. "I'm not sure."

I run back to my daughter's room to check on her. She fell asleep with her headphones on. Not sure that's a good thing, but at least she's not scared. I peer out her window to the backyard. The trees are whipping around and that roaring finally subsides.

Hazel sleeps through the whole thing.

Even the crash next door that rattles our house.

16

NICK

"Stay with Hazel. I'm gonna check on my neighbors," I tell Denise as I run out into my front yard. Car alarms blare up and down the street, and there's a ton of debris everywhere. Leaves and trash and tree limbs litter the neighborhood. It's hard to believe that all happened in the last few minutes.

At least the rain's subsiding. When I get to Abby and Paige's house, I'm about to pound on the front door when I hear a scream inside. Thankfully, the knob turns, and I'm able to get inside without kicking it in.

"Abby! Paige!" I shout.

"Back here!" a feminine voice calls out.

I head down the back hall where I find Paige and her boyfriend trying to open one of the bedrooms. The door is blocked.

"Abby's stuck," Paige says. "A tree fell through her wall."

What the fuck?

The door opens an inch, and from what I can tell, there's more tree in there than bedroom.

"Abby!" I yell. "You okay?"

Paige nudges her way in front of me to talk through the crack. "Nick's here. We're going to get you out."

When I hear the crying, my heart sinks. "Abby, hang tight. I'm on my way."

She calls out, "Nick, there's a huge tree limb braced against the door! It has me pinned to the floor."

Holy shit.

I turn to her roommate. "Paige, call the fire department. I'm gonna go around the side and see if I can get in through the window."

By the time I get to the backyard, it's pouring again, but the wind has died down. There's a cluster of live oaks between the houses, and one has pulled a few feet out of the ground and fallen through the roof. So much for climbing through a window. There is no window, just a gaping hole where the wall was sliced apart.

I peek through the gash and see Abby's bare legs on the ground. "Hang on. I'm coming."

"Be careful! There's glass everywhere."

After I yank off my letterman jacket, I throw it over the opening so I don't accidentally cut myself and climb through what used to be the window. I make a point to avoid the tree so I don't put any pressure on Abby. When I land, my feet crunch on the broken glass.

I rush over to her and crouch down. "Are you okay? Are you hurt? Are you bleeding anywhere?" Most of the tree landed on the bed, but there's a huge-ass limb pinning her down.

My heart is in my throat as I wait for her answer.

Her frightened eyes meet mine. "I can't breathe. It's heavy."

"Let's see if we can get it off you. It's not…" I almost can't say the words. "It didn't puncture you, did it?" Because if it did, and I lift it off her, I could do more harm. There's blood on her arms and legs, but I think it's from scratches and not deep cuts.

"I'm okay." She gives me a shaky smile.

I brush her damp hair out of her beautiful face. "Got yourself in another pickle, huh?"

She laughs and then groans. "Don't be funny. I don't have enough room to inhale."

"Is she okay?" Paige shouts through the door.

"She's in one piece," I yell back. Thank fucking God.

I don't know what I'd do if she was hurt badly.

"Why didn't you tell me you were friends with Nick Silva?" her boyfriend asks on the other side of the wall.

"It never came up," Paige says.

"But you could've gotten us tickets to the game."

"My roommate is pinned to the ground by a tree, and you're worried about football?"

I knew I liked Paige.

Turning to Abby, I decide we need some levity before this woman gives me a heart attack. "How do you always seem to get in these kinds of predicaments?"

"I don't know." She laughs weakly.

"I'm not sure how long it's going to take the fire department to get here, so let's see if I can lift the limb enough for you to scoot out." I take a pillow and use it to dust off the glass next to her. "Are you ready?"

She nods.

"On the count of three."

We count down together, and then I lift that damn thing with all my might.

"It's working." She scoots herself to the side until she's free. Then she collapses in a heap. She looks so fragile lying there in her t-shirt and boy shorts. The rain is still pouring through the roof, and her clothes are stuck to her damp skin.

After I set the limb down again, I kneel next to her. "Hey. You okay?" Her arms are bloody, and she's got leaves stuck in her hair, and when she sees me, her eyes get glassy. "Come here." I hold open my arms, and she rushes to me. I hug her close but try to be gentle. "Don't wanna hurt you."

Her shoulders shake as she cries, and I run my hand down her back. "That tree came out of nowhere. One minute, I... I was getting ready for bed, and the ne-next I was on the ground."

Jesus, that's a terrifying statement. Life's so fucking capricious sometimes.

I kiss the top of her head. "You're okay now. I got you." In the distance, I hear the arrival of the fire department. "Maybe we should get you dressed. Unless you're angling for more dates from firemen."

She laughs. "Shut up."

I get up and hold out my hand. She takes it, and our eyes meet, and I swear it's like I've been hit with a bolt of lightning. My heart races, and my skin gets clammy. What the hell is this woman doing to me?

It's probably just the adrenaline.

She slowly stands with a groan, but when she wobbles, I catch a glimpse of her perfect ass in that skin-tight underwear. After I make sure she can stand, I avert my eyes, only to see her nipples poking through her white t-shirt.

Clearing my throat, I let go of her hand and stare at the wall. "You sure you're okay?"

"Everything hurts, but I'm just glad I didn't get speared."

Fuck, I can't even consider that.

I motion to her destroyed room. "What do you need?"

"Um." She tugs down the hem of her t-shirt, which barely covers her flat stomach. "Everything?"

I studiously ignore her nipples poking through the damp fabric. Though I really fucking wanna look.

Averting my eyes again, I duck under the tree and make sure her dresser is accessible. "How 'bout we start with shoes and socks? Get what you need here, and I'll find your shoes and get you a bag."

"Nick?" I turn and see her holding her ribs. "I don't think I can get under that limb. It hurt when I sat up and stood, but bending forward hurts more."

She's worse off than I thought. "Hold tight. I'll get your things." I head to the closet and grab her backpack. "It's handy that our houses are almost identical." Then I return to the dresser. "I'm just gonna grab a handful of frilly stuff—underwear, bras, socks. Unless you have any special requests?"

I peek at her over my shoulder and almost laugh at the blush creeping up her pale neck.

"Abby?" When she looks at me, I smile. "You're alive. That's all that matters. Don't be embarrassed, okay?"

She lets out a breath and nods.

"Where's your phone?" I decide to distract her while I pack her clothes. "Is it over by you? Be sure to grab that and your charger."

I find some sweats in the bottom dresser drawer and grab her two bottoms, tuck one into her backpack and hand her the other.

"Paige?" I shout. "Can you pack some toiletries for Abby?"

"No prob. Listen, the fire department is here. I'm going to send them to your side of the house."

"Great. Thanks." I yank a blanket out of the closet and grab Abby's tennis shoes. I duck back under the tree and wrap the blanket around her shoulders and help her pull up her sweats. "You can change into something better after we get you out of here. Let's get your shoes on, though, or you might hurt your feet."

I kneel down, grab some socks from her backpack, and pat my thigh. "Up here, buttercup."

Her brows lift. "You're going to put on my shoes for me?"

"You can't bend over, so yes." I smile when she lifts her dainty little foot. "I like the pink polish." Reaching onto the bed, I grab a sweatshirt and dry her off. "Wet skin is how you get athlete's foot." After I tug on her sock, I help her slip on her shoe. We repeat the process with her other foot.

"Fire Department," a male shouts through the hole in the wall. "Anyone injured in there?"

"Yes, my friend got trapped by a tree," I call out as I tie Abby's shoelaces. "It's also blocking the bedroom door. I got her out, but she's banged up, and we need assistance evacuating her."

When I'm done, I turn and spot the fireman, who's surveying the damage through the hole. "Is she stable? Think she has any broken bones?"

"I think she's just banged up. She can stand, but she doesn't have the strength to climb. What if I hand her to you?"

"That works. We're ready out here when you are."

I turn to Abby. "Come on. I'll give you a boost through the wall." She pales, and I hope her fear is from needing to go through the hole and not from me. "I promise I won't bite." Then I wink at her. "Unless you want me to."

An embarrassed smile lifts her lips as she looks down. Hesitantly, she moves closer, and I hug her, because, my God, she could've died. "Glad you're okay, buttercup."

Her eyes meet mine, and my heart beats erratically. "Thanks for helping me."

"You're welcome. Now let's get you out of this crazy treehouse. I'm going to pick you up. I want you to reach through that hole where my jacket is so you don't get cut up more than you already are. Ready?"

When she nods, I help her through what's left of the window frame.

"I got her," the fireman yells from the other side.

Once she's out, I grab her bag and hand it to one of the other firefighters before I make my way over the wall. They've put Abby on a stretcher and are taking her vitals.

On the street, an ambulance parks behind the fire truck.

The flashing lights reflect off the wet street, and the sight is so familiar, I freeze. Chills come over me that have nothing to do with the rain.

My throat tightens.

My vision goes dark for a flash.

Bile pushes up the back of my throat.

Because for just a second, instead of a freaked-out Abby getting lifted into an ambulance, it's my dead girlfriend Gemma.

I stumble to the side of the house and vomit.

17

ABIGAIL

I SHOULD BE FOCUSED on Paige, who's frantically waving her hand while she argues with our landlord on the phone, but my eyes keep straying to Nick. He's holding Hazel and standing next to the window, staring out at the street.

Remembering how he climbed through my window last night, lifted a dang tree off me, and put on my shoes has me freaking out. And let's not forget how he picked me up and helped me through the window.

He smelled like that sandalwood and leather scent I love. His arms felt so safe. I hated letting go of him so the firefighter could evacuate me. I almost cried when the ambulance left without him.

For a split second, I thought he'd come with me, but that's stupid. He couldn't leave Hazel at home. After a night out with friends, he probably had a babysitter who needed to leave.

After I got to the ER, Nick texted several times late into the night. He wanted updates to make sure I didn't have any serious injuries. I thought based on all of those texts that the next time I saw him he'd lift me in another hug, but he's been reserved and quiet since he got here a little while ago.

"But my roommate just got out of the hospital." Paige looks at me and makes a face. "We don't have anywhere to go."

Marcus is sprawled on the opposite side of the couch from me, flipping through channels on the TV. "Paige, you can crash with me."

She covers the phone. "We've been dating since this summer. Do you really want me to move in? I've been known to be impulsive, but that seems crazy, even for me."

I chuckle, and then wish I hadn't because my ribs hurt. I must make a pained sound because Nick turns.

"You okay?"

"Nothing a few ibuprofen can't help."

Hazel kicks her legs, and he puts her down. She runs over to me, and before I can brace myself, she throws herself in my arms. My eyes squeeze shut as pain radiates down my rib cage. I didn't break anything, thankfully, but I definitely look like someone's punching bag.

"Shit," Nick mutters. "Hazel, be careful. Abby's hurt. You have to be gentle."

Her little head pops up and she frowns. "I huwt you?"

I swallow and attempt to smile. "I'm okay, Hazelnut. Really." I pat the seat next to me. "Want to play a new reading app on my phone?" I turn to Nick. "Is that okay? It has spelling games."

"Sure." He scoops up Hazel and seats her on the couch between me and Marcus. "Don't climb on Abby, okay?"

She nods. "I love apps."

"I know, kiddo."

I pull up the app and hand her my phone. "This has some of the words we were learning last week."

Marcus motions to Nick. "Just curious, bro, but do you think you'll make it to the playoffs? I wanna know where to put my money. I think y'all have a shot."

"Thanks, man. Gonna give it our best."

"Tough loss last year."

Nick's fist goes tight, then relaxes. He nods.

Marcus looks like he wants to talk football, but he's interrupted when Paige hangs up the call with a huff. "Mr. Owens says that it's too dangerous to stay here, that he wants us out by five p.m. He says the force majeure clause in our rental contract basically means that if there's an act of God, like that microburst that took out the tree and dropped it in Abby's bedroom, then he's not required to uphold our agreement."

Marcus flips through another channel. "What's a microburst?"

"I Googled it this morning. It's like a tornado, but I don't think there's a funnel. It's this shifting hot and cold air that's super unstable. It's what damaged our neighborhood last night."

I frown. "That's what uprooted a tree?"

She shakes her head. "Mr. Owens had his friend, some tree guy, come over this morning to check it out, and apparently there's black mold at the roots because no one ever rakes the leaves and crap in the yard, and I guess that hurt the live oak and made it susceptible to the high winds."

"Were we supposed to rake? I feel bad if it was our fault." The trees in this neighborhood are so beautiful, and to think we're responsible for one falling breaks my heart.

Nick folds his arms. "You've only been here since this summer. I'm guessing that problem started a while back."

"Y'all, what are we going to do?" Paige groans. "October is a terrible time to look for an apartment. Everything fills up at the first of the year, before summer school, or in August."

Marcus stands and wraps his arms around her. "I already told you to crash at my place."

She wiggles out of his hold. "But what about Abby? We're a package deal. Can she maybe sleep on your couch?"

Although Marcus keeps his expression blank, something

tells me he's not jazzed about this idea. "My cousin sometimes stays at my place, so I don't think I can swing that."

I give my roommate a sympathetic smile. "It's okay, Paige. Take what you can get. Maybe I can grab a motel for a few days until I figure out something. Perhaps student housing has some options. I really just need an apartment for, like, ten weeks."

"What happens in ten weeks?" she asks.

"I'm going to London. I meant to tell you yesterday when you were doing my makeover. I just bought the ticket." The excitement I'd had when I pulled the trigger has waned in the aftermath of so much craziness. It also means I don't have a ton of cash saved up for another apartment. "I wasn't sure I could go through with it since I'll be traveling by myself, but I'll take baby steps. This month, I'll get the plane ticket. Next month, I'll book the hostels."

"Hostels? You've got to be kidding." Nick frowns. "Aren't those dangerous? You're basically sleeping in a room full of strangers."

That is a bit terrifying, but I've spent the last few years being told what I can and can't do. I won't go down that path again. "I'm sure I can find places that aren't quite so... unstructured."

He scrubs his face. "Okay, that's probably a discussion for another day. Let's focus on where you're going to live for the next two and a half months."

Hazel grabs my arm. "Come live with me and Daddy."

Chuckling, I squeeze her in a gentle hug. "You're so sweet, and I love you to pieces, but you probably don't have the space." *Plus, I'd be lusting over your father the whole time. That can't be healthy.*

"Nick can make the space," Paige teases, and I shoot her a look. She winks at me. "Just think about it, Nick. Your babysitter will only be five feet away."

Hot embarrassment shoots through me. "Paige, the man needs his space."

Finally, I gather the courage to look at him, and he shrugs. "It isn't the worst idea."

So I can watch him date other women? What if he brings them home at night? What if I can hear them hooking up? The thought makes me nauseated.

I shake my head. "It's asking too much. I'm going to grab a room at that motel over by the east side of campus, at least for a few days. It'll give me time to find something else."

With a groan, I pull myself to a stand and motion behind me. "Going to pack a few things." I can get my bedroom door open since the tree guy removed the oak from the side of the house. It's stacked like firewood next to the fence now.

But when I get to my room, the destruction is so intense, I want to cry. There's sawdust and debris everywhere. My bedding is destroyed, shredded, and the gaping hole in the house is covered with a tarp. Scrabble letters litter the floor.

That tree could've killed me.

I close my eyes and take a deep breath. *I'm alive. I'm in one piece.*

Nodding, I try to take comfort that I have my health. If I'd been asleep in bed, I could've been impaled or maimed for life.

With the back of my arm, I wipe the tears that drip down my face. It's overwhelming to take all of this in.

It makes me realize how much time I've wasted caring what other people think of me. Worried they'd think I'm a geek or uncool. Worried I wouldn't fit in. Worried I wouldn't be the perfect girlfriend for Ezra, a man who couldn't give two shits about me.

Seriously, screw that.

Is this what they call an existential crisis?

My phone buzzes with a text from Roxy. She started texting

me first thing this morning. Paige gave her a heads-up about the tree episode.

Roxy: You're sure you're okay? You nearly died, girl. Don't die! That's crazy!

Me: I swear I'm fine. Thanks for checking on me!

Roxy: Let us know if you need anything. We love you!

It's funny how people in a solid relationship refer to themselves as part of a couple. *Let us know if you need anything.* I want to be an us.

Someone knocks on my bedroom door.

"Need help packing?" Nick asks as he pokes his head in. "I can carry your bags to your car." He has dark circles under his eyes. Did he get any sleep last night? He hasn't shaved today, and that scruff on his strong jaw makes me want to rub against him and purr.

"Thanks. That's really sweet of you." Surveying the damage again, I sigh. "Do you think my landlord will let me come back to get more of my belongings later? I can't take everything right now."

"If he doesn't, we'll break in and get it."

I laugh, knowing that he's probably joking. "Who knew you were such a renegade?"

He smirks. "It's true. I keep it hidden pretty well, but apparently, it comes out for you."

Biting my bottom lip, I try to restrain my smile. "If I haven't told you yet, I really appreciate everything you did for me last night."

"Couldn't let you get mauled by that tree. It reminded me too much of that old movie, *Poltergeist*. Ever seen it?" He shivers. "I'm a grown-ass man now, but that film still gives me the creeps."

Snickering, I grab a bag out of my closet and throw a few things in there. "Think you could carry those textbooks for me?"

I point to my desk. "I can carry maybe two at a time and make a few trips, but if you want to help..."

"Got it." He grabs the whole stack at once. It makes all of his muscles bulge and strain against his t-shirt.

We haul my stuff to my car before I find Paige and give her a huge hug. I whisper in her ear, "If living with Marcus turns out to be a mistake, come bunk with me, okay?"

She nods. "Are you sure you're going to be all right?"

"Nick said he'll follow me to the motel in his car and carry my things into my room so I don't hurt myself, so don't worry about me. You and I will grab lunch later this week."

She whispers back, "I still think you should make your move on him."

"You mean move in with him."

"Do I?" She laughs.

I'm still thinking about what she said when I pull into the Riviera Motel twenty minutes later. Nick and Hazel park next to me. He gets his daughter and meets me in front of the office.

"Hazel, cover your ears," he tells his daughter. When she complies, he points to the side of the building. "This place is a shithole. There's a drunk passed out over there."

"It's not so bad for the price."

He shakes his head. "I didn't save you from an oak tree just to have you mugged. I don't like this place, Abby." Grabbing my shoulder, he looks into my eyes. "Stay with me and Hazel. We'd love to have you."

My heart races at his nearness, and it takes me a second to process what he says. "That's asking a lot, don't you think? Do you really want me crashing on your couch for the next ten weeks?"

He thinks on that, then shrugs. "Maybe I can fit Hazel's bed in my room. Then we can move your bed into her room."

Hazel claps. "Yay! You-a staying with us!"

"Do you really want me to move in with you, Nick?"

He smiles, and it makes his green eyes twinkle. "It'll be fun." Slowly, my walls crumble. Especially when he wraps an arm around my shoulders and laughs. "I promise I'll be a great roommate. I'll even make us dinner tonight. What do you say?"

How can I refuse?

I don't know if this is smart, but I can't bring myself to say no.

18

ABIGAIL

"Dinner's served!" Nick yells, but when I enter the kitchen, he's tapping away on his phone. "Sorry, just wanted to check in with my dad. I swear, he doesn't take care of himself. Always works too much." He shakes his head, muttering, "*Terco como una mula.*"

"What does that mean?"

"He's stubborn. Like a freaking mule."

I laugh. "It's sweet that you look out for him."

"I'm hoping to get him to retire. It's one of the reasons I need to get drafted."

Ezra just wanted fame and fortune. It's refreshing to see that Nick wants to help his family.

After I get Hazel into her booster, I offer to help with the food, but Nick says he has it handled. A minute later, he slides plates of spaghetti and meatballs in front of me and Hazel.

"Eat up." He cuts up his daughter's food before he sits across from me.

"This looks delicious. Thank you." I bite into the most heavenly meatball I've ever tasted.

He chuckles. "Can't take credit for the meatballs. Cadence made those the other day."

Dang it, she really is a good cook. These are incredible, I grudgingly admit.

I feel weird asking about her, but since I'm living here now, I guess I'm not being a busybody if I inquire. "How's it going with her?"

"Awesome." He pours some milk in Hazel's cup. "She's super sweet, and Hazel loves her. And when she babysits, I end up with these incredible leftovers."

"Great." So, so great.

I cringe, hating that Ezra turned me into this jealous, crazy girl. Ironically, I never used to get jealous with my ex. I thought he was loyal, so there was nothing to worry about. "Sorry I can't cook much. I had a few bad experiences and decided it's probably best for humanity if I stay out of the kitchen."

Laughing, he helps Hazel twirl up some pasta on her fork. "I can really only make scrambled eggs, pancakes, and bacon. I'm pretty spoiled with the food the school provides for athletes. Hazel and I live off that most of the time."

"I've heard it's a good spread." I take a drink of water and then grab a pen and piece of paper off the counter. "How much do you want for rent? We probably should've talked about that first."

He shrugs. "Some nanny positions come with room and board, so I'm not sure."

"That's for full-time work. I only cover a few days."

He thinks on that a minute. "How 'bout you get back on your feet, get your deposit from your landlord, and then we can talk about rent. I wasn't planning on having a roommate, so I made sure to get a place I can afford. If you want to pitch in for groceries and utilities, though, that might be helpful."

"That's really generous." Too generous. I'll give him what I paid when I lived with Paige as soon as I get my deposit back, which will cover two months' rent. "If I'm your roommate, we should split up the work around here. Since I can't cook, can I help with the dishes? I can also sweep and mop once a week. That way Hazel isn't playing on a dirty floor."

"You don't mind doing that?"

I smile. "If I did, I wouldn't ask. If there's anything else you need, just let me know. Like, if you get behind on her laundry, I can do it."

He leans forward, a handsome smile tugging on his lips. "Remind me why you're not my full-time nanny?"

"Because I'm leaving in a few weeks."

His smile drops. Frowning, he pushes food around his plate. "What are your plans for after graduation? After your trip, I mean. Will you be returning to Charming?"

"I can't afford to stay here. Plus, my family is in San Antonio. I figured I'd move back home. Who knows? Maybe I'll get a nanny job abroad." I twirl my fork through the pasta. "It's funny because I was ready to go anywhere with Ezra, follow him to whatever city drafted him. That was a dumb plan. I'm a little irritated with my parents for not talking some sense into me."

"They must've liked him if they were on board with those plans."

"They *loved* him and his parents. They still hang out with the Thomases. I think they're harboring hope I'll forgive him. We were together for so long that they view him like a son. Plus, my mom was his counselor, and my dad was his math teacher in high school. Yes, they're mad at him for hurting me, but they think he's just young and dumb and has learned his lesson. That's probably my fault. I couldn't bring myself to tell them how bad it was, how many girls he…" I glance at Hazel and cut myself off. "You know. I was embarrassed to admit the truth."

Nick shakes his head. "Ezra doesn't deserve your forgiveness. Does that rat still call you?"

"No, thankfully. He's off terrorizing girls in Florida." I take a bite of spaghetti. "I guess you could say he taught me what *not* to do in a relationship. I've learned a lot. Even that tree episode was eye-opening."

"How so?"

"Life is short. Nothing is guaranteed. One minute you're getting ready for bed and the next—bam!—you're pinned down by an oak. So I'm not going to sit around and follow other people's rules for my life anymore. I'm going to make my own. And yes, going to Europe by myself is mildly terrifying, but what if this is my only chance? What if I move to San Antonio, start teaching, get married, settle down, and then never get that window to go again?"

Nick doesn't say anything, just stares at his food.

That's when I remember who I'm talking to and what he's been through. "I'm sorry. I don't mean to be so heartless. You and Hazel have been through a lot yourselves."

"No, you're right. You have to forge your own path in life," he says quietly. His eyes meet mine, and they're full of pain and something else I can't quite figure out.

Hazel, who's been munching away, giggles and flings out her hands.

Which are full of pasta, pasta that hits me in the face.

"Hazel Lynn Silva." Nick tries not to laugh as a noodle slides down my glasses. "Apologize to Abby."

I mock-growl at Hazel and tickle her. "You little monster."

"Sowwy!" She howls with laughter, and I ignore the sting in my ribs.

I'm a mess, but I'm grateful she broke up that serious conversation. Nick doesn't need to hear about my existential crisis right now.

After dinner, he gets his daughter cleaned up for bed. Tonight, I'm sleeping on the couch, and tomorrow, he'll move her stuff into his room and my bed into her former room.

I'm curled up on the couch, reading *Pride and Prejudice* for the millionth time. I pat the cover and admire the annotation flags sticking up from the pages in a pretty rainbow. I should be studying my Advanced Teaching Methods textbook, but I figure I almost died last night, so I'm cutting myself some slack.

My lips pull up in a smile when Mr. Darcy calls Elizabeth "tolerable" but not beautiful enough to tempt him. He fights the attraction so hard. It gives me sick pleasure that he has no idea love will kick his ass and make him eat those words.

I'm reaching for my textbook when Nick returns. "Want some ice cream? I think I have some butter pecan."

"I'd love some. Thanks."

He comes back a few minutes later with two bowls. After he hands me one, he sits on the other side of the couch.

"Sorry you got so banged up by that tree. How are you feeling? Do you need some ibuprofen?"

"I already took some. I'm feeling better." I'll just wear long sleeves until the bruises fade.

He takes a bite of his dessert. "So, uh, how did your date go last night? That was a date, right?"

"We met up with Paige's boyfriend's buddies. I'm not sure I would call it a date." I freeze with the spoon halfway to my mouth. I can't believe that was only a night ago. So much has happened since then.

"You gonna see him again?"

"Probably not. He was nice enough, but I didn't like the dynamic with him and his friends." There were too many times when they all but blew off us girls. "Plus, there were no fireworks."

"Fireworks, huh?"

"I know it sounds silly, but I think that chemistry is important."

"What about the firefighter? He seemed pretty into you." Swirling his spoon in the bowl, he glances at me.

I admit I enjoyed dancing with Shane, except I'm unfortunately even more preoccupied with my boss now than I was last night. "Shane's a nice guy. Maybe nicer than I thought he'd be, but I'm not feeling it. I guess I'm gun-shy after what happened with Ezra." I take a bite of ice cream before I have the guts to return the question. "What about you? How was your date? Will you see her again?"

He tilts his head slightly. "It was fine, but like you said, there were no fireworks."

I shouldn't be relieved, but I am. "What are you looking for in a girlfriend?" My face heats with the question, which is more forward than something I'd typically ask, but if a tree can fall out of the sky and knock me on my ass, I can afford to be more daring.

"Nothing too serious. Mostly just someone to hang out with for the next few months until I hopefully get drafted."

I cringe. "Not really selling it, are you?"

He huffs out a laugh. "Is casual dating really so bad?"

"I wouldn't know. I've only dated Ezra."

Nick chokes. "You're shitting me."

"Nope."

"How did you get through high school only dating him?"

"That's easy. I was a wallflower and a super nerd. And really shy. I'm still kind of shy, actually, and an introvert. I'd rather stay home on a Friday night and read or play Scrabble. Maybe crochet or learn how to knit."

I look up to find Nick staring at me. "It's okay to be shy. I can't speak for all men, but I prefer shy over aggressive."

"Do women get aggressive with you?"

"Yeah, but in a weird way. Like I'm a piece of meat they want for dinner."

"You poor sex symbol." We both laugh. I scoop another bite of ice cream. "If this is too personal, you don't have to talk about it, but how did you and Hazel's mom end up together? You were in high school too, right?"

His brows furrow as he stares off like he's looking into a window from the past. "Gemma was this beautiful girl I'd see in the hallway. Super artsy. Totally out of my league. One day she asked me to help her carry this huge painting to the auditorium for a student exhibit. We started talking, and that was it."

"Fireworks."

He laughs. "Yeah. The kind that knock you on your ass."

"And then y'all had Hazel at the end of your senior year?"

"Yup. Another kick in the ass." He smiles ruefully. "Even though Gemma and I were both scared shitless, Hazel was immediately the light of our lives."

"I'm so sorry for your loss," I say quietly. I don't know why I went down this road with him. He's probably still in love with her. I'm all choked up, and I didn't even know the woman. "You're doing a great job raising Hazel. I'm sure Gemma would be proud of you."

His jaw goes tight. "I, uh... Thanks. I try. Really fucking hard."

"Have you dated anyone since she passed? When was that?"

"Sophomore year in college. Three years ago this month, and, no, nothing serious since then. Not sure if I'll ever be ready for anything serious again, if I'm being honest with myself."

Which is probably why he'll only do casual now.

Because he's still in love with his dead girlfriend.

That motel might not be in the best part of town, but it's probably safer for my heart than living with Nick.

19

NICK

"Their blindside blocks are beautiful," Coach says as he replays the film footage of Northwestern, who we're playing this weekend. "Notice that there's no foul. He just slides in there between his running back and the two defenders on his tail to throw them off. There's not much body contact, no face mask grabbing, no tackle. He's just mucking up things for their defense, breaking their momentum."

He flips on the light as he heads back to the podium. "Our job is to anticipate those blocks and not get frustrated."

When Coach releases us to get taped up for practice, Jinxy mumbles, "Speaking of blocks, I got cockblocked last night. How am I not supposed to get frustrated?"

"Are you saying the apple cider vinegar didn't work?" I smirk.

"It worked. Mostly. But let's just say I tried a few things first that didn't go so smoothly, so I was... tender down there."

Maverick smacks him on the back. "Poor Jinxy. Did ya go one night without getting laid?"

As we head to the locker room, Jinxy laughs. "When you put it like that, maybe I am an asshole."

I chuckle and check my phone in case Abby texted me about Hazel. She sent a photo, a selfie of her and Hazel fingerpainting.

"Why you smiling so big?" Jinxy asks as he opens his locker. I show him the pic, and he lifts an eyebrow. "Be honest, bro. Abby's the reason you didn't go home with Cricket, right?"

"Cricket's a nice girl, but I guess I was kinda preoccupied last weekend. I just wasn't feeling it."

"Did your preoccupation have anything to do with your cute little nanny?"

Maverick chucks a dirty sock at Jinxy. "Who's the cute nanny?"

"You've met Abby," I say. "Blonde, glasses, likes to break into my house through the awning window."

"The one from Moe's, right?"

"Yeah."

"You sleeping with her?"

I make a face. "She works for me."

Maverick shrugs. "Is this really a problem?"

"Now that she lives with me, yes."

Jinxy's head jerks around. "When did this happen?"

"Saturday night when a tree crashed through her bedroom and nearly killed her. Now the house is unlivable, and her landlord kicked her and Paige out."

"Dude, it's fucking Thursday. I can't believe you've been sitting on this news all week. So Paige and Abby are both staying with you now?"

"Paige went to her boyfriend's place, and Abby was gonna stay at a motel, but it looked shady as fuck, so I brought her back to my house. Moved Hazel's crap into my room so she has her own bed. Abby's staying in Hazel's room."

"Convenient."

I ignore the innuendo in Jinxy's voice and tuck my phone in my locker. "She's only here a few more weeks, till the end of the semester, then she graduates. I actually need to find a babysitter to take her place when she goes." When I turn around, I find Jinxy and Maverick staring at me. "What?"

"I was just telling Mav you need to loosen up and that I self-appointed myself as team pimp to get you laid. Don't you think Silva could benefit from a little dick TLC?" Jinxy asks Maverick.

"Not this again," I mumble.

"It's true. Why don't you ask Abby to help you out? You said she's leaving soon. That's perfect. You'll have a live-in fuck doll, and when she graduates and moves out, no harm, no foul."

My jaw tightens. "Don't talk about her like that." Abby is one of the sweetest women I've ever met. She'd fucking die to know these assholes were discussing her like she was a sex toy.

Do I like living with her? Seeing her at the end of a long day? More than I'm willing to admit, but I'll never confess that to my teammates. They'll make a mountain out of a molehill.

Since that convo her first night at my house, I've been trying to put a little distance between us. I've never spoken about Gemma to another woman since she died. I don't know why I did with Abby. It freaked me out a little.

Then Gemma's mother Cynthia called me this morning, probably to talk about the anniversary of Gemma's death, and I let it go to voicemail. I texted back to apologize because I can't go down memory lane right now. I'll never get over what happened if she's constantly picking at the scab.

I've been feeling confused, so I don't need Jinxy getting in my face about my roommate, but he won't let it go.

His eyebrows lift. "You planning to date Abby?"

"No, but—"

"But nothing." Jinxy shuts his locker. "She's beautiful, sweet, and sleeping in the bedroom next to yours. Think of this as a mutually beneficial favor. She can fuck Ezra Thomas out of her system, and you can relax your ass for once. Then maybe we can win with more than a razor-thin margin this weekend."

It pains me to hear he thinks I'm barely eking it out on the field. I glance around the room and a few other guys are listening. "Do y'all agree? Do you think I'm barely cutting it? Be honest."

Guiltily, they look away, and my gut clenches.

Bowser clears his throat. "You're doing your best, bro."

"Fuck—" I cut myself off before I say something I can't take back and stalk out of the locker room.

"Come back," Jinxy yells. "Don't get butthurt. It's just a streak of bad luck. That's why I suggested sex. It'll loosen you up and—"

"It's cool. Gonna get taped up," I say to save face. But the conversation dogs me our whole practice. I can't stop thinking about it.

I don't believe in bad luck.

Or at least, I don't want to.

20

ABIGAIL

"You'd better not be biting your nails." Baylee gives me a look. "Not after I did that manicure."

I give her a sheepish grin and tuck my hands under my legs. "It's an intense game."

Baylee came over to give me a manicure and watch the Broncos play Northwestern. We're sitting on Nick's leather couch, munching on snacks, and I'm trying not to have a heart attack. Every time the Broncos gain some momentum, Northwestern matches their energy and comes from behind.

It's halftime, so I can catch my breath. At least now my lungs fully expand without that pinch in my side, and my bruises have faded to a lovely green color.

Glancing at the kitchen where Cadence and Hazel are cooking, Baylee whispers, "So how are things going with Nick? 'Cause I heard all about how he stormed the castle to get you out from under that tree."

Folding in my lips, I think about how to respond. I try to sound casual. "It's been good. Mostly. We get along pretty well."

She huffs. "Really? That's all you're going to give me?"

I've been bursting at the seams to talk about this with someone, and since Paige is always at cheer practice, I guess I'm doing this with Baylee. "If you tell anyone other than Paige I said this, I swear I'll hunt you down."

"Oh, this has to be good." She hops up and down in her seat.

"Just..." I glance at the kitchen. "You have to promise you won't talk about this with anyone."

"My lips are sealed. Just Paige."

Nodding, I take a deep breath. "Frankly, it's hard to be around him. He's such a great dad and a good person. And..."

"And freakishly handsome."

I hang my head. "Yes. *Sooo* handsome."

She cackles. "I knew it!"

"Shh." I don't want Cadence to overhear us. "I don't want to like him. I've been down this road before, and there's a steep cliff at the end. Getting involved with Nick is a terrible idea. Plus..."

Baylee shakes my arm. "Plus what?"

"He's been grumpy this week. Like, in the worst mood for the last few days. And it kills me. I want to make him feel better. I want to talk to him until his problems go away. So if I react like this when we're just friends, what would happen if we..."

"Got naked?"

"Yes. I'd be a nervous wreck until things inevitably ended." Which is why I bought a vibrator—I need something to deal with the tension. It just arrived today.

Her eyes go soft. "It's okay to be afraid. It's not like I have all the answers. I have my own relationship woes. Have you met Maverick Walker?"

"He's one of Nick's friends, right? A tight end?"

"Yeah, we grew up together in the same small town. In fact, Paige has always had a thing for Mav's older brother, Rhett."

"She told me about him."

Her eyes widen. "She must love you because she never talks about Rhett with anyone. Anyway, I've had a raging crush on

Mav since we were kids, but I've always been friendzoned. It sucks to watch him sleep around with jersey chasers who will happily swap him out for one of his teammates."

"I'm sorry. I don't know if this will help you at all, but ever since I found out my ex cheated on me, I've decided I have to do my own thing. I have to go after what makes me happy. I can't sideline myself, and I'm hoping the right man will fall in love with that version of me, the girl who goes after her dreams." I squeeze her hand. "So screw Maverick Walker. If he doesn't realize that he has a great woman right under his nose, then he doesn't deserve you."

"Thanks." She gives me a grateful smile.

"Who wants some homemade buffalo wings?" Cadence calls out from the kitchen.

"Oh! I do!" Baylee shouts. I give her a look, and she shrugs. "They smell good." She pats my arm. "Don't worry. I'm still rooting for you over the Stepford nanny."

"I shouldn't be jealous. She's just so dang perfect."

Cadence comes into the living room wearing a pretty sundress and pristine white apron. Her dark hair is pulled up in a twist. She's really beautiful. I can see why she was runner-up on *The Nanny Whisperer*. That's why I can't bring myself to watch the last season. I don't need more reasons to feel inferior to her. She sing-songs, "I have spicy buffalo, honey barbecue, ranch, and plain in case Hazel doesn't like the flavors."

Hazel runs in and wiggles her fingers, which are covered in sauce. "I want honey bawbecue!"

"Come here, Hazelnut." I whip out some hand wipes and clean her off.

Cadence lets out a sigh of relief. "Thank you, Abigail. I was sure she was going to wipe her hands on my apron, and it was giving me anxiety."

"Aren't aprons supposed to get dirty?"

She laughs. "I play a little game with myself to see if I can cook an entire meal without getting anything on it. I consider it a personal challenge."

Good thing she's never seen me cook. I somehow always manage to get flour in my hair. Once, it went up my nose.

Baylee piles her plate with wings and groans when she bites into one. "Oh my God. These are incredible."

Cadence holds the platter in front of me. "Are you sure I can't entice you? They're my mama's recipe."

"Fine. Twist my arm."

She squeals and holds it out for me while I place a few wings on my plate. I take a tiny nibble and try to keep the irritation off my face. It's not her fault I'm green with jealousy. "These are delicious. Thank you."

Hazel skips around the living room, and I have to admit that while Cadence gets on my nerves with her perfect apron and perfect hair and perfect chicken wings, I don't remember seeing Hazel this happy. That's the most important thing, I remind myself.

The third quarter starts, and I scoot to the edge of my seat. I really hope Nick can pull this off.

The whistle blows on the screen, and I lean to the side so I can see around Cadence. "Ugh, poor Nick. He just got sacked."

Cadence sets the platter down. "What does that mean? Sorry, I don't know much about football."

I spend the next ten minutes explaining the basics and then I return to the play that kicked off this conversation. "So right now, they're blitzing, meaning extra guys are rushing the quarterback, and that's why Nick got sacked once."

Yikes. Make that twice.

I hold my breath as I watch him slowly stand. Thank God he's okay.

Hazel is busy munching on her wings, which is good because I don't want her worried about her dad.

The game is tied again, and the temptation to gnaw off my new manicure is strong. "Northwestern keeps ramping up the defense. Nick's getting frustrated. I don't blame him."

"Why doesn't he just throw the ball?" Cadence asks, sitting down on the arm of the couch.

"Sometimes that's easier said than done. He doesn't have a lot of time after the snap to get the ball off. Add five or six huge guys gunning for him, and he probably feels that pressure. A bad throw might mean a turnover. I don't blame him for wanting to be careful." Although there were a few options he either didn't see or didn't think he could make, but I don't say that out loud.

It's fourth and twenty, so the Broncos kick. Northwestern catches the ball at the ten and runs it thirty yards. On the next play, the offense does a spectacular job blocking for the quarterback, who fakes a pass but then bolts downfield for another thirty yards. He has two guys running interference for him the whole way.

I stand and shout, "Come on! Tackle his ass!" Ugh, touchdown.

Hazel looks up. "You said a naughty wowd."

Shit. "I'm sorry. Football makes me forget myself."

Baylee giggles. "I had no idea you were such a fanatic."

I'm feverish. Sweaty. My hands are clammy and my heart is racing. Those wings are fighting their way back up my stomach.

Oh, God. When did this happen to me?

I know this feeling all too well. Dread swirls in my belly, and not just because we might lose the game.

By the time we reach the fourth quarter, I'm growling and yelling at the TV. "I can't watch this anymore." I flop backwards on the couch and cover my face, but as soon as the timeout ends,

I'm at the edge of my seat again. "Come on, Nick. Trust your offense. Dax is open downfield more often than not, you're just not seeing it. You have to make some long plays to spread the defense more. That'll get them off your back."

Northwestern has the ball, and they're driving the field, but a receiver bobbles it, and a quick Bronco knocks the ball away. They fight for it, running and tumbling until Lone Star State comes up with the ball.

"Yes!" We're all cheering and yelling.

Baylee and I hold hands as Nick takes the field with the offense. "You got this, Nick!" I don't know why I'm shouting at the TV. It's not like the man can hear me, but I like sending him good vibes.

It's fourth and sixteen at the Broncos' thirty-five-yard line. When the ball snaps, the O-line keeps the defenders at bay long enough for Nick to spot Dax downfield. He's under fire. Dax has two guys hot on his heels as Nick scrambles out of the pocket to try to get the throw off.

"Throw it!" I shout. There's only thirty-five seconds left.

Nick reaches back and releases it. The ball sails through the air in what has to be a forty-five-yard pass.

"Oh my God! Oh my God!" Baylee yells.

One of the defenders gets his hands on the ball but can't hold on, and Dax snags it. "Yes!"

We're all jumping and screaming as he runs it into the end zone for the win.

A few hours later, we've demolished the wings and ordered pizza. Baylee is drunk, and Cadence is getting tipsy. I won't drink because someone needs to watch Hazel, who's coloring.

She gets up with a yawn. "I have to go potty."

"Do you need help?" I put down my slice of pizza.

"I can do it."

"Holler if you need help." She's been such a good girl all day.

As Nick's SUV pulls into the driveway, Cadence leans over. "Does boss man have a girlfriend? I've been dying to ask you."

My heart falls. I knew she liked him. "I, um, I'm not sure." I go with something vague because I'm uncomfortable divulging something so personal about my employer.

That's weird to think when we're the same age and live together, but it's good to remind myself that he's my boss.

I'm so excited to congratulate him on the big win, but he's scowling when he opens the door.

"Nick!" Cadence flies off the couch and throws her arms around him. "Congrats! What a game. I almost died when you were sacked. Are you okay?" She pats him down like she's physically looking for an injury.

His brows lift, and his eyes meet mine. I look away because it's hard to watch another woman maul him.

I'm not sure what he does to disentangle himself, but he drops his stuff by the door. "Is everyone drunk? Or just you, Cadence?"

Baylee raises her hand. "Guilty."

I set my paper plate on the coffee table. "Cadence is off duty. I told her I could watch Hazel if she wanted a glass of wine to celebrate your win."

Nick glances around. "Where's Hazel?"

"I'm he-a, Daddy. Look! It's like Staw Waws."

I think she means *Star Wars*. Nick makes a weird sound, and I turn to him. His jaw is tight, and he looks pissed. "Hazel, where did you get that?" The sternness of his voice catches me off guard.

That's when I see what she's playing with.

My new, hot pink vibrator with the little rabbit ears.

"Oh, shit." Baylee elbows me. "Is it yours?" she whispers.

Cadence trots over to Hazel. "Where did you get that?"

Nick takes it out of his daughter's hands, and then, to my great mortification, it starts vibrating.

Cadence giggles and shoots me a look. "Guess you like 'em big, huh?" She ushers Hazel back to the kitchen.

I flop back on the couch and cover my face with my arm again. "Don't mind me. I'm just going to roll over and die."

When I finally brave another look, Nick is still holding my freaking vibrator, trying not to laugh. "I get the main part, but what's this for?" He flicks the rabbit ears.

"Shut up. Like you don't know."

He flushes. "Swear to God, I don't." Then he chuckles and hands it to me. "Sorry, that's kinda personal. Just ignore me. Got my bell rung pretty hard today." He runs his hands through his hair. "And I'm sorry Hazel got into your stuff. I'll talk to her."

I get up so I can put it away and maybe hide under my bed until I leave for London in December.

21

ABIGAIL

"You can't hide in your room all day," Roxy says.

I move my cell to my other ear. "Says you. You should've seen his face, Rox. I've never been so embarrassed in my life, and that's saying something." For the past hour, I've been catching her up on how I ended up living with Nick.

"I wish I could swoop by and pick you up so we could process this properly with some quality junk food."

My stomach rumbles in agreement. "I need to go eat. The house is pretty quiet, so maybe Nick and Hazel left." It's Sunday, and he usually tries to do something special with her to make up for the rest of the week when he has to eat, sleep, and breathe football. "Before I go, how's Marley?"

"She's getting so big. I'll send you some pics. Oh, and Billy says hi."

"How's he enjoying the NFL?"

"He's in heaven. I love seeing him happy." She sighs dreamily. "I just love him so much. Last year sucked, but now we're in such a good place. It was worth every bit of heartache. I'd do it all over again for him."

Roxy deserves her happily ever after. We both got played by

Ezra. I just hope I can find my HEA someday too. "I'm glad y'all are doing well. Thanks for checking on me. Send those photos of the baby."

After we hang up, I listen at my bedroom door to make sure I'm alone. When I don't hear anything, I tiptoe out to the kitchen, which gives me a clear view out to the backyard where Nick is jumping rope. Shirtless.

Holy hot eye candy, he's wearing gray sweatpants.

Sweat drips down his brow. Down his muscled chest. Down his six pack, and... and...

Wow. He's packing.

It's all right there.

Bouncing.

Up and down.

Again and again.

"Daddy!"

I jump back from the window when I hear Hazel's voice. She must be playing in the backyard while Nick works out.

I close my eyes. I should not be checking out Nick's impressive bulge while he jumps rope. *Bad Abigail.*

Maybe I have a few minutes to make breakfast before they come inside. I hustle around the kitchen to make some toast and pour a cup of coffee. I'm buttering my bread when the back door opens.

"Hey." Nick's out of breath.

"Hi." I'm not wondering if that's how he sounds after he has sex. Not at all.

"Hazel has something important she wants to tell you."

Oh, heck, no. Please don't bring up my vibrator.

I force a smile and turn around. Shoulders slumped, Hazel ambles to me. "Sowwy."

Nick wipes his face with a towel, and I'm momentarily distracted by his chest muscles that contract with the motion.

"For what, honey? Remember what we said? That you wouldn't go in Abigail's room without an invitation?"

Hazel sheepishly smiles. "Sowwy I went in you-a woom."

I kneel down and hug her. "That's okay. It used to be your room and will be again soon. I understand why you were confused. I really shouldn't have left that box on my bed. Lesson learned."

Nick grabs a glass of water, and I studiously ignore his incredible body.

The tension in the room is thick. I wonder if it's just me.

I clear my throat. "What are y'all up to today?"

"I'm taking Hazel to the park, maybe out for some ice cream."

"That's nice." I wait for him to ask me what I'm doing or invite me, but he doesn't. He's staring out the back window, scowling. He did a lot of that this past week for some reason. I want to ask him what's going on, but it's not my place.

Hazel tugs on his arm. "Daddy, can Abby come with us?"

I smile, which promptly disappears when her father's jaw tightens. "I'm sure Abigail has things she needs to do."

I'm back to being Abigail again.

Why was he so nice to me when I moved in with him if he was just going to turn around and be a dick? I swear, I'll never understand men.

Ignoring the sting in my eyes, I muster a smile. "Actually, Hazel, I have plans. Thank you so much for the invitation, though." The invitation her father clearly didn't mean to extend. I lean down to hug her. "Have fun, okay?"

I finish buttering my toast as quickly as possible and am reaching into the cabinet for a mug when Hazel's giggle makes me turn.

Nick's doing push-ups in the living room while Hazel sits on his back. "Faster, Daddy."

"Slave driver."

Funny how he doesn't have that edge with his daughter. Just with me.

Did I do something wrong?

Maybe stop staring at the man while he does push-ups.

After I pour my coffee, I scuttle back to my room and grab my phone to send Paige an S.O.S.

Me: Nick's being weird. I think he's mad at me.

Paige: Because his daughter found your huge vibrator?

My face goes scarlet. Baylee wasted no time telling Paige about the vibe incident.

Me: I blame you for telling me I had to get one!

Paige: Your eyeballs will roll back in your head, I promise.

Me: I'm scared to use it. What if I don't like the rabbit ears?

Paige: That's the best part!

Me: Now I feel weird using it. Like Nick will know.

Paige: *laughing emoji*

My phone buzzes with a reminder that I have a tutoring session in an hour.

Me: You can joke all you want, but he's being standoffish this morning. Like he's mad at me. You're right. It's probably because I had a huge sex toy lying around that his daughter found.

Paige: Maybe he fantasized about you using it.

I suck in a breath. Closing my eyes, I can see him lying in bed without a shirt on. His hand would rub his strong chest and then dip down beneath the sheets. He'd grab his thick erection on a groan, and start—

My phone buzzes in my hand, and I almost drop it.

Paige: If you don't like that model, there's a smaller toy you could start with.

All of this talk about sex toys is making me heated, and since I don't have any time to relieve the problem, I'd better focus. The last thing I need is to be turned on when I'm sitting in the library, proofing someone's essay.

Me: I have to go to a tutoring session. I hope Nick leaves soon or I'll have to face Mr. Grouchy again.

Paige: Wear something cute and flirty.

Me: Why? I'm just going to the library.

Paige: Because it'll make you feel good. And if you feel good, you won't give a shit that Nick's being an asshole. Remember how awesome you felt after that makeover?

She makes a solid point. I don't want to sit here all wound up over what Nick may or may not think about me.

Me: What's cute and flirty? Jeans and a t-shirt?

Paige: What about that pink top with buttons? It's casual but nice. Pair that with some dark jeans. Hair up in a messy bun, but you should swipe on some mascara and lip gloss.

Messy bun. Light makeup. Nothing crazy. I can do this.

Me: Thank you!

Paige: Please kiss him already! He's probably grumpy because he wants you! You're graduating soon. Make the next few weeks count.

My heart races when I think about kissing Nick. But do I really want to get involved with him when I know he doesn't want anything serious?

I sit at the edge of my bed and consider that. Before the tree incident, I would've said no, but now? I'm not sure. What if it's really fun? What if we have great sex? What if we're really good together? I've never had a fling before.

I've always thought I couldn't do a hookup because I'd get attached, but I don't know that for sure since I've never experienced one.

Would it hurt to try?

My whole body tingles at the thought.

I'm probably jumping the gun. He likely wants someone like

Cadence who looks like a pretty princess and does everything perfectly.

Realizing I'm running out of time, I run around my room and get ready. When I come out, I find Nick doing Hazel's hair.

He's sitting on the couch, and she's sitting between his legs, watching a cartoon while he puts her hair in a ponytail.

"Is it okay if it's crooked?" he asks.

"No." Her little mouth purses.

"What if it's the best I can do?"

She sighs. "I guess that's okay."

"Just teasing, gingersnap. It's straight." He kisses the top of her head. "There. All done."

Holy swoon. What is it about a dad doing his daughter's hair that's so sexy?

I wave awkwardly. "Hey, guys."

Nick does a double-take when he sees me. I pat my hair, worried I didn't pull off the "cute and flirty" look Paige suggested. "What?"

"Nothing." He frowns. "You look nice. That's all."

If I look nice, why does he look so pissed about it?

I push up my glasses. I didn't want to deal with contacts *and* mascara today. "Thank you. Have fun at the park. I'll be back late."

I was right—living with Nick was a bad idea.

22

ABIGAIL

EXHAUSTION PULLS at my lids as I drive home. It's after midnight, and I smell like chicken-fried steak and Italian dressing. I love Moe to pieces, but I'm not sure how many more shifts I can handle. Juggling classes, taking care of Hazel, and tutoring is plenty. The extra money for my trip would be nice, but not if I die of exhaustion first.

I park on the street. Nick's house is dark except for a small light in the kitchen that we leave on at night.

I'd love to march straight to my room and collapse in bed, but if I don't take a quick shower, my bedding will smell like Moe's, and I'll have to wash the sheets. So after I get a drink of water, I grab my pajamas and clean undies and set them on my bed.

My phone buzzes with a text.
Moe: Did ya get home okay?
Me: Yes, thanks! Goodnight! :)
He texts all of the staff who work late to make sure we get home safely, which I appreciate.

Yawning, I head to the bathroom, close the door, and crank the shower. After I strip out of my clothes, I toss them in my compartment of the hamper, which has three sections, one for each of us. Then I step under the steaming hot water and groan. It feels so good. I lean against the wall and let the water pummel me. I'd give anything for a back massage right now.

After I wash off, I grab my towel that's hanging on a wall hook and dry off. Once I'm done, I glance at the counter.

Wait. Where are my pajamas? Didn't I just grab them out of the dresser?

Dang it. I think I left them on my bed. Frustrated, I wrap the towel around me, flip off the light, and head back down the hall.

Oof.

I bounce off something hard.

Heart pounding, I somehow manage not to scream.

Big, calloused hands wrap around my shoulders. "Shit. Sorry, Abby."

I barely manage to keep the towel wrapped around me. "You scared me, you big oaf."

He chuckles. "Maybe if you were looking where you were going…"

I'm tired and cold and confused and in no mood for his flirty smile.

I poke him in his hard chest. His warm, hard, *bare* chest. I whisper-yell at him, "Listen, mister. You don't get to be mean to me all week and then break out the charm when you feel like it. One minute, you're making me dinner and we're friends, and the next, you're growly and irritable and ignoring me. Are we friends or not? I get that I'm your employee, but that doesn't mean you can be a beast whenever you feel like it. Because I don't like getting whiplash."

It's dark, so I can barely see him except for the light coming down the hall from the kitchen, but I think he's frowning.

I sigh. "Do you want me to move out? I don't want to be a burden. I'd rather us get along."

"Fuck," he mutters.

"I... I can move my things tomorrow night. That motel wasn't so bad." I swallow down the hurt.

His paw moves to cup my jaw. "That's... No. I don't want you to move. I'm sorry, Abby. I've been an asshole."

"What's going on? Why are you mad at me?"

He tilts my head up.

That's when I realize how close we are. How his chest is heaving. How he's looking at me like I'm an ice cream cone he wants to lick up.

How I'm only wearing a towel.

His thumb grazes my cheek. "Can I be honest?" That growly low voice makes chills break out along my arms.

I nod. "Please."

"You're driving me crazy."

It's my turn to scowl. For a second, I'd thought he was into me, but clearly that's not what he meant. "There's no need to be rude. If you don't think I'm a good roommate, you should just say that."

He chuckles again and shakes his head. "Not that kind of crazy, you little nut. This kind." He backs me up against the wall, and I suck in a breath when he presses his beautiful, hard body against me.

That bulge I'd admired this morning is pointing straight up in his pajama bottoms and is now pressing against my stomach.

Oh! I grab his shoulders and let out a sigh of relief. "Thank God, because I've been going out of my mind." His nose grazes my shoulder, and I moan and bring him closer. "Is this a good idea? I work for you."

"It's a terrible idea, but I'm tired of fighting this. I've been thinking about you all week. How sweet you look first thing in the morning. How good you are with my daughter. How gorgeous you looked on that date with another fucking man."

He growls and wraps his arms around me and sucks on my neck. "Were you on a date tonight? Is that why you were out late?"

Breathless, I shake my head. "N-no. I had to work."

Good thing I'm leaning against the wall because my legs probably won't hold me up right now.

"Are you sure you want to do this?" he asks against my temple.

My nails dig into his shoulders. "Yes."

"We have to be quiet, and we can't let Hazel know something's going on between us. You're leaving soon, and I don't want her to be disappointed when you go."

Cue the record scratch.

The euphoric cloud I was surfing on a minute ago lights on fire and crashes to the ground.

Of course he doesn't want anything permanent or long-term. He just wants to bang.

I look away. Can I do this knowing it ends at the end of the semester? If I walk away now, will I always regret it?

That's a sobering thought. My ex slept with half of Charming while I sat at home like an obedient girlfriend. This is my chance to experience the passion I never had with Ezra.

I take a deep breath. Do I want a smoking hot affair with the most beautiful man I've ever laid eyes on?

Yes.

Will it break my heart when it inevitably ends?

Probably.

Do I care?

Not in this moment.

As I struggle to keep the towel on, I push Nick back and stare up at his handsome face. "I have some rules of my own. If we do this, I'd better be the only woman you're sleeping with. I don't share. If I find some girl crawling all over you, we'll be over right then and there. And I'm not cool with you flirting with other girls. We might not be in any kind of formal relationship, but I won't put myself at risk with someone who only thinks with his dick. Been there, done that, and I'd rather work out my frustrations with my vibrator than go there again. Do you agree to those terms?"

His eyes go hot. "I like this feisty little version of you."

"I'm not joking, Nick," I huff. I'm not sure where this burst of bravado comes from that has me throwing down ultimatums left and right, but I don't care. "We're monogamous while we do this. If you decide you'd rather bang some fangirls after a game, you'd better end this first or so help me, I'll—"

"Yes. Now shut up." He lifts my chin as he presses me against the wall again. "I had no idea you had such a saucy fucking mouth."

His thumb drags against my bottom lip, and I promptly nip him. "Don't play me."

A smile tugs at his lips. "I won't, buttercup. I promise."

23

NICK

It takes everything in me not to fuck Abby in the hallway.

She's staring up at me with fire in her eyes. I've certainly given her every reason to be pissed at me. Between my teammates ribbing me and the anniversary of Gemma's death coming up later this month, I haven't been in a good headspace.

All the more reason to distance myself from my new roommate. Abby's looking for something long-term. That's not me.

Except she's so damn tempting.

But she's a big girl. If she thinks she can handle it, who am I to question her?

I have to admit that Jinxy's right about one thing. With Abby's looming trip and her move back home to San Antonio, that gives us a solid deadline. This way, neither of us gets hurt. We can have a little fun before we graduate without getting all tangled up in feelings.

Reluctantly, I agree that Jinxy's also right about me being wound too tight. Yesterday's game was a shit show. Sex will help me relax, and then I can focus on football. Hooking up with Abby kills two birds with one stone.

But I'm also dying to be with this woman. She's driven me to the brink of insanity with her cute little smile and shy demeanor. I've been going out of my mind since I saw her vibrator. Then today, thinking she had a date tonight almost sent me over the edge.

I keep waiting for the panic to set in. For that voice in my head that always tells me hooking up is wrong. That I belong to Gemma. That I can't move on.

For the first time in three years, it's quiet.

I gently grab Abby's face and tilt her head back. "We go at your speed. Whatever you're ready for."

Her luminous eyes stare back at me as she nibbles her plump bottom lip. "I'm cold. Can we stop standing in the hallway?"

I chuckle. Did I think she was shy? Because the woman in front of me with her towel hanging dangerously low on her luscious curves has been giving me shit ever since she stepped out of the bathroom. I love that she's a straight shooter.

With a hand on her back, I walk her to her bedroom. I close the door behind me and lock it.

She shivers. "Should I put on something warmer than a towel?"

I trace my finger across one of the bruises on her arms. I plan to kiss each and every one of them tonight.

I take her glasses off her lovely face and place them on the bedside table before I wrap my arms around her small frame. "Do you need clothes if I plan to warm you up?" I dip my mouth to hers, and she instantly throws her arms around my neck. Her skin is damp, and she smells like peaches.

Our tongues slide against each other. Slowly. Decadently. Like we have all the time in the world.

I want to savor every moment. I want to remember her minty taste and soft skin and sweet peach scent.

Because someday soon, she'll be just a memory. This is what

I have. Right here. Right now. The next few weeks. And I aim to make the most of every night I have with her.

She arches into me, pressing her tits into me as I kiss her. We both moan, and suddenly we can't get close enough. Her hands are in my hair, and mine are on her round ass as I grind her against my cock.

The feel of her in my arms is drugging. I've never been this out of control with a woman.

I take her damp hair out of the messy bun on top of her head. It falls in curtains around her. "Beautiful." I stare into her eyes as I drag my finger along her chest, just above the towel. "Can I take this off?"

She nods. Her breaths come in quick puffs, which I hope means she's as turned on as I am.

The wet towel falls at her feet, and I finally let myself look down her gorgeous body. Her full tits are high with hard, pink nipples. She has a slender stomach, curved hips, and a trim blonde bush between her thighs.

Her legs cross. "I don't shave that all the way."

"I don't care. I'd want to put my face there if you had a jungle."

She laughs and her breasts bounce in such an enticing way, I have to reach out and grab them. "Christ, you have great tits. I've been obsessed with them since they streaked across my window."

Her small hand runs across my arms and chest. Down my stomach. Until it cups my hard-on. "If we're making confessions, did you deliberately jump rope this morning in *gray* sweatpants? Because I'd be lying if I didn't admit I've been replaying that in my head all day."

She likes me in gray sweats? Noted.

Groaning as she strokes me through the thin pajama

bottoms, I grab her wrist. "I need to make you come first before you do that or this evening will get cut short."

She frowns. "I need to warn you about something."

My back stiffens. "What's up?" Maybe she's changed her mind. I take a deep breath, hoping I don't have to jerk off in the bathroom.

"It's hard for me to come."

That's not what I was expecting her to say. "Hard as in you can't get yourself there on your own? Or hard as in no one else has gotten you there?"

"The latter."

Ezra really is a tool.

I kiss her forehead. "That sounds like a challenge, baby, and I love challenges. Oh, and I finally figured out what those rabbit ears were for." Her face gets that adorable blush, and I drag my thumb over her smooth cheek. "Let's see if I can do a better job than your vibrator."

Chuckling at her expression, I tip her back until she sits on the bed. "Slide back, but keep your ass near the edge."

She does what I ask, but frowns. "Like this?"

"Now lie down."

Demurely, she keeps her legs together after she reclines. Sweet, beautiful girl.

Kneeling in front of her, I pat my shoulders. "Up here."

"Up here what?"

"Put your feet up here."

Her eyes widen comically. "What?"

I'm going about this all wrong. It's been a while, and I'm obviously rusty at this whole seduction thing.

"Relax. If you don't like something, tell me." Reaching down, I grab her dainty ankle and raise it to my mouth where I kiss and nibble her skin. I drag my mouth up her calf. Up her knee. Up her smooth thigh.

Glancing up, I catch my breath. Because she's so fucking gorgeous. Chest heaving. Nipples hard and pointed to the ceiling. Damp hair a messy tangle across her bed.

I dip my face between her thighs and lick across her swollen flesh. Then I wrap my arm under her other thigh. Both of her feet automatically rest along my shoulders, opening her. Fortunately, her bedside lamp is on, so I can see her sweet little pussy. It's puffy and pink and glistening.

With one finger, I drag the tip through the wetness. She sucks in a breath and arches her back when I graze her clit.

"Remember, you have to be quiet. No screaming."

She glances down at me. "I've never screamed during sex."

"Yet." Ezra obviously didn't know what the fuck he was doing.

The dubious expression on her face is another challenge, one I fully expect to win. Maybe not tonight because I'd rather not wake up Hazel, but at some point, I aim to get Abby Dawson screaming my name.

I lick around her swollen clit, and her legs tighten around my head. Smiling, I widen her legs again before I take slow laps up her slit. "You taste so good, buttercup."

She makes an incoherent sound, and I smile. Reaching up, I grab her full tit and squeeze and mold it. Her hips lift, and I take the hint and get back to work.

I spread her again and circle that hard nub. Abby's quiet groans make me so fucking hard that I have to grind myself against the edge of her bed for a little relief.

When I know she's warmed up, I slide one finger into her tight hole. Her toes curl on my shoulders. I curl that finger, and she yells, "Nick!"

"Shh. Baby, you have to be quiet." I'm grateful my daughter sleeps pretty deeply. I'm praying she doesn't stir.

"Sorry!" Abigail whispers. "That's intense, though."

I lift my head. "Too much? Do you want me to stop?"

She shakes her head. "Just... go slow."

Nodding, I duck back between her legs and I work her over with that finger. When her thighs fall open, I add a second one, little by little, and tap against her g-spot. I watch my fingers disappear into her pretty pussy, and my cock throbs. She's so warm and tight and wet.

"Oh my God. Oh, wow. What? Wait. Don't stop." Her hands clench my hair.

Chuckling, I finally focus on her clit, licking and sucking it in time with the motion of my hand, and her whole body goes tight as she arches back on a screech.

She pulses, and I keep thrusting and licking until she's spent.

Abby groans when I slide out of her.

I lick her off my fingers and wipe my face. I try to tame what I know is a smug grin on my face before I crawl over her. "That good for you, buttercup?"

She yanks me down, and I fit between her thighs that tighten around me. "So good." Abby looks away. "Actually, I've never come like that before."

Taking her beautiful face in my hands, I turn her back to me and kiss her. "I'm honored to be your first."

The caveman in me rears his head and beats on his chest. It makes me wonder how else I can make her come for the first time. I aim to find as many ways as possible before she leaves.

I lean down to kiss her, and when she sucks on my tongue, my cock swells. Grinding my erection on her, I relish what it feels like to be with a woman again. Soft, sweet curves. Her peachy, feminine scent. Her beautiful, long tresses. It's fucking heaven.

Her fingers wind in my hair, and she uses her grasp to pull my head away so she can bite my neck. It makes me so damn hard.

"Can I grab a condom?" I don't wanna assume she wants to fuck the first night.

"Please."

I'm about to slide off her when I realize what I need to do and hang my head. "They're in my bedroom. In a drawer right next to Hazel."

Just thinking about my kid kills the mood.

She drags me back down to her and brushes her nose against mine. "What if we save that for next time?"

Damn. I guess I might need to make a trip to the bathroom after all.

"Of course. This is probably a lot for one night."

I push up, but stop when she grabs my arm and yanks me down again. I barely stop myself from crushing her. We both laugh, and she shakes her head. "I didn't mean you should go. I mean, what if we do something else? Like…" She chews her bottom lip. "Maybe we take off your pajama bottoms and you keep grinding? If I can trust you to stay on top?"

"Fuck, yes. I can stay above ground." That sounds hot as hell.

She giggles, and I want to soak it up. Abby's fun in bed. Sweet. Super sexy. And so fucking responsive.

I kneel and shove down my bottoms before I take my dick in hand. The tip is weeping, and I slide that wetness over my crown.

Her eyes are glued to the motion of my hand as I jerk off between her legs. But this isn't how I wanna come.

I lie on her again, and she groans when the root of my cock nestles between her thighs. She's wet enough to handle this. Using my hips, I slide back and then up again.

Her breath catches, and she arches beneath me. I lean down to suck on her tits. "Can you come like this, baby?"

"I—I don't know." Her voice is shaky.

"Try."

Kneeling again, I grab a pillow and stick it under her ass. Then I spread my legs to lower myself to her hot little pussy. Using my thumbs, I spread her apart and nestle my dick against her.

Then I slowly thrust. She's making those noises again as her head turns one way, then the other. Her hands clench her comforter.

"We look so good together, buttercup. You're gonna take my cock so well. I can't wait." I don't know where the hell these words come from. I've never been a dirty talker, but Abigail makes me want to fuck her until her screams rattle the roof.

Guilt tugs at my chest. I didn't mean to play games with her this week.

I'll make it up to her, one orgasm at a time.

Lowering my dick until the head nudges against her clit, I focus there until she's panting and moaning.

I'm about to warn her to be quiet when she slaps a hand over her mouth and comes with a muffled yell.

I drop down to her and thrust in earnest. This time, I slide from root to tip against her wet folds. It's fucking heavenly. She jams her hands in my hair, and when we kiss, she sucks my tongue again.

That's all it takes for me to erupt all over her stomach. Dropping my head to her shoulder, I laugh.

"What have you done to me?" I shudder in her arms as I ride the incredible orgasm.

She chuckles. "I was going to ask you the same thing."

Her voice is hoarse. I made it that way. The caveman in me beats his chest again.

I could get used to this.

Maybe too used to this.

Good thing we only have a few weeks.

24

ABIGAIL

PAIGE LEANS OVER THE TABLE, eyes wide. "So did y'all go all the way?"

I glance around the West Campus cafeteria. We're just finishing up our lunch. "No, but what we did was..." I close my eyes as shivers race through my body. "Amazing."

Two days later and I'm still obsessing over the way Nick touched me.

When I look at Paige, she's smirking. "Can I just say I knew you two would be perfect for each other? Y'all are going to have beautiful babies someday."

My heart sinks. "It's not like that."

"What do you mean?"

I clear my throat. "We... um... we decided we'd only hook up until I left for London."

"Why the hell would you agree to that?"

I love that my friend is pissed on my behalf. "Because he doesn't want anything serious or long-term."

"He told you that?"

"The night I moved in with him, we had this unexpected heart-to-heart. I worked up the courage to ask him what he was looking for in a girlfriend. That's what he told me—he wants casual. And before you get up in arms, I get the feeling he's still hung up on Gemma."

Her shoulders slump. "His ex."

"His daughter's mother who *died*. That's not an ex. It sounds like she owned him, lock, stock, and barrel. His commitment to her is beautiful and tragic, and hearing him talk about her broke my heart." I brush my bangs out of my face. "I can't compete with that. So we decided we'd have fun until I leave for my trip. And to underscore the point, he even told me he didn't want Hazel to know that we're kinda seeing each other."

She balls up a napkin and tosses it on the table. "This is unacceptable."

"Do I wish he wanted more? Absolutely. But I'm not going to pressure him. Nick has enough responsibilities. I'm just going to try to enjoy myself. I've never had a fling before." I shrug. "I can handle it."

Paige doesn't look convinced. If I'm being honest with myself, I'm not all that convinced either, but I don't want Paige to be down on Nick.

"Remember when you told Marcus that you didn't want to move in with him since you hadn't been dating long?"

"Yeah." She takes a sip of her water.

"This would be worse. Nick and I went from zero to one hundred in, like, fifteen seconds. So I don't blame him for not wanting to dive feet first into a relationship with me. But he promised to be monogamous, so that helps."

I don't tell her this is the first time Nick's gotten into anything remotely serious since Gemma passed. That seems too personal.

"Boo." She shakes her head. "That boy is going to rue the day he lets you go, mark my words."

Judging by how fast he left my room after we were done the other night, I'm not so sure. Don't get me wrong—he cuddled and was sweet. But he looked like he was itching to go. I couldn't really fault him since he has a five thirty a.m. alarm.

"Speak of the Devil." Paige motions to the other side of the cafeteria where a few of the football players walk in.

I immediately find Nick. He's talking to some girl, and my claws descend.

But she's not hanging all over him. He nods at her, and she trots off. I take a relieved breath.

I really need to get my feelings in check.

Nick's not Ezra, I remind myself. My ex chose to cheat. It wasn't the women's fault. No one knew he had a girlfriend. So I can't get catty with girls over Nick. He's either going to be true to our agreement or not, and then it's over.

The thought dampens my excitement to see him. When he spots me and walks over, I don't leap out of my seat and smother him in a hug like I want to. I give him a careful smile.

But the smile he gives me? He might as well announce he had his face between my thighs.

Just before he reaches our table, Paige whispers, "Holy shit, Abby. Do you see how he's looking at you?" Paige fans herself.

After what he told me about not letting Hazel know that we're seeing each other, I'm totally shocked when he comes to our table and leans down to kiss me. "Hey, buttercup."

I open my mouth to say hi, but nothing comes out.

Paige laughs. "Hey, Nick. How's it going?" She smirks at me. "Ya left my girl here speechless with that kiss."

He chuckles and motions for me to scoot over. When I do, he drops down into the booth next to me, wraps his arm around my shoulders, and tugs me to his chest. "I haven't seen Abby in two days. Kinda miss my roommate."

"Roommate? Sure. Let's go with that." She rolls her eyes. "Ouch."

I give her a look and mouth 'sorry' because I didn't mean to kick her so hard. Turning to him, I scramble to think of a question. But he's so close and he smells so good, it's difficult to think. "How was your study session last night?"

Nick put Hazel to bed, and then Cadence watched her while he left for a late-night study group. The night before, I had a shift at the diner. So today is the first time I've seen him since he licked me to the best orgasm of my life.

My face heats just thinking about it. I'm so lost in my own head, I almost miss his response.

"It was a waste of time. Everyone was arguing about how to break down the assignment, so we didn't get much done." He leans close to me. "Would've rather hung out with you."

Paige fans herself again. "You two are a five-alarm fire."

I shoot her another look, and Nick chuckles. "Abby and I definitely have chemistry."

Is that what this is? Is that why my heart beats erratically and I'm clammy all over? Because of chemistry?

I glance around, noticing that his friends are watching our table. "I thought you didn't want people to know about us?"

His head jerks back. "When did I say that?"

"You said you didn't want Hazel to know anything, so I took that to mean you want to keep this quiet on campus too. I mean, I never see you at school, but I figured..."

His voice lowers. "You're not my dirty little secret, Abby. Just because I don't want Hazel to know doesn't mean we have to sneak around everywhere else." He scans the room. "We don't usually come to this cafeteria, but it's not too far out of my way for lunch. I can meet you here sometimes."

Paige, the little shit stirrer, taps the table. "Almost like a date."

I glare at her, and the glee in her eyes is unmistakable. She's making more of this than she should. Nick doesn't want to go on dates. He just wants companionship and sex. I got that memo loud and clear.

So I'm one hundred percent shocked when he shrugs. "I mean, yeah. I don't have a lot of time in my schedule or we could leave campus. Do something fun."

"Do you do anything for fun?" I ask dryly.

He shakes his head. "Smartass."

"What's next for you this afternoon, Nick?" Paige asks sweetly. "Because Abigail here doesn't need to be anywhere for an hour, whereas I have class in ten minutes. So bye, darlings. Love y'all." She blows me a kiss and flounces off.

Nick chuckles. "She really wants us to happen, huh?"

"You have no idea. Just ignore her."

I finally get the courage to look at him, and when our eyes meet, my heart leaps in my chest.

He nods slowly. "I don't have to get to the locker room for a bit."

"I'm taking over for Denise later today, as you probably know, but I need to pick up a packet in the library first. Want to come with me?" Because that sounds so exciting.

"Let's go."

When he stands, my eyes go straight to his ass, which is encased by the perfect pair of worn jeans that cling to his muscular rear. Would it be wrong to bite it?

"Eyes up here, buttercup." His sexy smirk makes me huff.

"I wasn't checking you out."

As I come to a stand, his giant hands land on my shoulders. "Really? Because I'd be lying if I said I wasn't checking you out in your cute little outfit. Turn around."

I'm wearing another Paige ensemble—a scoop-neck shirt and a Goodwill skirt I bought for ten dollars with some strappy sandals. It's really nothing exciting, but she always manages to pair my outfits really well so I look less like a homeless librarian and more like a normal college student.

She made me box up all of my khaki pants when I moved to Nick's. Paige wanted me to donate the clothes, but I'm keeping them just in case I need something comfy.

I do an awkward twirl before I crash into him. "I'm not good in heels."

He sets me upright with a chuckle before he tosses an arm around my shoulders. "Let's get you to the library before I bend you over this table."

Oh, good golly.

Would he really do that?

I'm shockingly amenable to the suggestion. I mean, if we weren't surrounded by dozens of other students.

As we cut across the cafeteria, Jinxy shouts something to him that makes Nick grumble under his breath.

"What's that about?"

He shakes his head. "Just Jinxy being an asshole."

I can't help but notice that every single woman turns to watch us pass. Ugh, then that cheerleader Tiffany, who gave me crap at Moe's, runs up to him. She gives me a funny look before she turns to Nick. "Good luck this weekend! I'll be cheering just for you."

This is where Ezra would've hugged his fangirl and let her fawn all over him while I stood there like a lamppost.

But Nick, who never lets go of me, smiles politely. "Thanks. Appreciate the good vibes."

And then we're off again. I let out a breath I didn't realize I was holding.

"That girl doesn't like me," I tell him once we're outside.

"She doesn't like anyone."

I don't state the obvious—that she more than likes him—

because I know that sounds insecure, and I don't want to come off like a needy basket case.

A brisk wind whisks across campus, and I shiver and pull out a button-down sweater from my bag. As I tug it on, I notice that Nick is only wearing a t-shirt. "Aren't you cold?"

He shrugs. "I'll be sweating my ass off in a little while. I don't mind the chill."

It makes me realize I haven't seen him wear his letterman lately. The football guys basically live in those jackets.

When I'm done putting on my sweater, he grabs my hand, and we resume our trip to the library.

I almost have to pinch myself. Nick Silva is freaking *holding my hand*. Not because I asked him to, but of his own accord.

Butterflies erupt in my chest, and I barely keep myself from skipping.

Cool your jets, Abigail. This doesn't change anything.

Who am I kidding? It changes everything.

25

ABIGAIL

I EXPECT Nick to take off when we reach the library, but he patiently waits with me while the librarian checks for the packet I need for my class.

But when she returns, the title on the handout doesn't match what's in the syllabus. When I point this out, she shrugs. "This is what I have down for the course. Why don't you grab a table and double-check the materials?" She glances around the room, but every single table is full. "Follow me. I'll open a study room for you." Nick and I follow her through tall bookcases into the shadowy back, where she unlocks a door. "Here you go. Take your time. If this isn't correct, just return the packet."

The door clicks closed behind us.

I put the folder on the small table. There's a floor-to-ceiling window that overlooks the quad on the opposite side of the door.

I'm about to tell Nick he doesn't need to stay with me when he wraps a muscular arm around my waist and nuzzles my neck. "This was a brilliant idea."

Goosebumps break out along my arms, and I tilt my head back. "Don't you have to go?"

"I probably have twenty minutes before I need to haul ass across campus." He turns me around, and there's a question in his eyes that I'm eager to answer.

Hopping up on my tiptoes, I wrap my arms around his neck and pull his handsome face down to mine. "Why, Mr. Silva, do you need a tutor?"

His lips graze mine as his hands find their way under my skirt and he grabs my rear. "As a matter of fact, I do. How are you at oral reports?"

I giggle and pull him closer. He smells so good, like sandalwood and soap. "Hmm. I'm not sure how advanced I am at oral. Maybe I could demonstrate, and you could critique my methods?"

Humor dances in his green eyes. "Where do I sign up?" He grabs a handful of my hair and tugs my head back so he can kiss me. "But I have a rule, Miss Dawson. You have to come first."

Apprehension skitters through me. "Nick, we don't have time. What if I can't... you know? Let me just take care of you."

His thumb slowly sweeps across my cheek. "Let me try."

"Okay, but—" My acquiescence is apparently all he needs before he slips his hand into my panties. "Oh." I suck in a breath as he slides a thick finger inside me. "Wow, okay. We're doing this."

He chuckles in my ear. "Let me make you feel good." We turn, and he leans me against the door while he works one finger, then two, in and out of me. All the while, his hand grazes my clit. "You're so wet. You feel so good. I can't wait to fuck you."

I shiver in his arms. "I can't w-wait either." Panting, I bring his mouth to mine and we kiss like we're about to rip off each other's clothes. But we can't. We're in the middle of campus. This is insane, and so dang hot.

Just when I think I can't get more turned on, he palms my boob and pinches my nipple. "Oh!" I gasp.

"Shh. No screaming in the library."

I lift my leg around his hip, and his hand goes deeper. "I'm gonna... Nick... Don't stop..."

"Come for me, baby. Come on my hand. Let me feel that pretty pussy pulse around my fingers."

His dirty words do the trick. The orgasm rocks through me so hard, I almost fall to the floor, but Nick braces me as I quake and groan. Once I'm done, he removes his hand and licks his fingers.

"You're a dirty, dirty man," I say. "I kinda love it."

He grins. "Glad you enjoyed that, baby." I'm sweaty and laughing when he sets me to rights. "So I'll see you tonight?"

"You can't leave yet." I motion to the very obvious erection straining his jeans.

Pulling out his phone, he glances at the screen. "I need to leave soon."

I throw his cell on the table and push him against the door. "Let's see if we can break the record for how fast you can come in my mouth."

Who is this girl who demands to give her guy a blow job? I don't recognize myself, but given the heated look Nick gives me, he's into it.

I drop to my knees and unbutton his jeans. I laugh at the huge bulge.

"Buttercup, you shouldn't laugh at a man's junk."

"I'm amused that you were going to try to walk across campus with this weapon in your pants."

I take him out of his boxer briefs and almost swoon at his huge dick. It's tall and thick with a swollen crown. Glancing up at him, I smile as I lick his tip.

Groaning, he grips my hair and tilts my head back. "Stick out your tongue." I do as he asks and he taps himself on me. "Fuck, you look good like this."

"You have like five minutes before you have to go. Shut up and let me blow you." I grab his base as I lick him like a lollipop. Then I take him in my mouth and suck his swollen crown before I go deeper.

I keep him deep until my eyes water, and then I come up for air.

I repeat the motion, and Nick makes a strangled noise as I pull him to the back of my throat. "Abby, I'm..."

He tries to back away, but I grab him and send him deeper. That's all it takes.

Erupting down my throat, he tilts his head back against the door with a groan.

A sudden knock makes us freeze, but he's still pulsing in my mouth. I swallow him down as fast as I can.

"Is someone in there?" a lady says on the other side of the door. "A group has the room reserved this afternoon."

"We're coming," Nick chokes out, and I chuckle around him.

Two minutes later, we gather our things and book it out of the library laughing.

We pause in the middle of the quad and stare at each other. I'm momentarily embarrassed about what we just did.

He motions toward the stadium. "I'm going this way."

"I'm headed that way." I point toward the opposite direction.

He nods. I don't know what I expect, but it's not the way he grabs me and kisses me until I'm out of breath again. "See you at home, buttercup."

Then he pats me on the ass and runs off to practice.

I swoon all the way home.

I'm in so much trouble.

26

NICK

"Do it one more time!" Coach shouts from the sidelines.

At the snap, my O-line holds the defense in check while I glance at my options. Maverick jukes one way, then the other before he races downfield. A defender gets loose and is about to mock tackle me when I get the ball off on a long pass.

The ball sails in the air and descends just as Mav looks up and leaps up to catch it over his defender.

"Yes!" I hold my hands up. Hopefully, I can nail this shit tomorrow against the Longhorns.

Jinxy shouts, "That's what I'm talking about."

Coach blows the whistle. "Great job, gentlemen. Hit the showers. Get here on time in the morning." He grabs my shoulder as I guzzle down some water. "Whatever you're doing to mentally prepare, keep it up. You're on fire this week."

As we head for the locker room, Jinxy elbows me. "Gee, wonder how you're preparing for your game. Could it have anything to do with your sexy little roommate?"

Dax shakes his head. "Man, lay off. Nick's just finding his stride. Don't be a dick."

Am I more relaxed because Abby and I have been messing

around? Maybe. I can't rule it out entirely. Really, I just like hanging out with her. She's fun, and she helps me relax. I enjoy riling her up.

And I really enjoy making her come.

But I have no plans to dish about that with anyone. I smirk at Jinxy. "How's your taint, bro? Did you get that death smell to go away?"

Everyone roars, and his ears go red. "Yeah, yeah. Laugh all you want. I printed the recipe to clean your taint, if anyone needs it. Think I'm gonna sell it on Etsy like they do for baked goods. I'm gonna be rich. That apple cider vinegar shit works, but if you soap up afterward with something minty, your dick tastes like dessert."

Dax snorts. "Jinxy's homemade taint cleanser recipe!"

"I have a jug of it in the shower if you wanna try it." Jinxy looks around, waiting for someone to take him up on his offer.

Bowser shrugs. "I'll give it a go. Can't ever have your taint area too clean. The ladies will appreciate my fresh scent."

I cover my mouth to mask my laugh.

Once we're in the locker room, I check my phone. I have a message from Cadence.

Do you want me to get Hazel ready for bed?

I check the time. **No, I can do it. I'll be outta here soon.**

Hazel needs a bath, and I've read some scary-ass statistics about children drowning in the tub. I don't really trust anyone to do what I should be doing. My daughter's life isn't worth the few extra minutes I'd get to relax.

When I get home, my munchkin is coloring on the couch with Cadence. I'm hoping Abby's home. Her car is here, but sometimes Paige picks her up.

Hazel leaps off the couch and wraps her arms around my leg. "Daddy!" This right here is the best part of my day. My daughter is my number one fan, and I'll never take that for granted. Everything I do is for her. Every sacrifice, every sleepless night I've spent with her when she's sick, every time I've rocked her to sleep, it's all worth it when I see her bright smile.

"Hey, kiddo. Did you have a good day?" I ask as I drop my stuff and swing her into my arms.

She kisses my cheek. "Yup. I ate pasghetti and some apple stuff."

I love that her life updates always pertain to food.

Cadence pushes off the couch. "I made a homemade apple cobbler. Would you like a bowl?"

"I'd love some, but if I eat anything before I get her bathed, I'll crash face first on the couch." Her shoulders slump. Damn. I don't mean to make her feel bad. "But I'm sure it's amazing. Looks like Hazel enjoyed it."

This is usually where Cadence takes off, but she seems to want to say something. I put Hazel down and scruff her hair. "Can you go get your bath toys from your bedroom? You can play with three tonight." If I don't give her a limit, I'll find five thousand toys sitting in the tub when I get in there.

"Okay!"

I smile as she stomps down the hall, passing Abby, who wanders into the kitchen wearing her cute little pajamas. Her hair's up in that messy bun I love. Her glasses are perched on her nose. Fuck, she's adorable.

When she sees me, I get another luminous smile. "Hey, roomie," she calls out.

It's crazy that we live together, and I've barely seen her in the last few days. I've been living off memories of that hot-as-hell blow job she gave me in the library. It's like she sucked the soul out of my body, and I still haven't recovered. We've been texting, but that's just building the anticipation for the next time I can get her alone.

Knowing that Cadence can't see my face, I wink at Abby

before I turn back to Cadence, who looks nervous for some reason.

"Nick, hey, I was wondering..." Her hands flex, and I'm immediately on guard. I hope she doesn't quit. I feel like we've just gotten into a good routine. She lowers her voice. "I hope this isn't too forward, but I was wondering if you'd like to do something together this weekend. Maybe after your game?"

Fuck, no.

Cadence is a beautiful woman, no doubt, but I'm not interested.

From the corner of my eye, I see Abby freeze in the kitchen before she darts back down the hall. Thankfully, Hazel is in my room right now.

I try to keep my face expressionless. "Thanks for the invite, but I'm sorta seeing someone."

Her eyes widen. "Oh my God. I'm so sorry. This is awkward."

"Not at all." It's totally awkward, but the woman works for me, and I need her to stay on because Hazel likes her. "We're cool."

I'm tense as she runs around the living room gathering her things. Finally, she leaves, and I blow out a breath.

I check on my daughter, who has all of her toys splayed across my bedroom. "Which ones should I play with?" she asks.

"I don't know, honey. Maybe pick the dinosaurs tonight."

"Nah. I want the mewmaids."

"Or pick the mermaids. Give me two minutes. I need to ask Abby a question about her schedule."

She doesn't bother looking up, which means she's debating which mermaids to pick, and that could take a while since she has several. I head into the hallway and knock on Abby's door.

"Come in."

I poke my head in. Abby has a blank expression on her face. After I close the door behind me, I take her in my arms. "I told

Cadence I was seeing someone. Didn't say it was you because I wasn't sure if that would make things weird, but she got the message."

Her eyes soften. "Really?"

"Yes."

She toys with my t-shirt. "How was practice?"

"Great." I lean down to kiss her, and she moans softly and presses herself into me. I could get lost in this sweet woman if I'm not careful. Maybe it's a good thing we're both so busy. Pulling away, I rub her back. "Want to study later? I wish we could just hang out, but I have an essay I need to finish. I doubt I'll have time tomorrow night 'cause I'm always pretty braindead after away games, and I want to use Sunday to do stuff with Hazel."

Abby smiles. "I have to read a few chapters tonight too."

I like that she's so studious. Nothing against party girls, but it's refreshing to be with a woman who doesn't mind staying home on a Friday night.

"Gonna give Hazel a quick bath, and I'll meet you in the living room once I get her to bed."

I finally get my kid in the tub with her mermaids. I wash Hazel's hair and condition it. "Close your eyes while I rinse." She clenches them shut while she clamps a hand over her nose. I tilt her head back and wash out the product. Then I turn on the detachable showerhead and hose her off. "Circle, circle." She wiggles around while I spray her down. "Towel." Hazel holds out her arms while I wrap her in a towel.

I set her down on the closed toilet seat and spray in extra conditioner and comb it through. Blow-dry her hair. Put her in her pajamas. Help her brush her teeth. I carry her to her room and set her down on her twin bed that sits adjacent to my queen.

"Which book do you wanna read, gingersnap?"

Her lips purse. "I like the one whe-a she has long hai-a."

Which ones have long hair? "*Rapunzel*?"

"The other one."

"*Tangled*?"

"Yup!" She hops up and down.

I love how excited she gets for a book I've read her a hundred times. I tuck her under the covers, flip on her fairy night-light, and lie down next to her. "In a galaxy far, far away…"

"That's not *Tangled*, Daddy."

I chuckle. "Are you sure? Because there's a princess in that story, and she has long hair too."

When I'm done reading *Tangled*, she yawns. "I want to be a pwincess."

I kiss her forehead. "You're already my princess." That gets me a sleepy smile. "Night, sweetheart. Love you."

"Love you too, Daddy."

Gently, I close the door behind me. I might be exhausted, but I'm grateful I could squeeze in Hazel's bedtime routine tonight. I know she'll grow up fast, and then one day she'll be off on her own, so I have to make the most of the time we have now.

Abby's curled up on the couch with a textbook in her lap, a pen behind her ear, and a highlighter in hand. My little sexy nerd is hard at work. "I need a snack, or I'm gonna die. Can I get you anything?" I ask.

She shakes her head. "I'm good, but I made an extra sandwich for you. Unless you're in the mood for something else." There's a plate on the coffee table with a roast beef sandwich loaded with veggies and a bottle of water.

"How did you know what I wanted?" I sit next to her and shove half the sandwich in my mouth.

"I saw you eating that last week. Thought it looked good, so I made one for myself this evening. Wasn't sure if you'd be hungry, but if you weren't, I figured I could eat it for lunch or something."

"You're the sweetest." After I swallow, I lean over and kiss her forehead. "Cadence's cooking is great, but it's kinda rich. I'm a simple guy. I like easy stuff. Sandwiches, soups, salads. Unless you wanna bring me some chocolate icebox pie?"

She laughs. "I'll bring you a slice from Moe's Sunday night."

When I finish eating, I slide the empty plate back on the coffee table and turn to Abby. "Before I forget, are you still cool to watch Hazel tomorrow? I know I already confirmed, but I'm paranoid about Saturday coverage after Felicia bailed that time. Away games give me extra anxiety. I'm never sure what time I'll get home. The Austin traffic is always terrible."

Abby grabs my hand and gives it a squeeze. "We're good. Hazel and I are going to pre-game with some buffalo wings, compliments of Cadence. We're going to braid each other's hair, watch you kick UT's ass, and then cap off the day with an assortment of art projects. If I'm really lucky, she'll want to learn how to play Scrabble with me."

I tug her into my lap. "You're awesome at this nanny thing. I can't believe I almost didn't hire you."

"I did ram you with my car." She threads her fingers through my hair and kisses me softly.

"And yet you're a paragon of responsibility. Man, I misjudged you. I'm sorry for being an ass."

"Hazel is the center of your universe. I don't blame you for being cautious. It's what makes you a great dad." She leans closer to graze my neck with her teeth. "And now we have to do homework."

I growl and adjust myself when she slides off my lap.

She chuckles and grabs her textbook. "Maybe tomorrow night we can have a celebratory... thing after you beat UT?"

"A *naked* celebratory thing?" I lift an eyebrow.

Her laughter grows as she nods. "Definitely naked." She snaps her fingers. "Now get to work or no more blow jobs."

"Damn, you're tough, woman."

I pull out my laptop and try to concentrate, but I find myself glancing at Abby every few minutes.

"Nick Silva, get to work."

Nodding, I turn so I can't see her in my peripheral vision. I revise my assignment, then print it.

"Do you need someone to proof?" she asks.

"Would you mind?"

"Not at all."

I study her pretty profile while she reads. In my mind, I map out places on her body I want to kiss or lick or bite. Like that pale spot on her shoulder, or the soft skin behind her ear, the inside of her wrist. What does she taste like there?

The thought is jarring.

I'm not used to thinking this way about women. Not even Gemma. We were kids when we had a child together. Barely adults when she died. I loved her with my whole heart and soul, but I'm starting to wonder if a man's ability to love expands as he gets older.

And if I'm being really honest with myself, my relationship with Gemma wasn't perfect. Sometimes we argued a lot. Having a kid is stressful as fuck, but we did the best we could. It was my first serious relationship, so maybe I've idealized it since I had nothing else to compare it to.

I'm just not sure I should compare what I had with Gemma to whatever I'm doing right now.

I scrub my face with my palm.

This thing with Abby is messing with me. We've been an item for less than a week, and I can admit this is more serious than I intended. Obviously what Abby and I have going on is more than a friends-with-benefits situation, like we discussed.

I'm just not sure what to do about it.

I'm not ready to let Abby go, but I'm also not sure I'm capable of more.

The here and now is easy. Study together. Grab dinner from time to time. Mess around when we can. Have a few laughs.

It's the long term that scares the hell out of me. I tried long-term, and it landed my girlfriend in the bottom of a ditch where she drowned in a few feet of water.

Christ. I pinch the bridge of my nose.

Life isn't fucking fair. If anyone knows that, it's me. So as much as I'd love to make post-graduation plans with the beautiful woman on my couch, I'm not sure I can.

Maybe the answer is to not think about that for now. Abby agreed our arrangement ends this winter when we graduate, so I'm going to plan for that. It's the only way for me to enjoy what we're doing.

So when she yawns and says she's going to bed, I walk her to her door and kiss the hell out of her.

Because our days are likely numbered.

27

ABIGAIL

Baylee, Hazel, and I all hold our breaths as the Broncos make the field goal. "Yes!" I shout when the ball goes through the uprights.

We do a little dance across the living room and hoot and holler. It was a close game, but unlike last weekend, Nick killed it. He looked so confident out there and scored four touchdowns against a great team. UT is our biggest rival because they're so close. I bet parties are erupting across town right now to celebrate our win.

On a commercial break, they do a slow-motion clip of Nick taking off his helmet and smiling at the camera.

Holy swoon fest.

"Girl." Baylee elbows me. "Hope you're enjoying that hot daddy."

"Shh. Little ears." Fortunately, Hazel is now preoccupied with the art project I have sprawled out on the coffee table, but I don't want to take any chances. You never know what kids will pick up. I motion to the kitchen, and Baylee pulls up that clip on her phone. It's already trending on social media.

"He has great hair."

"It's super soft and smells so good." I could drown in his scent and die a happy girl. That's madness, but I'm too happy to care. I'm so proud of him. I know he's struggled this season, but the guy who stepped out on that field today was a different man.

After I get Hazel to bed, I'm glued to ESPN where they rehash the game. It's basically a highlight reel of Nick kicking ass, but there are some nice plays by Jinxy, Dax, and Maverick too.

Baylee stares longingly at the TV screen when Mav leaps into the air to catch a pass. "I would do anything to get rid of these feelings. Why do I have to love that idiot?"

I hug her. "For me, I had to get in touch with all of the crappy things Ezra did while we were dating. Everything from mocking me for liking school to banging every girl in a ten-mile radius. It helped that my friend Roxy showed me their texts. It made me realize I didn't know him at all." I'll never forgive Ezra for using me to play better football. What kind of asshole does that?

Baylee sighs. "Part of me wishes we could sleep together, and I could get him out of my system. You know, maybe he's bad in bed or has a little weenie, and then I'll be inoculated."

I laugh and rest my head on her shoulder. "That's not a terrible idea. Unless having sex makes you fall harder. Hey, want to play Scrabble with me?"

She side-eyes me with a snort. "How about Uno? That's more my speed."

"Okay."

I've just dealt the cards for the third time when headlights spill through the window. Nick's home. When he opens the door, I leap into his arms. "Holy shit, you were crazy amazing out there today!"

He laughs and sets me down, then pauses to look around. "Where's Hazel?"

"Asleep."

"Perfect." Then he tilts me in his arms and kisses me senseless.

The crunch of popcorn makes me turn my head. Baylee is watching us with a giant smirk. When I give her a look, she laughs. "What? This is a good show. Don't let me interrupt."

Nick chuckles and sets me upright with a pat on my ass. "I almost grabbed us some burgers on my way home, but I wasn't sure if you'd want that. My phone died, so I couldn't call. I just wanna check on Hazel, then I'll run out and grab us some dinner. You're welcome to join us, Baylee."

She rolls her eyes. "I have a better idea. Why don't y'all head out to 'grab some burgers,' and I'll babysit for a while."

With a devilish gleam in his eyes, he looks at me, and I laugh. "Baylee, I owe you. Call me if Hazel wakes up, though she usually sleeps like she's in a coma."

"Thanks, Baylee," Nick says as he wraps an arm around my shoulders. "What can we get you from the restaurant?"

She lifts a dubious eyebrow. "You're really going out to get food?"

He chuckles. "Eventually."

"Burger, everything on it, and fries. Thanks."

I grab a sweater and try to calm my excitement while Nick checks in on Hazel.

When we get outside, I realize he's driving a truck instead of his Outback. "Is this yours?"

"No. I borrowed it from Bowser so I could haul some sand tomorrow. I want to make a sandbox for Hazel in the backyard."

Ugh, he's so sweet.

We jump in the truck, but when he pulls out of the driveway, he heads in the opposite direction of the restaurant. We head down some winding dark roads until he pulls into a wildlife preserve. The sign says it's closed, but there's nothing that bars cars from entering. He parks along the far corner of the parking lot under a giant oak tree.

The moment he turns off the ignition, my heart leaps in my chest. This is it. We're going to have sex.

I turn to him and fight the blush that's working up my neck. "This truck isn't big enough for this. If I climb onto your lap, I'm going to end up with a concussion from hitting the ceiling."

He laughs and kisses the back of my hand. "I was actually thinking we could do a little stargazing in the back. Just wanted to spend some time alone with you without worrying about my daughter or football or school for five minutes. We don't have to do anything."

Disappointment crashes through me. Living with him is making my hormones go insane. I was never a sex-crazed girl with Ezra, but for some reason, I want to pounce on Nick and do all the naked things all the time.

Slow is good, I remind myself. *Slow means we're building something.*

He comes around to the passenger side and helps me out. Then he lowers the tailgate, removes a tarp, lifts me up to the edge, and joins me. There's a huge gym mat on the bed that he slides closer, which makes this pretty comfortable. With our legs dangling, we lean back on our arms and stare up at the million stars in the sky.

I bump him. "What inspired this little trip?"

"Our options are pretty limited. We could go to a bar, a restaurant, or the drive-in, but I've been gone all day, and I figured a movie might take too long. And I'm not in the mood to be around crowds. I'm always pretty tapped after a game. I just want quiet." He threads our hands together. "When I borrowed Bowser's truck, he mentioned that his old girlfriend always liked to stargaze back here, so when Baylee offered to babysit, I thought this might be fun. I probably should've brought snacks, though."

My insides go all gooey. Granted, he didn't call *me* his girlfriend, but he's taking me on a girlfriend-type excursion, so this all points in the right direction.

I lean against him. "This is nice. We'll grab food later."

The wind blows, and I shiver.

"You cold?" He jumps off the back and returns a minute later with a blanket. He hops back up next to me and spreads it over our laps. "I didn't realize it was so chilly out tonight."

"What happened to your letterman? I never see you wear it anymore." He's sporting a hoodie over a t-shirt and some jeans.

He winces. "Kinda got torn up."

"That sucks. What happened?"

"It's not a big deal."

"Seriously, how did it get torn?"

He looks down. "It's my fault. Remember when I used it on the ledge of your window to get you out of your bedroom?"

"Yes," I say slowly.

"It got shredded by the jagged glass."

My eyes instantly well. "Why didn't you tell me? I'm so sorry." Those jackets are so expensive. Usually several hundred dollars. I remember Ezra complaining about it once.

"It's cool. I just can't afford to replace it yet."

I make a mental note to buy him a new letterman, even if that means I have to cut my trip short. That sounds dramatic, but the dollar isn't as strong in England. I figured out that a hundred US dollars only gets me seventy-five pounds. So I'm going to need more money than I had anticipated.

It shouldn't be a problem since Nick's been so laid-back about me paying him rent, but my old landlord is dragging his feet refunding my deposit, and I just found out my transmission needs a bunch of work. As long as I don't have to drive down to San Antonio, I can put that off for a while.

I'll figure something out, even if I have to pick up more shifts at Moe's.

With my palms, I wipe my eyes. "I feel terrible."

"Aww, babe, it's okay." His arm drapes around my shoulders, and he tugs me to his chest. "Don't worry about it." My throat feels tight, and I struggle to swallow. I nod to buy myself a minute, but he turns my chin, and then I'm staring into his beautiful green eyes. "Don't cry over this, Abby. Please. You're kinda breaking my heart."

A fat tear rolls down my cheek, and he swipes it away, then leans in to kiss me. It's sweet. Soft. Just a gentle graze.

For some reason, sitting under the dark sky full of stars, I can sense how fragile this is. Nick and I are tethered together with the thinnest of strings, gossamer strands that could break at any moment. We're basically tied together right now because of circumstances. It's not like he would've asked me out of his own accord. Living together transformed our dynamic. That dang tree crashing through my bedroom changed everything.

Deep down, I know this is a fluke. That we might not make it beyond graduation.

It's what we agreed to, but I can't help wanting more.

And I'm too afraid to ask him if he wants me to come back after my trip.

Another tear falls.

"Hey, come on now. I can't handle you crying, buttercup."

I take a deep breath and decide to shove all of this into the deepest recesses of my heart. I wanted a hot fling, so I'm going to take what I can get. I'll deal with the consequences of that decision later.

Sniffling, I laugh. "I'm just crying because I bet a hundred bucks on UT today."

Nick laughs like he knows I'm full of it. "Abigail Dawson."

"Kidding."

He tackles me back, and I squeal as he tickles me senseless. "You naughty girl. I'm gonna make you pay for that one."

I end up on my back, and he comes up over me, settling between my legs. It's dark out but clear, so the moonlight lets me see the handsome man in my arms. I try to catch my breath, which billows up in the chilly air. "I'm cold. You should warm me up."

His nose drags against mine. "You are cold."

Reaching down, he drags the blanket over us. When he reaches under my shirt, I squeal again. "Your hands are freezing!"

"That's what you get for betting on UT."

I tangle my fingers in his hair and drag his mouth to mine. "You know you're the only man on that field I'd ever bet on, right?"

His eyes go soft, and he nods. "Thanks, buttercup."

After he takes off my glasses, he dips his head to kiss me. I open to him right away. His tongue lazily strokes mine as his hand makes its way up my shirt. When he palms my boob, I arch into him. He kisses down my neck, pausing to suck on that tender skin.

"Up." He backs away to help me out of my button-down sweater and t-shirt, but then he slips the sweater back on me. "That way you're not cold while I worship your tits."

I laugh and lie down again, loving how he holds my boobs up to his mouth and bites my nipples.

He groans against my skin. "Christ, you make this sweater look sexy."

It's just a button-up red sweater, the kind I plan to wear when I teach.

Through our jeans, I feel his giant erection against my hip. I run my hands under the back of his shirt and then tug it up. "If I have to take off my shirt, you do too."

He shrugs off his hoodie, then reaches back and drags off his shirt. "Scoot up the bed so if my face lands between your legs, I don't fall off the back."

Laughing, I comply. When he crawls over me again and wraps us in that blanket, I sigh with happiness. Why does he feel so good? Why does this feel so right?

Dipping his face, he sucks and licks my boobs while my fingers trace the bulging muscles in his shoulders.

Our hips move against each other until we're both panting. When I can't stand it any longer, I nudge him. "Take my jeans off."

His eyes go molten. A minute later, I'm lying in the bed of the truck in my open sweater and a pair of bikini underwear.

I drag my finger down his stomach and flick open the button on his jeans. He kicks them off, and he's left wearing boxer briefs that strain against his erection.

We come together again, almost entirely skin to skin. His body heat feels so good in the cold air. I wrap my legs around his waist as we kiss.

He makes his way down my body, licking and biting my breasts and stomach and hips until his nose is pressed against my mound.

I help him shove off my panties and he opens me up, pausing to swirl my wetness around my opening. Then he flicks his tongue against my clit until I cry out.

"Nick," I pant. "I don't want to come like that. Come here."

He kneels between my legs and pulls out a condom. When he's wrapped up, he strokes his dick through my damp core. "Lift your knees to your chest. Open that pretty pussy for me." My clit throbs at the request. I bite my bottom lip as I do as he asks. "That's a good girl."

Inside, I preen. I love being Nick's good girl.

Our eyes meet as he taps my clit with his thick cock and then he's at my entrance. His swollen head notches into me, and I gasp. "Relax," he whispers.

"You're too big." Like, holy crap, it's a snug fit.

He pauses. "Do you want me to stop?"

"No. Just... I need a minute." He kisses me, long and slow, until I wiggle beneath him because I'm ready for more.

"You can take it." He sinks in another inch, and we both groan. "That's it, baby. Take my cock. You're doing so good."

I shiver, delighting in his dirty words.

Leaning up on one arm, he glances down. "Look at you stretch around me. So fucking beautiful, Abigail." He watches as he works himself in. I widen my legs because his cock's enormous. Just when I think I can't take any more, he licks his thumb and swirls it against my clit, and I gasp again, sending him deeper. "Fuck, you're tight." He makes this feral sound in the back of his throat that makes my nipples get harder. I hold him to me so I can adjust. "You okay, baby?"

"Keep going." Then his hips move back, and I'm not ready for the emptiness. "Nick."

"I'm right here, buttercup." When he thrusts in again, I moan. This is too much and not enough.

"Oh, God." I reach for him.

Bracing himself on his forearms, he leans down to kiss me as he works himself in and out of me. My legs close around him. He lifts his hips, angling himself so his base drags against my clit.

"Don't stop," I groan. "Faster."

Our bodies slap together in the quiet night. He grunts when he bottoms out. I'm so full, almost painfully so, but the drag of his length against my core makes me shudder in delight. I've never come like this before. It's crazy that I'm so close. But he fills me up so much and taps at something inside of me I didn't even realize was there.

And when he leans down to suck my nipple, I come apart on a scream. "Yes!"

I quake and moan and quiver around him as he pounds into me. His dick gets impossibly bigger just before he finds his release and shoves his face into my neck.

Wrapped around each other, we pant. As our slick bodies start to cool, I trace his spine with my finger.

When he lifts his head, his sleepy eyes make me smile. "Was that too hard? Didn't mean to get so outta control," he rasps.

"It was perfect." I lean up to kiss him.

So perfect, I'm not sure how I'll ever let him go.

28

NICK

Abby's nails drag down my back, and I thrust harder. I have her backed up against her bedroom wall. Her bed makes an ungodly noise when we try to have sex there, so we can either fuck on the floor or against the wall. Tonight, we decided to stay upright.

Her blonde hair is a glorious, tangled mess as it hangs down her pale shoulders. Her tits play peekaboo behind those soft strands, bouncing with every thrust. "Jesus, you're gorgeous."

We've spent the last week fucking like animals every night. I can't get enough of this woman. She makes me goddamn ravenous for her.

Glancing down, I watch my cock sink in and out of her tight hole. Fuck, I can't watch or I'll blow too soon.

I squeeze her ass. "Baby," I grit out. "Need you to come."

Her legs tighten around my waist. "It's okay. Go ahead," she pants. "Don't worry about me."

Like hell I'm coming before she does. That's not how this works. "Open your mouth." When she complies, I stick my finger on her tongue. "Suck."

Her eyes go round at my command, but she does what I ask.

Why is that so fucking hot? I love how much she wants to please me, which is why she deserves to come first.

I drag my finger out of her mouth and move my hand down to her ass again, where I rub it against her asshole.

"Nick!"

"Shh. No screaming." My girl is a total screamer. "Just relax. If you don't like it, we'll stop." The concerned look on her face makes me pause. "Do you trust me?"

She immediately nods.

"If you hate this, I'll stop. I promise."

Her hands wind through my hair. "Okay, try again."

I wiggle my finger against her again until I pass that tight ring. "You ever do anything back here?"

"N-no."

"Is this okay?"

She nods slowly. "Better than I thought."

"Arms around my neck. Hold on."

I bounce her on my cock while I fuck her ass with my finger, and it only takes a minute before she comes with a cry, which I smother with a kiss so she doesn't wake up the whole neighborhood.

Her pussy squeezes me so damn hard, I let myself go. "Yes," I grunt. "You feel so fucking good." I kiss her while I throb inside her.

By the time we're done, she's laughing against my shoulder. I've learned that orgasms sometimes make her laugh. I smile against her forehead. "That good for you, buttercup?"

"So good, Nick. I'm going to fall into a coma in a minute." She grabs my face and kisses me. "Are you sure this wasn't too much? I don't want you tired tomorrow."

I slowly ease her off my dick and set her on the ground. "Sex helps me relax. Clears my head. I'll be great tomorrow."

She gives me a sweet smile, and I pat her on the ass. "Let's go clean up."

Afterward, I crawl into bed behind her for a little while. She snuggles up against me, and I run my fingers through her long, soft hair. I think through the game tomorrow, the plays I hope to execute, and I visualize passing over traffic and not always picking the easy route.

Like some fucked-up fairy tale, though, when the clock on her bedside table hits midnight, it's time to go.

I hate this part, but I can't sleep in Abby's bed. If Hazel wakes up, I don't want her to find me here. I kiss Abby's forehead and pull the blanket up to her shoulders before I slide out of bed.

The next morning, I'm making Hazel breakfast when Abby wanders out in her pajamas. "Morning. Did you sleep well?" I smirk because I know damn well she slept like the dead after we had sex.

She blushes adorably and nods. "Yeah, thanks. And you?"

"Slept great."

Abby heads over to Hazel and hugs her. "Morning, Hazelnut. What are we going to do today before we watch Daddy's game?"

Fuck, I like it when she calls me Daddy.

Hazel's mouth purses. "Can we play in my sandbox? I wanna make some castles."

"Absolutely. That's a great idea."

I place a plate of scrambled eggs and bacon on the table. "I hope you two didn't forget about the Nut Festival this evening."

Hazel's eyes widen. "Can I have a candied apple?"

"Sure. If I can have a bite."

"I'll share it with you, Daddy."

"Thanks, gingersnap." I kiss the top of her head. "Okay, ladies. Gotta run. Wish me luck today." Michigan is ranked number two in the country. I have my work cut out for me.

Something strange passes over Abby's face, but it's gone in a flash. She clears her throat and gives me a small smile. "You don't need luck, Nick. I'm sure you'll kill it today."

I almost bend down to kiss her before I catch myself. Instead, I squeeze her shoulder. "Thanks, buttercup. Hope y'all have a great afternoon. I'll see you after the game."

IT'S BEEN A HIGH-SCORING GAME, but I can't point to any big mistakes by either team. It's the third quarter, and we're down by three points, but I wanna get the win in the books. I wipe the sweat from my eyes and jog to the huddle. "Sell those routes. We can do this."

I call the play, and we stalk back to the line of scrimmage.

After the ball snaps, I fake a lateral pass while I scope out my guys in a matter of seconds.

Jinxy is on the ground.

Dax is tangled up in defenders.

My tight end Finn can't shake loose.

Which leaves Mav, who pivots away from the free safety and makes his getaway. There's a defender in my face, but I get the ball off just in time.

The pass has just the right amount of arc and lands in Mav's outstretched hands around the twenty.

"Yes! Come on!"

Two defenders are on his ass, but Mav charges up the seam and into the end zone.

We take the lead and never look back.

I'm wiped out by the time we get to the post-game press conference, but over the fucking moon about the win.

Coach starts taking questions once Mav, Dax, Jinxy, and I sit at the conference table.

"Coach Santos, your team never got rattled today," one

reporter says as he reviews his notes. "It was close until that touchdown by Maverick Walker in the third. After that, your guys seemed turbo-charged. Can you describe what happened?"

He nods. "We're really coming together as a team. My defense kept Michigan at bay, and my offensive line is hungry. Maverick Walker has great instincts out there, and that catch motivated everyone. After that play, the whole team was hyper-focused on finishing strong. Nick Silva spearheaded that effort. He's done a great job all season, but I think you just saw him level up, which is what you want when you get closer to the playoffs."

After a question for Mav, the reporter turns to me. "Nick, you looked really poised out there today under pressure, as opposed to the Northwestern game where you were sacked twice and struggled to connect with your receivers. What would you say has brought on this change?"

Jinxy coughs. "His nanny."

It's under his breath, but I hear it. I shoot him a look, and he smiles like an idiot. Thank God the reporters didn't hear what he said.

Leaning forward, I speak into the microphone at the table. "I'm not sure if you guys have noticed, but we have a pretty spectacular coach." Everyone chuckles, even Coach. "Mostly, I just try to listen to him and trust my guys. I have one of the best offensive lines in the country, and I'm honored to play with them. I'm just trying to be the best quarterback I can be and take one game at a time."

Another reporter raises his hand. "Nick, just a follow-up, but you're also a single father. How much does that role affect your performance on the field?"

Coach covers the mic in front of him as he leans toward me and whispers, "You don't need to speak about anything regarding your daughter or being a father."

"It's okay. I got this," I tell him quietly. Coach has had a few single fathers on his team over the years, and he's protective about our privacy. My situation is a little different because everyone knows what happened to Gemma, but the reporters who cover us at Lone Star State are usually respectful.

I clear my throat to give myself a moment to gather my thoughts. "If anything, being a father makes me a better player. I have to be on top of my life, both at home and on the field. I can't be a slacker." I don't mention how not having the right babysitters at times has messed with my head.

But knowing that Hazel is with Abby right now makes a huge difference. That woman would jump in front of a train for my daughter. It helps me have the headspace so I can focus on what I need to do.

I smile to myself. I'm not sure when Abby became such a central part of my life, but I hope she's here to stay. I must be getting a second wind because I'm itching to get home so I can take my girls to the festival tonight.

I'm enjoying my post-game high until I get to my locker and pull out my phone.

Missed call from Cynthia Kendrick.

Hanging my head, I close my eyes.

I usually stay in touch with Gemma's parents, but getting some space this fall has been good for my mental health. Talking to Cynthia and Charles reopens too many old wounds.

They probably want to video-chat with Hazel or get together for Thanksgiving. I'll text them later.

I hope they'll understand why I can't see them until the season is over. Thinking about Gemma and the accident screws me up, and I can't afford any more fuckups this fall. I've deliberately not thought about her this semester.

Gemma, I'm sorry. Please forgive me. I'll always hold you in a special place in my heart, but if I want to live and do right by our daughter, I need to let you go.

A text comes in from my father.

Congrats, mijo. Estoy orgulloso! He's proud.

Thanks, Dad! Glad you could watch.

I wanna ask him how he's feeling and if he's staying on top of his bills, but I don't wanna bum him out, so I drop it for now. I hope I'll be able to help him retire so he doesn't work himself to the bone.

I'm still trying to shake off the lingering sadness of that missed call from Cynthia when I think about tonight and how I get to hang out with Hazel and Abby.

My smile returns.

29

NICK

ABBY and I swing Hazel between us as we wander between the booths. The annual Nut Festival showcases local arts, crafts, and baked goods, usually featuring pecans.

"Daddy, I wanna stuffed animal." Hazel yanks her arm free to point at a booth full of unicorns. Awesome. That's exactly what I need. A giant pink unicorn to stuff into our bedroom.

I'm about to redirect her attention when she folds her hands under her chin. "Please."

Oh, hell.

Abby sees my expression and snickers.

I rub my face. I'm not sure when I got wrapped so tightly around my daughter's finger, but it is what it is. "All right. Come on." I pick up Hazel and the three of us head to the Magical Unicorn Forest where I'll have to spend my scholarship money to try to win a stuffed animal.

Some of the guys on the team see us and head over. They're hanging out with Paige and Baylee. The girls hug, and Dax pats me on the back. "I see a giant unicorn in your future."

"Uncle Jinxy!" my daughter screeches.

Jinxy holds out his arms to Hazel, and she leaps at him. It

makes my heart stop, the way she has such little regard for her own safety. When Jinxy puts her on his shoulders, I grouse, "Don't drop her."

He looks affronted. "C'mon, Daddy. I got good hands. You know this."

"Dude, don't call me Daddy."

The guys laugh.

I chuckle and lay down the money. Abby takes out her phone. "Y'all, stand closer so I can grab a photo." My teammates and I huddle up, and Hazel leans over to put her arm around my shoulders. "Oh my God, that's adorable. Smile!"

The girls then squeeze together to take a few selfies.

After everyone's done taking pics, Mav, Finn, and I step up to the basket toss. It's ten bucks for ten balls. The basket isn't too far, but the angle is tricky. If you throw too hard, the ball pops right out, as Mav just illustrated. You need a pretty soft touch, and a little backspin wouldn't hurt.

Mav ends up with five in the bucket and a small bear, which he gives Baylee, and Finn gets seven, so he lands a medium-sized prize, which he hands to Paige.

When my first ball pops right out, Jinxy hisses, and I shoot him a dirty look, which only makes him laugh.

Hazel leans over to kiss my cheek. "Come on, Daddy! You got this!"

I nail the next nine balls, which makes my daughter squeal with glee when she gets the giant pink unicorn. She can't even hold the damn thing, it's so heavy. I help her heave it into the air, and the guys all cheer.

"Daddy, I have to pee," she announces.

That's the thing about kids. They constantly eat, pee, or puke. I'm hoping nothing she eats tonight upsets her stomach.

Abby offers Hazel her hand. "I can take her to the bathroom."

After I hoist the unicorn under my arm, I wink at her. "Thanks, babe."

I don't mean to call her by an intimate nickname. It just slips out, but Hazel's too busy jumping up and down on one leg like she's about to burst to notice my slip-up.

Hand in hand, Hazel happily trots off with Abby. They look so sweet together. Almost like Hazel is Abby's daughter, a thought that immediately makes me feel guilty.

I probably should've gotten therapy in the aftermath of what happened to Gemma. I justified it because I was so busy trying to keep my child fed and diapered while attempting to piece my life back together, but now I wonder if it was smart to put that off. I definitely have issues I need to work through at some point.

It's concerning that the only way I feel like I have a shot at football is if I stay in the present. I can't think about the past or worry about the future. It's like I need blinders so I stay in the moment. I'm not sure that's healthy.

And this thing with Abby? The sex is insane. We combust whenever we come together. I've never experienced anything like it. I vacillate between feeling grateful as hell I found her and guilty as fuck that the sex is so damn good.

Gemma and I had sweet sex. I was the only guy she'd ever slept with, and it's not like I'd had a ton of experience when we started dating in high school. But I wouldn't describe it as feral, the way Abby and I get sometimes.

Granted, we've only been seeing each other for two weeks, but I feel like Abby and I have been dancing around each other for a while. We've had a connection from the beginning. It's been easy to work together and be friends, so leveling up with her feels like the most natural thing in the world.

The guys wait with me. Everyone's shooting the shit. I'm leaning against the booth, about to check my messages, when Tiffany wanders up to me with a few of her friends.

"Hey, stranger," she purrs as she drags her hand down my arm, which I promptly move.

"What's up?"

She holds open her arms. "Don't I get a hug?"

"Kinda have my hands full here." I show her the unicorn, and her eyes widen.

"That's fucking adorable. Can I have it?"

"Sorry. My daughter already called dibs."

I look to the guys to get me out of this, but they're heatedly debating some fantasy football regulation.

Tiffany sidles closer while her friends stay back. This can't be good.

"Jinxy," I call out. "Didn't you say you were looking for Tiffany?"

Because I can't handle this girl tonight. She does not take no for an answer.

He saunters over to us. "Hey, gorgeous. What are you doing with this bum?"

"I was hoping Nick was free tonight. I just got a Brazilian wax, and I thought he could check it out and tell me if he liked it."

My jaw tightens. I already told her I was seeing someone the other day when she threw herself in my lap while I was trying to eat lunch.

"Tiffany, like I said, I'm seeing someone."

She juts out her lower lip. "You only live once, Nick. Don't you wanna have a little fun? You're always so uptight."

"Not the last two weeks," Jinxy teases.

Tiffany drags her hand down my chest, and I shift the stuffed animal so she has to step back. Honestly, this whole thing is pissing me off. I can't imagine how women deal with this kind of shit all the time.

Jinxy tosses his arm around her shoulders. "Just be patient, babe. It's nothing serious. Nick will be a free man come second semester."

What the fuck does that mean?

When she wanders off to hang out with her friends, I whack Jinxy on the shoulder. "Why the hell did you say that?"

"Because it buys you time." He taps on his temple. "No one ever recognizes my genius. See, by then, you and Abby will be settled in that weird little domestic thing you have going on, and poor Tiffany will be looking to rebound. Don't worry. I volunteer as tribute to soothe her aching soul with my minty-fresh taint."

I bust out laughing. "You're so fucking weird sometimes."

He beats on his chest. "I'm weird *all* the time, bro. It's a mantle I wear proudly."

When Abby and Hazel return, Paige points to a ride. "Who's going with me?"

I follow her finger. *Oh, fuck no.* "That looks dangerous."

The Magic Carpet Ride is on some kind of pendulum that swings in a circle. The riders strap in, facing the crowd, before they're whipped up and around.

Abby hops up and down and claps. "That looks like fun." She gives me one of those sweet smiles I can't resist. "I'll be right back." She hooks her arm in Paige's before they run off to the ride.

As I watch the ride spin around, my stomach tightens. "I have a bad feeling about this."

I'm about to drag her back when Mav elbows me. "Come on, buzzkill. Let your girl enjoy herself."

Does everyone know Abby and I are dating? Not that I care, but it's weird getting attention for dating someone.

The girls walk up some small stairs and onto the platform that holds the ride. It's all one giant contraption. Jesus, that thing looks rickety.

Hazel tugs my hand. "Can I go too?"

With one arm around her unicorn, I lift her with my other. "Honey, there's a height requirement for that ride." At least, there should be. "I can take you on the Teacups when they're done." That's a safe little kiddie ride where no one will get whiplash or hurl. "Besides, I need you to keep me company."

She smiles and squeezes my neck. "Okay, Daddy. I keep you company."

Baylee graciously grabs the unicorn before I let it drag in the dirt. "I can help you until they get back." She shivers. "Carnival rides give me the creeps."

Maverick elbows her. "Come on, Bay. Don't be a wimp."

She holds her hand out. "If you have a death wish, go for it, but that carnie looks like he's barely sober."

Those words send a chill straight through me. I study the ride operator, hating that Baylee's right. He's sipping something out of a giant plastic container that I suspect isn't soda.

I wander closer, hoping I'm wrong. He's not wobbling or being weird. Now that I'm a few feet away, I realize the ride operator doesn't look drunk, just tired. I'm an asshole for thinking the worst, I suppose. I just worry. I let out a relieved breath.

Paige and Abby strap in as the rest of our group joins me to watch.

"I wonder how many people puke at the top? Are we in the strike zone?" Jinxy muses.

Dax shoves him closer. "I don't know, but maybe you can test that theory."

They horse around while Hazel and I watch as the ride starts to swing, one way, then the other. The riders squeal and yell in anticipation.

I try to smile. *Abby's enjoying herself. That's good. Calm the fuck down.*

But when they reach the top and pause upside down, my

heart stops. The ride launches into motion again, and this time keeps spinning.

I let out a laugh. Here I am, being a stick in the mud. I roll my eyes at myself.

I'm about to ask Hazel what she wants for dinner when there's a loud metal groan. Then a sudden snap. I look back at the ride that's spinning, but it's no longer spinning upright.

The whole goddamn ride is leaning back.

Everyone on the ride screams, but this time it's in terror.

I don't pause to think. I hand Hazel to Baylee and run to the ride as I yell to the guys, "Help me!"

I don't know if this will work or if it's insane, but I can't just stand there and do nothing while the ride tips over. I'll never fucking forgive myself if Abby gets hurt on this thing.

The base of this contraption is lifting off the ground. There's a small staircase and a metal enclosure to keep people from falling off the platform. The guys and I grab the rails on the enclosure to stabilize the damn thing as I yell to the operator. "Turn the ride off!"

"I already did! It has a shutdown sequence. Hang on!"

My heart beats in my throat as the guys and I are lifted off the ground with the motion of the ride, but our weight is enough to keep it from tipping over. Fortunately, it only does one more full rotation before it slows.

The girls are crying when they wobble off. I sweep Abby into my arms and pick her off the ground. "Buttercup, are you okay?"

She sniffles into my neck. "I don't know what happened. One minute we were having a blast, and the next I thought we were going to crash. I swear, my whole life flashed before my eyes."

In a blink, I'm standing on that desolate road next to Gemma's car as it sits upside down in that ditch.

It makes me wonder what would've happened if I hadn't been here tonight, or if I'd taken Hazel to ride the Teacups while

Abby and our friends rode this fucking death trap. What if nobody had helped them?

I set Abby down, and our friends surround her while I wander behind a booth to puke.

Jinxy and Dax find me a few minutes later.

Dax hands me a napkin. "You okay, man? That shit was intense."

Jinxy shakes his head. "Y'all are like that movie."

"What movie?" I ask as I spit on the ground.

"You know, that one where everyone dies." Dax elbows him, and Jinxy frowns. "What? It's true. First, Abby hits him with her car. Then a tree almost smashes her in her bedroom. And now she nearly gets demolished on a carnival ride. But bad shit always happens in threes, so you're probably fine."

The rest of the night, I try to play it off, pretend I'm okay, but inside, I'm the same guy who watched his girlfriend's cold, limp body get carried off on a stretcher.

And there wasn't a damn thing I could do about it.

30

ABIGAIL

On a gasp, I wake and reach for Nick, but the other side of the bed is empty.

Sunlight peeks through the blinds as I try to calm my racing heart. I don't often have nightmares, but given what happened last weekend, I'm not surprised I'm still freaked out by that carnival ride.

The whole dang thing almost tilted over. I've seen video of it. Nick rushed to stabilize the base and called for his friends to help. That's probably the only reason I'm alive right now.

This is the second time the man's rescued me. I've never wanted to play the role of damsel in distress, but I'm grateful I'm still on this planet to gripe about it.

I reach for my phone. No messages.

Hmm.

Sliding my finger across the screen, I flip to Nick's thread. Since Saturday night, he hasn't texted anything personal.

I put Hazel's new vitamins on the counter.

I'll be home late. Can you make sure Hazel brushes her teeth?

Did Hazel eat dinner yet?

If I scroll higher, he's a different person.

Looking forward to seeing you, buttercup.

Wanna grab dinner later?

Too bad we have to be quiet tonight. *devil emoji*

When Paige texts a few minutes later, I decide I can't brood about this all week. I need help figuring out what's going on. I have a doctor appointment later today, but maybe we can squeeze in lunch.

I drive like a granny to school because as long as I keep my car in first or second gear, my clutch doesn't slip. Fortunately, I take suburban streets and never need to hop on the highway.

Once I reach the cafeteria, I scan the room, hoping to catch Nick on his lunch break, but I don't see any football players. Paige waves at me from across the room.

I join her at the booth, leaning over to hug her. "Hey, thanks for meeting up."

"No problem. Want some of my taco salad?"

"I brought a sandwich, but thanks." After I shrug out of my jacket, I pull out my food, but I'm too twisted up inside to eat. "I need your input. I think Nick wants to break up. Not that we're together exactly. You know what I mean."

"Not entirely."

I lower my voice. "We sleep together. We're friends. I take care of his daughter. I guess that's friends with benefits, but we said we'd enjoy our time together before I'm done with school this December and leave for England. And he promised he wouldn't explore any extracurricular activities with other girls while we're doing what we're doing."

"But you have feelings."

My eyes sting. "Yes. Too many feelings."

She reaches across the table to squeeze my hand. "He was pretty upset Saturday night. He looked like Hercules, holding up that ride until the other guys joined him."

Nodding, I look at my lap. "I feel bad I went on that dumb thing. He said it looked dangerous, and I thought Nick was just being Nick. He thinks everything is dangerous. I figured it's because he doesn't want Hazel to get hurt, but now I wonder if it's something else."

"Like what?"

I nibble on my bottom lip. "Maybe something to do with Hazel's mom. We've only talked about Gemma once, about how they met, not about how she passed. Last year, when he transferred, everyone said she died in a car crash, but I don't know much more than that." I shake my head. "I'm probably grasping at straws. He just seems so remote this week."

"Maybe the carnival triggered him somehow. Tragedy tends to stay with a person."

"Yeah." I peel back the label on my water.

"Do y'all still sleep together? Sorry, I know that's personal."

"We do in the sense that he holds me in bed, but we haven't had sex since the accident. And he's not chatty then either. He says he's tired and wants to think through his upcoming game."

She takes a bite of her salad. "I'm a terrible rug sweeper sometimes, so take this with a grain of salt because it's easy for me to tell you what to do. But I would probably sit him down and tell him how you feel, or at least what you've noticed, and see what he says. Because it's obviously eating away at you."

I rub my clammy hands on my jeans. "We don't have that much time together before I leave, and I don't want to waste it."

She gives me a sympathetic smile. "And you're hoping he falls in love with you in the meanwhile."

"Well, of course." We both laugh. "All right. Enough about me. How are things going with Marcus?"

She shrugs. "It's okay. He works a lot and socializes with his friends more than I'm comfortable with, but I guess no relationship is perfect. I'm not in a position to complain since I have cheer practice every night and games every Saturday." After nibbling on her food, she waves her fork. "He's just never free when I am. Unless he wants sex, and then he's available. But why couldn't he take me to the Nut Festival last weekend? Because he wanted to grab pizza with his bros and bitch about fantasy football."

"I've never understood the obsession with fantasy football."

"Thank you."

I check my phone. "I'd better eat. I have a doctor appointment in a bit."

Concern etches her face. "Is everything okay?"

"I want to switch birth control because I've been getting headaches. I'm not sure if that's the answer, but I'd like to try that rather than popping ibuprofen all the time."

Loud laughter on the other side of the room makes us turn.

Paige looks at me. "Now's your chance to talk to Nick."

He's with several football players and a few girls from the cheer squad. "Ugh, why is Tiffany always hanging around them?"

"Just ignore her. Go on over there and tell him you need to chat for a minute, and then drag his ass outside."

I push my glasses up my face. "Thanks. I appreciate the play-by-play because I never know what to do in social situations." I shove my food back in my bag and tug on my jacket. "Here goes nothing."

"You got this."

I make my way across the cafeteria.

When I reach the guys, Dax elbows Nick, then smiles at me. "Hey."

"Hi, Dax."

When Nick sees me, his face goes blank. There's no smile or light in his eyes. It hurts. I swallow and motion behind me. "Can I talk to you a minute?"

Somehow, Tiffany manages to cut across the group and hook her arm through his. "Nick's busy. Make yourself useful and go wait tables at Moe's."

Nick growls. "Stop being such a bitch to everyone, Tiffany."

She gasps, and he shakes her off.

I'm momentarily comforted when he puts his hand on my back as we walk away. I don't stop until we're outside. But as soon as we're alone, he drops his hand.

Awkwardly, I point to a bench.

He nods, but doesn't sit right next to me and throw his arm over my shoulders. No, he settles on the opposite side and turns to face me. "What's up?"

I want to go for subtle, but I'm a geyser of word vomit and hurt feelings. "What's up? You mean aside from you being M.I.A. all week? I mean, sure, you're around, but even when you're with me, you're a thousand miles away. Talk to me, Nick. I thought we were friends."

He looks away. "It's been a rough week."

I wait for him to expand on that, and when he doesn't, I sigh. It's like that, huh? "I'm going to make this simple for both of us because I don't like playing games. Are you saying I've overstayed my welcome and you want me to move out? Or that you don't want to hook up anymore? Because I can have my things out tonight."

The alarm in his eyes momentarily soothes my ruffled feathers. "No, I don't want you to move out, Abby. I just don't know how to talk about my shit. I've found that the only way I can play football is if I block out all the trauma, drama, and distractions and focus on two things—my kid and the game. That's it."

I nod slowly. "So I'm a distraction, and maybe trauma too after what happened at the carnival."

He scrubs his face. "I'm not explaining this right."

"Then spell it out. Say what you mean even if it'll hurt my

feelings. I'd rather know the truth than guess. I'm not good at guessing. Because my mind goes straight to you having other interests, like Tiffany or some other woman who's been hounding you." Okay, maybe not Tiffany because he just told her off, but there are girls all over campus who would be only too happy to jump into his bed.

His eyes close. "Shit. I'm sorry. Nothing could be further from the truth." He reaches for me, and next thing I know, I'm in his arms. "It's not you, buttercup. I swear. You're the sweetest thing in my life right now. I'm sorry I'm being a prick."

He kisses my temple as tears stream down my face. I don't mean to cry, but I'm so relieved that he's opening up to me, it feels like a dam of emotion has burst in my chest. "I figured you had moved on and... and... didn't know how to break it to me."

"Aww, baby, no. I'm so sorry I gave off that vibe." His hand moves up and down my back.

We sit there in silence for a long moment. The breeze is brisk, and I shiver.

He stares across the quad. "You know Gemma died in a car crash, right?"

I sit back so I can face him and grab his rough hand. "Yeah, but I don't know any other details."

"That night, we had an away game. It was a two-hour drive. She was supposed to follow the team home, but she got tired of waiting. It was raining hard by the time we left." There's that thousand-mile stare again, but beneath it, I see the pain. "The police think she swerved to avoid a deer, and she flipped her car over. It landed in a ditch with two or three feet of water." He swallows. "Where she drowned."

"Oh, God." I can't imagine experiencing that kind of devastation.

"Our bus drove up as the ambulance pulled her out, but it was too late."

I wrap my arms around him. "I'm so sorry."

He dips his face into my neck. "This week was the third anniversary of her death."

"Nick." I squeeze my eyes shut. That explains so much.

"And when shit happens to you—that tree through your window or you going on that carnival ride—all of a sudden, I'm back on that country road in the rain."

Here I am thinking we're so good together when I'm really a huge trigger. "What can I do to make things better?" It pains me to say this, but now that I understand where he's coming from, it would be selfish to pursue this with him if he's not ready. "As much as I love living with you and taking care of Hazel, if you would rather find someone else to—"

"No." Gently, he cups my face. "I just need some time to recalibrate, I swear. I've been thinking it's long past time to talk to a therapist about this. We have a team psychologist on staff, and I have an appointment with him later this week. I wanna get through this without driving you away or fucking up my season."

I nod and try to smile. "That sounds like a plan."

A plan that could take months or even years to help him untangle that trauma.

I only have weeks before my trip, and given what he just shared about Gemma, I'm not sure I'll get an invitation to stay with him when I return from England.

31

NICK

"Close you-a eyes, Daddy." Hazel giggles from the kitchen.

"They're closed."

Her feet pad across the hardwood floor, stopping in front of me as I sit on the couch, dressed like a shepherd. The itchy wool costume makes me wanna scratch myself against a tree trunk, but I'm happy to endure it for a few hours.

It's Friday night, and while I'd love nothing more than to chill on my couch before I get to bed early so I can be ready for tomorrow's game, I want my daughter to enjoy some trick-or-treating first. She's sacrificed so much so I can play football. She deserves to do something fun.

Abby suggested that we walk around the neighborhood this evening and said she'd take care of the costumes.

Things have been awkward between us all week, but I'm hoping tonight will help us get back to our laid-back vibe.

"Daddy!" Hazel squeals. "Open you-a eyes!"

My daughter holds out her hands. She's dressed in a black leotard and leggings with huge cotton balls glued all over her smock. Pink and black ears jut out from a white, wooly cap. "Aww. What a beautiful little lamb."

Abby clears her throat with a saucy smile on her face.

Okay. Wow. "Are you a milkmaid?" Because, Jesus, I wanna get up close and personal with her incredible rack right now.

"No, silly. I'm Little Bo Peep." She presses her hands down her skirt. "Is this okay? Paige helped me get the costumes together."

"You two look incredible."

It's really inappropriate to have an erection right now, but Abby's so damn hot in that getup. She's wearing a pink gingham dress that laces up the front with a fitted bodice, a lacy apron, and white tights. Her long, blonde hair cascades over her shoulders in pigtails tied with ribbons.

As I check her out again, I notice something's different, more than just her outfit. "You fixed your glasses." I almost miss the little bundle of white tape on the corner. "They look great."

She smiles and traces a finger over where they were once broken. "Not too nerdy?"

"Not at all." Funny how I used to think they looked a little geeky. Now I just think she looks smart and really fucking beautiful.

"I realized I'm actually pretty fond of this pair."

When Hazel turns away to grab her jack-o'-lantern, I kiss Abby's forehead. "I am too." I take in her outfit once more and try to keep my jaw from unhinging because Abby's a total smokeshow. "My shepherd costume makes sense now."

"Baaa!" My daughter twirls in the middle of the living room. "Let's go!"

Her happiness is infectious, and I find myself smiling for the first time this week. As my daughter skips to the front door, I hug Abby. "Thanks, buttercup. You're the best."

The shy smile she gives me makes my heart race. Damn, this woman is addictive. I've tried to get some space this week to work through my shit, but I can't stay away from her anymore. It's been killing me to tuck her in at night and not fuck her senseless, but it felt wrong to use sex to feel better.

After I tell Hazel to put on her coat, I whisper in Abby's ear, "Don't change out of the costume when we get home."

The look she gives me makes me grateful I'm wearing this getup because it would be really awkward to go trick-or-treating with a giant stiffy.

Abby wants us to take photos, so she has me kneel down next to Hazel to snap a few. Thankfully, this family-friendly moment is an instant boner-killer.

"Join us. We'll take a selfie." I motion her closer.

With my daughter in my left arm, I wrap my right one around Little Bo Peep. She holds her hand out with her camera, and we yell, "Cheese!"

Then I take a few of her and Hazel. They look so damn sweet together.

I dash off pics to my dad and Cynthia. When Gemma's mom immediately texts back, anxiety shoots up my spine, but she only thanks me and says Hazel looks adorable.

Abby and I once again swing Hazel between us as we head out. All the neighborhood kids are running from house to house. When we reach the first one, I hand my daughter her jack-o'-lantern. "Remember to say thank you when you get a treat, and don't eat any of the candy until we can check it at home."

She nods and skips up the walkway.

"Ring the doorbell," I call out from a few feet away. As I watch her wait for our neighbor to answer, I lean over to Abby. "Do you think this is okay? Or should we go with her?"

"We're right here. If she needs help, you can step in."

I rub the back of my neck. "I realize I'm overprotective and need to chill my ass out, but how do you know what's too much?"

"You have great instincts when it comes to Hazel. Trust yourself." She gives me a sweet smile and squeezes my arm. "This is age appropriate. If she was a little younger or shyer, we could go up to the house with her. We're close enough to keep her safe, but far enough away to let her do her thing. I think you're giving her the perfect amount of independence. She's going to grow up to be a confident young woman someday. Just watch."

Thank God I'm doing something right. Some days I feel like I'm barely keeping this train on the tracks.

Abby's phone buzzes with a text, which she reads and thumbs a response on the screen. "Just Paige asking if we want to go to a Halloween party."

Damn, I hope she doesn't wanna go, but that's a selfish thought. Abby is young and beautiful, and she shouldn't be tied down if she wants to be social. "You don't have to hang out with us all night."

She nibbles her bottom lip, like she's afraid to say whatever's on her mind. "I'd rather spend the evening with you and Hazelnut than a bunch of drunk frat boys."

Abby's been tentative with me all week, even after we spoke on campus. I hate that I've created this weird energy between us.

Hazel trots back waving a candy bar in her hand.

"Nice job." Abby high-fives my daughter, and we head to the next house.

While we're waiting for Hazel to do her thing, Abby fidgets with her apron. "So, um, did you get a chance to talk to the team psychologist about how you've been feeling?"

Instantly, I freeze up. I don't know why. Normal people talk about their feelings, but I'm starting to realize I've been emotionally stunted since Gemma died.

I work my jaw back and forth. "I touched base with Coach, who said he thought a few sessions might be a good idea." Coach Santos is a good man. He called me last Sunday after he found out what happened at the Nut Festival to make sure Abby and I were okay. "But when I spoke to the team psychologist, he said tapping into deep trauma in the middle of the season might not be the smartest move. He thought I should do some meditation instead and deal with the rest in the offseason. We reviewed a few techniques he wants me to do if I get stressed or triggered."

She gives me a tight smile. "Great. Whatever helps you."

I get the distinct feeling she's disappointed. "I have one last shot to get drafted, Abby. I can't do anything that might compromise my season."

"I didn't say you should."

My daughter is digging through a huge box of candy, presumably looking for the one she wants. I lower my voice. "Football has to be the priority in my life. If I don't get drafted, it's like... like Gemma died for nothing." I don't mean to make that admission, but now it's out there.

Abby swallows, then glances down at the ground. "I can see how losing your girlfriend would make you feel that way. I'm so sorry, Nick."

Hazel skips back to us. "I have two candy baws now, Daddy!"

Her giddy voice hits me like a bucket of cold water. What am I doing talking about Gemma right now when I'm trying to give our daughter a fun night? "Congrats, honey. Great job."

I take her hand and try to smile as she skips alongside me. Silent, Abby follows behind us.

Jesus, I'm fucking this up.

When we reach the next house and Hazel runs up to ring the doorbell, I grab Abby and pull her close. "I'm sorry. Forgive me for ruining this evening. I'm doing everything wrong here." After

I check that Hazel is looking away, I lean over and kiss Abby's forehead. "You've gone through so much trouble to make Halloween special for my daughter. Let's not talk about my baggage and just have fun. You don't have that much more time before you leave for your trip. Like, what, six weeks? We should make the most of this."

I get another tight smile. "Sure, Nick."

Confused, I rub the back of my neck. What did she want me to say? I thought this is what she wanted? To have fun together until she left?

As we wander up and down the street for the next hour, Abby slowly starts to relax again, and by the time we get home, she's smiling and chatty.

When I open the front door, the scent of apples and cinnamon hits me.

"I left some apple cider simmering on the stove," she says as she takes off Hazel's coat. "I saw it on Pinterest, and since it only had a few ingredients, I didn't think I could mess it up. Who wants some?"

Hazel jumps up and down. "Me! I do!"

I nod. "That sounds great. Thanks."

My daughter scampers after Abby. I duck into my bedroom to change out of my costume and then crash on the couch in a pair of pajama bottoms and a t-shirt. Hazel crawls into my lap with her bucket of candy.

She starts counting it. "I got so much chocolate."

"You sure did, munchkin. Gonna share with dear ol' Dad?"

Her little lips purse. "Hmm. I'll think about it."

"You little rascal." I tickle her and roar like a monster, and she squeals in delight.

"Okay! You can have some!"

"It's late, kiddo, and if we eat too much sugar, we won't be able to sleep. You can have one piece tonight, but we have to brush our teeth really well."

After I inspect the candy to make sure no psycho tampered with them, we both enjoy some chocolate.

Abby sets down a tray of hot apple cider. There are two big mugs, and one small one. Hazel can't have a huge drink before bed or she'll have an accident.

"Thank you," I say as I reach for my mug. "Smells delicious."

The beaming smile she gives me fills my chest with something I can't describe. I haven't wanted to please a woman since Gemma. Being with Abby twists me up in knots and soothes my soul at the same time.

This thing with my roommate was supposed to be fun and easy, not complicated.

But when I see the affection shining in her eyes, I know we're hell and gone from uncomplicated. Especially when she sits on the couch next to me and my daughter crawls into her lap.

Because Hazel loves Abby.

Abby gently unpins the wool cap on Hazel's head. She compliments her on how well she trick-or-treated. On how polite she was by saying please and thank you to our neighbors. On how proud of her we are that she's such a big girl.

Fuck, I think I love Abby too.

Dread, thick and suffocating, chokes me, and I scrub my face with my palm.

The last woman I loved died a horribly tragic death.

And it was all my fault.

How the hell can I get into another relationship when I'm not sure how I'll protect Abby?

An alarm goes off on my phone. It says, *Set two alarms for tomorrow morning.*

I have a game I need to mentally prepare for. I can't sit here all night losing my shit over this thing with Abby. I have to focus, or I can kiss the NFL, my daughter's future, and my father's retirement goodbye.

Leaning my head back, I stare up at the ceiling. I know how to survive. I've done it before. I just have to shove all of this emotional shit down until the only thing that rises to the surface is the game.

The team therapist is right. I need to focus on football.

32

ABIGAIL

STARING at the clock isn't going to make Nick come to my room.

Frustrated, I sit up in bed.

Damn him for getting my hopes up. Why did he ask me not to change out of this stupid costume if he wasn't planning to come see me?

After I set my glasses on the bedside table, I pull on the ties that hold up this dress and yank it over my head, but it gets caught on my boobs, so I spend another five minutes trying to wrestle it off.

By the time I'm done, I'm too tired to get off the rest. I stare at my reflection in the mirror. I'm dumb for spending money on this lingerie, but it's so pretty, I couldn't resist. It's a matching bra and panty set in white lace with matching garters and thigh-high stockings. I've never worn garters before, but Paige thought this looked super sexy, so I bought it.

I guess she's right about doing stuff for myself. She's always saying I shouldn't dress up for a man, but because it makes me feel good.

But that doesn't minimize my irritation at getting stood up.

I shrug on a robe, tie it in the front, and shuffle out to the kitchen. I was so excited to see Nick tonight that I forgot my glass of water, and now I'm parched.

After I fill my glass and take a few sips, I freeze when I hear the click of a door down the hallway behind me.

Don't get your hopes up, Abby. He's probably going to the bathroom. Another door clicks, and disappointment that I'm right hits me like a tidal wave.

Well, I'm not going to beg him to spend time with me. Deciding I need to return to my room before he's done in the bathroom, I whirl around and nearly have a heart attack because Nick's right behind me.

"Hey. Didn't mean to scare you." He chuckles as he puts his hands on my shoulders. "Sorry it's so late," he says with a deep, gravelly voice. His hair is sticking up every which way.

I try to calm my racing heart. "I didn't think you were coming."

He tugs me to his chest and wraps his arms around me. "Sorry, buttercup. Fell asleep when I was putting Hazel to bed."

Closing my eyes, I breathe in his sandalwood scent and try not to get emotional, but I can't handle being jerked around. "Is this dumb? What we're doing?"

He kisses my temple. "Probably. But I can't bring myself to let you go."

I swallow past the knot in my throat. "I feel like I should have a sense of self-preservation and move out."

His hold tightens. Then he steps back, but moves his hands back to my shoulders and leans down to look into my eyes. "I know I'm not an easy man to be with, but don't give up on me." He shakes his head. "I just need some time to work through some stuff. Can you do that? Give me a little more time?"

I'd give him all the time in the world if I didn't think I'd get my heart decimated in the end.

But my mom always says good things are worth fighting for,

and I see so much goodness in Nick, from the way he takes care of his daughter to the way he always looks out for me.

I realize there's no guarantee here. Nick's made no commitment to me, but I also know he's not a fickle man. And I trust him. I know he's not carousing with other women like my ex did.

But more than that, I love him, and love doesn't give up.

"I can give you more time. Just please don't jerk me around."

He nods. "I promise."

I wrap my arms around him and listen to the beat of his steady heart. "Do you need to go to bed or do you want to come to my room?"

Nick has a game tomorrow, and it's late, so I don't get my hopes up.

He nuzzles my neck. "I was hoping I'd get an invitation."

I snicker. "Is this a late-night booty call?"

"Only if you're offering." He presses his huge erection to my belly, and my eyes widen. "I mean, it's been a while. Can't blame me for being excited."

Chuckling, I take his hand and lead him back to my bedroom. My small lamp is on, which makes me nervous. I've never worn lingerie for a man before. Will he think it looks dumb?

The lock clicks behind me.

His arms drape around my shoulders. "I've missed you this week."

"You've been in my bed every night."

"You know what I mean." He turns me around and then... stares at my face.

"What?" I feel my cheeks heating.

He drags a finger under my jaw and down my neck. "You're a beautiful woman. Do you know that?"

I stare down at my stockinged feet. "Thank you."

He lifts my chin. "And I dig that you're shy sometimes."

Smiling, I shrug. "What can I say? I'm the whole package." I mean that one hundred percent facetiously.

"And that costume you wore tonight?" He shakes his head with a wolfish grin. "Gotta say I'm excited to strip it off you."

I wince. "I got tired of waiting for you, so I took it off."

"Naughty girl." He pats my ass. "But that makes me wonder what you're wearing under this robe."

"You'll have to open it and find out."

Slowly, he drags a finger down the front of my robe, parting the two folds. I shrug it off my shoulders until it falls to the floor.

"Goddamn, Abigail. Were you wearing this all night under your costume?" His eyes slowly descend over my body, pausing at my breasts, stomach, and thighs, before they meet mine again.

"Yes, I wore the lingerie under my Little Bo Peep costume."

"Good thing I didn't know or I never would've gotten rid of that erection."

I palm the giant bulge in his pajama bottoms. "The problem seems to have returned."

He grabs my jaw and kisses me. I moan as he palms my boobs and tweaks my nipples through the lace.

"Need to see more of you," he says as he pulls my boobs above the lace of my bra. "Christ, you look good like this. Turn around. Let me see the back."

With my heart pounding, I do as he asks.

I smile when he curses. I've never worn a thong before, and clearly, he likes this one.

He moves me in front of the mirror over my bureau as he cups my breasts. "Look at how fucking sexy you are." After he kisses my shoulder, he bends me over and drags his lips down my back, then bites my ass, making me gasp.

For a minute, he fumbles with my underwear until he drags them down my legs.

Oh, I get it now—why Paige said the thong had to go over the garters. This way, the stockings stay on.

He toys with the ribbons on my thighs as he nibbles along my inner thigh. Then his thick finger spreads my wetness around before he sinks it into me, and I moan.

"No screaming."

I can fully admit that every time we come together, Nick makes me want to scream in delight. The man knows what he's doing. I've never had orgasms like the ones he gives me. Even that rabbit vibrator doesn't feel as good as the real thing.

I bite my bottom lip as he thrusts one finger, then two, deep inside me. He taps my g-spot each time, and I shiver. Reaching down, I rub my clit.

"That's right, baby. Get yourself there." Then he drags his thumb against my asshole.

"Oh, God."

But when he stuffs me full with a third finger and bites my right ass cheek, I disintegrate. Bright light flashes behind my closed lids as he works me over. It's a good thing I'm braced on my bureau or I would collapse to the floor.

I'm laughing by the time I'm done. He turns me in his arms and holds me to his chest as I smile sleepily.

"Mm. That was amazing. Dang near forgot my name," I mumble against him.

His chest rumbles with a laugh. "I love making you come. Especially when you make those little noises."

I look up at him. "What little noises?"

"The ones you make when you're trying not to scream." The smug look on his face makes me laugh again.

Lifting up on my toes, I wrap my arms around his neck and kiss him. "Thank you for my bedtime orgasm."

We kiss for a long moment until he starts grinding his huge erection against me. "Will you be a good girl and suck my cock?"

I've never been crazy about giving blow jobs before, but it's like I have dick fever now, especially when he calls me a good girl.

Nodding, I happily drop to my knees and pull him out. "Take off your shirt." He quickly complies, and I smile when his thick, long length juts out almost to his belly button. I drag my nails down his chiseled stomach as I lap at the drop of precum dripping down his tip.

He grabs a fist full of my hair and holds my head back while he taps his cock on my tongue, and everything in my body tightens. I love the feral look in his eyes. I love that I do this to him. That I make him lose control.

"How deep can you take me, baby?"

I suck his crown and lift an eyebrow. "I'm not sure. Why don't we find out?"

He watches me as I lick up and down his swollen length before I wrap my hand around his base and take him into my mouth. "Mm."

When I pull him to the back of my throat, he hisses and drops his head back.

All of his muscles go taut as I take him as far as I can go. He's so beautiful like this, with long, lean lines of muscle that flex and tighten. I can't take my eyes off him. I swallow around him, and he lets out a deep groan.

When I come up for a breath, he looks down to watch me. I lick up and down his length, lick his fat tip, then take him down the back of my throat again.

He thumbs my lip. "Love watching you stretch around me." I respond by tonguing the underside of his cock, and he sucks in a breath.

I'm about to reach for his balls when he pulls out. "Don't wanna come this way." He offers his hand and helps me to my feet. "The wall or the floor?" It sucks that my bed makes too much noise because a mattress would be nice.

"How about my beanbag?" It's not that big, but it should fit him comfortably, and I plan to be on top tonight.

I push him back and he drops back, landing with a grunt. I crawl over him and sprawl across him, loving the heat of his body and how his sprinkle of chest hair rubs against my skin. The angle makes my boobs look huge, and I don't miss the look of appreciation in his eyes as my breasts drag up and down as I grind against his dick.

We kiss as he grabs my ass and helps me move. The thickness of his cock feels so good, I shudder.

"Sit up," he says. I move up enough for him to squeeze my boobs to his mouth so he can suck and bite them. Once he's given both ample attention, he pushes me back. "Get on."

"What about the condom?"

"Oh, shit. Thanks for reminding me." He reaches into my bedside table, where we moved them, and pulls out a packet. After he rips it open with his teeth and rolls it over his thick length, he holds the base of his dick as I lean up and angle him toward me. I always forget how big he is, how insane the stretch is, and it takes a minute to squeeze him in. I gasp. "This is intense."

I've never been on top with him before, and his endowment is significant.

"Take your time," he says, his voice gravelly.

But I can't slow down because everything is throbbing again. So I start to bounce. Each drag of his cock against me takes me one step closer to the ledge.

His eyes are riveted to my boobs as they bounce in his face, but then he tells me to lean back.

Reaching behind me, I brace myself on his thighs. When I look down, I realize Nick can see everything like this. His neck is taut, his eyes wild, his attention glued to where his dick stretches me wide open.

I lift my hips, up and down, and it's his turn to grunt and groan.

But when he licks his thumb and circles my clit, I lose control. "Yes! Yes!"

With his other hand, he grabs my hip and quickens our pace, and a few thrusts later, I shatter around him. A second later, he follows with a curse, but I'm still pulsing. We cling to each other as we ride out the orgasm.

Finally, I collapse on his chest. We're sweaty and spent, and I'm utterly content when his arms wrap around me. I'm half-asleep when he nudges me.

"Sorry. Gotta take care of the condom, baby."

It hurts to move because my legs have been wrapped around his waist for the last half hour. I manage to crawl off him and curl up on the beanbag.

"Fuck." He grunts.

Hmm. That wasn't a sexy fuck. That was a pissed-off fuck.

I crack open my eyes. "What's wrong?"

He's holding his dick. "The condom broke."

Yawning, I shrug. "I'm on the pill." He knows this.

The grooves on his forehead deepen. "So... we're okay?"

"Yes. Now stop frowning at me, Nick. You're ruining my after-orgasm glow."

He chuckles, and I smile.

When he leaves to clean up, my smile widens because he has to have feelings for me. Why else would he ask me to stay here when I offered to move?

One way or another we're going to get through this. We're going to happen.

It's just going to take a little more time.

33

ABIGAIL

"Ted, turn down that TV! I can't hear Abigail!"

I pull the phone back from my ear before my mother makes me deaf. "Mom, we can chat later if you're busy."

"Don't be silly. I barely talk to you as it is. How are things with the family you work for?"

She was so excited when I told her I got a nanny job. I never told her that the 'family' was a single dad and I had moved in with him. If she'd heard a tree nearly smashed me to bits and my sexy-as-hell neighbor-slash-boss had invited me to live with him, she would've been on my doorstep, demanding I return to San Antonio.

Needless to say, I haven't mentioned he's another football player.

I love my mother, but I wish I had siblings so she wasn't always so focused on me. I'm in my last semester of college, for Pete's sake. Even though I've lamented moving to Charming a million times, I'm starting to appreciate having more independence. I love my parents, but I need space to work things out for myself.

"It's great. I love Hazel to pieces. She's adorable."

"I just wish you didn't have to work so much. I can't believe you're still taking shifts at the diner."

"I have to work if I want to eat more than ramen when I'm in Europe." It's hard to choke out those words. I mean, I want to go. Of course I do. It's been a lifelong dream, but the closer I get to my departure, the more anxious I get that Nick's not going to invite me to stay with him once I return.

"I still don't understand the rush to go this winter. Why not wait until the summer? You're going to miss Christmas with the family."

I've explained this so many times. "The summer is when all the tourists go. I won't get the same experience. Plus, I want to see the Christmas markets."

"You and those markets. Did you change your mind about coming home for Thanksgiving next week? I'm making that oyster stuffing everyone loves."

The thought of that mushy stuffing makes my stomach roil. "Mom—"

"I was going to let your grandparents sleep in your bedroom, but if you're coming—"

"I didn't change my mind. I can't visit until the end of the semester." I'll be home for a day or two before my flight leaves for London.

She sighs. "Look, I know you don't want to discuss this, but Ezra's parents say he's visiting, and this might be your only chance to patch things up."

Not this again. "Mother, he *cheated* on me."

"That boy was young and stupid. I'm sure he's learned his lesson. His parents say he asks about you all the time."

"He just wants to win football games," I mutter.

Pause.

"What does that have to do with anything?"

I don't know why I'm protecting that asshole. "You know how he's superstitious, right?"

"Of course. I gave his parents the name of a good therapist to help him with his OCD, but I'm not sure they ever called. Maybe he didn't need it. He's coped quite well, all things considered."

"Let me put it this way. Ezra and I started dating in high school because the day after we..." Messed around? Made out? "The day after we kissed, he won his football game. That idiot thought it had something to do with me. Like I was his good luck charm or something. *That's* why he dated me so long even though he was bedding half of Charming behind my back and truly had no affection for me. *That's* why he asked me to marry him, Mother. Not because he loved me. Not because he cared for me or thought I was special. But because he thought I helped him *win football games.*"

"That... What?" Silence. "You're kidding me."

Now she gets it.

"I would never joke about this."

"Oh, Abigail. Honey. Why didn't you tell me?" She sniffles.

It's been long enough that this situation doesn't completely humiliate me anymore. "I was embarrassed. I was dating a guy you and Dad loved. Someone you helped in high school. You're best friends with his mother. I guess I didn't want to rain on everyone's parade, but that's dumb. I was only hurting myself by not being honest."

"I'm so sorry. Can you forgive me? Next time I see that little dumbass, I'm going to give him a piece of my mind."

"Forget Ezra. He's not worth the time or aggravation. But that's why I don't want to see his parents."

"I'll call them right now and uninvite them from Thanksgiving dinner."

I tug on a loose thread at the hem of my t-shirt. "That's not in the spirit of the holidays, though, is it? I love Beth, and I doubt she knows the truth about her son. If you choose to tell her, that's on you. I don't want to be involved. I just want to move on with my life."

By the time I get off the phone, I feel like a weight has been lifted from my chest. I had no idea this was bothering me so much. I'm relieved I finally had that conversation. It was long overdue.

In the living room, I hear voices. Cadence is watching Hazel this afternoon.

I wander out to the kitchen where I see Denise dropping off Hazel from preschool.

Denise waves bye, and I brace myself for Hazel to plow into my legs for a hug. "Hey, sweetheart. How was school? Did you learn a lot?"

"Yup. I told my teacha I know my ABCs."

"You certainly do."

"Can I listen to music?" The kid loves her headphones.

I turn her toward Cadence, who's looking at me funny. "Ask Cadence, honey. She's in charge this afternoon."

This always gets tricky because I can obviously help, but I don't want to step on Cadence's toes.

The other nanny gives me a tight smile before she turns to Hazel. "Sure. I'll call you in a little while for lunch."

"Okay!" She skips down the hallway.

"How's it going?" I ask Cadence.

"Fine."

I've gotten the distinct impression she doesn't like me. So she really won't like this request, but I don't have the funds to cater Thanksgiving. I push up my glasses as I gather my courage. "Can I ask a favor? It's kind of a big one, and you can totally say no."

"You're scaring me."

I chuckle. "It's not scary, I promise. But I was wondering if you could possibly cook a turkey and some sides for Nick and

Hazel. They can't go see his father because Nick has a game and needs to stay in Charming. And you already know I'm no good in the kitchen. I can pay for all the ingredients and help out by watching Hazel while you cook."

She gives me another funny look. "It's you, isn't it?"

"What's me?"

"You're the one Nick's dating."

I open my mouth, but nothing comes out. While neither Nick nor I have done anything to hide that we're sorta seeing each other, we've never been affectionate around Denise or Cadence, and certainly not Hazel, aside from a few hugs when she's not paying attention.

When I don't say anything, Cadence laughs. "I don't know who you think you're fooling. I see the way you moon over him when he comes home."

"I... we're... I mean, we're friends."

"Sure." She rolls her eyes. "Okay, so you want me to make him Thanksgiving dinner? One I'm assuming you'll enjoy with him?"

What's the point in lying? "Yes, I probably will."

"Fine. Whatever. Write down what you want. We'll make it on Wednesday, so it's fresh. I'll need your help with Hazel."

"Thanks." I pull out some paper and a pen. "Listen, please don't say anything to Hazel about this thing with her dad."

"I'm not an idiot."

This is going well. I look down at my shoes, not knowing how to make this less awkward.

She sighs. "I don't mean to be a bitch. I'm just annoyed he didn't pick me. I'm awesome."

I laugh at her honesty. "I'm just as shocked as you are. You're so beautiful and such a good cook, and I'm... a big nerd who's accident-prone."

"Girl, no." After she wipes her hands on a dish towel, she

glances down the hall to make sure we're alone and then lowers her voice. "I'm just being an asshole about this because I like getting my way. He's hot, and I thought he'd be down for some fun. But you're awesome too. I'm not saying you're not. You taught Hazel her alphabet, and I watched you teach her how to use scissors and do all those cool crafts. I watched you sew her Halloween outfit and do that little crochet project. You even designed a book of activities for her. You have plenty of great skills, and deep, deep, *deep* down, I'm happy for you."

We both laugh, and I try not to seem too shocked when she hugs me. I mean, yeah, that activity book was cool, but it consisted of assignments I designed for my student teaching last spring. I just sent it off to one of those print-on-demand places so I could have everything in one place for Hazel.

Cadence pulls out the bread, cheese, and butter. "Want a grilled cheese? I'm making some for Hazel and myself."

"That would be great, thanks. I have to go to the library to tutor someone in a bit. Let me go get my things together."

After we eat, and I help a baseball player with his English essay, I trudge to the student store at the Athletic Department. I finally have enough money to do this.

The girl at the counter smiles at me. "How can I help you?"

"I need to replace my friend's letterman jacket. I tore it, and since I can't live with that guilt, I'd like to buy him another one. I can do that here, right?"

She pauses. "Yes, but they're really expensive."

"I know." I called ahead to double-check the price.

"You'll need to fill this out." She hands me a form where I have to spell the athlete's last name, include his number on the team, note which sport he plays, and select the jacket size. When I hand the paper back to her, her eyes widen. "You ruined *Nick Silva's* letterman?"

I suppose I should've prepared myself for this. "It's a long story, but yes."

She makes a face, like I'm an idiot, and she enters the info into the computer. "It won't be ready for a few weeks. Do you want to pick it up, or should we mail it?"

In three and a half weeks, I'll be in Europe. "Maybe you should mail it." I jot down Nick's address.

"It'll be four hundred and fifty-two dollars with tax and shipping."

Even though I knew the price ahead of time, the sticker shock still gets me. With a sweeping sense of nausea, I hand her my debit card.

If we don't work out, I'm going to feel like such a fool.

No. That's a bad way to look at this. Nick saved me that day. He crawled over broken glass and lifted a dang tree off me. He ruined his jacket in the process. This is me returning the favor.

When I get home, I'm still debating whether I should be spending that much when I don't have the money to fix my transmission, but I'm hoping that problem can wait until I return from my trip. Is it wrong to pray my family gives me cash for graduation?

Regardless, I need to pay Nick rent for the time I've stayed here, and I just got my deposit from my old landlord, which will help. Maybe I can pick up a few more dinner shifts at Moe's.

Nick and Hazel are reading a book together on the couch when I come through the front door. I'm about to gush about how adorable they look when I remember how Cadence said I moon over Nick. That can't be attractive. I don't want to moon.

I give them a moderate smile, nothing too toothy. "Hey, guys. What's up?"

My insides go all gooey when Nick beams at me. Seriously, this man has a drop-dead-gorgeous smile. "Whatcha doing next Saturday afternoon? 'Cause I have two tickets to my last regular season game. I thought you and Baylee might enjoy coming to see us play Clemson."

"Are you serious?" When he nods, I want to jump up and down. Maybe cartwheel, though I'm not sure I know how to do one. Since we started seeing each other, Nick hasn't invited me to a game or given me tickets, which are super in demand since the Broncos are undefeated. I can't express how proud I am of Nick. He's been on fire out there on the football field, winning his last several games with decisive victories. "I'd love to come. Thank you."

Hazel gets up to hug me, and I bend over to wrap my arms around her. "Hi, sweetheart."

"I have to potty."

After I kiss the top of her head, I point to the bathroom. "Hurry. You don't need my permission."

When she's gone, Nick reaches to the side of the couch and pulls out a box, which he hands me. "There's just one requirement next weekend. You have to wear this."

Hesitantly, I take the box from him. My fingers tremble as I open it.

It's a Bronco jersey. Number twelve. Nick's number.

My eyes instantly well, and I blink quickly as I hold it against my chest because I'll cherish it forever. "It's beautiful." Which is such a dumb thing to say.

He chuckles. "Try it on."

I shrug off my coat and then pull the jersey over my t-shirt. It's snug on my boobs, but otherwise, it fits well.

"That," Nick says with a giant smirk, "looks fantastic on you."

"It's a little tight."

"In all the right places."

He gave me his jersey.

I let out a relieved breath because we're finally moving in the right direction.

34

ABIGAIL

Baylee nudges me. "Want another nacho?"

"No, thanks. I've eaten too much junk food today." I press a hand to my stomach to calm it.

We're sitting on the fifty-yard line in the third row. It's a packed house. There have to be seventy thousand people in the stadium. The energy is electric. Charming is out in force to support our team.

It's sad that I dated Ezra all those years and he never once invited me to see him play in college. I asked dozens of times if I could come, and he always gave me some crappy reason why I shouldn't. The fact that Nick wants me here today means more than he'll ever know.

But I'm not sure how much more excitement I can handle. I'm hoarse from screaming, and my stomach hurts. I'm glad it's halftime. I need a breather.

Baylee's eyes narrow. "You don't look so good. Don't hurl on me."

"I'm just anxious. It's such a close game."

Close but incredible. We're ahead twenty-five to twenty

against Clemson, the only other undefeated team in the country, in the last regular season game before the playoffs.

I start to bite my thumbnail, but Baylee slaps it out of my mouth. "No. Friends don't let friends ruin a great manicure."

Holding up my hand, I smile. It's just white polish, but it looks pretty. "I did do a nice job. Thanks for helping me."

She brought me supplies and showed me how to use everything. Apparently, I was applying too much at once, which is why I always smudged it before it dried.

I point to the sideline. "Look at Paige go. She's amazing." I watch my friend flip up on top of a guy who holds her up by one leg. She lifts the other up to her head. "If I did that, my girl parts would tear in two."

Baylee laughs as she waggles her brows. "Since we're on the subject of getting torn in two, how are things going with Nick? Any closer to staying in town second semester?"

I avoid talking about my sex life because there's no way I'm sharing that with anyone. Though, for the record, it's the best sex I've ever had. I squirm on my seat, a little sore from our antics last night. "We had a great Thanksgiving dinner this week, and of course, he gave me tickets to today's game along with this jersey."

"Oh, wow. I didn't realize he gave you the jersey with his number. Girl!"

We giggle.

But then I sigh. "Unfortunately, he hasn't said anything about plans after the holidays, so I've decided to bite the bullet and ask him. I know he wants to focus on football, but he has a month between this game and the playoffs, so I don't think asking what he wants to do will put too much pressure on him. Besides, I need to apply for teaching jobs. I've been putting it off, but I can't do that much longer. I need to know if I should apply here or in San Antonio."

"Are there jobs teaching second semester?"

"There are always maternity leaves." At least, according to my parents. "I can substitute-teach if I have to. What about you and Maverick? Any closer to wrangling that boy into submission?"

Baylee rolls her eyes as she points to a cheerleader on the sideline. "My sources say she's the flavor of the month."

I hug her. "We need to find you someone who appreciates you." Mav is handsome, but as someone who dated a grade-A player, I know the heartache isn't worth it.

The whistle blows, kicking off the third quarter, and we scream when the Broncos charge out onto the field.

By the fourth quarter, both teams have scored, except one of our receivers fumbled a pass, and Clemson scooped it up and ran it in for a touchdown, so now it's thirty-two to thirty-four with less than two minutes remaining. We have possession and the time to score, but the teams are so evenly matched, nothing is guaranteed.

I press a clammy hand to my forehead.

"Are you sure you're okay?" Baylee asks. "You're paler than usual."

"It's so close, I might puke."

She slurps up the rest of her soda and hands me the empty container. "There's ice in there. Press it to your face to cool off."

I shouldn't be overheated. It's fifty degrees, according to the jumbotron.

"Thank you." I just know how important it is to Nick to end the season strong. Sports commentators tore him up last year, questioning his consistency, questioning his abilities, questioning whether he has what it takes to win a championship.

So even though he's been incredible this year, I wonder how much of a toll those critics have taken on him.

I hold my breath for the first snap. Nick dodges a defender as he checks his options, but he's out of time because Clemson is rushing. He manages to break free and pass the ball just before he's tackled.

The ball sails through the air toward Dax, who's on the twenty-yard line. He has two defenders on top of him. His arm stretches up, and he catches it.

"Oh my God!" I shout as Baylee and I and seventy thousand other people freak out.

Dax somehow manages to stay on his feet and run it in for a touchdown.

I hug Baylee when we make the extra point. There's still time on the clock, but the Bronco defense keeps them from gaining any momentum until the clock runs out.

When it's over and I'm done screaming my head off, I let out a sigh of relief. The Broncos are undefeated.

Which means tonight is the perfect time to talk about plans in the new year.

Baylee screams his name, and I look up and see Nick walking by on the field.

In my head, I have this fantasy where he hops up onto the stands, pulls himself over, and kisses me.

But all he does is wave.

I smile and wave back.

I'm not disappointed... too much.

SWEATY AND PANTING, Nick and I collapse in bed. I'm so tired, I can barely move. I don't know how he had the energy to do what we just did after today's game.

"What're you giggling about?" His gruff voice in my ear makes me grin.

"Just happy." I snuggle against his chest and do my best to

keep my eyes open. "I'm so proud of you."

"Thanks, buttercup." He kisses my forehead, and I close my eyes and breathe in the scent of his skin.

Ask him. Don't chicken out.

My heart kicks in my chest. "I wanted to talk to you about something."

"Hmm."

It takes me another minute to gather my thoughts. "I was wondering what your plans are for second semester." I take a deep breath. "I'd like to stay in Charming. I know you and I haven't really defined what we're doing, but I thought if you'd like to make us official, I could start applying to teaching positions here for the spring. What do you think?"

I stare into the darkness and try to get my heart to stop pounding while I wait for him to say something.

"Nick?"

Nothing.

Closing my eyes, I brace myself for the worst-case scenario. For him to tell me he's still not ready to make any plans or that he's really not ready for a relationship or that he has to focus on the playoffs. Honestly, each of those scenarios pisses me off.

When I can't stand the silence anymore, I lift my head and face him.

The man is sound asleep.

A wave of relief hits me, and I laugh.

Well, I guess we're not doing this today. I snuggle back into him and close my eyes.

He lets out a sigh and wraps his arms around me, and I smile. The warmth of his body makes me so drowsy.

I'll wake him in a little while so he can return to his room. It just feels so good to lie together like this. I don't want to let him go.

I'll wake him. I will. In... just... a few minutes...

35

NICK

THERE'S A WARM, naked body lying across my chest. Abby.

I smile and pull her closer as I yawn and peek at the clock.

When I open my eyes, I expect to see the bright numbers shining through the darkness, not the morning sun spilling through the windows.

Fuck.

"Daddy!" Hazel howls from down the hallway, and I scramble out of bed. Where are my pajama bottoms?

I barely get them tugged on when the door flies open and hits the wall. Jesus. "Hazel, what's wrong?" Her eyes are bloodshot, and there's vomit down the front of her shirt. Shit. Her bottom lip juts out and quivers before tears spill down her chubby cheeks. "Aww, honey, come here."

Kneeling, I open my arms and she runs to me, sobbing. I hold her head to my chest as I check out the bed situation. Wide-eyed, Abby's clutching the blankets to her chest. She mouths, "Sorry."

Frustrated, I nod. It's not her fault I didn't wanna leave her bed last night. "Come on, Hazel. Let's clean you up."

I pick her up and whisk her out before she asks any questions. At some point, I'll need to have a conversation about me and Abby, but I'm not quite ready to do that with my four-year-old. I'd like to ask her how she feels about me having a girlfriend long before we discuss the birds and the bees.

Assuming Abby wants to return to Charming when she gets back from Europe.

My gut sinks just thinking about it.

Her trip is around the corner. I'm a fucking idiot for not asking her about her plans sooner. I don't know why I've had my head up my ass all semester. Hopefully, we can talk after I get my daughter cleaned up.

That takes a while because she threw up all over her bed, on the floor, and in the hallway.

How much food can one little girl vomit?

After I bathe Hazel and dress her, I set her up in the living room with some cartoons and ginger ale while I clean up the puke in my bedroom. Abby must've cleaned up the hallway. I stick my head in her room to thank her, but she's on the phone, so I take a quick shower because I reek like sex and puke.

When I'm done, I throw on some jeans and jog out to the living room to check on Hazel. "How's your tummy? Any better?"

She nods. "Can I have some toast?"

"Yeah." That's a good sign.

Abby wanders out in some duckie print pajamas. "Is she okay?"

"Better."

She presses a hand to her stomach. "I was feeling sick yesterday too, but I figured it was the junk food at the stadium. I hope I didn't give her a stomach virus."

"She's probably fine now that she's thrown up."

Abby lowers her voice to a whisper. "Did she see anything? In my bedroom?"

"I don't think so." Thank God. "That was a close call. I can't believe I forgot to lock your door last night. I just need to get my ass up out of bed sooner." Abby looks like she wants to say something, but the doorbell rings. "You expecting someone?"

"No."

I hand my daughter her breakfast before I open the door.

"Nick!" Gemma's mom Cynthia holds open her arms while I stand there, frozen. "It's so good to see you." Behind her are Gemma's father Charles and sister Monica, who looks so much like Gemma, it's jarring.

When Cynthia realizes I'm not wearing a shirt or expecting company, she looks away. "We're so sorry for dropping by like this, but when I couldn't get you on the phone, I wanted to check up on you and Hazel. We were down in Austin visiting one of my cousins over Thanksgiving, so we decided to stop by here on the way home."

"It's good to see you." It is. It just always rips out my heart. "Come in." I hug the women and shake Charles's hand as they enter.

When Cynthia sees Hazel, she rushes to her and immediately starts crying. "Baby, it's Grandma."

Guilt immediately chokes me for not staying in touch better this fall. "She's been sick this morning, so you might not want to get too close."

"Nonsense," she says as she sits next to my daughter and hugs her.

"Hi, Gwandma," Hazel says.

A throat clears. "Hi, I'm Monica, Hazel's aunt."

Christ. Monica introduces herself to Abby, who has a deer-in-the-headlights expression plastered on her face as she fidgets with the hem of her duck pajamas.

Monica is glancing between me and Abby. I'm not wearing a

shirt, and Abby looks like she just rolled out of my bed. I scrub my face with my palm.

How the hell do I introduce Abby? As my girlfriend? Which we still haven't discussed yet. That's one hundred percent my fault, but it still doesn't change my predicament here. And if I say she's my girlfriend, will that upset Cynthia more? But this is not the way I wanna break it to Hazel. Do I say Abby's my babysitter? Except how the hell do I explain her outfit?

I go with the truth. "This is my nanny Abigail. She lives with us."

There. Short and sweet. And, more importantly, not a lie.

Abby's eyes cut to me, and I can see the hurt and disappointment in them.

Shit, this isn't going well. I should open my mouth and dislodge my foot, but I'm afraid I'll make this worse.

She awkwardly waves at everyone. "I'm heading to work in a bit, but it's nice to meet y'all." Then she turns and scurries out of the room.

Monica eyes me. "She's cute."

Abby's fucking gorgeous, but I'm not stepping in that trap. I motion for Monica and her dad to have a seat. "Can I get you guys anything to drink?" When I'm in the kitchen, I grab a sweatshirt that's hanging on the back of a chair and pull it on.

After I've gotten everyone some coffee, Abby darts by in her Moe's uniform. "Have a nice visit."

She doesn't look at me. Just leaves.

Inside, I groan. I'll talk to her later. I can only handle one dumpster fire at a time.

36

ABIGAIL

My legs are lead blocks as I drag myself around the diner. I feel like a zombie, forcing smiles and going through the motions, all the while obsessing about what happened this morning at Nick's.

He called me his nanny.

Not his girlfriend.

Not his friend.

Not his roommate.

His nanny, the most impersonal option.

Maybe Nick didn't want to make waves with Gemma's family, or maybe he wasn't ready to say it in front of Hazel. I get it. But seeing as how I'm on the cusp of leaving for Europe, that hit me hard.

"I didn't order this." The woman in front of me makes a face. "I don't eat bacon. Those poor little pigs."

I don't have the patience I need for this job today, and my throat is hoarse from screaming at the game. "I'm so sorry." I place the pancakes with the extra bacon in front of her boyfriend and move his plate with the turkey bacon in front of her. I don't question her decision to forgo pork while enjoying fowl. "Can I get y'all anything else?"

Her boyfriend rubs his temple. "Got anything for hangovers? We partied a little too hard last night. Had to celebrate the Broncos' win."

That pulls a smile from my lips. "It was a phenomenal game." I might be upset with Nick, but I'm still his biggest fan. "Do you feel like beer or a mixed drink?" We just got our liquor license last month. Moe's hoping to boost sales with booze and fried appetizers, and it's working. That's why he begged me to come in to cover a double shift today at the last minute.

After I rattle off the drink options, I head to the back to get the customer's beverage.

"Can I get a mojito?" I call out to Moe as I use a napkin to remove a smudge in my glasses.

"It's only ten in the morning," he says as he scrambles eggs on the grill.

"I'm not their mom, Moe. You need a sign that says 'no alcoholic beverages sold before a certain time' if you don't want to sell it this early."

He rolls his eyes. "Why do ya always have to be so practical?"

I laugh and steal a French fry. "Put a cork in it, and get my drink."

He chuckles. "Flip these pancakes and I'll make it."

Frowning, I step up to the grill. "I'm not qualified to do this. What if I mess them up?" When he returns, he sighs at the mangled pancakes, and I shrug. "I tried. And you need a bartender."

After I drop off the mojito, the bell rings, and the noise in the room doubles with cheers. Jinxy, Mav, and Dax strut in, and Jinxy charges around the room with his arms in the air like a heavyweight boxer who knocked out his opponent.

I approach the group as the door opens again and Tiffany and Sheryl join them. "It'll be a wait for one of the booths."

Tiffany rolls her eyes, but Dax smiles and says it's not a problem. Jinxy throws his arm around my shoulders. "Hey, cutie. How's it going? Did ya see me kick ass yesterday?"

I cough from the fumes. "Jinxy, are you already drunk this morning, or is this from last night?"

"Yes." He shrugs, wobbles, and leans on me, the weight of him almost throwing us both to the ground. Fortunately, Dax reaches out and keeps us upright.

The group waits outside, and I'm finally able to seat them. They want a round of drinks, and I wrangle another waitress to make them because our orders will fall behind if Moe steps away to make that many beverages.

When I serve them, Jinxy practically chugs it. "I'm still celebratin'."

"I can see that. What can I get y'all to eat?"

The five of them are seated in the circular booth. Tiffany's all up in Jinxy's business right now.

He waves his drink at me. "We owe you, Abby Cadabby."

Abby Cadabby? Isn't that a Sesame Street character? "You owe me, huh?" He's drunk. I hope he's not driving today. I'll pull Dax aside later and make sure.

"You're single-handedly responsible for the Broncos going to the championship game."

I whip out my pen and notepad to jot down their orders. "Okay. Humor me. How did I manage this feat?"

"You did *all the things* to our boy."

Dax elbows him hard. "Shut the fuck up, man."

Tiffany has an evil smile on her face. "Don't tell him what to do. Spill the beans, Jinxy, baby."

He practically purrs at her. "Just saying that Abby should get the credit for fuckin' Nick senseless so he could relax and focus on football."

I glance around, embarrassed to be having this conversation in the middle of the diner. Lowering my voice, I ask, "He told you I fucked him senseless?" Nick's friends saw us together several times, but I'd never imagine he'd speak about our relationship so crassly. *Unless he's just using me for sex.* I press my hand against my stomach and look at Dax. "Nick said that? He used those words?"

"Ignore Jinxy. He's drunk. He doesn't know what he's talking about." But the sympathy in his expression makes me think there's some truth to what his friend is saying.

Jinxy bangs on the table. "The hell I don't. Our boy got his shit together 'cause Abby was putting out. C'mon. We all know he's bangin' his nanny. In fact, I told him he should. That it would help clear his thoughts and get him to chill the fuck out." And then he adds, "She's our little lucky charm."

Lucky charm? I blink several times as I try to catch my breath. *Not this again.*

With a toss of her hair, Tiffany cackles. "That's why you said to be patient because he'd be single come second semester!"

Oh my God. Is that true?

Have I been wrong about Nick all this time? Have I been sleeping with a man who talks about me like I'm some whore? Like I'm disposable? Like I mean nothing?

Was he stringing me along, putting off making any decisions about our relationship because he never planned to have one with me?

I stagger back.

This is just like Ezra.

I fell for another man who doesn't love me and likely never will.

ABIGAIL

Paige holds a box of tissues in front of me.

"Thanks." I sniffle.

"What happened after Jinxy word-vomited all of that stuff?" she asks.

"I ran to the bathroom and cried. Asked another waitress to cover my section, then told Moe I had a stomach virus. He had enough help. It's not like the nights I covered the entire diner by myself."

We're hanging out in her boyfriend's apartment. Marcus is out of town for a few days, so Paige is letting me crash here while he's gone. We're curled up on his couch as I regurgitate everything that happened today.

Baylee returns from the kitchen where she's been whipping up some snack called Puppy Chow. It's basically cereal, powdered sugar, peanut butter, and chocolate. I grab a handful and jam it in my mouth.

"This is amazing. I'm going to eat the whole bowl," I say as I crunch away.

"I used to make it for Maverick all the time in high school. It's his favorite. Now I make it for everyone but him."

I chuckle and wipe the tears that spill down my cheeks. "Savage."

"But necessary." Baylee sits on the floor in front of us and looks me over. "Maybe it's best that you found out the truth before you uprooted your life for this guy."

Paige shakes her head. "Is it possible Jinxy misremembered what Nick said? Or twisted it around somehow? You said he was drunk, and Jinxy talks shit when he's sober. I think he's taken too many hits to his head."

"You're right," I say slowly. "It's possible." But then I remember the look in Dax's eyes when Jinxy was going off. "Except I feel like Dax was trying to cover for Nick. Like he was trying to defuse the situation. And he had this look on his face like he felt sorry for me."

"Maybe he felt bad this was going down in front of that bitch Tiffany."

"Maybe." I bite the inside of my cheek. "It just makes me question everything, like how we almost always have sex the night before a game. Nick even said it helps him relax."

Paige squeezes my arm. "But don't most guys think that? You need to talk to Nick. Put your cards on the table. Ask him if he said all that. Ask him if he's serious about you."

I flop back on the couch. "He told Gemma's parents I'm his nanny. He couldn't have sounded more impersonal if he was introducing his grocer."

Baylee taps her phone on the coffee table with a long, manicured nail. "Have you ever checked out his old girlfriend's social media?"

I lift my head. "No. Should I have?" I figured if Nick wanted me to know something, he would've told me, but maybe that was naive.

She shrugs. "If it's not set to private, why not?" She flips over her phone and punches in the code. "What's her name again?"

"Gemma Kendrick. I think that's her last name."

Paige shakes her head. "I'm not sure this is a good idea."

Baylee shushes her. "It's a fucking awesome idea, and I'm glad I thought of it. Our girl needs to know what she's dealing with. If I was in her shoes, this is the first thing I would've done after I banged him." She scrolls around for a minute. "Found it." A minute later, she hisses. "You're right. This is probably a bad idea."

"You can't say that now." I hold my hand out. "Gimme the phone. Please. Whatever it is, I want to see it with my own eyes."

Wincing, she holds it to her chest. "This is going to make everything worse."

I swallow past the lump in my throat. "I'm tired of burying my head in the sand. I'd rather face this head on."

I tell myself I can handle it, but nothing prepares me for image after image of Nick and Gemma and their lovesick smiles. Or the shots of Nick, bare-chested, holding Hazel. Of the pics of Gemma gazing at Nick like he's her whole world. Of him grinning at her like he's never been happier.

All the photos stop around the week she died.

Two seconds later, I burst into tears. Because of what he lost. Because of how much he's been through. And because he'll probably never be really and truly mine. "He doesn't smile like that with me." He's beaming in every pic like he won the lottery.

I feel so stupid. Here I was, worried he'd succumb to the charms of some woman on campus when the truth is, he's probably still in love with Gemma.

Baylee sits on the other side of me, and she and Paige squish me in a hug, and my friends let me cry.

"I... I was just about... about to ask him if he wanted me to move in with him permanently." I sniffle. "I'm so glad I didn't. That's probably the last thing he wants."

My phone vibrates on the coffee table, and Nick's name flashes on the screen.

I watch it with an increasing sense of dread.

"Don't you want to answer it?" Baylee asks.

"No." Between Jinxy's comments and Gemma's Instagram, I feel so dumb. When it stops ringing, I text him that I'm staying with Paige tonight and that I'd like to talk to him tomorrow after practice. And then I turn off my phone.

I don't know how I'll face him or what I'll say, but maybe after a good night's rest, I'll find the words.

Because I don't have them tonight.

38

ABIGAIL

By morning, I'm feeling better. Paige was right. I shouldn't have looked at Gemma's social media.

I'm still upset about everything, but I can admit that my emotions got the best of me yesterday. It was a lot to process—Gemma's parents, Jinxy's comments, Tiffany, and those photos—all in one day. It overloaded me.

But I'm not holding my breath. I don't think Nick is going to make some deep declaration of love, but he's probably not the asshole I thought he was yesterday. He's been good to me. I know he cares.

That doesn't mean he wants to date me, though.

I close my eyes. *Please don't let what Jinxy said be true.* Because if it is, we're over. I don't see how we're not.

After class, I finally have the courage to turn on my phone. My eyes widen when I see that I have a ton of texts, the most recent from Denise. She says to call her ASAP, which I do.

"What's wrong?" I say as soon as she answers.

"Thank goodness you called me back. My father-in-law had a heart attack, and my husband and I have to catch a flight to Chicago, but Hazel needs to be picked up from preschool. I tried Nick and Cadence and got voicemail for both."

"Give me the directions, and I'll go now."

I've never driven Hazel around or picked her up, but Nick installed a car seat for her in case I ever needed to. He probably didn't want me driving her, given our fender bender last spring, but he never outright told me not to. I'll drive super slowly, just to be safe.

He'll see I can handle it.

When I pull up to the school, Hazel gets the biggest smile on her face when she sees me. "Hey, Hazelnut. Are you feeling better today?" I ask.

She hugs me and nods. "Better!"

"I'm so happy to hear that, honey. Let's get you checked out." I talk to her teacher for a few minutes and show her my ID. Fortunately, I'm one of the people who has permission to pick up Hazel.

See, silly? Nick won't mind you driving his daughter.

But after I get Hazel strapped into her car seat, I'm afraid to make any mistakes. I'll never hear the end of it if something happened to Hazel while I was driving. I'm so apprehensive, the car behind me honks to go faster. I don't know why I'm so paranoid about this.

"Okay! Hold your horses." I press my foot on the accelerator, and the whole car jerks several times. What the hell?

Shit. That's probably my transmission.

My car's never done this before. I've kept it in first and second gear without a problem, but this is worse than my clutch slipping.

Please, please make it home.

We're on the edge of campus. Students are jaywalking en masse, probably trying to get to class on time, and one dummy almost gets hit by an SUV. Has no one ever heard of a crosswalk?

"Abby, my tummy hurts again."

Ugh. "Do you think you might puke again?" Please say no.

She's quiet for a long minute. "Maybe."

Dang it.

I'm a bundle of nerves as I drive. The car jerks whenever I stop at lights and sputters along the way like it's having a hard time locking into gear. This is not good.

A van is waiting to turn at the intersection I'm stopped at. I have my blinker on, prepared to make a right as soon as that van clears it.

I inch forward. "Hang on, Hazel. We'll be home in just a bit."

"I don't feel good, Abby." She lets out a loud burp, and I look behind me.

"You okay?"

"Yeah."

"Did you puke?"

"No."

Thank you, Jesus.

The van clears, and I hit the gas to make my turn.

Almost home.

But there's a loud crunch of metal, and my car jerks to the right. Hazel screams in the back, and I yank the wheel to keep from going off the road. The van in front of me swerves, which seems to drag us down the road. Eventually, we come to a stop.

"Hazel! Are you okay?"

"Y-yeah, but my neck huwts."

Damn it. "Okay, baby, hang on."

At first, I'm not sure what happened, how I ended up tangled with that van, but then I see it. The utility trailer that was attached to the rear.

The one I just smacked into.

I thump my forehead onto my steering wheel.

Pretty sure Nick is going to lose it when he finds out what happened.

39

NICK

We're just wrapping up our team lunch when I get a slew of texts and messages. For some reason, this side of the field house is a cell phone dead zone.

I'm relieved to see a message from Abby.

Yesterday was a shit show. My plan had been to take her and Hazel to lunch, then try to get some time alone with Abby and ask if she wanted to make plans with me for the future, to see if she'd like to stick around second semester.

Then Hazel got sick and almost caught us in bed together.

Things went downhill after that.

Abby took off so fast when Gemma's family stopped by, and I haven't had a chance to smooth things over. She was obviously upset. I admit I didn't handle things well. I was hoping to talk to her when she got home last night, but she stayed with Paige, which I'm guessing can't be good.

My heart skips a beat when I read her first message.

We were in an accident.

Who's we? Her and Paige?

But it gets worse.

Hazel might have whiplash.

The EMTs are taking her to the hospital.
I'm so sorry!!!

My vision goes blurry, and I have to lean against a pillar. Why was Abby driving Hazel? Denise is supposed to pick her up from preschool.

Oh, fuck. Hazel's in the hospital.

I bolt across the field house and out into the parking lot. People call out my name, teammates asking where I'm going, as I jump into my car and take off. All of the worst-case scenarios rush through my head. I try calling Abby, but it goes straight to voicemail.

By the time I reach the hospital, I'm jumping out of my skin with worry. A nurse directs me through the ER and when I reach Hazel's room, the sight of my little girl lying on that gurney, pale and still, makes bile push up the back of my throat.

"Hazel?" I force my legs forward and take her cold hand in mine.

Relief pours through me when she opens her eyes. "Daddy?" The moment she sees me, she starts to wail. She's wearing a thick neck brace.

"Honey, don't move. Let me talk to a doctor. Does your neck hurt?"

"Y-yes."

Why is she here by herself? "Where's Abby?"

"The police took her."

I close my eyes. The little voice in the back of my head that warned me months ago that she shouldn't be driving Hazel gets louder. "Let me find the doctor, okay? They probably want you to lie still until they can check you out." I dry her tears. "I'm here now. I promise everything is going to be okay." It'd better fucking be okay because I don't know what I'll do if it's not.

Her lower lip quivers, but she whispers, "Okay."

"I love you, Hazel. And I'm so proud of you. You're doing great."

Another tear drips down her cheek. "Love you too, Daddy."

"I'll be right back. I promise I won't be gone long, okay?"

My phone keeps buzzing in my pocket, and I finally grab it. There are several messages from Dax. He missed the team lunch for some reason.

Bro, is Abby okay? I think she was in an accident this afternoon.

This is her car, right?

Then he sends a short video. Someone else must've been driving him because it's shot from the passenger side as he passes an ambulance, Abby's car, and some kind of utility trailer that's attached to a van.

I'm immediately relieved when I see Abby standing next to her car talking to a policeman. Thank God she's okay.

But then I see her car.

It's shredded, like someone took a can opener and sliced open the driver's side panel.

What the fuck happened? She and Hazel could've been killed.

My breath shallows. I'm not sure I can handle losing anyone else I love in another car wreck. The lights flicker, and I realize it's me, not the lights.

Hazel. I told her I wouldn't be gone long.

I stagger toward the nurses' station, but stop short when I see Abby talking to a cop a few feet away down another hallway. Her back is to me.

"Miss, the driver behind you says you were driving erratically," the policeman says.

She was driving erratically? My jaw tightens.

Abby shakes her head and mumbles something, but I can't make it out. The cop jots down notes. "So you think your car was jerking back and forth because of your transmission? How long have you known you had a problem?"

She looks down. "Several weeks."

Fuck. Abby drove Hazel when she knew her car was having trouble?

"And you didn't think you should get that fixed?"

"I couldn't afford it. As long as I kept it in first or second gear, the clutch didn't slip."

Her clutch was slipping? Why the hell didn't she mention that?

The cop frowns at her. "If you couldn't afford it, you shouldn't have been driving the vehicle."

My thoughts exactly. It's bad enough that she drove it, much less picked up Hazel.

Her shoulders slump, but she doesn't say anything.

"What about the utility trailer?" he asks. "You didn't see it? Because the van had the right of way."

Jesus, Abigail.

Her voice wavers, like she's about to cry. "I was afraid the little girl I take care of, Hazel, was going to throw up."

I don't hear the rest of what she says, but the cop says, "So you thought she was going to vomit, and then you turned around to look at her—in the middle of an intersection?"

I almost don't hear her response because blood is pounding in my ears.

"That's—no, that's not how it happened. You're twisting around my words."

"I'm trying to figure out why you would hit the gas and ram a utility trailer in the middle of an intersection when he had the green light and the right of way."

Her voice rises. "I didn't see the trailer. Just the van, which I thought had cleared the intersection. Why would I deliberately hit it?"

"Look, bystanders say you darted into the middle of the intersection after driving erratically and struck the trailer. Fortunately, you passed the field sobriety test, but after talking to everyone involved and witnesses, I'm going to have to write you a ticket."

"What? No. I swear I didn't see the utility trailer, and my transmission is why my speed wasn't consistent."

"Ma'am, you shouldn't have been driving that vehicle in the first place."

"But the jerking didn't start until today."

The cop gives her a look like he doesn't believe her. He tears off a sheet of paper and hands it to her. "You're lucky I'm not giving you a ticket for reckless driving. That's a class B misdemeanor, punishable by up to thirty days in jail."

She gasps. "Jail time!"

"Consider yourself lucky."

Livid doesn't begin to describe what I'm feeling right now.

When he walks away, I say her name.

Because we have to talk. Now.

40

ABIGAIL

"Abigail."

My stomach falls when I hear Nick's voice. I turn around and prepare myself for another interrogation. Hopefully, he'll understand. I just need him to listen to me and not jump to conclusions, but the moment I see his face, dread forms in the pit of my stomach. "Did... did you hear that whole conversation?"

His nostrils flare. "What I heard is that you drove Hazel in an unsafe car. What were you thinking?"

My eyes well with tears, and I curse under my breath. Now is not the time to cry, but I can admit I'm a basket case after everything that's happened today. Lifting my glasses, I wipe my eyes. "I was thinking that Denise couldn't pick her up, and she couldn't reach you, so rather than leaving Hazel at school, I skipped class and picked her up myself." I've never skipped class. Not once.

His jaw works back and forth. "See, the thing about staying at school until perhaps Cadence could get her is my daughter would be safe."

I can't hold back the tears anymore. "You're okay with Cadence driving her but not me?"

"She has a perfect driving record."

I already know Cadence is perfect in every way, but it's good to know Nick prefers Cadence over me.

He pinches the bridge of his nose. "The cop said you were driving recklessly. So much so that he had to give you a fucking field sobriety test. That you, what, blew through a red light to turn? That you couldn't just wait until you had the green light?"

"Did you hear the part about Hazel almost throwing up?"

"Did she? Did she vomit?"

"Well, no, but—"

"Then why are you blaming her for your accident?"

I knew I shouldn't have expected Nick to understand what happened today. "I'm not blaming her. You're twisting everything around. That's not how it happened."

"Why didn't you just fix your transmission if it was so bad?"

Because I bought your letterman instead, asshole. Because I was going to pay you the rent I owed you. Because I wanted to eat more than ramen on my stupid trip, a trip I don't even know if I can afford anymore.

But my mouth won't cooperate. I can't force out the words. And even if I did, he won't believe me.

A choked sound comes from the back of my throat, and I burst into tears. "Does it matter?"

He doesn't say anything at first, but then he looks away, a pained expression on his face. "I'm sorry, Abby. I know you had a terrible afternoon, and I'm glad you weren't hurt, but... I don't think you should watch my daughter anymore."

I suck in a breath. *He doesn't want me around Hazel?*

This is what it feels like to get stabbed in the chest.

I knew this man was going to break my heart. I'm so stupid.

With the back of my hand, I try to wipe the tears, but the torrent keeps coming. For some reason, it's at this moment I remember Tiffany's cruel words that Nick doesn't want me around in the spring anyway. That, according to Jinxy, Nick was just banging me to win football games. And let's not forget that he introduced me as "the nanny" to Gemma's parents.

"I guess you don't need your lucky charm anymore, hmm? You've already won all of your games." Because, obviously, this is a breakup. It's not like Nick wants me to stay at his house when he doesn't need me to babysit anymore.

Why am I standing here crying when he obviously doesn't give a damn about me?

He frowns at me. "What does that mean?"

Rolling my eyes, I sneer, "Ask Jinxy." I shake my head. "It's funny that I thought you were such a great guy."

Turning on my heel, I head for the exit.

"Abby, wait."

I start to run, and he doesn't follow me.

Why am I not surprised?

41

NICK

A MILLION TESTS LATER, I finally get the green light to take Hazel home. She yawns in my arms as I carry her out of the hospital.

When we exit the ER doors, my lungs expand for the first time since I got the message Hazel was in a car accident.

Hands down, today was the second worst day of my life. I'm just grateful my daughter is okay. The doctor says she'll be sore for a while.

After I get her situated in her car seat and I start my SUV, my first instinct is to call Abby and let her know we're headed home.

Except...

I cringe. I said some pretty harsh shit to her this afternoon.

Tilting my head back on the seat, I stare at the roof. Maybe I should get her some roses or buy her dinner. But I'm not sure that'll cut it.

"Hazel, when Abby picked you up from school, did your tummy bother you?"

"It stawted to huwt."

I get a sinking feeling in my chest. "Honey, did you think you might puke?"

"Yup. I kept buwping."

Shit. I totally railroaded Abby when she tried to explain how she was worried about my daughter. And now that I'm sitting in my car, as I think about the logistics of Hazel in the back seat, if I heard her burping after puking the day before, I'd be twisting back to check on her too.

I pinch the bridge of my nose.

If I got that screwed up, what else did I get wrong?

I'm still not crazy that Abby was driving with a jacked-up transmission, but she said it only started malfunctioning today. The cop didn't look like he believed her, but why didn't I? She's never lied to me before.

On the other hand, she did admit her clutch was slipping before today... I blow out a breath. She was probably trying to get some more mileage out of the damn thing. Transmissions are expensive to fix. I can't blame her for hoping she could keep it running longer.

When I put all of that together—her car acting weird and Hazel burping in the back seat—it's no wonder she might've been a little distracted. But Abby is the most responsible person I know. She always takes great care of my daughter. Always does fun activities with her. Keeps her well fed and clean. Listens to her when she chatters.

Even when I think back to the fender bender we had last spring when Ezra was harassing her, I have to admit it wasn't entirely her fault. That parking lot was dark, and I was parked at a weird angle. I can see how she didn't notice me in her rearview mirror.

There's a reason why I put a car seat in her vehicle. It's because I trust her.

So why the fuck didn't I give her the benefit of the doubt today?

God, I'm a dick.

As I drive home, I think about how I can make it up to her.

Apologizing is a good place to start, but what else? I know I hurt her feelings. I should've waited until we were home, when I had calmed down, to talk about what happened, but I was really pissed when I heard the cop recapping everything from his notes.

That's no excuse, though.

Abby's car isn't in the driveway when we pull up. Maybe she had it towed to her mechanic's.

When we cross the threshold, I'm about to call out her name, but the house is quiet and still.

Something's not right.

I situate Hazel on the couch. "I'll make you some dinner in just a bit." I click on her favorite show and then head to Abby's room.

Which is empty.

Most of her stuff is gone. Her clothes. Her shoes. Her toiletries. She only left behind her bed and three other things.

The beanbag still sits in the corner, and in the center of the bed is the jersey I gave her and a thick envelope of cash. There's a note. It says, "Here's my part of the rent and utilities. Sorry it was late."

That's it. That's all it says.

Abby left. She's gone. And it's my fault.

I sit on the bed and drop my head into my hands.

What the fuck did I do?

42

NICK

"So you won't tell me where Abby is?" I ask Baylee as I pace in the backyard. I had to call Maverick to get her number. Paige wasn't answering, and Baylee's the only other person I thought might know something.

"Nick, let me put it this way. When you pull your head out of your ass, then we can talk."

"I've left her several messages apologizing."

"That's not enough."

I shake my head. What the fuck does she want from me? "Look, I obviously upset her with how I handled the car accident."

"Here's a hint. You were an asshole long before that."

"What did I do? How can I apologize for something if I don't know what it is?"

She hums in the back of her throat. "Why don't you ask Jinxy?"

I freeze. What the hell does that mean? "Abby mentioned something about Jinxy this afternoon."

"Ding, ding, ding."

"And you're not going to tell me what it is?"

"Why should I help you? You broke her heart. Congratulations. Hope football is worth it."

Click.

Damn. I broke her heart?

But what does football have to do with this?

I pull up Jinxy's number, but get his voicemail. "Hey, it's Nick. I need to talk to you about something. Call me back."

The asshole doesn't call back.

I lie in bed all night and replay that conversation I had with Abby in the hospital. Why wasn't I more patient? Why didn't I hug her and tell her I was grateful she and Hazel were okay? Why did I assume the worst?

But more importantly, why haven't I told her I love her?

My heart pounds and my eyes sting. I can't believe I lost her, and this time it was my own damn fault.

I can admit it to myself now—I love Abby. With my whole heart and soul. In a way I've never experienced before.

That's what I've been having trouble processing. That I love her more than Gemma. Seeing her parents on Sunday drove that home.

I'll always have a special place in my heart for Hazel's mom, but being with Abby makes me realize how much Gemma and I glossed over things to be together for Hazel's sake. In the wake of her death, I think I romanticized our relationship because it felt wrong to remember the times we argued or bickered. And after we had Hazel, we argued a lot.

Being with Abby is like what I expected my relationship with Gemma to be like, but it never was, and that made me feel guilty as fuck.

Everything about Abby felt right, from having her live with us to the way she clicked with Hazel to how she always seemed to understand the pressure I'm under.

When my alarm goes off in the morning, I'd love nothing more than to pull the covers over my head, but I have to get to the field house to weightlift, and since Denise isn't back from Chicago yet, and Cadence can't help this morning, I need to bring Hazel with me.

The doorbell rings, and I see a FedEx truck in front of my house. When I open the door, the delivery guy hands me a tablet. "Sign here." Then he hands me a giant box.

I don't remember ordering anything online. I set the box on the coffee table and tear it open.

It's a new letterman jacket.

I hold it up and turn it around. It has my name, number, and football patch. Did Coach order this for me? He was irritated with me a few weeks ago for not having my letterman for a team picture, and I had to borrow one and hide the fact that it wasn't really mine.

It's sucked to not have my jacket, but I couldn't spend that much money to replace it.

At the bottom of the box, there's a slip. When I read the names, I wince. "Jesus." My name is listed under "Ship To" but Abby's name is listed under "Paid By." My eyes widen when I see the amount.

That girl has busted her ass waiting tables all semester so she could go on her trip, and instead of saving up for that or fixing her car, she bought me a new letterman.

Of course, I had to lecture her yesterday about not repairing her transmission. No wonder Baylee wants to lop off my balls with a rusty blade.

I grab my cell and pull up Abby's name. When I get voicemail again, I clear my throat. "Abby, I know you don't wanna talk to me, and I don't blame you. I was an asshole yesterday. I can't apologize to you enough. I got your gift today. I received my new letterman. Baby, thank you. You are such a thoughtful woman, and I don't deserve you. Please call me back. Let me make this up to you."

As much as I'd love to sit on my ass today and wallow, I need to get Hazel up. I trudge into the kitchen and pour some coffee. As I chug some down, I stare at the calendar on the fridge. We have a month before our quarterfinal playoff game. Finals are next week.

But the date I can't stop thinking about is two weeks from tomorrow, the day Abby leaves for London.

I'm not sure how to track her down, but one thing is clear—I have to talk to her before her flight.

Or I might never see her again.

43

NICK

Hazel yawns, and that parental guilt I'm so familiar with spreads through my veins.

"Sorry you have to come to work out with me this morning," I tell her as I unclip her car seat. I hate that I have to drag Hazel around campus, starting with my early morning weightlifting session. The doctor said he doesn't want her running around at school for a few days. I wish I could keep her home today, but I can't slack before the playoffs. I'll carry her so she doesn't overexert herself.

I already gave Coach a heads-up I was bringing Hazel with me, and he said it wasn't a problem.

"It's okay, Daddy. I'll col-a."

I love this kid. She's so understanding. "Which coloring books are you going to work on today?"

Her little lips purse. She takes coloring very seriously. "Cindawella or Snow White."

"Will you do one for me? So I can put it in my locker?"

She gives me a brilliant smile. "Yes! Can I make one for Abby?"

My heart sinks when I think of her empty bedroom. "Of course." Now I just need to find her.

"When's she coming home?"

"Hopefully soon, honey."

I'm grateful Hazel doesn't really understand what's going on. I told her Abby was going to visit her parents for a few days.

I head for the trainers' offices, which surround the weight room. I'll be able to keep an eye on Hazel while I work out because it has giant glass windows. There's an extra desk she can use.

"Honey, I'll be right out here weightlifting. If you need anything, just open this door and call out to me, but don't go anywhere. The field house is too big for you to go wandering around. Promise me you'll stay put."

"I pwomise."

I pick her up and point out the machines I'm using this morning so she knows where to look. "I won't be far. Work on that picture for me, and let me know if your neck hurts." I brought ibuprofen if she needs it, and we'll use a heat pack when we get home later.

"Okay! I'll col-a a good picture for you, Daddy."

I pause. She's starting to say her Rs correctly. "That's my girl." I get her seated and kiss the top of her head.

Dax is on a treadmill a few steps away, so I ask him to keep an eye out for Hazel while I change in the locker room, and I'm back in less than two minutes.

When I return, I hop on the machine next to him. "Thanks for watching her, man." I turn up the treadmill and warm up with a jog.

"Don't take this the wrong way, but you look like shit."

I let out a weak laugh. "I feel like shit, so you're not off base." I hate talking about my personal life, but I could use some advice. There are only a few other guys here, and they're on the other side of the room. "Abby moved out yesterday. I said some stupid shit to her after the accident, and when I got Hazel home from the hospital, she was gone. But she left the jersey I gave her and rent money."

He hisses. "Damn. Sorry to hear that."

"I know I upset her, but moving out? That seems extreme. Especially after she went through the trouble of buying me another letterman."

"Those are expensive as hell. That girl must really love you."

The thought that Abby might reciprocate my feelings shoots a streak of hope through me. If she loves me, maybe we can work this out. Maybe she'll hear me out. Maybe she'll forgive me.

"I feel like a giant asshole for yelling at her. I know she loves Hazel and would do anything for her. I don't know why I lost my cool."

We run in silence for a few minutes before he glances at me. "Cut yourself some slack. You and Hazel have been through a lot. I get why you blew up at Abby. You can make it up to her. Just be sure to grovel."

I turn up the treadmill. "I'd be happy to if I could track her down." After a minute, he gives me a look. "What?"

"Did, uh... Did she mention what happened at Moe's on Sunday?"

"Please don't tell me something terrible went down because Gemma's parents stopped by that morning." I wince. "I introduced Abby as Hazel's nanny."

"Shit. Well, this is worse. I figured she would've hashed it out with you Sunday night."

That makes the hair at my nape stand on end. "Hash what out? She stayed with Paige Sunday night, so we never talked about whatever happened at work."

"Don't shoot the messenger."

This gets worse by the minute. I stop the treadmill and turn to Dax. "Spit it out." Just then, the door opens, and several of the guys join us. I spot Jinxy clowning around with Maverick over by the water fountain. "Does this have anything to do with Jinxy?"

Dax pauses his machine. "I'm not a fan of ratting out friends, but I think you need the whole picture if you wanna win your girl back." After he glances over his shoulder, he lowers his voice. "But take this with a grain of salt. Jinxy was drunk off his ass."

"On a Sunday morning?"

"It's more like he never stopped drinking the night before. Anyway, Abby was our waitress, and he said something like she deserved the credit for our win. That she was your lucky charm."

Frowning, I look over at Jinxy. "What does that mean?"

Dax makes a face, then glances away. "Jinxy thanked her for fucking your brains out so you could focus on football."

"What the fuck?" I literally feel the pulse in my neck. "What exactly did he say?"

"Something about how we all knew you were banging your nanny. That he encouraged it because it would clear your thoughts and get you to relax. That she put out and helped you get your shit together." I'm gonna kill that asshole. "But it gets worse," he says again.

"How the hell could it get worse?"

"Tiffany was there." Christ. Nothing good happens when that girl's around. "She was like, 'Ohhh! That's why you said he'd be single second semester.'"

I close my eyes. "Jinxy said that to Tiffany at the carnival. He told me it was to get her off my back so Abby and I could work things out."

You know that expression, seeing red? When Jinxy struts by with a giant smile on his face, that's what happens. I see red.

"Motherfucker." I leap off the treadmill and slam him to the wall. I'd love nothing more than to punch his teeth in, but my daughter is a few feet away. I glance over there, and she's blissfully ignorant that I'm seconds away from kicking Jinxy's ass. "Why the fuck would you say all that shit to Abby at the diner?"

His eyes widen. "I—I... shit. I don't know, bro. It just slipped out." He holds up his hands. "I was drunk. I thought she'd be like all the other girls who want some football dick. Grateful she had a role in your success."

I shove him back against the wall again. "I love that woman, you asshole. I think I wanna marry her someday." The honesty of that statement shocks the hell out of me, but as I consider those words, it feels right. I want Abby in my life. Permanently.

"Jesus, bro. I'm sorry. How was I supposed to know that? You're sealed up tighter than Fort Knox. Maybe if you shared your feelings once in a while, I'd know—"

"You'd know you shouldn't treat women like trash?"

He holds up his hands. "Let Jinxy make it up to you."

"Stop talking about yourself in third person, Jankowitz."

His mouth drops open. "Why would you call me that? I thought we were friends. That's just mean."

"It's your name, asshole."

"Hey, you two!" Coach yells as he points at me and Jinxy. "Hallway. Now."

I look around the weight room, and all the guys are watching us. Fuck. I've never fought with a teammate before, much less weeks before the playoffs. I'm pretty sure Coach is gonna rip us new ones.

Jinxy and I walk over to Coach, and I immediately apologize for disrupting everyone's morning.

"What's going on?" he asks.

When Jinxy opens his mouth, I give him a look that shuts

him up. "I've been dating this girl Abby, Abigail Dawson, one of the women who takes care of Hazel."

Coach's eyebrows lift. "Ezra's ex?"

"Yes, sir."

Jinxy makes a noise of disbelief. "You never said you were *dating* her."

"I don't need to explain my shit to you." Even if Abby and I never formally solidified things, I was in her bed every night. That woman is mine. My inner caveman seethes and beats his chest.

Coach holds up his hands between us and motions for me to continue, so I explain what this idiot told Abby.

Coach glares at Jinxy when I'm done. "You really said those things to that sweet girl? What the hell is wrong with you? I'm going to tell Roxy and she'll light your ass on fire."

I forgot his daughter is friends with Abby.

"No! Don't do that. Please, sir. Roxy's little, but she's fierce."

"You should be scared of her." Coach crosses his arms as he stares down Jinxy. "You have bathroom duty for the next two weeks."

I chuckle as a look of horror grows on my teammate's face. "You mean I have to clean the toilets every day?"

"I expect them to sparkle in the morning. By the way, I'm ordering the team chili dogs tomorrow."

"What?" Jinxy's eyes widen. "No, Coach. Not chili dogs!"

Coach must be pissed because we usually get grilled chicken and veggies for team lunches.

He points a finger in my teammate's face. "And I'll be sure to tell the maintenance crew not to touch the toilets. Maybe you'll learn a little respect. Son, I never want to hear you talking to a woman like that again. I want to win football games, but if you graduate and don't know how to conduct yourself, I've failed my job."

"Sorry, Coach."

After Jinxy walks away, Coach turns to me. "I understand why you're upset, but you either need to hash things out with Jinxy and get over it, or set your feelings aside until the playoffs are done." He rests his hand on my shoulder and gives me one of those looks. "I'm relying on you to put the team first."

Isn't that what I've always done? Maybe if I'd put Abby first, even once, she would've given me the benefit of the doubt and stayed to work things out.

44

NICK

My professor points to the tray, and I drop my exam in with the rest of the finals. "Good luck in the playoffs," he says.

"Thank you, sir." I smile even though I don't feel like it.

Abby's been gone eleven days, and each one is more torturous than the last.

It's given me a lot of perspective. This entire semester, I've been obsessed with football and making the playoffs. That's nothing new. What's new is now that I've had an undefeated season and am days away from achieving a lifelong dream, I can't seem to find any joy in it.

After practice, I drag my ass home. I get Hazel to bed and then flop on the couch.

I grab my phone and stare at Abby's number. Pretty sure she blocked me. I'm so tempted to call her, but what can I say if she doesn't wanna talk to me?

A knock on the door has me leaping off the couch. My heart is in my throat as I open it. Except it's not Abby. It's Jinxy, Dax, and Maverick.

"What are y'all doing here?" And why is Jinxy carrying a whiteboard?

They push past me, and Mav smacks me on the back. "We think you've been moping long enough."

"I'm not going out tonight, so if that's why you're here—"

"It's not, bro." Jinxy puts the whiteboard on my coffee table. "We wanna help you win your girl back."

I blow out a breath. "Don't you think you've done enough? Are you here because you're afraid I won't play well without Abby in my bed? Because if that's why—"

"I swear it's not. I feel bad for being an asshole. Just wanna make it up to you. To Abby too. So I thought I'd gather the hive mind and see if we could figure out something. That's why I brought the whiteboard and ordered us some pizza. My treat."

I'm out of ideas, so I guess it can't hurt to see what my friends think. We sit around my living room, and a few minutes later, the food arrives. The guys woof it down, but all I can do is think about how much I've messed up with Abby. "I'm not sure she's even listened to my messages."

Jinxy grabs a pen, writes my name on the board, and draws an arrow to the word 'Blocked.'

"Thanks for spelling that out for me," I say dryly.

"What about her friends? Paige and Baylee. Who else does she hang out with?"

I shrug. "Maybe Cadence? But she says she hasn't spoken to Abby. I've already tried calling Paige and Baylee. Paige won't return my calls, and Baylee told me to pull my head outta my ass."

The guys chuckle and Mav smirks. "My girl is feisty as fuck."

His girl? "Are you two a thing?"

"Nah. We grew up together. Have always been close."

Jinxy lifts an eyebrow. "Close as in you've stuck your dick in her?"

"Watch your fucking mouth. Baylee is out of your league, so don't even think about trying to get with her."

Hmm. I'm sure there's a story there, but Mav's love life is none of my business, and I'd like to keep it that way.

I clear my throat. "Jinxy, remember what Coach said, that you need to watch how you talk about women? Not sure you want to continue cleaning the toilets."

"Oh, shit. You're right. I'm sorry I talked about Baylee like that, Maverick."

Mav rolls his eyes, and Dax chuckles, then looks at his phone. "Okay, let's focus 'cause I have a date in an hour. Has anyone seen Abby since the day of the accident?"

Anytime I'm on campus, I can't help looking for her. "I haven't. I was hoping she'd stop by the cafeteria, and I've even walked around the Education building a few times, but I haven't spotted her anywhere, not even the diner. Moe told me she gave away all of her shifts." Which isn't like her at all. I hate that I'm the reason she flipped her life around. That she's been so upset about what happened between us, she disappeared.

Jinxy helpfully writes M.I.A. on the board.

After discussing this with my friends for the next twenty minutes, I start to think it's a hopeless cause. "Is it possible she went home already? She could've wrapped up her finals this week."

"Where does she live?" Dax asks.

"San Antonio. I'd drive down there this weekend if I knew where her family lived."

"You should definitely take her flowers."

Jinxy writes 'flowers' and 'dick pics' on the board, and I shake my head. "Dick pics?"

"Bro, it works for me every time. You should try it. Maybe set some nice mood lighting and find your best angle. Show her what she's missing. You could dress it up in a little outfit, like one of those Wiener Warmers or get yourself a nice top hat for an elegant yet jaunty vibe."

A top hat. For my dick.

Dax snorts, and I have a hard time not laughing.

Mav tilts his head. "Depending on what you're working with, it can be effective."

What the hell is wrong with my friends? I ignore the dick pic suggestion. "I'm not sure flowers would cut it at this point, but I can't even do that without her address."

Jinxy points at me. "That's what we should focus on. What you're gonna do to get her to forgive us."

"Us?" I ask.

"Yeah. I don't want her to be mad at me. She's gonna be your woman, and you'll be all domesticated, but if she doesn't forgive me, I won't be invited over to your shindigs, and Jinxy hates being the odd man out."

I think about how to get her to forgive me. "I wish I could prove Abby didn't cause that accident. Because I researched utility trailers, and they cause all kinds of accidents if they're not hitched properly."

Jinxy scratches the back of his head. "What about a Triple-A membership? That way if she gets in another fender bender, her car can get towed for free?" He taps his temple like he's a genius and writes 'emergency roadside service' on his dumb board.

"Hold up." Dax taps on the coffee table. "I know someone who has her address back home."

"Who?"

He makes a face. "Your favorite person. The one guy I'm sure you're dying to talk to."

I slouch back on the couch. "Ezra."

Mav lets out a whistle, and Jinxy sketches a dick and balls with an arrow of what I can only assume is spooge that points to the name Ezra Thomas.

Shit. Now I have to call that asshole.

Dax smacks me on the back. "Let us know how it goes."

Jinxy throws his arms around me. "For real, bro."

I pat his shoulder. "You're laying it on kinda thick, Jinxy."

"I have a guilty soul. I'm trying to make amends here."

Mav yanks Jinxy away and yells, "Good luck," as they head out the door.

After I lock up, I grab my phone and pull up that douchebag's number. What do I say to him? He made my life hell on the team last year with all of his little passive-aggressive tactics. I pace up and down my living room a few times to gather my thoughts.

As much as I hate this guy and loathe the idea of needing him for anything, I love Abby more.

Here goes nothing.

Ezra answers on the third ring. "Well, well, well. If it isn't Nick Silva. What the hell do you want?"

"Nice to talk to you too, man."

"Cut the crap."

I rub my jaw. "I need a favor."

"Fat chance I'm gonna do you one."

"Then let me put it this way. I need a favor for Abby." When he doesn't say anything, I glance at my phone. Did he hang up? "Hello?"

"What's wrong with Abby?"

I'm surprised by what sounds like genuine concern in his voice. "I'm gonna be honest here, okay? She and I have been seeing each other, and I hurt her feelings. I didn't mean to be an asshole, but now she won't call me back, and I really need to talk to her. I know you two go way back, and I was hoping you'd give me her address in San Antonio."

He chuckles. "Fuck off. I'm not helping you with shit."

I take a deep breath to keep calm. "Ezra, you and I have had our differences, but that has nothing to do with Abby. She was a great girlfriend to you, and how did you thank her? You slept with every girl in Charming while you were fucking engaged. You stomped on that poor girl's heart when all she did was support you." Just thinking about how he treated her makes me want to kick his ass. "The least you can do is help me right now. All I want to do is apologize to her in person. That's it."

He's quiet again. "What do I get in return?"

Jesus, he's a prick. I want to tell him maybe it'll lessen his time in hell, but that probably isn't a productive thing to say. "Maybe she'll hate you less."

He sighs. "She really does hate me."

How did Jinxy phrase it? "Think of this as a way to make amends."

"What if you piss her off more by showing up?"

"I plan to beg for her forgiveness."

He hums. "Did you cheat too?"

"Fuck no. I'm not an idiot."

"I'm just not good at impulse control. It's not my strength, bro." Ezra sighs again. "I know I was a terrible boyfriend."

"So... will you help me?" *Please*. I close my eyes, hoping that something I say resonates with him. "I love Abby, and I don't know what I'll do if I lose her."

After a beat of silence, he laughs. "You sound so fucked right now. What the hell? Fine. But if she gets pissed when you show up, I'm gonna deny helping you."

Thick, hot relief pours through me. Ezra's a grade-A asshole, but I can't deny that this is huge.

Now I just need to get Abby to forgive me.

45

ABIGAIL

My mom nudges me. "Honey, pass the popcorn."

I set down my crochet needle, grab the bowl from the side table, and hand it to her.

She wanted to watch *It's a Wonderful Life* this afternoon. That's her go-to holiday movie. My dad escaped to his workshop in the garage while I've been crocheting emotional support pickles. I've made a half dozen so far.

A coffee commercial comes on. The young man returns from military service and sneaks into his parents' house, presumably on Christmas, and makes a pot of coffee. His little sister tiptoes down to the kitchen, sees him, and runs into his arms.

My tear ducts sting, and I try to wipe them without my mom noticing, but she side-eyes me when I sniffle. "Are you crying because of a coffee commercial?"

"Nope. Just some dust in the air."

The look on her face tells me she doesn't believe me. "Are you sure you're okay? You've been so quiet since you got home. You didn't want to play Scrabble last night, and this morning, when I handed you a plate of waffles, you looked at me like I was the Devil."

I chuckle. "Sorry, Mom. My stomach hasn't been right since I got food poisoning. I think I had some bad nachos. And then everything with Nick threw me off my game."

When I got home yesterday, I finally gave her the basics of my living situation. That I worked for a single dad who I started dating, that we broke up, and that I really didn't want a lecture.

To my surprise, all she did was hug me.

"I bet you just need a good probiotic." Then she clenches her faux pearl necklace and whispers, "Abigail, I can't believe you were dating Nick Silva. Ezra's mother is going to poop her pants."

"Please don't say anything to her. Nick and I are over anyway." It was just easier to tell my mom I was dating Nick than to explain he and I had crazy monkey sex without any kind of commitment.

Her lips tug down, and she grabs my hand. "I know you don't want to talk about it, but I'm here if you change your mind."

"Thanks."

"If you want to visit your friends while you're in town, you can borrow my car."

"Aren't you afraid I'm just going to plow it into a utility trailer?" Because the worst things constantly happen to me. Baylee was worried about my trip, so she saged me to cleanse me of my bad juju before I left Charming.

Mom wraps me in a tight hug. "I'm just glad you and Hazel weren't hurt."

When I told my parents I totaled my car, I assumed they'd be pissed, but they were only worried I'd been injured. My mom even drove out to Charming to pick me up after my last final yesterday.

I try not to think about the accident. It reminds me of that argument with Nick, and I'll do anything to not think about him.

My mom nudges me again. "Maybe tomorrow we can get your phone replaced."

"Tomorrow's Sunday."

"Oh, then on Monday. I'm officially on winter break too."

"Sure. If you want." I accidentally left my phone at a laundromat the day after I moved out of Nick's house. By the time I figured out I had lost it and returned to the Laundro-rama, it was gone. I didn't have the money to replace it and was still too upset to pick up shifts at Moe's, so I figured I'd just wait until I got home to get another one.

I've been wondering what Nick's messages said. He'd left me a few before I lost my phone, but I hadn't had the guts to listen to them. But it's not like any good could come from that. It's clear Nick's still in love with Gemma. The sooner I come to terms with this, the better. I spent the first few days crying myself to sleep and moping. It still hurts, but I guess it will for a while.

I'll survive. It doesn't feel like that at the moment, but I will. In the meantime, I just want to sit on this couch in my pajamas until I leave for London on Wednesday.

When the doorbell rings, my mom looks at me. "Are you expecting anyone?"

"No. I'm all yours this weekend."

She squeezes my arm. "After the movie, we'll go for barbecue. That'll make you feel better."

My stomach lurches, and I try to smile. "Sounds good."

She peeks through the peephole. "Mercy."

I chuckle and slouch deeper on the couch. It's good to be home. I've missed my mom and her weird little ways. She always says mercy when someone's hot. "Who is it?"

"I think this one is for you." She opens the door. "Hello."

"Hi, Mrs. Dawson. Is Abigail here?"

My eyes widen when I hear that deep voice. *No way. There's no way that's Nick. He doesn't even know where I live.*

"And who would you be, dear?" my mom asks sweetly.

"Nick Silva, ma'am. And these are for you."

Holy crap. I'm not hallucinating.

"These flowers are gorgeous. Thank you, Nick. I'm Gail. Come on in. Make yourself at home." The door closes. "Abby! A handsome young man has brought us flowers. Unglue yourself from the couch."

I close my eyes. It's a mother's job to embarrass her children, I suppose.

With a deep breath, I sit up and take stock of what I'm wearing. Thick socks, duckie pajama bottoms, and a t-shirt that says "Introverts unite... separately, in your own homes." I dust off popcorn crumbs from my clothes and push my saggy bun back.

Defeat makes my shoulders droop. Would it have been so hard to get dressed today and look nice? No, I have to look like a homeless nerd.

Whatever. I might not be wearing my exterior armor, but that doesn't mean I'm not strong. I don't need clothes to be tough.

I set aside my yarn and crochet needle and stand up. It takes me a moment to turn around, and the first sight of Nick is a punch to my solar plexus. He's wearing jeans and a Bronco sweatshirt that strains across his chest and shoulders. His hair is messy like he's been running his hands through it.

I've missed him so much. My eyes burn, but I tighten my jaw and wrap my arms around myself.

"Abby."

That's all it takes, him saying my name, for me to burst into tears.

Next thing I know, his strong arms come around me.

"Honey," my mom says, "I'm going to check on your dad. Nice to meet you, Nick."

Traitor.

"Nice to meet you too, ma'am." His deep voice is so soothing, I almost forget all the terrible things that happened between us.

Wait. No. I won't just flop like a wobbly deck of cards.

I push him away and adjust my glasses. "You can't just sweep back into my life and pretend everything is okay."

He holds his hands up. "I'm not here to pretend. I promise. I came here to get all of our baggage on the table and see if we could work things out." His giant palms cradle my face, and he gently dries my tears with his thumbs. "I said some horrible things to you that day at the hospital, words I'll always regret. I'm so sorry. You've been nothing but supportive and wonderful, and you didn't deserve my suspicion. Clearly I have issues I need to work through."

I lower my face and rest my forehead against his chest. I'm almost too tired to stand. "You really hurt me, Nick."

His arms tighten around me. "I'm so sorry, buttercup. I handled everything wrong, but I'll do anything to prove to you how much I love you."

I stop breathing, and my head pops up. The honesty in his expression is so open and bare. I want to believe him, but I'm afraid to believe in us anymore. "Don't say things you don't mean."

"I'm not lying. I love you so much, it hurts. Not having you at home is killing me. I left you, like, fifty-two messages. I finally stopped because I didn't want you to think I was stalking you."

Pushing out of his arms, I take a step back. "How can you say you love me when you're still in love with Gemma?"

His brows furrow. "Why would you think that?"

"You introduced me to her family as the nanny. Then I did a deep dive on her Instagram. You were always smiling so wide in those photos. You were so happy with her. You never smile like that with me."

He swallows and nods slowly. "Can we sit down?" When I don't immediately agree, he whispers, "Please?"

Ugh, fine.

I curl up in the corner of the couch, and he takes a seat in the middle, close but not suffocatingly so. I grab a throw pillow and hold it against my stomach. There's something I need to ask before we wade into our baggage. "Is Hazel okay? You texted me she was, and Paige did some reconnaissance for me and said she was fine, but I want to hear it from you."

He nods. "She's great. She was only sore for two days. She didn't even need a cervical collar. I think she was mostly afraid of all the attention she got from the police and paramedics and then the doctors at the hospital."

"I feel terrible she was hurt." I can barely say the words, I'm so choked up.

"Baby, she's fine, I swear." He tries to grab my hand, but I pull it back to wipe my eyes. I'm not ready for him to touch me.

"Explain what happened with Gemma's parents, and please don't gloss over the details. I need to know what I'm dealing with." I tighten my arms around the pillow. "I want to be someone's number one pick, not your plan B."

Looking down at his lap, he shakes his head. "I'm sorry I made you feel like a fallback option. You've never been that for me, I swear it." He blows out a breath. "Was I happy with Gemma? Yes, but we also fought a lot. We'd both dated around before we got together, but we were the other's first serious relationship. At first, it was fun, but a baby changes everything. We went from being carefree, stupid kids who were focused on our goals to being parents and college students trying to take care of a small human. It was intense."

I don't say anything, and he continues. "Gemma was an extrovert. She loved partying and going out, and she wanted everyone to think we were the perfect couple. She would take fifty photos to find the perfect image to post. Even today, I don't have any social media. After talking to the press and fans at a game, the last thing I want to do is interact with more people. Gemma never understood that. It drove her up a wall that I just wanted to stay home on the weekends."

"You do like hanging out at home."

He gives me a cautious smile. "My relationship with you is easy in ways it never was with Gemma. You get my need to focus on football and try to solidify a future for my family. You get that I genuinely enjoy being a hermit sometimes. And you understand Hazel in a way no one else does. It kills me that she asks about you every day and I don't know what to tell her."

At the thought of sweet Hazelnut asking about me, my throat closes up again. I have to take a few deep breaths before I can continue. "What about Gemma's parents? Why call me the nanny? You could've called me a friend or roommate."

"I'll admit I panicked. That wasn't how I wanted to broach the subject of me dating with Hazel, so I went with something safe. But after you left, I leveled with them. Hazel had gone to the kitchen, and I told them that you and I were seeing each other. I was afraid how Cynthia, Gemma's mom, would react because she's a crier. Every time we video-chat, she cries, and that's one of the reasons I distanced myself. I couldn't handle the guilt."

"The guilt?"

"The guilt of having feelings for you." He levels me with a stare. "Feelings that I've never experienced before. The guilt of moving on. I never thought I was capable of falling in love again, and when I did, I felt guilty as fuck that I never had that same intensity with Gemma."

"Do you just mean the sex or actual feelings? Because if you just mean sex—"

"Is the sex amazing between you and me? Out of this fucking world. But no, I don't just mean the sex, Abby. I swear."

I look down. "Did you get with me because you thought sex would relax you and help you play football? Because Jinxy told me that all of your friends knew you were, quote, 'bangin' the nanny.'"

He rubs the back of his neck. "Did I tell Jinxy I was open to hooking up with someone? Yes. You saw me out at the Buck 'Em Brewhouse that night, but I wasn't feeling it, and I wasn't about to sleep with someone I didn't vibe with. For the record, I'm not a fan of hookups. That's never been my scene, but I considered it because I didn't think I could handle a relationship. Did Jinxy say sex would help me focus on football and chill out? Also yes. But I told him I wouldn't consider going out with you because you were my nanny. The only reason that changed is because you moved in with me, and I couldn't fucking help myself."

I bite my bottom lip to keep from grinning at his admission. This is the most open he's ever been with me, and my heart is practically fluttering.

He grabs my hand. "I swear I would never talk about the intimate things that happened between us with the guys. Jinxy saw you and me hanging out, and he thought I looked happy—which I was—and more relaxed on the field. He put two and two together. Jinxy and I got into it because I was pissed when I heard he was talking shit about you and letting Tiffany think I was somehow using you for sex."

Nodding, I process everything he's shared with me. I suppose it's my turn to be vulnerable. "Do you remember when I told you that Ezra called me his lucky charm?"

He winces. "That's what Jinxy called you, isn't it?"

"Yes. What I didn't tell you is that this was the whole reason Ezra dated me in the first place." I explain how Ezra was so superstitious that he believed us being an item had something to do with him winning his dumb football game in high school and securing the starting QB position. "So even though I don't think he ever had feelings for me, he freaking asked me to marry him because he was so irrational. That's why I couldn't come home Sunday night. When Jinxy told me I was your lucky charm and that you were with me for sex, I felt so stupid. I thought maybe you were using me like Ezra did."

"Jesus, Abby. I'm sorry." He takes my hand and tugs me to his chest. "I know I said some stupid shit at the hospital, but I couldn't figure out why that would make you move out. By the time Hazel got discharged, I knew I needed to make a big-ass apology to you. I was shocked when I got home and you were gone. Now I get it. The way I reacted to the accident was the last straw."

I close my eyes, but I don't say anything.

Stroking my back, he whispers, "Baby, I've missed you so much." We're quiet for a long stretch. "You're right about me needing therapy. I booked someone for the new year. It was the earliest I could get an appointment."

"Have you ever talked with a therapist about Gemma?"

"No. I just gutted it out and took one day at a time and basically shut down. I don't think... I don't think I could deal with the truth."

Frowning, I look up at him. "What truth?"

He takes a deep breath. "That I'm the reason Gemma died."

The look of grief on his face makes me take his hand in mine. "But you said it was an accident. You didn't drive her car. You were on the bus, right?"

His eyes get a faraway look in them as he stares across the room. "I guilted her into coming to my game that night. She wanted to hang out with friends. Gemma wasn't a huge football fan, but I told her if she loved me, she'd support me, which is a stupid thing to say to a young mom who's trying to stay afloat. But as you and I both know, I often say stupid shit at important moments in my life."

I squeeze his hand. "You don't need to feel guilty. You were young too. I see how hard you work to take care of Hazel while you juggle school and football. You were doing your best. Gemma would be proud of you."

He swallows. "Thank you. That means a lot to me."

"At least you wanted her at your games. I never understood why Ezra didn't want me to see him play. Now I understand. It's because he didn't love me."

"Ezra's a fool, but I have to admit he did me a solid."

I lean back. "What does that mean?"

"No one knew how to get ahold of you. Your friends basically told me to fuck off. So the guys and I got together and brainstormed how to track you down. Dax suggested calling Ezra, so that's what I did."

My eyes widen. "You didn't."

"Swear to God, I did."

I don't even know what to say. "And he just gave you my address?"

"No, it wasn't that easy. At first, he told me to fuck off, but then I reminded him that he was a shitty boyfriend to you. That he owed you for being such a prick. I think he actually felt bad."

"Huh. And here I was thinking he was a sociopath."

Nick laughs. "I don't know that he's not."

My parents come stomping back in from the garage. They're the two quietest people I know, so they're obviously trying to give me a heads-up.

I scoot back from Nick so I don't make my mom clutch her fake pearls again. "I should warn you," I whisper. "My parents are huge football fans."

"That's cool."

We both stand as my mom sweeps into the room all wide-eyed and bushy-tailed. "Nick, this is my husband Ted."

Dad pushes his glasses up the bridge of his nose, then reaches out to shake Nick's hand. "Hell of a game against Clemson, son."

"Thank you, sir."

I'm filled with pride for Nick. "I was there, Dad. It was even better in person."

He shakes his head. "You lucky duck."

Nick puts his hand on my back. "Sir, I was wondering if I could take Abby out for a drive. Maybe get a bite to eat."

My dad puffs up like a little rooster. "I'm sure she'd love that."

"Hello? I'm right here." My parents are acting weirder than usual.

Mom motions to me. "Honey, why don't you go change out of your pajamas. We'll grill Nick in the meanwhile."

Nick chuckles, and I let out a breath of relief that he's not weirded out.

I turn to him. "If you talk about football, they won't care about anything else."

My mom clucks. "Not true. I have every intention of asking him if he's the reason you've been so upset."

Nick's smile drops, and I grab his hand again and give him a hesitant smile. "I think... we're working things out?"

He takes a deep breath. "I should've introduced you as my girlfriend that day with Gemma's parents. I'm sorry I didn't."

My heart beats erratically as we stare at each other, and I clear my throat. "Is that what you want?"

"More than you know."

Behind me, my mom squeaks the way she does whenever we watch romcoms. "Y'all are too cute! Aren't they cute, Ted?"

"They're almost as adorkable as us," my dad says.

Nick and I laugh. "Go get your coat so I can take you on that date."

I lift my eyebrows. "A date, huh?"

"It's long overdue."

ABIGAIL

"You feel like eating ice cream?" Nick asks as he drives. "It's not too cold for that?"

"Not when I'm all cozy warm in your letterman." I saw it sitting in the passenger seat, so I stripped off my coat and tugged it on. "Besides, I've been craving butter pecan all week."

He chuckles and squeezes my hand as he drives with the other. "Thank you for the jacket. You're the sweetest." He's quiet as he drives for a few minutes. "I got the letterman the day after you left. I was so fucking miserable. I texted you a million times. Did you read any of them?"

I'm starting to feel bad I took off the way I did. "No. At first, I wasn't ready, but then I lost my phone when I was doing late-night laundry at that twenty-four-hour Laundro-rama."

"Baby, that place is dangerous. Weirdos loiter around there."

"I swear I was careful, and Paige was with me." I snuggle deeper into his jacket. "So what did you text me?"

"Why don't you grab my phone and look." He motions to the dash where it's sitting in a cupholder.

He gives me his code, and I tap it in.

Hazel is fine. She's just sore. I thought you'd want to know. That's the only text I already read.

I glance at him sheepishly. "I'm sorry I never texted you back after you told me that Hazel was okay. I thought you were going to yell at me."

"I'm the one who's sorry."

"I'll forgive you for yelling at me if you can forgive me for driving Hazel in my car. But I swear it never jerked like that until literally minutes before the accident."

"I know, baby." His brows furrow. "Maybe next time tell me if you need something so we can figure it out together. I could've helped you fix your transmission."

My eyes water. It's overwhelming to know that he has my back. "Okay." I go back to reading his texts.

Abby, call me back when you get this.

I'm sorry about this afternoon. I was an ass. I know you'd never deliberately do anything to put Hazel in harm's way. Please forgive me.

Why did you move out? I know I was being an idiot, but I thought we had something special. Didn't we? Call me and let me know you're okay. I'm going out of my mind.

I know I hurt you. I'm sorry. Come home.

With the back of my hand, I wipe the tears and then adjust my glasses. "I feel bad. I didn't mean to make you worry. I'm sorry I took off without talking to you first. I was really hurt and genuinely thought we were over. I spent a lot of time talking to Ezra after I found out he was a serial cheater. I guess... I wanted to preserve some dignity this time. He made me feel so pathetic, and I wanted to avoid feeling that. But... you're not Ezra." A sob escapes me.

He takes one look at my face and pulls over into a parking lot. When he turns off the engine, he opens his arms. "Come here."

I crawl over into his lap and wrap my arms around his neck. After several minutes, I finally calm down. "Do you really think we should date? We're terrible at this."

He rubs my back. "I meant what I said, Abby. I love you. And I'm willing to do what it takes to prove that to you. Will you let me?"

"I'm scared, but I love you too." I stare up into his beautiful green eyes. My heart pounds in my chest. "Does this mean I can take care of Hazel sometimes? Or drive her around? Because if you don't—"

"Shh." He puts his finger over my lips. "Of course. I trust you, and I'm sorry I lost my mind that day at the hospital."

I still feel guilty I put Hazel in harm's way, even inadvertently. The cop made a good point that I shouldn't have been driving in a car that needed work. "I know my priorities this semester were out of whack. I should've fixed my car instead of funding my trip to London, but I just felt so desperate to reclaim that part of me I lost when I dated Ezra." I shake my head. "I don't know if that makes sense."

"Of course it does. Maybe we could both use a little therapy to work through our issues."

I think about that a moment. "You're right. I'll look into that. I was also thinking that maybe I could take a defensive driving course."

"That's a great idea." He kisses my forehead and whispers, "Say it again."

I wrinkle my nose. "I'll take a defensive driving course?"

He laughs. "No, the other thing."

My heart flutters. Oh, that. "I love you, Nick."

The smile he gives me makes me fill with warmth. He leans down to press a gentle kiss on my lips. "I missed you, buttercup."

"Missed you too." I suddenly feel shy, and I have no idea where to go from here. "What do you want to do second semester? Do you want some space so you can focus on the playoffs and the draft? I can stay with my parents, and—"

"No. I want you at home with me and Hazel." He kisses me again. "I told her I was coming here to try to talk you into coming back to Charming with me. I asked her how she would feel if you and I dated, and she clapped and hopped up and down and howled that she loved you."

I smile. "You told her?"

"Yeah. I mean, I knew there was a chance you would slam the door in my face, but I wanted to take a leap of faith. I hoped we could work things out eventually."

It hits me all at once. "I'm leaving for London in three days."

He frowns. "Then move in with me when you get back. And please, please be careful on your trip."

"I promise. I got a travel buddy, a girl named Yvette, who's also an education major. I don't want you to worry while I'm gone."

"I'll worry no matter what, but that'll help. Would it be too much to ask you to text me each night? Just to let me know you got back to your hostel okay?" He has a hard time saying the word 'hostel.'

"I can definitely text you. I'm getting a new phone tomorrow. And my aunt has all of these miles on her credit card and said I could use them for a hotel, so you'll be happy to know I won't be staying in hostels."

"Oh, thank God."

I laugh, and he gives me another one of those killer smiles. I chew the inside of my cheek. "I have a court date for my ticket on the twenty-ninth. My parents have been really great. They said they'd loan me the funds to pay for it, and my grandmother gave me money for my trip. So, as it turns out, I'm not going to live on ramen when I'm in London."

"Jinxy wants to help you with your traffic ticket."

"That... doesn't sound helpful. And I'm not his biggest fan right now."

"Something I'm sure he regrets. When Coach found out about the stupid shit he said to you, he made him clean the toilets in the field house for two weeks. But even before that, I think Jinxy felt bad, and he called me this morning to tell me about his plan to make it up to you. I'll explain more over ice cream." Nick runs his thumb over my cheek. "Will you come to my bowl game? It's in Houston on the thirty-first."

Oh my God! His bowl game! I can barely contain myself. "Are you inviting me?"

He grazes his lips across mine. "If you'll say yes."

"Yes!"

His soft kisses grow heated, and within minutes, I'm writhing in his lap. He groans and drops his head to my shoulder. "Buttercup. We have to stop."

I glance around, and the windows are fogged. I suppose having sex in a car is not ideal. "Want to come home with me? I can probably talk my parents into going out to dinner without us, and I can give you a tour of my bedroom."

He chuckles. "As enticing as that sounds, I don't want to have sex until after my bowl game."

"What?"

His eyes go serious. "I don't want you to worry that I have ulterior motives. That I'm with you for any other reason than because I love you and want to be with you."

I think on that for a moment. Then smile. "That's really thoughtful. Okay." I grab his handsome face and kiss him. "I guess it's a good thing I'm leaving for twelve days because I'm not sure I could keep my hands off you otherwise."

He lifts his hips, which nudges his huge erection against my thigh. "Trust me. I know the feeling."

We eventually get out and walk hand in hand to the ice

cream shop. Once we get our order, we sit at a small table in the corner. I'm so happy to see him, I keep smiling.

After I devour my scoop, he pulls me into his lap again. "Would you like to go to a bookstore next? There's something I want to get you."

"A bookstore?" I get downright giddy. "Really? I love bookstores."

He winks at me. "I know."

ON OUR WAY HOME, I hold the sack of books Nick got me to my chest. "Thank you. I love everything you got me."

"My pleasure, buttercup." When he pulls in front of my house, he leaves his SUV running.

I didn't realize how late it is. The sun is setting.

Then it hits me. I'm going away and won't see Nick for over two weeks.

But before I have a chance to get sad, he clears his throat. "This might sound stupid, but I've been wanting to do this for a while." He fiddles with his radio until a slow country song comes on, which he turns way up for some reason. Then he comes around to my side, opens the door, and holds out his hand. "Wanna dance?"

Oh, heavens. Could the man be any dreamier? I place my hand in his, and then he walks me to the front of the car where he pulls me close, and we sway in front of his headlights.

As I close my eyes and rest my head against his strong chest, I smile. Because life has a funny way of working out sometimes.

47

ABIGAIL

My nose is cold, I'm jetlagged, and my stomach is queasy, but the moment Yvette and I reach the Tower Bridge walkway and stare out the lattice windows, I forget my discomfort.

"Breathtaking," I whisper.

An incredible view of London stretches out before me as I stare at the River Thames, which snakes through the city. I whip out my phone and snap several photos before Yvette and I take some selfies. I'm not much for selfies, but I figure a trip to London warrants a few.

As Yvette takes video for her travel blog, I text Nick a quick note letting him know what our plans are this afternoon and that I'll upload photos for him tonight.

He immediately responds even though it's barely six in the morning back home. **So glad you're having a blast, baby. Be safe!**

I grin and tuck my phone away. As much as I miss him, I'm glad Nick can use this time to focus on the playoffs.

Yvette holds up her map and points at the horizon. "That's London Bridge. Did you know they used to put the heads of decapitated prisoners on spikes there, like William Wallace and Thomas Cromwell, as a warning not to start trouble?"

I shiver. "Having your head on a spike is a great reason to avoid a life of crime."

She regales me with more historical tidbits while I jot down notes and color code them in one of the journals Nick bought me. Since he couldn't come on this trip, he told me he'd be with me in spirit and thought I could use my journals to share this experience with him when I got home.

Sighing happily, I stare out the window again as I hug the book to my chest. As much as I miss him, I'm excited to have this great adventure on my own to prove I can do it.

When we reach the Tower of London, I make a very undignified little squeal of happiness. "You can almost feel a thousand years of history wafting off the brick."

We decided we'd start with some major monuments first before we hit up more literary sights, but we've also grouped some attractions by location for maximum efficiency. Yvette and I are both book nerds, and we spent the majority of our flight here figuring out our itinerary, which is what I used my other journal for.

We're going to visit the Globe Theatre, the Charles Dickens Museum, Poet's Corner at Westminster Abbey, and a dozen other sights if we can swing it. We're saving the best part for last and plan to see Jane Austen's house the day before we leave since it requires a train ride out to Alton and then a long walk to Chawton.

As much as I was hoping to do a side trip to Germany to see their Christmas markets, Yvette doesn't want to leave England, and I'm not crazy about going by myself. I promised Nick and my parents that I'd be safe, so my one concession is not taking that solo trip. I'm not crazy about braving Heathrow alone with the holiday crowds anyway. Fortunately, London has its own

Christmas markets. Cutting that trip will also help me stay within my budget.

Yvette hooks her arm in mine. "We still need to figure out when we can do a high tea."

"You just want a reason to get one of those mugs we saw in that gift shop."

"Are you kidding? I want *all* of those mugs. Like 'Fifty Shades of Earl Grey,' or 'I'm bad to the scone,' or maybe 'Don't be chai.'"

"I think I want 'Sticks and scones may break my bones.'"

We both laugh.

London is awesome.

48

NICK

"Show me more, Daddy." Hazel scoots closer, and I wrap an arm around her shoulders and pull out my phone.

"Here's where Abby went to see Big Ben."

"Who's Ben? I don't see him."

"It's the clock, honey."

Her nose wrinkles. "That's a silly name for a clock."

I laugh. "Maybe Abby can tell us the story behind that. Did I show you this photo?" I read her the caption. "'Sitting on that bench in Notting Hill. Have you seen the movie?'"

"What does that mean?"

"She's asking me if I've seen the movie that was shot there." Abby set up a private Instagram so she could share her photos with me. I broke my social media ban and made a private account to respond to her posts. I never thought I'd say this, but I'm really enjoying how we use it.

We talked a lot about it beforehand because she didn't want to trigger my anxiety since she knew how I felt about Gemma's social media, but this seemed like a fun way for her to share her trip with me.

"This is the Kingston Christmas Market she was excited to

see." I stare at Abby's beautiful face. I feel like she's smiling just for me. "And these are pics of her journal pages where she's writing about her trip."

That's why I took her to the bookstore. I wanted to buy her some journals and pens to show her I support her trip and this great adventure. Her ex never supported anything she did, and I aim to be the exact opposite even if it takes me outside my comfort zone sometimes.

"Can I see more?"

I kiss the top of Hazel's head. "Sorry, gingersnap. I need to go pick her up from the airport."

"Why can't I come?" She juts out her lower lip.

"Because we'll be getting home late, but you can see her in the morning. She's really looking forward to seeing you, though. I spoke to her a few nights ago, and she said she got you a little present."

My daughter's eyes light up. "I love presents!"

Sometime in the last few days, Hazel started saying her Rs correctly. I can't wait to tell Abby. There's so much I want to talk to her about.

I try to refresh my screen, but there are no new posts from yesterday, which unnerves me because Abby has been posting daily. She texted two days ago to say she was really tired and fighting a cold. She's bummed she won't make it to Jane Austen's house, but that requires a train ride, and she doesn't think her stomach can handle it.

She's been fighting stomach issues ever since Hazel caught that bug just after Thanksgiving. I hope it's just stress and nothing more serious.

The doorbell rings, and I let Cynthia in and kiss her cheek. "Thanks for watching Hazel tonight."

"It's my pleasure. I'm so happy this is working out."

"I can't tell you how grateful I am." When Gemma's family

stopped by last month, Cynthia and her husband told me they wanted to help out more, so they're renting an Airbnb in Charming for the next month so I can focus on the playoffs. Part of the reason she was always upset when we spoke on video chat was because she missed us, and this will give her time to bond with Hazel.

I hug my daughter. "Be a good girl."

"I'm always a good girl." She looks at Cynthia. "Right, Grandma?"

"Right!" Cynthia laughs.

It's a relief to have family looking after Hazel. This year, for the first time, the playoffs have expanded from four teams to twelve, so if we win our bowl game this week, we still have to play a semifinal round next week to determine who plays in the championship game at the end of January. It's a hell of a lot of travel.

I grab the bouquet of roses out of the fridge, then the placards I wrote. As I'm making my way out the door, Cynthia calls my name. "I can't wait to spend more time with your girlfriend. She seems like a sweetheart."

Hazel nods. "We love her."

I smile. That we do. "Thanks, Cynthia." It means a lot to me that I have her blessing. Obviously, I'd date Abby without it, but knowing Cynthia and Charles support me no matter what has unburdened something inside me.

By the time I hit the road, I'm starting to worry because I haven't heard from Abby. I figured she'd text when she changed planes in New York. A million worst-case scenarios filter through my head. But when I realize I'm being negative, I flip on the radio and try to change my thoughts. While I haven't had a therapy session yet to deal with all of my personal baggage, I've been listening to podcasts on grief and anxiety, and it's helping me get perspective.

When I reach the San Antonio airport, I wipe my clammy hands on my jeans and make my way to baggage claim. I check my phone again but don't have a signal. That could be what prevented Abby from messaging me, I realize. I try to calm my ass down as I watch people retrieve their luggage.

Finally, travelers from Abby's flight gather by the carousel.

My heart is in my throat as I watch people descend the escalator. I don't know why I'm nervous. As I check the placards for the tenth time, I roll my eyes. Yeah, I'm doing something kinda goofy and romantic, but I just want to make Abby happy, and I think this will put a smile on her face.

When I spot her, I swear my heart stops. I can't help the huge smile that spreads on my face. Abby's so damn beautiful. She doesn't see me yet, and I take her in. She looks like she's lost weight. From the pics and video clips she posted, she went all over London.

She's staring down at her feet, frowning. She must be exhausted.

I'm surprised she's so pale after being out and about sightseeing.

At the bottom of the escalator, she gets off, then glances around, and I remember to hold up my sign and walk closer.

She looks at me, does a double-take, and laughs when she reads her name on the placard.

"Are you Abby Dawson?" I ask like a dumbass, but I don't care if I look like a fool. I want this woman to know I'm all in.

"Why, yes, I am."

I move that sign behind the next one that reads, "Will you be my girlfriend?"

Her eyes go soft and dreamy. Yeah, I put that look on her face. "I thought I already was your girlfriend."

I lean over and kiss her. "Is that a yes? Because I got thinking, and I don't remember actually asking you to make this official." I hand her the bouquet of roses. "I don't want you to have any doubt about us. So I figured I should ask."

She swallows, and a flash of fear crosses her face. "Nick, I..."

When she doesn't say anything, I take her hand. "Did something happen? Are you okay?"

Abby takes a deep breath. "I guess my answer to your question depends on you." She reaches into her bag and pulls out a box. "It depends on how... on how you feel about this."

Okay, I'm freaking out a little. I thought she would smile and laugh and we'd be good to go.

I take the box and open it.

Inside are... are... five pregnancy tests.

My eyes widen. They're positive.

Holy shit. I might need to sit down. But before I lose it, I see the fear on her face again, and I wrap my arms around her. I have no clue how we're going to handle another baby, but I immediately know I want one with Abby. "Yes. I'm all in." I kiss her forehead. "I'm all in for two a.m. feedings and doctor appointments and diaper changes and whatever else comes our way. Because I wanna do it all with you."

Surprised, she leans back. "Really?"

"Yes, really." I can't believe the words coming out of my mouth right now, but it's the truth. I didn't want more children before Abby, but having her in my life has changed everything.

She sniffles. "I just figured it out. My period has been super light, but I couldn't get over that stomach bug. And then, the other day, I smelled something that turned my stomach again, and one of the passengers on the bus tour, this nice older lady, gave me a funny look and asked if I was pregnant. Of course, I ran out and got five tests." She tilts her head back so I can see her beautiful, tired eyes. "They're all positive."

I lean down and kiss her again. "Do you know what this means?"

"What?"

"You can't get rid of me now."

She laughs, then her expression gets serious. "I want you, but I also want this baby, which I know is crazy because we're young, and you have Hazel."

It's the biggest shock for me when I tell her, "I want this baby too. You and me, we'll be a family. I meant what I said—I'm all in on this. I love you, Abby, and if you're willing to give me this incredible gift, I swear you'll never regret making a commitment to me." I take her face in my hands. "I want you to know that I'd pick you to be the mother of my children. I don't want this happy accident to diminish the fact that I would choose you, okay?"

Her smile grows. "Okay."

"Now let's go home."

49

ABIGAIL

The minute Cynthia leaves, Nick closes the door, presses me up against it, and kisses the daylights out of me. "God, I've missed you."

I run my fingers through his thick hair. "I've missed you too. Maybe we could go on a trip like that together sometime. To England or France or Italy. I'm glad I went, but the whole time, I kept wishing you were with me so I could share it with you."

He smiles. "I'd love that. I showed Hazel your photos, and she has a million questions."

"I can't wait to see her." I press my hand to my stomach.

"Are you feeling okay?"

"Yeah, just nervous about my court appointment tomorrow. Do you really think Jinxy's brother will come through?"

"He's supposed to be the best guy in town to handle this sort of thing."

"I can't believe he's doing this pro bono."

"Jinxy is paying his brother with playoff tickets. And don't feel bad. He owes you for stirring up all that shit. It's the least he can do."

I nod, then notice the Christmas tree in the corner. "I'm sad I missed opening presents with you and Hazel."

He grabs my hand and tugs me to the other side of the living room where there's a pile of gifts. "We waited."

My eyes sting. "You're so sweet." I wave at my face. "Now I understand why I've been so emotional. And jeez, Nick, I wonder if it happened that time the condom broke. I was so dismissive, but I had just started new birth control. What if it was my fault? I told you we were fine, but—"

"Baby, it's all good. I'm starting to think you and I were meant to be. So don't stress about the details."

He looks genuinely happy, and I finally start to relax. Nick and I are really happening. I'm so relieved he took the baby news well.

I throw my arms around his neck. "I love you so much. And I know you were stressed about me going on a trip by myself. Thank you for trusting in my abilities. I might've had a little help. Baylee saged me to get rid of my bad juju so I wouldn't have any more mishaps."

"Saged?"

"She burned sage and waved it around me while she said this prayer. Apparently, it's something her family does. All I know is I'll take whatever good vibes she wants to send my way."

"Good vibes are always appreciated." He rubs his nose against mine.

I nibble his bottom lip and lower my voice. "I know we agreed we wouldn't have sex before your game, but we'll have more time to abstain. I know you're going to make it to the championship again. It's just been so long since we've..."

"Fucked each other's brains out?" he asks with a laugh.

"Yes. So what do you think? Can we bang like bunnies tonight and then hold off until the quarterfinal game? Though..." I kiss him, then rub my nose against his. "If I can bring you any luck at all, I'm happy to do so. I know you're nothing like my ex, and I'm sorry I didn't just talk to you after that convo with Jinxy at the diner."

Nick hugs me tight. "We'll get better at this. I swear." He gives me a heart-stopping smile. "I'm so glad you're home. Let me grab the rest of your stuff from my car."

"I'll go take a quick shower. Meet me in my bedroom in half an hour?"

"You mean *our* bedroom."

I pause. "You want me to sleep in your bed?"

"If that's okay? I already told Hazel you would stay with me. She thinks we're going to have sleepovers."

I can't help but hop up and down on my toes. "I don't know how much sleep you're getting tonight, but yes!"

Giddy, I jump in the shower and scrub off the travel grime. When I'm done, I wipe the condensation off the mirror and stare at my naked body. Holding my stomach, I turn one way, then the other.

I don't think I look that much different.

That's when it really hits me. *I'm pregnant with Nick's baby!*

Nothing could make me happier than his sweet response at the airport when I gave him my news. I was so worried on the flight, but he completely erased my fears with his confidence in us.

With a towel wrapped around me, I tiptoe to his room and open the door. He's lying in bed in his jeans and t-shirt, scrolling on his phone. He puts it down.

"Do I look pregnant? I think my boobs are bigger." I take a fortifying breath and drop the towel. I want to be brave with my man.

His eyes heat and the intensity of his stare makes goosebumps break out on my skin. "I'm not sure. Maybe you should touch them."

"Good idea." I grab my boobs and lift them while I watch Nick's eyes go positively feral. I pinch my nipples and moan. "Definitely more sensitive."

"Are they? So if I suck them, do you think it'll feel good?"

I feel a gush of wetness slick between my thighs. "So good."

"Maybe you should turn around and let me check out the rest."

As I fight a smile, I do a slow turn. He makes a growling sound before he scoops me into his arms. We end up in a tangle on the bed.

He presses hot kisses to my lips before I open to him and our tongues slide together. We kiss until I'm out of breath, and then he leans down to suck my nipple. Shivers run through me as he pulses each suck. I'm already so turned on, I could explode. His rough palm runs down my back, along my ass, and dips between my legs, where he grips my thigh and opens me. A second later, his finger drags along my crease, and he groans. "Buttercup, you're soaked."

"Apparently, pregnancy makes me really horny." I reach down and rub my clit because I can't wait anymore. He leans back to watch.

"You know what I found when I was unpacking the boxes your parents gave me?"

I never unpacked, so my parents just let him collect the small stack of boxes and bring them back to Charming. "I have no idea, but thank you for unpacking. That's the last thing I have the energy to do right now."

He reaches over to his bedside table, opens a drawer, and pulls out my new rabbit vibe.

Use a sex toy with Nick? My heart races in anticipation as I giggle. "I'm game if you are."

"If you hate it, we can stop."

I nod. "Just go slow."

"Spread your legs."

I do as he asks. At first, he just licks his lips and stares. But then he flicks on the vibe. "Let's leave off the rabbit part." He grabs some lube from the drawer, but he can't get the wrapper off.

I laugh and take it from him and slice it off with my nail and hand it back to him.

After he drizzles a little on the tip, he settles between my legs. "Open yourself with your fingers."

This is so intimate, but as I stare into his eyes, I'm not afraid. I trust Nick to take care of me. To love me and protect me. That makes all the difference in the world.

I spread my pussy lips apart and suck in a breath when he drags the vibe against me. "I... Oh, wow. I can come like this."

"Not yet. See if you can hold off."

He lowers it to my entrance and slowly dips it in and out. The vibration is nice, and when he works it in, I moan. "This is good, but it's not as thick as you."

Nick smirks. "I know." We both laugh, but his laughter stops when I grab my boobs and tweak my nipples. "Fuck, you're gorgeous."

He spreads my legs apart more and leans down to drag his tongue against my swollen flesh.

"Nick!" I squeak and arch back while my hands grip the sheets. "Don't stop."

"Don't worry, baby. I have no intention of stopping."

50

NICK

Abby arches back as I stretch her with her vibrator. I lick her clit, and just as she's about to explode, I back off.

She huffs and gives me a dirty look. "Nick Silva, you'd better make me come right this minute."

I try not to laugh. Her indignant pout is adorable, and I love that she's comfortable enough to let me do this. I've never used sex toys in bed before, but holy hell, this is hot.

"Calm down, baby. I wanna watch you take this vibe. You should see how good your pussy looks right now." I make a point to drag it slowly in and out. She's really wet, which makes this easy. Then I slowly circle her clit with my tongue. Her hand grips my hair and she tugs me closer.

"Can I come now? Please?" she wails softly.

"You asked so sweetly, buttercup. Yes. You can come." Who knew I got off on these kinds of dynamics? But based on the glassy-eyed, flushed expression on Abby's face, she's into this too.

Leaning down, I flatten my tongue against her clit and do long, slow licks that make her squeal.

Within seconds, she detonates, shaking and shivering and writhing on the bed as her head tosses this way and that.

When she's done, she gives me a contented, sleepy smile. "That was amazing."

I set the vibe on the side table, flop down next to her, and pull her into my arms.

My cock throbs in my jeans. We haven't had sex in more than a month, and I'm wound tight, but I remind myself that she's pregnant and tired from her trip. So I ignore my erection and kiss her forehead. "Love you, baby."

"Love you too." All of a sudden, her eyes widen. "What about you? It's your turn."

"You're tired. I don't want you to overdo it."

She leans up on one arm. "Get rid of your clothes and take me to pound town."

I laugh and pull her closer. "Are you sure?" She rolls her eyes, reaches for my t-shirt, and yanks it over my head.

"Do you know what pregnant women need, Nick?"

"What's that?"

"Vitamin D. Give it to me, Nick. I need it. Do you know how long I've been craving this? You have no idea."

It's a rush to know my woman wants me as badly as I want her. I unbutton my jeans and kick them off, along with my boxer briefs. My cock bobs against my stomach. "He's happy to see you."

She scoots down, grabs my dick, and gives me a long lick from my balls to my tip. "I'm just as eager for a reintroduction," she says before she sucks me into her warm mouth.

"Baby. Fuck, that feels good." I watch her suck me, lick my tip, and tongue my slit with an enthusiasm that makes my balls go tight. "Stop or I'm gonna bust on your face."

She laughs and moves up to straddle me. "You say that like it's a bad thing."

Holy shit. My dick swells as I think about all the things we're gonna do together.

"Buttercup? Since we're talking about cravings, can I fuck your tits?"

Her eyes widen with something akin to glee. "Where's the lube?" She flops back in bed, and I pat the bed until I find the bottle.

She pinches her nipples as I drizzle it back and forth between her cleavage. Then I scoot up the bed and straddle her. She licks her lips as she watches me drag my cock through the liquid.

"Hold them together."

Grabbing herself, she squishes her tits to my flesh as I begin to thrust. The sight of my thick cock sliding between her incredible breasts makes my balls pull tight again. After a few minutes, I have to stop. "Wanna come inside you. Not like this."

She grabs my arm and pulls me down to her until I wedge myself between her thighs. "Then bang me how you want." She reaches between us and angles me toward her pussy. "Is it weird I'm excited to feel you without a condom?"

That's right. We don't need condoms anymore.

I smile and kiss her. "Not weird at all."

After I notch myself into her tight hole, I slowly sink into her body. "Tell me if something is too much." Jesus, she feels incredible bare.

"I'm good. Keep going."

Her face is flushed and her damp hair is a tangle. Her nipples are beaded and tight, and her pussy is snug and wet. It's like I've died and gone to heaven.

Carefully, I pull out and thrust back in, and within a few minutes, her eyes are no longer sleepy. They're hazy with lust.

I lean back to watch my cock shuttle in and out of her tight sheath. Each thrust makes her glorious tits bounce. "Baby, can you come again?"

"I don't know."

"Try. Spread your pussy open." With one hand, she spreads her lips. "Now rub that pretty little clit with your other hand." I drizzle more lube on that spot, and her fingers go to town with tight, fast circles. I pump harder, faster, and she tilts her head back with a cry and lets go.

I try to hold out, but she's squeezing my cock in these tight pulses that feel so fucking good. I drop down to her so I can feel her tits on my chest and her warm tongue in my mouth.

Her arms wrap around me, and I chase my release and tip over the edge when she lets out another cry.

We pulse together, one heartbeat between us.

Keeping us joined, I roll us to the side and pull her into my arms. I stare down at my beautiful girl. "I love you, Abby. I'm so happy you're home." Reaching down, I press my hand to her stomach. "And I'm already in love with our baby. Thank you for the best Christmas gift."

Sighing, she gives me a sleepy, sated smile. "I love you too, Nick."

As the morning light creeps through the blinds, I reach for Abby, but her side of the bed is empty. I toss on some track pants, make a quick stop in the bathroom, and head down the hall where I hear her and Hazel chatting.

I lean against the wall and stare at my girls, who are curled up together on the couch.

Hazel leans against Abby as they stare at her phone. "Tell me about the Christmas place again."

"The Kingston Christmas Market? Gosh, it was so beautiful.

I went in the evening, and there were a thousand little twinkle lights. Look. Here's a picture."

"I love those lights," Hazel says, like she's ready to swoon.

"I do too." Abby pauses. "Would you like some twinkle lights in your room? Maybe on the ceiling so they look like stars?"

"Yes!"

"We'd need to ask your dad first, but if he likes the idea, I saw this really cool bedroom with those lights, and it looks so magical."

My daughter claps in excitement. "I love magical!"

I chuckle. "Morning, ladies."

"Morning, Daddy! Can I have twinkle lights? And can we open Christmas presents?"

"We can do it tonight." I sit on the other side of Abby and kiss her cheek. "Morning, baby."

"Hi, honey. Can I give Hazel what I got her in England? She's been waiting so patiently."

Hazel folds her hands together like she's praying, and I laugh. "Okay. One gift."

She leaps off the couch and dances. I'm grateful she's not fazed by me and Abby being together. The three of us feel so right. I guess we always have.

Abby retrieves the present and hands it to her. "It's delicate, so you have to be gentle."

"I can be gentle." Hazel rips off the paper, opens the box, and squeals. "She's so beautiful!" She pulls out a marionette in a fluffy pink dress.

Abby takes the wooden controls and untangles the strings to the doll. "If you like this, I found directions to make our own. We could put together a play and do all of the parts ourselves."

"I wanna do that! Yessss!" Hazel throws herself at Abby, almost knocking her over.

With my heart in my throat, I reach out and steady them.

"Hazel, you have to be gentle with Abby too, okay? Don't pounce on her."

Jesus, I was protective of Abby before she got pregnant. Now I wanna tape her down in bubble wrap.

My eyes meet hers and there's so much love shining back at me, I swear it swells my heart.

We decided to wait to tell everyone about our news. I'm excited to shout it from the rooftop, but I'm also grateful to have this time just for ourselves.

I glance at the clock. "Hazel, Cadence is coming to watch you for a few hours while Abby and I go take care of something, but Abby will be back to hang out with you this afternoon while I go to practice."

"Okey-dokey." She doesn't bother looking up from her doll.

I take Abby's hand and lead her into the kitchen, where I kiss her until she's panting. "Good to have you home, buttercup." I pat her on her shapely ass. "Now go get dressed for your court appointment. We need to leave in an hour."

She tosses her arms around my shoulders. "Thank you for coming with me. I'm so anxious about it."

I hug her close. "It's going to be fine, no matter what. If we have to pay the ticket, so be it, but maybe Jinxy's brother has an ace up his sleeve."

She leans back. "*We'll* pay the ticket?"

"Families watch out for each other." I press my lips to her forehead. "And you're family now, so yes, *we*."

EPILOGUE

THREE WEEKS LATER

NICK

SWEAT STINGS my eyes as I glance at the clock from the sidelines. We're tied with LSU at thirty-four points with five minutes remaining in the national championship.

I take a moment to soak in the fact that I got here again and look back at the stands where Abby, her parents, and Hazel are sitting. Abby and Hazel are wearing their game faces with black grease strips under their eyes. My girls look fierce.

I wasn't going to bring Hazel, but she really wanted to come, and I know she'll be safe with Abby and her parents. I figure this is a once-in-a-lifetime opportunity to see her dad play, and I'm grateful Abby talked me into it.

My girlfriend's wearing my jersey, of course, which I can't wait to strip her out of later tonight, and since Gail offered to babysit so Abby and I could unwind and hopefully celebrate, we'll actually have a night all to ourselves.

She must sense me staring because Abby waves at me, and I hold my fist to my heart, which I told her would be my sign to her when I'm out on the field.

She's been my rock these last few weeks. Helping me watch film. Keeping Hazel busy with fun activities. Making sure my workout clothes make it to the washer and don't stink up my gym bag. I've never had anyone look out for me before. It's incredible. But the best part is how much fun we have together. I'm so fucking grateful that woman ran into me with her car.

Speaking of car accidents, Jinxy's brother handled her case like a boss when he showed up to court with subpoenaed footage from the street cameras that showed the utility trailer swerving all over the street behind the van. It likely wasn't hooked up correctly, which is why it drifted so far into Abby's car. The trailer also didn't have the required reflective lamps on the side panels, which explains why Abby might not have seen it since it was so low to the ground.

Unfortunately, because of the police report from when she struck my SUV last April, she still has to take a defensive driving course. She planned to do it anyway, but at least now, there's no additional fine.

And when Jinxy helped me wrangle extra tickets to today's game so Abby's parents and Hazel could join her, he officially got himself off her shit list.

Coach calls a timeout and our defensive line huddles up. Even though I'm not on the defense, obviously, I want to hear Coach's direction. He makes some adjustments and then points to the field. "Let's execute, gentlemen. You've got this." He's hoarse from screaming.

I shout, "Let's go, Broncos!"

This game has been a one-eighty from how we played last year. Me scoring four touchdowns and not getting sacked has helped.

Now we just need to win.

I'm too amped up to sit down, so I stand next to Coach.

"You're playing great, Nick," he tells me when he sees me out of his peripheral vision.

"Save the compliments for after the win, Coach." That's the kind of shit he always tells us.

He chuckles, nods, and pats my back. "You've learned well, Padawan. I think you're ready to graduate to Jedi."

It's my turn to laugh. Coach and his *Star Wars* references.

The whistle blows, but our D-line stops them in their tracks. On the next play, LSU loses five yards. But on the third snap, their QB throws a forty-five-yard pass that's taken in for a touchdown.

Damn. But with two thirty remaining, there's still time. After they make the extra point, it's forty-one to thirty-four.

After the punt return, we have the ball on the LSU twenty-yard line. Our O-line surrounds Coach as he covers his mouth with his clipboard and yells out the play.

On the first down, we get eight yards. Then five more on the next. When we huddle, I call the play, then look at my teammates. "Do you know what I see when I look at you guys?"

"What?" Jinxy shouts.

"The best college football team in the country. Now let's get out there and win."

I can see it in their eyes. They think we can do it.

I know we can.

There's thirty seconds on the clock at the snap. I drop into the pocket and fake a pass to Jinxy, who cradles air and makes like he's headed down the right side of the field. That's when I throw over traffic and aim for Dax deep in the end zone.

I watch it arch over him. He has two guys on his ass, but he snatches that ball out of the sky and nails that touchdown.

Hell yes!

Now we're down by one point with fifteen seconds on the clock.

Coach calls a timeout. It's our last one. LSU has two more. Coach taps on his clipboard. "We're going for the two-point conversion. Just like we practiced. You can do this in your sleep."

I turn to the guys. "It's time to break some hearts, gentlemen."

We pile our hands in the middle and shout, "Broncos!"

But when we line up, the Tigers call a timeout, obviously to adjust now that we've shown our cards. Coach switches a few people around too, and we head back out.

On a two-point conversion, we line up at the three-yard line. *It's only three yards, Silva. This is a walk in the park.*

The ball snaps, and I drop back one step before I throw a pass to Maverick, who hangs on for a touchdown, but the refs blow the whistle.

"Prior to the snap, LSU called a timeout."

Oh, fuck.

I gather my guys. "Don't let that get to you. Great play, Mav. Let's do it again. We just have to be a little more creative." I make two adjustments, and we line up again.

But this time, when the ball snaps, I cradle it, and as I'm checking my options, I see the opening.

And I run.

It's only three yards, I tell myself as I dodge a defender.

Two yards.

One.

Touchdown!

The stadium erupts. We take the lead with ten seconds remaining.

They never get more than five yards on each of their two possessions, and we win the game.

It's pandemonium in the stadium. Of course, we have to nail Coach with a bucket of Gatorade, and then I look toward the stands. It takes me a minute, but I finally spot Abby. I race over to the railing, leap up, and pull myself over. The crowd cheers when my girlfriend jumps into my arms.

Panting, I kiss her. "We did it."

"I'm so proud of you." She grabs my face and peppers me with more kisses. "I knew you'd win."

With my other arm, I pick up Hazel and kiss her cheek. "How'd Daddy do?"

"So good! I'm proud of you."

"Aww, thanks, kiddo. Have you been behaving up here?" I ask as I put my girls down.

"She's been an angel," Abby says with a huge grin.

I motion behind me. "Need to go do the post-game media thing, but I'll see you back at the hotel." She nods. I spot her parents over her shoulder and hug them. "So glad you could come today."

"Are you kidding?" her dad Ted says. "You just made my whole year."

Abby sets Hazel down on her seat, and I lean over to hug my daughter again. "Be sure to listen to Abby and Miss Gail, okay? I'll see you in a little while, and we'll grab dinner, okay?"

Hazel gives me a thumbs-up.

I laugh, then turn to kiss Abby on the forehead. "See you in a bit, baby."

She leans in and whispers, "We have to make up for what we didn't do last night."

With a chuckle, I wink. "Oh, I haven't forgotten."

ABIGAIL

"Fuck, you look good like this," Nick groans as he takes me from behind.

I hold myself up against the headboard as best I can. "The jersey does it for you, huh?"

"You have no idea. All of your clothes should be labeled with my last name."

A blissful smile spreads on my lips as he sucks on my neck. "That feels so good, but I didn't bring any turtlenecks. Careful."

He chuckles as he leans back and grips my ass. "A turtleneck in Miami might be hard to explain."

After his huge win this afternoon, we had dinner with Hazel, my parents, Coach Santos, and a few other players before we locked ourselves in my hotel room, where we've been reconnecting ever since. I owe my mom for offering to watch Hazel tonight.

I'm about to say something about turtlenecks when Nick reaches around to circle my clit with his fingers, and I lose all coherent thought. I arch my back, and he hits that spot that makes my eyes cross. A moment later, I come so hard, my legs quake beneath me, and he has to hold me up so I don't smash into the headboard.

His hold tightens until my back is flush against his chest. With another groan, he bites my shoulder and molds my boobs with his giant hands. I'm just coming down from my orgasm, but when he swells between my legs with his release, that somehow sets me off again.

By the time we collapse in bed, I can't stop giggling. "You have a magic dick. I didn't know I could come like that."

"I'm looking forward to finding all the ways to make you come." He hauls me up over his chest and kisses me. "I love you, buttercup."

"Love you too."

"Just want to point out that I won today without boning you last night."

I laugh and lean up to kiss him. "I caught that. For the

record, I never doubted you'd win. And now your phone is blowing up with calls from A-list agents. Do you know who you're going to choose?"

"I have a phone call with a few former players—Billy Babcock, Michael Oliver, and Ryder Kingston—tomorrow morning. They're gonna give me some pointers. Coach said he'd be happy to be on that conference call."

Wow. Of course I know Billy because he's engaged to Roxy, and he's killing it as a rookie. Michael and Ryder are also superstars on their respective NFL teams.

"I'm so happy for you." My eyes prickle, and I sniffle.

"Us. Be happy for *us*, baby, because you're a big reason I'm here." He shifts and cups my belly. "You brought me back to life, Abby. I know that's probably a cheesy thing to say, but it's true. I feel like I'm finally living again. Part of living is taking risks. I understand that now. I'm still not crazy about taking risks, but it helps that you and our littles make me so happy."

Our littles?! "I'm so excited I'm having your baby." Tears spill over my cheeks.

He runs his hand up and down my back until I get over my emotional outburst. He gets that I just need to cry sometimes.

"Did you still want to tell your parents and Hazel tomorrow?" His gruff, post-sex voice is so sexy.

My parents love Nick. I'm sure they'll have the usual apprehension about us being young, but I think they'll be over the moon about being grandparents. "Is that okay? Or do you think it's too soon? I brought that t-shirt for Hazel in case we decided to do this."

He kisses my forehead. "I'm ready when you are."

"How do you think Hazel will take the news?"

"She'll be ecstatic. She loves you, and I think she'll love the idea of being a big sister."

"What about your dad?" Nick's father couldn't come to the

game—the cost of the travel and hotel was just too much—but he's been texting Nick all week and telling him how proud he is.

Nick smiles. "He likes being a grandpa. I don't think he'll have a problem. And once he retires, he'll have more time to spend with our kids."

Our kids. I love the sound of that.

Life is good, I think drowsily. I fall asleep with a smile on my face.

THE NEXT MORNING, Nick has to get up early to do that conference call. After I get dressed, I pop down to Paige's room. She's packing and getting ready for her flight home this afternoon. It's been such a crazy few days. Even though we've both been in Miami for the game, I've barely seen her.

"You looked awesome yesterday. I love that routine y'all do during halftime," I tell her as I sit on her bed. "I took some video for you."

"Thank you. That was thoughtful." She folds her jeans and tosses them in her luggage.

"Do you think you can make brunch with me and my parents in a little while? Nick and I have some news, and I want you to be there if you can make it."

Her eyes widen. "What kind of news? Girl, are you pregnant? Because Baylee told me she thought you had a bun in the oven like two weeks ago."

"Damn it. I wanted to surprise you." Baylee has some kind of third eye because she always gets these weird feelings.

Paige squeals and practically tackles me in a hug. "I'm so happy for you! Oh my God, you and Nick are going to have gorgeous babies!"

I smile like a lovesick fool. "I'm so happy."

"Just think. You didn't want to work for him, and now you're having his babies and hearts across campus will break." She gasps. "I almost forgot to tell you. Guess who got in a cat fight the night before last."

"Who?"

"Tiffany. She was blowing some guy in his hotel room when his *wife* tracked down his weaselly little ass. Wifey was so pissed, she grabbed Tiffany by her hair and slammed her to the ground."

"Holy crap."

"And then Tiffany missed the game because she broke her jaw and had to get it wired shut."

We look at each other, and a slow giggle builds between us.

I clear my throat. "I would never wish anyone an injury..."

"No. Of course not. But..."

"But if it had to happen, I suppose Tiffany has some bad juju coming to her. Maybe she'll want to hire Baylee to sage her."

Paige cackles. "Baylee wouldn't sage Tiffany if she offered her a million dollars."

Just then, her phone buzzes with a call. I glance at the screen. "It's Rhett." That name rings a bell. "Isn't that the guy you were in love with in high school?" Her brother's best friend, I think.

"Ugh, don't remind me." She sends it to voicemail. "Leave me alone, Rhett Walker!"

When it rings again, and she turns off the ringer, my eyebrows lift. "So... you're never planning to talk to him?"

"Not if I can help it. Abby, I grew up in a small town, the kind of town where everyone knows your business. Literally every single person knew I had feelings for him in high school. It was so humiliating. I have no idea why he's calling now, but he can leave a message instead of hanging up like a weirdo, and if it's important, I'll text back. Besides, Marcus will go crazy if he finds out I talked to Rhett. He's so jealous all the time. I don't get it. I didn't think we were that serious, but if a guy so much as talks to me, he gets incensed."

That's concerning. "Maybe y'all should break up."

"I tried, and he was like, 'Paige, baby, I need you in my life.' He was so thoughtful and sweet for, like, a week. And then he became aloof again. I don't get it. He confuses me."

"If you change your mind, Nick and I can help you figure out a place to stay until graduation. I don't want you living with Marcus if he's unpredictable."

"I'll probably move in with one of the cheer girls next month. We're gearing up for nationals. I'll tell him I need to focus." She glances at the clock. "What time is your brunch?"

"It's getting late. We'd better go. And act surprised when I tell everyone I'm pregnant."

She squeals again with excitement and hugs me.

We bring down her luggage, and Nick and Hazel meet me in the lobby. He leans over to kiss me, then greets Paige while Hazel holds her arms open to me.

"Hey, Hazelnut." I lean down to hug her. "Did you have a good night?"

"Yup. Miss Gail gave me some coloring books and new crayons."

"Ohh, fun. You'll have to show me your work later."

My parents wave to us from the entrance of the attached restaurant. I take Hazel's hand and introduce Paige to my parents. Then we grab our seats at a round table.

Nick tells us about his conference call with Coach and the former Broncos. "They gave me some great advice about picking an agent and the draft. I've narrowed it down to three possibilities."

My dad sips his coffee. "Have all of those agents reached out to you already?"

"Yes, sir."

On the TV screen over the bar, ESPN is recapping yesterday's game. Jinxy, Maverick, and Bowser are sitting in one of the booths, and they ask the bartender to increase the sound.

The sportscaster says, "Nick Silva not only had the game of his life, he had the best season of his college career. He's a strong contender for the Heisman this year and likely a first-round draft pick."

Jinxy points to my boyfriend. "Yeah, baby! Who's the man?" Their teammates hoot and howl in agreement.

Nick chuckles. I grab his hand under the table. "I'm so proud of you."

"Thanks, buttercup."

I take out the activity book I made for Hazel and hand her some markers. It might be a while before we get our food.

My dad clears his throat. "So, Nick, are you planning to whisk our daughter away this summer after you're drafted? What are your intentions exactly?"

Oh dear God. I cover my face with the menu, embarrassed.

My mom smacks Dad. "Really, Ted? That's how you segue into that conversation?"

Nick smiles. "It's okay. Yes, sir, I am planning to whisk Abby and your grandbaby away with me when I'm drafted, if it's okay with you. But you and Gail will always have an open invitation to visit."

My dad scratches the back of his head and turns to Mom. "Did he say grandbaby?"

Mom's eyes widen and she grabs her faux pearls. "Are you pregnant?" she whispers.

"Pregnant?" Dad goes pale. "How did that happen?"

Paige covers her mouth with her hand to choke back a laugh.

Mom elbows him. "Darling, I love you, but please stop."

Then she turns to me and clasps her hands together. "Am I really going to be a grandmother?"

I grin. "Yes. I'm due this summer."

Hazel is still oblivious about our conversation. Nick picks her up and hands her a little gift bag. "Munchkin, open your present."

Her head darts up from her activity book. "Present?" She makes grabby hands and, a second later, has the t-shirt out.

I help her unfold it. "Want to read this with me?" I point to the words as I say, "'World's Best Big Sister.'"

Nick leans over to Hazel. "Do you know what that means? You're going to be a big sister."

Her eyes dart to me, then back to her dad before she squeals. "Can we have a girl? Then I can put her in pretty dresses!"

I brush her hair out of her face. "We don't know what we're having yet, honey, but we're going to need help with names. Do you think you can help us brainstorm?"

"Yes! Can I wear the shirt?"

"Sure." I tug it over the one she's wearing and she beams proudly.

My mother dabs her eyes. "Congratulations, darling!" She jumps up to hug me and Nick, and, after a few tears, sits back down next to my dad, who gives me a hesitant smile.

"That's great, Abby. Your mom and I are happy for you. I'm just surprised, that's all."

I get up and hug him. "It's okay, Grandpa."

He laughs, and as I'm making my way back to my seat, Nick snatches me and seats me on his lap.

Then he turns to my parents. "I know this is all out of order, but at some point, I'd like to give Abby my last name too, if she'll have it. But I figure we have enough on our plate right now. Just... I want you to know I love her, and I'm very serious about our relationship. She and our children will always be my number one priority."

Our children!

My throat goes tight, and I look up at him. "Can we have more than one? I've always wanted a large family."

He leans down to kiss me. "Whatever you want, buttercup. I think you're going to be a great mother."

I give him a dreamy smile.

Sometimes a girl has to kiss a few frogs to find her prince. In my case, I just had to hit him with my car.

BONUS CHAPTER
A YEAR AND A HALF LATER

ABIGAIL

"Are you sure you have everything you need?" I ask my mom as I gather the kids' toys and drop them in a basket.

"We're fine. Go have fun." She winks at Nick, who's patiently waiting for me in the doorway of the London hotel room.

My dad lowers his newspaper where he's going over the headlines with our daughter Janie, who's cradled in the crook of his arm. She just turned one. "Where's the trust?" my dad asks. "Granny and Grandpa have a whole afternoon of fun planned for the kids."

"Mommy, where are we going tonight?" Hazel jumps off the bed and wraps her arms around my leg. I swear, I'll never get tired of hearing her call me that.

She started calling me Mom last fall when we moved to Houston after Nick was drafted. (And that sportscaster was right —he got drafted in the first round *and* nabbed the Heisman.)

At first, I was worried about how Cynthia and Charles would take hearing Hazel call me Mom, but they've only been supportive and kind. I told them they were always welcome to tell Hazel about Gemma. Hazel knows her biological mom is Gemma. I told her I'm honored to be her bonus parent.

Nick scoops her up. "Gingersnap, tonight's a surprise."

We're taking her to ride the London Eye, which is a giant Ferris wheel that overlooks the city. I kiss her cheek. "I promise you'll enjoy it. Why don't you make me some artwork for my office?"

She smiles. "Do you want some rainbows this time?"

"That sounds great. You know I love lots of color."

As much as I wanted to teach after college, having two small children took most of my focus and energy. I taught that spring semester after I graduated while Nick prepped for the NFL combine and conditioned. I enjoyed it, but the whole day, I found myself waiting for when I could be home with Nick and Hazel.

Turns out, I'm really good at making educational materials for young children. Some of the moms in our playgroups saw my activity book and asked for copies. So I started self-publishing educational books for kids, and I'm having a blast. The best thing is I can do that from home while nursing Janie. Being home has helped us give Hazel more stability since her dad has to travel so much during the season.

After I hug Hazel and kiss the baby and double-check she has enough breast milk, Nick drags me out of the hotel room.

"They'll be fine," he assures me as we hop in our rental car.

I close my eyes because I can't handle driving on the wrong side of the street. "So you're not telling me where we're going?"

"I'll give you a clue. It's an hour and a half away."

I crack open my lids to side-eye him. "That could be anywhere."

He chuckles, grabs my hand, and kisses the inside of my wrist. "Patience, buttercup."

When city streets turn into suburban roads and lush green

hills, I realize it doesn't matter where we're going. With the windows down and the fresh air breezing through the car, I'm happy. As exciting as Nick's first NFL season was, as proud of him as I was for getting Rookie of the Year, I'm grateful to have this quiet downtime with my favorite person.

There's really no place I want to visit except...

I gasp. "Are we going to Jane Austen's house?"

Nick's thousand-watt smile makes my heart go pitter-patter. "Yup."

Giddy, I hop up and down in my seat. I'm so excited, I forget to be afraid of the oncoming traffic. "Are you serious?"

"Why do you think I read *Pride and Prejudice* last year?"

"Because it's a great work of literature?"

"Because I wanted to see what Jane Austen was all about since you love her so much. And since I love you, the things you find important are important to me."

My throat tightens. "Nick." I wave my hand in my face so my eyes don't tear up.

He chuckles and laces our fingers together. "It took me a while to figure out what all of her fancy language meant, but it was a pretty cool romance. Not as cool as ours, but how can anyone top us?"

"No one has a romance as great as ours, but if you're any sweeter, I might need you to put another baby in my belly, and I think we have our hands full right now, so cut it out."

I love the smile that puts on his face.

Nick and I have come a long way since I was his nanny. We both got therapists to work through our baggage, and I'm happy to say we've never been stronger as a couple. He'll probably always be concerned about my safety and our children, so I do my best to reassure him and avoid anything excessively risky. I also talk to him if I'm feeling insecure instead of jumping to conclusions. He knows he can't control everything, and he's learning to enjoy life more instead of worrying so much.

When we get to Jane Austen's house, Nick has me wait in the lobby while he talks to the tour guide. I think he wants to know where we can do lunch. After that, we take the full tour. By the time we're done, I'm filled to the brim with interesting details about my favorite author.

Afterward, we sit on a little bench in her garden.

Nick has his arm wrapped around my shoulder, and I'm drowsily snuggled into him. "This was amazing. Thank you."

"I figured next season might be even busier than last year, so I wanted to bring you here before our lives got crazier." He kisses my forehead. "You know you mean the world to me, right?"

"I'm mildly obsessed with you too."

"Only mildly?"

"Well, if the truth be known, I'm just shy of stalker-level in love with you."

He laughs and squeezes me tight. "Close your eyes. I have a surprise for you."

"Another one?" I sit up and look at him. "What is it? I don't think anything can beat coming here."

"We'll see about that. Close your eyes. Don't cheat."

"Yes, sir." I comply.

He scoots away, and a minute later, he says, "Open them."

I blink into the bright sun, but he's no longer next to me.

He's holding a Scrabble board as he kneels in front of me. The Scrabble tiles read, "WILL YOU MARRY ME?"

"Oh my God!"

Nick sets down the board and takes my hand in his. "In the words of Mr. Darcy, 'You must allow me to tell you how ardently I admire and love you,' Abigail Dawson." He kisses my wrist again. "You've captured my heart and soul. What is mine is yours, starting right here," he says, putting his hand on his chest.

"But can I give you one more thing? Can I give you my last name? Will you marry me?"

I sniffle. "I'd be honored to be your wife."

Reaching into his pocket, he pulls out a small, velvet black box.

When he opens it, I gasp. "That's beautiful."

"A princess ring for my princess." He slides it on my finger. "I would've done this sooner, but I wanted to take you somewhere special."

Launching off the bench, I toss my arms around him. "I'm going to make you so happy."

Dipping his head, he gently grazes my lips with his. "You already do."

WHAT TO READ NEXT

Thanks for reading! If you enjoyed Blindside Beauty, I hope you'll consider leaving a review. I try to read each one.

To stay up-to-date with my new releases, be sure to subscribe to my newsletter, which you can find on my website, www.lexmartinwrites.com.

Next up is Paige and Rhett's book! If you're in the mood for small town romances that feature a family of broody ranchers, you're going to love my new series, Wild at Heart, which kicks off with **Stealing Hearts.** You can get your copy on my website.

If you want to start at the beginning of the Varsity Dads series, be sure to check out The Varsity Dad Dilemma, which is a USA Today bestseller. Keep flipping to read the synopsis.

THE VARSITY DAD DILEMMA
A USA TODAY BESTSELLER

What's worse than having Rider Kingston, the star quarterback, give you the big brush-off because he doesn't want to get serious? You'd probably think living across the street from him where you get a firsthand view of his hookups, right?

That's what I thought. Until someone drops off a baby with a note pinned to her blanket that says one of those jocks—either Rider or one of his roommates—is the father. The problem? Baby mama doesn't mention which of these numbskulls is the sperm donor.

I wouldn't care about their paternity problems—not the slightest bit—except my brother lives there too. Which means that adorable squawking bundle might be my niece, and there's no way I'm leaving her unattended with those bumbling football players.

They need my help, even if they don't know it yet. Once we solve this dilemma and figure out who's the daddy, I'm out.

I'll just ignore Rider and those soul-searing looks he gives me every time I reach for the baby. He broke my heart three years ago. He won't get a second chance.

∼

The Varsity Dad Dilemma is a sexy, small-town sports romance novel from USA Today best-selling author Lex Martin. Readers are raving about this passionate, angst-filled enemies-to-lovers romance, and the smoking-hot chemistry between Gabby, the slightly nerdy Latina with a take-charge attitude, and her surprisingly sweet former fling, Rider. Who knew that he actually had a heart of gold underneath that deliciously ripped, well-defined exterior?

"Gabby and Rider have great chemistry and their banter is HOT. While she had loathed everything about Rider since freshman year, there was no denying the physical attraction they had towards each other... If you are looking for a college romance that brings the laughter, with loads of sexual tension and plenty of heart melting moments, check this book out!" – Reader Review

ACKNOWLEDGMENTS

I can't believe this series is over! I loved every minute with these Varsity Dads, and I hope you did too.

Personally, I really enjoy hearing what inspires authors, so I thought I'd share some inspo for Blindside Beauty.

I have social media to thank for two situations. The carnival accident was a real incident in Michigan a few years ago. No one was hurt thanks to bystanders who steadied the base of the ride. That awning window scenario came across my story feed, tits and all, and the moment I saw this video, I knew I needed to include it in a book.

That bumper situation came compliments of a personal experience. I was in a fender bender in college and accidentally took off my dad's bumper on his old van. He used bungee cords and duct tape to tie it back on, and drove it around like that for years. Every time I saw it, I cringed because it reminded me of that day. (Side note: My husband always tells me to use crappy things that happen to me in books so I can turn them into something positive. So that's how the bumper ended up in Blindside Beauty.)

Speaking of crappy things, the live oak crashing through

Abby's room is a combination of personal situations too. A drunk driver drove through my old bedroom at my dad's house. Fortunately, I wasn't there at the time. And two live oak trees recently fell in my yard and landed on my house during a storm, thanks to black mold, which we didn't know was a problem. (Apparently, the roots of live oaks need lots of sunlight, and if your canopy is too thick or you don't rake often enough, mold can grow. Good to know!)

My husband and I also nearly drove through a microburst once. We pulled over to the side of the road, and a minute later, trees had fallen everywhere. We were lucky to have been unharmed.

I also want to note that although intersection cameras were banned in Texas in 2019, municipalities are allowed to use them until their contracts expire, so that's how Charming ended up with footage that helped Abby's case.

With each book, there are always so many people to thank, but I have to start with my sweet husband Matt. He never complains when I randomly cut him off to tell him a story idea or nag him to help me think of titles. He's seriously the best, and I love him to pieces. He and my daughters are my entire universe, and I'm so grateful for our family and their support. I also have amazing parents who always encouraged me to write. They're the best!

I have a great team of people who help me reach the finish line: my agent Kimberly Brower, editor RJ Locksley, proofreader Julia Griffis, photographer Lindee Robinson, cover designer Najla Qamber, alternate cover designer Janett Corona, Candi with Candi Kane PR, and Jen DeJong and Olivia Rose with Grey's Promotions.

A huge hug to my dear friend and PA Serena McDonald. She's the best sound board, beta reader, and comic relief. Thanks for everything you do for me, Serena!

In addition to Serena, I have a fantastic team of beta readers who are so generous with their time and help me craft the best books possible. Leslie McAdam, Victoria Denault, Christine Yates, Riley Kelm, Jess Hodge, Jan Corona (who also helps me with my Spanish), and Chelle Sloane (who double checks my football scenes)—thank you for kicking the tires on my stories and helping me craft the best books possible!

A big thanks to my cousin Misty and her husband Waylon for helping me with some car questions.

Lastly, huge tackle hugs to my readers in Wildcats, my ARC team, author friends, fans, bloggers, and influencers who've spread the word about my books. Thank you so much for the book love!

While the Varsity Dads series is complete, I'm not done with some of these characters. You'll see Paige, Baylee, and Maverick in my new series, Wild at Heart. Get ready for Stealing Hearts, which is Paige and Rhett's story!

ALSO BY LEX MARTIN

Wild at Heart:

Stealing Hearts (Paige & Rhett)

Varsity Dads:

The Varsity Dad Dilemma (Gabby & Rider)

Tight Ends & Tiaras (Sienna & Ben)

The Baby Blitz (Magnolia & Olly)

Second Down Darling (Charlotte & Jake)

Heartbreaker Handoff (Roxy & Billy)

Blindside Beauty (Abigail & Nick)

Texas Nights:

Shameless (Kat & Brady)

Reckless (Tori & Ethan)

Breathless (Joey & Logan)

The Dearest Series:

Dearest Clementine (Clementine & Gavin)

Finding Dandelion (Dani & Jax)

Kissing Madeline (Maddie & Daren)

Cowritten with Leslie McAdam

All About the D (Evie & Josh)

Surprise, Baby! (Kendall & Drew)

ABOUT THE AUTHOR

Lex Martin is the *USA Today* bestselling author of Varsity Dads, Texas Nights, and the Dearest series, books she hopes readers love but her parents avoid. A former high school English teacher and freelance journalist, she resides in Texas with her husband, twin daughters, a bunny, and their rambunctious Shih Tzu.

To stay up-to-date with her releases, stop by her website and **subscribe to her newsletter,** or join her Facebook group, **Lex Martin's Wildcats.**

www.lexmartinwrites.com

Printed in Great Britain
by Amazon